Sheila Norton lives in Chel~~~~~ and part-time in Torquay worked for most of her lif~~~~~ secretary, until retiring earl~~~~~ on her writing.

Sheila's first novel was published in 2003. Before starting to write novels, she had over a hundred short stories published in women's magazines.

Sheila enjoys hearing from readers and can be contacted through her website: www.sheilanorton.com, where you can also ask to be added to an email mailing list for updates about Sheila's books and writing life.

Winter at Cliff's End Cottage

Sheila Norton

PIATKUS

PIATKUS

First published in Great Britain in 2021 by Piatkus

1 3 5 7 9 10 8 6 4 2

A CIP catalogue record for this book
is available from the British Library.

ISBN 978-0-349-42985-4

Typeset in Sabon by M Rules

Printed and bound in Great Britain by
Clays Ltd, Elcograf S.p.A.

Papers used by Piatkus are from well-managed forests
and other responsible sources.

MIX
Paper from
responsible sources
FSC® C104740

Piatkus
An imprint of
Little, Brown Book Group
Carmelite House
50 Victoria Embankment
London EC4Y 0DZ

An Hachette UK Company
www.hachette.co.uk

www.littlebrown.co.uk

In memory of my lovely mum, Kay, who (as well as teaching me to cook — 'Auntie Nellie's' Christmas cake recipe at the end of this book was actually hers) — always encouraged my ambition to become a writer despite such a thing being unheard-of in our family. She passed away in 2007 at the age of 87, but not before seeing the publication of my first six novels, a source of immense pride to her. The men and women of her generation were an amazing inspiration to us all. Thanks, Mum.

1

Holly

JANUARY 2018

The house is small but solid looking, with a grey slate roof and whitewashed walls. You can see it from quite a long way off, across the fields as you approach up the lane towards the top of the cliff – especially during these cold months of winter, when the trees are bare and there's nothing but the gloomy sky and the circling seagulls interrupting the view. It's on its own, a bit of a landmark, sitting up there so close to the edge. Sometimes on winter nights it's almost like a lighthouse looming out of the darkened sky; a warning, letting us know we're approaching something. Approaching the end of the lane – but more than that. The end of everything.

I've lived in Hawbury Down for most of my life, and although I've never been inside Cliff's End Cottage before, I know all about it. Everyone around here knows about the crazy old lady who lives in the house perched on the edge of the cliff, who refuses to move out even though half her garden has now gone into the sea and the environmentalists don't think it'll be long before the rest goes – followed by the house itself. People come up here to Hawbury Top, as it's known, local people as well as visitors to the area. They come up this tiny dark lane riddled with potholes, bringing their cars as far as they can, until the lane peters out, and then walking the rest of the way up the track on foot. And they simply stand on the edge and stare. It's a sight, all right. The waves crashing down below, where over decades, over centuries, they've been eating away at the base of the cliff, destabilising the clifftop from beneath, until bits of it crumble and topple into the sea.

People were up here taking photos earlier this month when a tremendous storm, combined with a high spring tide, finally sent an overhanging section of Mrs Jackman's garden, including her potting shed, down to the hungry sea below. They stared, they took their photos, and they went away muttering about the stupidity of the woman who still insisted she wasn't going to move, saying she'd know when it was time. I was there myself. I'd like to say my curiosity was purely professional, but to be honest I was being just as nosy as everyone else. I'd never met Stella Jackman before, and I wasn't going to believe all the outlandish rumours and ridiculous myths that circulate this town about her, but I *was* intrigued. And that day, some of us who were up there on the clifftop did get to see her – the woman some people refer to as 'The Witch of Cliff's End', because of the weird wailing noises reputed to sometimes come from her cottage at night – for a few moments when she came out of her front door to call her cats. She was just as I'd imagined her: small, with wiry grey hair, and a weathered look, as if she'd been outdoors her entire life. On the spur of the moment, I took my chance, rushing towards her as others held back, pretending they weren't watching.

'Excuse me . . . Mrs Jackman,' I gabbled. 'I'm Holly Brooks, I'm a feature writer for *Devon Today*—'

'Oh, you are, are you?' she said, looking me up and down. She started to turn away, but I went on, desperately trying to detain her:

'I was rather hoping you might agree to have a chat with me – about your home, and the terrible damage from last night's storm—'

'My home's fine,' she said calmly. 'No damage.' She met my gaze and added, 'No chat.'

Well, at least I'd tried, I consoled myself as she went back inside, closing the door behind her.

'I don't think so,' the editor of *Devon Today*, Frances Small, said in response to my phone call, without trying to hide her boredom and irritation. She wasn't nicknamed as Frosty Fran behind her back for nothing. She'd listened in silence as I'd outlined my idea for a feature on Mrs Jackman and Cliff's End Cottage. 'There's been enough written already about that house. Enough pictures of it too. Coastal erosion has been done to death. Find me something new.'

Although I'm a freelance writer, Frosty Fran's one of my most important clients and my feature submissions to *Devon Life* are normally accepted – and I really needed something to be accepted as soon as possible, if I wanted to avoid going into my overdraft again. Even with my cleaning job on the side, it's tough at times. Trouble was, I knew Fran had a point. And to be fair, even if she'd grasped the idea with open arms, I had yet to persuade Mrs Jackman to talk to me.

'What if I try a different angle?' I blurted out, without having even thought it through. 'A more *personal* angle. I mean, she – Mrs Jackman – must be in her eighties, and people say she's lived there all her life. She must have some stories to tell. As well as explaining why she won't move.'

There was silence for a moment.

'Are you sure she'll talk to you?' Fran said eventually.

'I'll find a way.' I swallowed back my doubts. I'd *have* to find a way.

'So send me the story when it's written. I'll think about it.'

I sighed. If she didn't take it for *Devon Today*, there were other markets I could try. And now I'd suggested it, I liked the idea of trying to talk to Mrs Jackman about her life in Hawbury Down. But despite my determination to keep pushing away at her until she agreed, I had a feeling I'd need to start more gently, and build up the pressure gradually if necessary. So I wrote a short, friendly note to her saying I'd love to talk to her about her long life in Hawbury Down, because I was just interested for personal reasons, and she didn't have to agree to being interviewed for the magazine. I asked her to call me if she fancied a chat. I clipped my card to the note and went back to deliver it through her letterbox. It was a cold, rainy day, about as bleak and dark as it gets, the bare trees up on Hawbury Top bent against the wind, and there was no sign of her or the cats this time, and nobody hanging around taking photos. I wasn't particularly optimistic about getting a response from her, but I was prepared to give it a bit of time before following up with another attempt. To my surprise, just over a week later, she called me.

'I don't know what you want,' she said, 'but I suppose you'll keep on at me until I agree. Come on Tuesday. Eleven o'clock.'

And here I am, on her doorstep.

2

Stella

I'm not a fool, whatever Miss Holly-I'm-A-Journalist-But-All-I-Want-Is-A-Little-Chat might think. She's obviously still after her story, and she thinks she's going to get it by the back door, by a softly-softly approach, talking about *my long life in Hawbury Down*. How does she even know how long I've been here? I should have just thrown her little love letter straight in the bin, but something about it intrigued me, even if it did exasperate me at the same time. I found myself wondering about her. Wondering how long she's lived here herself, who her parents are and whether I know them, why the hell she's interested in me – or rather, in my house – and why a young girl like that wants to work as a journalist, nosing into other people's business. Well, I haven't got much else to think about, these days. Or, to be honest, many people to talk to. Life gets wearisome when you reach my age, especially in the coldest months of the year. The cold wind up here chills my very bones, making me ache all over, body and soul. Sometimes I think winter will never end.

So, eventually, I called her. 'Come on Tuesday at eleven', I said. She won't stay too long that way; she'll be wanting to get away for her lunch.

It's been a while since I had a visitor – apart from the nosy ones who hang around outside the house, looking down the cliff edge, taking photos, staring at my windows. They don't realise I'm watching them from behind the curtains. But an actual visitor, coming into the house, sitting down and talking to me – I must admit, getting the little note from Holly Whats-Her-Name made me stop and think how long it's been since that's happened. Years ago, I used to get visits from ex-colleagues at the school. And friends from the Cats Protection place where I used to volunteer. But I suppose over the years they've all retired too. We've lost touch. And a lot of them probably aren't even alive anymore. That's one of the sad things about living to what we used to call a *good old age* – you outlive everyone. You don't have any friends left.

Anyway, although I don't like admitting it, I feel kind of jittery while I'm getting dressed this morning. I don't know whether to put my better trousers on, and a decent shirt, one I've ironed. Normally I can't be bothered much about what I wear. Nobody sees me. I shouldn't care what this young woman is going to think of me, but nevertheless I do a bit of tidying up, brush the cat hairs off the table and chairs, move Gracie from where she likes to sit, grooming herself, on the top shelf in the kitchen, and shoo her outside with the other two, in case this Holly person doesn't like cats. Or if she has an allergy – they all seem to have allergies these days. Just before eleven o'clock, I put the kettle on and warm the teapot. I get down the cake tin, lift the lid and peek inside, feeling silly all of a sudden. Why have I gone to all this trouble? The girl only wants to write some daft story about me for her job. Maybe I'll save the cake till this afternoon and eat it on my own.

The doorbell makes me jump, and I nearly drop the cake tin. I go to the door and usher her in. She's got dark hair, very pale skin, and she's pretty in that too-skinny way they are these days. She

6

smiles and reminds me who she is, as if she thinks I'm so bloody senile I've probably forgotten.

'I'll take my shoes off,' she offers, unzipping her coat. I tell her not to bother. I'm aware I'm probably sounding a bit snappy. I feel flustered, having her coming into the house, wafting perfume and flicking her long hair.

'Sit down,' I say curtly. 'Tea? Or do you prefer coffee?'

'Oh!' She looks around her through the open door into the sitting room, and I follow her gaze, seeing the thin old carpet and the shabby, worn sofa and armchairs through her eyes. The cats have, over the years, done what cats do – their claws have pulled threads in the fabrics, their damp fur has left dark marks on the cushions. The legs of the table have scratch marks in them. It hasn't bothered me. I prefer their company to the idea of having a perfect home.

'Um, what kind of tea do you have?'

I stare back at her. 'The kind you make a pot of tea with.'

'Right. Sorry.' She gives a little laugh of embarrassment. 'I . . . I was thinking about herbal teas – only because they're what I normally drink myself. But of course, ordinary tea is fine. No milk or sugar, thank you.'

Herbal teas. They're not tea at all, in my opinion, just fancy fruit drinks. I sniff as I turn back to the teapot, put in a spoonful of tea each plus one for the pot, wait for the kettle to come back to the boil, then fill the pot and put the tea cosy on. When I look back at Holly, she's sitting down at the kitchen table, watching me. Probably never seen anyone make real tea before.

'We can go in the sitting room,' I say, 'while the tea draws.'

She follows me and sits in one of the armchairs. I can see she looks as awkward as I feel, and something inside me softens slightly – but only slightly. Isn't she supposed to be a journalist? Aren't they supposed to be tough and ruthless? She looks like an anxious little girl, sitting there in her tight jeans with her toes together and her hands in her lap. No notebook, or recording thing, unless she's hidden it. It seems she's keeping up the pretence that she only wants a little chat – *off the record*, that's what they say, isn't it?

My radio's playing in here – I put it on earlier, to listen to some music while I tidied up, and it's probably a bit loud for her, so I go to turn it off.

'That was nice music,' she says – being polite, I suppose. I doubt she knows much about classical music.

'It's the first movement of *Eine kleine Nachtmusik*,' I tell her. '*A Little Night Music*. Mozart.'

'Oh.' She looks blank but nods. 'One of your favourites?'

I can't help smiling now, despite myself. The memories that particular music evoke always make me smile. 'My absolute favourite,' I say. Then I catch myself, and move on abruptly:

'Anyway, what exactly do you want to talk about?' Straight to the point. No sense in shilly-shallying around.

She smiles back now. 'Well, for a start I wondered how long you've been living here – in Hawbury Down, and in this house. Have you been here for your entire life? You must have some stories to tell.'

'Must I?' I say. 'What sort of stories?'

'Well, stories about Hawbury Down. What it was like here when you were younger, how it's changed . . . your memories, and so on.'

'I see.'

Holly sits back in her chair, as if she's waiting for me to start. I feel weary, weary of this nonsense before it's even begun. What's the point? Can I really be bothered to drag up a few ancient memories just to satisfy this girl? Just so she can write something for her paper or magazine?

'I'll pour out the tea,' I say, to delay the conversation for a bit longer. I hesitate, then add – because it will have been a waste of time making it if I don't – 'Want a slice of cake?'

'Oh!' She looks surprised. 'Cake? Really? Well, thank you, that's nice of you.'

She probably never eats it. Probably thinks it's fattening, or not vegetarian enough for her. I go into the kitchen and cut us a slice each, whether she decides she's going to eat it or not, pour out the tea and carry everything into the sitting room on a tray. Holly sits up, looking guilty.

'I should have carried that in for you.'

'I'm not totally helpless,' I mutter, putting the tray down on the little table between our chairs. She's looking at the teacups, a strange expression on her face.

'Proper cups and saucers,' she says wistfully. 'My gran used to use them.'

Since when did cups and saucers become something only older people use? I push a plate of cake towards her and her eyes open wide with surprise.

'This is home-made, isn't it!'

'Yes. Cherry and almond.' I wonder if home-made cakes are something else she's not used to. Another thing she only associates with old ladies. 'You're not allergic to nuts or anything like that?' I add quickly.

'No. It looks delicious.' She takes the plate, picks up her slice of cake and nibbles it politely. 'It's lovely,' she says with a smile. Then she puts her plate down again and gives me a more business-like look. 'So: where shall we start? Were you actually born here – in Hawbury Down?'

'No.' I wipe crumbs from my mouth. This'll spoil her little story. 'I was born in London. In the East End.'

'Oh, really?' she says. 'When did you move to Devon, then?'

'I was evacuated as a child. During the war.' I glance at her, wondering if she understands. 'World War Two. Children were sent to the countryside, to escape the Blitz. The bombing.'

'You were an evacuee! That's really interesting.'

'It wasn't always much fun at the time,' I retort.

Suddenly I don't want to talk about it anymore. I don't want to talk at all. I put my cup down so abruptly, tea slops into the saucer. 'I'm sorry, I've changed my mind.' I get up, trying not to look at her. 'You'll have to go.'

'Oh. OK, of course.' She follows me back to the kitchen and out to the front door. I'm already holding it open for her. This was a stupid idea. Stupid of me to agree to it. I shouldn't have got her hopes up.

'Goodbye,' I say, still not looking at her. I don't know why I feel bad about it. She shouldn't have wheedled her way into coming round here.

She's stopped on the doorstep. I can't close the door while she's still got one foot inside.

'Thank you,' she says. 'For the tea, and the cake. It was nice to meet you.'

'You're welcome,' I mutter.

'I just ... just wondered why you agreed to me coming round,' she goes on. She sounds genuinely interested rather than being put out about it. 'I mean, if you really didn't want to talk to me – about your life, your past, whatever – why ask me to come? Why make me tea? Why bake that lovely cake?'

I nearly don't answer. But then I glance up at her, and there's something about her gentle expression, the kind look in her eyes, that makes me blurt it out.

'If you must know,' I say, 'it's my birthday. I'm eighty-three today. So I made myself a cake. I'm glad you liked it.'

She puts a hand on my arm, her eyes clouding with sadness. Damn it, why did I tell her that? Now she's going to go away thinking I'm a pathetic, lonely old woman who invites strangers round to share her birthday cake.

'Goodbye,' I say more firmly, giving the door a little push so that she moves her foot out of the way. As soon as she's off the doorstep, I close the door and walk back into the kitchen. What a waste of time that was. Never mind. I'll have another piece of cake later on. Wouldn't do to let it get stale.

3

Holly

Poor thing. She's lonely, obviously, and I'm not surprised – living up there all on her own like that, at her age, stuck in that chilly old house that – even inside – feels somehow as if it's literally teetering on the edge of the cliff. I know it's ridiculous, but just sitting in her lounge, I could almost feel how unstable it is, how very fragile its grip on that cliff might be. And what a shame that she has to invite a complete stranger to share her cake, just to have company on her birthday. Eighty-three! It was stupid of me to think she'd make anything other than real tea, in a teapot, and have anything other than home-made cake; my gran was exactly the same. It brought back such memories. I'm sighing as I walk back down the track to my car. Gran's birthday was at this time of year, too. January the twenty-ninth– less than two weeks' time. She'd have been seventy-eight. She's only been gone a year and I still miss her so much, enough to bring tears to my eyes now that have nothing to do with the cold, sharp wind whipping across Hawbury Top. It's always colder up here than down in the town, of course, and on a freezing winter's day like this, there's ice on the puddles that formed in the potholes from yesterday's rain, and frost glittering on the bare branches of the trees. Beautiful in a sparkly Christmas-card kind of way, but also enough to make me shiver as I hurry to get into the car and turn up the heating.

I don't want to start crying about Gran again. I think instead about Mrs Jackman's change of heart today. It was pretty sudden – just as I was enjoying her cherry cake, too. She obviously didn't want to talk about being evacuated, and of course I understand that perhaps she has some unhappy memories about it. Perhaps the people she stayed with weren't kind to her, and no doubt she missed her own parents.

It would have been a perfect story for *Devon Today*; but I have to respect her feelings. It's a pity, as I'd have loved to know more about it, anyway, just out of my own curiosity. Did she stay in Devon after the war? Or did she come back years later? Why move away from London to come back down here, if her time as an evacuee 'wasn't much fun', as she put it?

My copy for a regular slot on another magazine is due so I'm busy enough for the rest of the day. It's a nature monthly, and although I was lucky to get the chance to write it, I'm beginning to run out of ideas. There's only so much you can say, the third year you're describing what to look out for in January. I manage my word count, thanks to the brave little snowdrops I admired, poking their way up into the frosty air as I walked down from Hawbury Top this morning. And I'm just in time to go and pick Maisie up at three-fifteen.

'Good day?' I ask as she throws herself into my arms outside her classroom. 'Do your coat up, Mais. It's freezing.'

She fumbles with the zip and I pull her hat down over her ears. She skips along beside me, chattering about maths, and play time, and lunchtime, and which naughty kid in the class was told off by the teacher. She hasn't put her gloves on – she hates wearing them – but her little hand is warm in mine, her cheeks glowing pink with health and happiness. Sometimes, at times like this when I know she'd be furious with embarrassment because of the other children around us, I have to fight the urge to pick her up and smother her with kisses. It's a never-ending source of amazement to me that she's so perfect, the most perfect little girl in the world – and she's mine. She's far and away the best thing that's ever happened to me, despite being the last thing I wanted at the time.

It's not until night-time, when Maisie's in bed, that I start to think about Mrs Jackman again. I imagine her now, alone in that house, with the wind whistling outside and only her cats for company – how many does she have? Two? Three? I didn't see any of them this morning. Does she even have a TV? I didn't notice. I try to imagine her life, and can't help the inevitable comparison with that of my gran. Gran was so different. She was an extrovert, a chatterbox, full of laughter and fun and wisdom.

'Holly,' she used to say to me, 'don't mope. Life's too short, girl.'

It was too short to spend it moping over things I couldn't have, too short to cry over a boy who didn't want me, too short for regrets. She was right, wasn't she – and sadly, life *was* too short for her. She shouldn't have died at only seventy-seven. It was far too soon; she was still so full of life. Whereas Mrs Jackman . . .

I stop myself there, shocked by the direction of my own thoughts. What about Mrs Jackman? I still don't know the first thing about her, but I'm making assumptions, based on rumours around the town, and one short meeting with her. I've assumed she's not just lonely, but also a miserable old bag who doesn't like people or want them around. That she insists on staying up there on the edge of a collapsing cliff out of sheer cussedness, and, worse, that if she's lonely it must be her own fault. But now I'm remembering her tea tray, set with a cloth, china cups and saucers and milk in a little jug. The home-made cake on a plate. The way she

14

made the tea – three spoonsful of tea leaves in the warmed pot, just like Gran did. I couldn't take my eyes off her while she was doing it, because in this instant-gratification, *tea bag in a mug without even sitting down* world we live in, I wanted to treasure that sight, the memory it evoked. Whatever else Mrs Jackman is – miserable old bag or not – she's alone, and lonely, and it's her birthday, and I might be the only person in Hawbury Down, or even the only person alive, who knows about it.

As soon as I've dropped Maisie off at school the next morning, I head straight to the flower shop on Fore Street and choose a small posy of yellow and white freesias – nothing too fancy, just bright and cheerful. The florist ties the stems with yellow ribbon and wraps them in cellophane.

'Do you want to include a card?' she asks.

I hesitate. What would I write?

'No,' I decide. 'I'll say . . . what I want to say when I deliver them.'

She smiles at me and says that'll be nice. I wonder what she'd say if she knew who I was taking the flowers to. I wonder, too, whether Mrs Jackman knows what they say about her in the town – that they call her a witch and spread silly rumours about those ghostly noises coming from her house at night. How do these things start, and why do people repeat them?

I put the flowers on the back seat of my car and drive, again, to the end of the lane to Hawbury Top, turning my coat collar up around my neck against the cold as I trudge up the narrow track to the house, avoiding the icy patches of bare rock. There's sleet in the air and it stings my face. I wonder what the hell I'm doing.

Mrs Jackman comes to the door wearing a chequered overall and some brown slacks. There's no burst of warmth from inside the house indicating that she might have the heating on, or a fire lit. She blinks at me in surprise.

'Oh. It's you again,' she says. She looks down at the flowers I'm holding out to her. 'What's all this?'

'For your birthday. I'm sorry it's late, but obviously I didn't know about it until I was leaving. But I wanted to ... well, to say happy birthday for yesterday.' She's staring at me, silent, so I add: 'A birthday should be a thing to celebrate, shouldn't it?' – and to my surprise, she gives a little gasp, blinking fast, as if I've said something outrageous.

I feel awkward now. Was this a mistake? Too late I wonder if she'll think I've only done it to persuade her to talk to me for the magazine. I thrust the posy towards her and at least she takes it, passing it from one hand to the other as if she's making up her mind about it.

'Well,' she says, just as I'm about to say goodbye and turn away. 'Well, these are very nice. I suppose I should say thank you. And I suppose you'd better come in.'

She holds the door open wide for me. And here I am, back in her little blue kitchen again, with its ancient-looking electric stove and old-fashioned crockery cabinet with glass doors, as she puts the kettle on and gets down the china cups and saucers.

'Let me carry the tray this time,' I say. 'Shall I put the flowers in a vase for you?'

And she's actually smiling as we go into the sitting room.

4

Stella

What a surprise – flowers, for my birthday. I can't even begin to think when I last had flowers bought for me. And it nearly took my breath away when she said those words: *A birthday should be a thing to celebrate.* It's exactly what *he* said to me – all those years ago, when I turned eighteen. How strange, to hear it said again now. Now I'm at the age where birthdays don't mean a thing, don't bring any excitement at all, just a reminder of the cold hard truth of another step into old age. Still – it ... touched my heart, in a funny way.

I'm not stupid, though. I suppose the girl's still just after her story and this is another way of trying to get round me. But it's nice, anyway. Especially after I shooed her away yesterday. Well, there's still some cake left so she might as well sit down and have a slice with me. I'm having to move two of the cats off the chairs while she carries the tray through.

'Oh, don't worry about that!' she says, seeing me trying to brush the hairs off the cushions. She puts down the tray, bends down and starts stroking Vera, who's winding herself around her legs. 'I love cats. What's his name?'

'She's a girl. Vera. They're all girls,' I say, nodding at Gracie, who's trotting over towards her now to get her share of attention. 'This one's Gracie.'

I can't help warming to her a bit, seeing her pet my girls.

'How many cats do you have?' she asks, smiling.

'Three. You might not see anything of Peggy. She spends most of her time outdoors. Doesn't mind the cold as much as these two.'

'Ah, they're lovely,' she says. 'Nice names.'

'Singers,' I tell her. 'I named them after famous singers. Gracie Fields, Peggy Lee, Vera Lynn.'

She looks blank. I might've known.

'Famous during the war, and after,' I explain. Why should she have heard of them? 'A bit before your time.'

I glance at her again. I wonder how old she is. In her twenties, I suppose – probably early twenties. She looks so young, sipping her tea, perched on the edge of her chair, almost as if she's scared she's going to fall off it at any minute. Perhaps she really thinks the house is wobbling on the edge of the cliff. All that silly nonsense people talk about it.

'Eat the cake, Holly,' I say more gently. 'It'll only go to waste.'

She smiles and thanks me, starting to nibble her slice of cake around the edges like she did yesterday. She hasn't even taken her coat off. There's a bit of a draught in here when there's a cold wind blowing. That window needs fixing. I'm used to it, but she's so skinny, not an ounce of fat on her, she probably feels the cold. I sigh, and to my own surprise, find myself saying:

'Sorry about yesterday. I was tired. Couldn't be bothered with it – talking about the war. Not that I can remember much about it. I was too young, really.'

'That's all right,' she says. 'I was intrigued, that's all, when you said you'd been evacuated. My gran used to talk to me about the old days a lot, but she was too young to know much about the war. She was born in nineteen-forty.'

She looks down at her plate, blinking fast, pushing the remainder of her cake from side to side, and I guess:

'Has your gran passed away now?'

'Last year,' she says, still looking down.

Poor lass. She must have loved that gran of hers. I wonder what it would be like to have a granddaughter myself, to sit down with me, asking for stories about 'the old days'. As if she knows what I'm thinking, Holly suddenly looks back up at me and asks:

'Do you have any family? Children, or grandchildren?'

'No,' I say automatically, without thinking. Then I remember, struggle to hide a little smile, and find myself adding, 'Not . . . well, not really, no.'

She probably wonders if I'm away with the fairies – not even knowing if I have family or not. But it's too soon. I've only known about it myself for a few weeks and I'm still not even sure I believe it. I'm definitely not ready to share it with someone I've only just met.

'So—' she puts her head on one side '—how do you manage? I mean . . . sorry.' She goes a bit red. 'But I can see your knees hurt, when you walk. My gran had arthritis too. How on earth do you get your shopping – living up here on your own? Do you order it online?' She looks around her. I can see her mind whirling. *No computer. Not even a TV. How on earth does this old girl cope?*

'No, I don't order it *online*,' I say scathingly. 'I order it over the phone, from the Co-op in town. They deliver it every Friday.'

'They carry it up, from where the lane runs out?' she asks, looking impressed.

'No, of course not! I have to walk down the track and meet the delivery driver there, with my shopping bags.'

'You're joking!' she exclaims, although I'm clearly not. 'Wouldn't they help, if you paid them a little bit extra?'

'No, they wouldn't. I wouldn't ask anyway. It's a ten-minute walk each way, they're busy, and I've got all the time in the world. They do help me load the shopping into my bags, though.'

'But what about when it's raining? And cold, like it is now?' She looks so appalled, I almost want to laugh. 'You can't ... with your poor legs, and carrying heavy shopping bags ... it's so steep coming back up that track!'

'I'm used to it,' I say, shaking my head. She doesn't have to know how much I dread Friday afternoons. They call me to say they're on their way. It just gives me time to put my coat and boots on and walk down to meet them. She's right, of course. The track *is* steep, and it's hard going when it's cold and wet. I try not to order anything heavy, but now I don't grow my own veg any more, I do like a couple of potatoes and a cabbage. And a bag of flour every week for my baking. 'There was a time I used to walk down into town, buy everything I needed every day, and walk all the way back up,' I tell her. 'But I can manage with a delivery once a week now. And the milkman comes right to the door – only twice a week, that's all I need, I don't have much milk in my tea; but he brings my eggs too, to make my cakes. So I manage.'

'You never learned to drive?' she says.

'No, never. Never wanted to.'

'And you've lived here all this time, doing your own shopping like that?' She makes it sound like a miracle. I could be offended, but I'm not. I actually find myself laughing.

'Well, I've lived here – in this house – since nineteen-fifty-six,' I tell her. 'Before that, I lived on a farm, the other side of the town. There! That's what you wanted to know, isn't it? What you were asking me yesterday.'

'I'd like to hear *anything* you *want* to tell me about your life.'

20

She pauses, meets my eyes, and goes on: 'But I understand, if you don't like talking about the old days.'

'Well, it's not as if I've got anything much else to do,' I say. I glance at her again. 'Aren't you going to take your coat off? Are you cold?'

'It's fine,' she says. But she gives a little shiver, huddling into her coat, and I sigh and get to my feet. These young girls don't dress properly, that's the trouble. They don't wear vests in the winter. Me, I go into my thermals from the end of October and don't leave them off until at least April. And I've got blankets for putting over my knees in the evenings if it's really cold.

'Oh, please don't—' she calls out, clearly embarrassed now, as I go over to the fireplace and switch on the electric fire. 'I expect that's expensive. If you don't normally—'

'Let's just have it on for a few minutes,' I say. I must admit it's lovely when it's on, but I try not to use it until it gets dark. That was always the rule: light the fire when it gets dark, not before. I'd have to lay it in the morning, before I went to school – carefully piling on the kindling wood, adding the balls of screwed-up newspaper, and the layer of coal – so that, in December, when it was starting to get dark before I even got home, it'd be all ready to light.

I sit back down again and Holly slips her arms out of her coat. The room will warm up quickly now I've got both bars of the fire on. I hope I don't fall asleep.

'So where do you want me to start?' I say.

She looks back at me apologetically, probably still wondering if I'll show her the door again. But I won't. I feel a bit more like talking now. I'm getting used to her, and to be honest, I'm beginning to like it – having someone to talk to.

'How old were you?' she asks. 'When you were evacuated here?'

'I was about five and a half. It was September nineteen-forty.

Same year you said your gran was born.' I nod at her sympathetically. 'The war had already been going for a year—'

'I think it started on the first of September, nineteen-thirty-nine, didn't it?' she says.

'That's right. And the first wave of evacuations started as soon as Germany invaded Poland. But a lot of those children were brought home again when the bombings didn't happen straight away, like everyone had expected. Then when the Blitz did start, they had to be re-evacuated.'

'Is that when you were sent away?'

'Yes. Because I was so little, my mother didn't really want me to go. It was mostly school children who were being evacuated. A lot of them got sent in class groups, with their teachers, but I hadn't even started school yet. I was due to start that month, so she decided it would be best to send me away then so I could start at the right time, at a school in the country. Some mothers were evacuated with their children, but my mum couldn't leave London, because she was looking after her own mother – my grandmother – who was poorly, and lived down the road.'

I pause for a second, glancing at Holly, remembering again about that gran of hers who's passed away. Sadly, I don't really remember my grandmother at all.

'My father was away at the war, of course,' I go on. 'He was in the RAF. And the Blitz had got bad by then. Houses all around us were being hit every night. My mum wrote to an aunt and uncle in Devon, who I'd never met, and asked if they'd take me in. As it happened, the twelve-year-old daughter of one of our neighbours was being evacuated to Devon at the same time, and my mother decided this girl was sensible enough to look after me on the journey. I had a little suitcase packed, a gas mask and a cardboard sign with my name on hung round my neck, and I was put on the train.'

'You must have been terrified,' Holly says.

'I don't remember, really. I probably thought it was an adventure, like going on holiday. But I do remember getting off the train, and meeting my great-aunt for the first time.' I laugh. 'I think I probably *was* terrified then!'

September 1940

Torquay railway station, Devon

'Hurry up, hurry up! What's the matter with you? Walk properly, I can't stand dawdlers.'

Stella looked up at the woman in the blue coat who was rushing her along the platform. She couldn't understand what the woman was saying. Her voice was different from her mum's, and her nan's, and everyone else she'd ever known. And she was *huge*. Not just tall, but wide, with massive arms and legs. Stella couldn't stop staring at her. Her mum, and all the women in the neighbourhood where she'd grown up, had been thin and gaunt from hard work and surviving on rations – but at least they'd been cheerful, not like this inexplicably angry woman.

'How old are you now?' the big woman asked Stella as they left the station and walked towards a bus stop.

'I'm five an' a half,' she said importantly.

'Right. You might be of some use, then, when you're not at school, although I don't suppose you've got much idea about life on a farm.'

Stella puzzled over this as they waited for the bus. All she knew about farms was what she'd seen in her books. Pictures of cows, sheep and haystacks had as much to do with life in Bethnal Green as pictures of the moon might do.

'Are you my auntie?' she asked once they were settled on the bus, remembering what her mum had told her.

'Yes. Your great-aunt.'

Stella had only found out about this auntie when her mum sat her down and explained that she was coming to live in Devon.

'Auntie Nellie,' she said out loud. 'You're Auntie Nellie, ain't you? Mummy said so.'

The woman nodded but didn't respond. She was staring straight ahead.

'Why ain't you never been to our 'ouse?' Stella persisted.

'Curiosity killed the cat,' snapped Auntie Nellie. 'And talk properly. You're not in the slums now.'

There were so many things Stella didn't understand in that short response, she hardly knew where to start. Which cat, and why was it killed? What was wrong with how she talked? What were slums, and when had she been in them? She instinctively realised already that it wouldn't help to ask any more questions, that it would only make this auntie even crosser. She shifted uncomfortably on the rough seat of the bus. She was tired after her long journey and wanted a drink.

'Stop wriggling about,' said Auntie Nellie, without looking at her. 'Sit still and behave.'

The bus had left the town behind now, and they were travelling through open countryside, the like of which Stella had never seen before. Vast open spaces, fields with cows in them, like in her books, and occasionally a tiny village where the houses had gaps in between them and some of the roofs looked like they were made of straw. Finally, Auntie Nellie dragged her off the bus again and they set off along a deserted country lane. Several times Stella stumbled as she tried to keep up.

When they came to a little house standing on the edge of a huge field, Auntie Nellie finally stopped and unlocked the door.

'Home,' she announced as they went inside. Stella wondered why she didn't sound happy about it. If she could only see her own home at that moment, she knew she'd have been smiling till her face hurt. 'I'll show you your room.' She led the way up a narrow staircase. Stella followed, watching her great-aunt's huge girth as she ascended the stairs, wondering how on earth she didn't get stuck halfway up.

She was shown to a small room with just enough space for an iron bedstead and a chest of drawers. Auntie Nellie laid Stella's little suitcase on the bed and opened it up.

'Put your things away in the drawers,' she told her. 'Then you can come back down and help me in the kitchen.'

Stella laid her few spare clothes into the drawers, laid her two books on the chest, tucked her nightie under the pillow, and sat her teddy bear on top of it. Then she went back downstairs, through the living room and into the kitchen. She could see her aunt, through the door into the scullery, peeling potatoes and dropping them into a big saucepan.

'Has your mother taught you how to lay the table?' she asked Stella.

'Yes.'

'Get the cutlery out of the drawer here, then. There's a cloth in the other drawer. And three table mats.'

Three? Stella frowned. Who else was having dinner? She hoped it might be another little girl.

She'd only ever *helped* her mother set the table, so she struggled a bit with trying to do it on her own. She couldn't remember which sides of the table mats the knives and forks went, and she was too scared to ask.

'Knife on *this* side,' whispered a voice behind her suddenly, making her jump and almost drop the cutlery.

She spun round to find a man smiling down at her. He was as thin as her aunt was fat, with a red face, bright-blue eyes and a shock of fair hair.

'Hello,' he said out loud now. He spoke in the same funny voice as Auntie Nellie, but he sounded a lot more cheerful. 'I presume you'll be young Miss Stella from London?'

'Yes!' she giggled.

'Jimmy? Is that you?' her aunt called out. 'Did you bring the cabbage?'

'Aye.' The man winked at Stella, and, throwing a huge cabbage from hand to hand as if he was juggling with it, walked through to the scullery.

'Wash your hands and face, then,' Stella heard Auntie Nellie telling him. 'Has that child managed to set the table?'

'Aye, she's made a good job of it. What's for supper?'

'Rabbit, what d'you think? Not that it's ready. I've had to go down to Torquay, to bring that child back. It was chaos down there, soldiers everywhere. Look at her!' she went on without bothering to drop her voice. 'Doesn't look like she's had a wash since midsummer. And she talks like a ragamuffin.'

Stella felt the itch of tears in her eyes and wiped them quickly with the back of her hand.

'I don't talk like a muffin,' she protested.

'I was talking about you, not to you,' Auntie Nellie said. 'Speak when you're spoken to.'

'Nell,' she heard the man say quietly. 'Go easy. She's only a littl'un.'

'Yes, and what are we supposed to do with a littl'un, tell me that?' her aunt replied. 'With the harvest to get in, and his lordship up at the big house watching every jug of milk and every cabbage we take for ourselves – how are we going to feed another mouth, you tell me that?'

'We'll manage, Nellie. We always have done. I couldn't say no. She's my niece's kid, when all's said and done. And there's plenty of rabbits; I've shot a couple more today.'

'*Shot* them?' Stella gasped, forgetting all about speaking when she was spoken to. 'You shot the rabbits? Shot them dead?'

Stella had never seen a real rabbit, of course. The only rabbit she was familiar with was Peter Rabbit, hero of one of her favourite story books, which she loved her mum to read her at bedtime, so she was aware that rabbits got chased, and put in pies if they were caught. Rabbit meat was often served for dinners in her home – and her neighbours' homes too – but she'd never made the connection before. Now, though, as Auntie Nellie dished up the dinner, and the man laughed – not unkindly – at her horrified expression, she folded her arms across her chest and stuck out her lower lip.

'I'm not hungry,' she said.

'Come on, little miss Stella,' the man coaxed her gently. 'You've got to eat.'

'She can go without,' her aunt retorted. 'I'm not putting up with fussy eaters.'

'Aw, have a heart, Nell. It's her first day. She's tired out. Just let her have some tatties and cabbage.'

'A slice of bread and a cup of water is what she'll get, nothing else. You can take it up to her after you've eaten. Up to bed, miss, if you're not having dinner.'

Sniffing back tears, Stella went up to her room, got into her nightie and sat on the bed, hugging her teddy as tight as she could to stop herself from crying. It was cold in the little bedroom and she slid her legs under the rough grey blankets and pulled the heavy eiderdown over herself. She must have dozed off, because the next thing she knew, someone was whispering close to her ear:

'Stella!'

She blinked awake. It was long past blackout time, and the room was so dark that she could only sense, rather than see, the man – Jimmy – bending over her.

'Sit up,' he was whispering. 'I've brought you bread and jam, and a cup of milk. Don't tell your aunt.'

'Thank you!' she whispered. She took the cup from him and swallowed most of the milk straight down, before taking a bite of the bread and jam. The jam was delicious! Mum hadn't been able to get any at home for so long that she'd forgotten what it tasted like. Her mouth was watering while she ate it.

'Good girl,' the man whispered. 'Better now?'

'Yes.' She smiled. Thank goodness she had a friend. 'Who are you?' she added curiously as she lay back down.

'Why, I'm your Great-Uncle Jimmy, dear,' he said. 'I'm your nan's brother.'

'Uncle Jimmy,' she repeated, remembering now. Her mum had told her about him. 'Goodnight, then,' he whispered. 'God bless. Back to sleep, now. If you need a wee, there's a pot under the bed, right? You can empty it in the privy outside, in the morning. Tomorrow's another day, right?'

'Tomorrow's another day,' she repeated inside her head as Uncle Jimmy softly closed the door behind him. She liked the sound of that. Tomorrow Auntie Nellie might be in a better mood. And she might not have to eat dead bunnies.

5

Holly

'She sounds absolutely awful!' I say. Mrs Jackman has stopped talking and she's leaning back in her chair, looking like she's miles away. Remembering. What horrible memories they must be. No wonder she didn't want to talk about it. One of the cats – the black one, Vera – is curled up on her lap, and Mrs Jackman is stroking her little twitchy ears, while the cat purrs in her sleep. The ginger-and-white one, Gracie, is lying in front of the electric fire, her paws stretched out in front of her as if she's sunbathing. 'How could anyone be so unkind to a little girl? It's shocking. You poor thing.'

To my surprise, Mrs Jackman gives a snort of laughter.

'Shocking? No. She was a grumpy old bat but she wasn't used to children, and she hadn't wanted to be lumbered with me. And children weren't mollycoddled in those days; we were expected to do as we were told, or else.'

'But you were so little!' I protest. 'And away from home – moving in with complete strangers—'

'Yes. That was hard. And the thing is . . .'

She hesitates, shaking her head, and then goes on quietly:

'It sounds silly. But the thing is, that's my earliest really clear memory. Meeting her at the station, and going back to the farm with her. And then the fuss about the rabbits.' She gives a short little laugh. 'Ah, don't look so worried. I have other memories – happy memories – about my life here in Devon. Lovely memories that came much later.'

She's smiling, her eyes actually twinkling behind her glasses. I'd love to know what happened later in her life that's making her look like she's got a wonderful secret, but I sense she doesn't want to get ahead of herself. And anyway, maybe I'm missing something, but—

'Didn't you go back home to London, your parents, after the war?' I ask her.

'No,' she says abruptly. She gets up and goes to turn off the electric fire. 'It's warm enough in here now.'

I think it's my cue to leave. I don't want to outstay my welcome – it's been surprising enough that she started opening up to me. Equally, I feel awkward about just walking out on her now that she seems to have got a bit upset. But she suddenly turns back to me, smiling again.

'I got used to it, you know,' she says. 'Got used to that miserable old bugger. There were a lot worse off than me. Uncle Jim was nice. And besides, I had some good times while I was growing up there. I got to like the farm, and the countryside. It suited me better than I expected.'

'Then I'm glad.' I get to my feet, pull on my coat, give her a smile and add: 'And thank you for telling me about it. I . . . won't write about it, by the way. I promised you I wouldn't, and I won't.'

'Think I care, one way or the other?' she retorts. But I'm getting to know her now. I know when she's putting on a front, pretending she doesn't care about something. There's a sensitive soul behind that brusque façade.

'No, it's . . . what you've been telling me about; it's personal, isn't

31

it? But I appreciate you sharing it with me. I do find it interesting – sad, but interesting.'

She doesn't meet my eyes for a moment. Then she shrugs and says, in the same off-hand manner: 'Well, you'd better come again, then, hadn't you? If you want to hear some more. Not that I can understand why it's so fascinating, for a young girl like you – listening to an old woman's ramblings about her childhood.'

I hesitate. I'd like nothing more than to come again, of course. She's right – I *am* fascinated. And I'm genuinely not even considering making a feature out of this now. It wouldn't feel right. I'll tell Frosty Fran I've had no luck with an interview. I just want to sit with Mrs Jackman and her cats again and hear some more of her story. I know I shouldn't. I should be staying at home, working on other ideas, trying to win another commission so that I can get paid for something. As it is, I'll have to catch up with my other regular work after Maisie's asleep. But Stella's starting to get to me: not just her story, but her attitude to life, the way she seems to shrug off difficulties and get on with things. I admire her, just as I admired my gran. I admire their generation: their grit and their spirit. But of course, I don't tell her any of this. I just smile and agree:

'OK, Thank you, I'd like that.' Then I have an idea. 'Why don't I come on Friday, and bring your shopping? To save you walking down to meet the delivery van?'

'Think I'm too old to do it, do you?' she says sharply.

'No. I think you're amazing. You're probably tougher than me! But if I'm going to come and see you anyway, what's the point of both of us walking up the track?' I can see her hesitating, so I press on: 'Look, I'll give you my phone number, then you can call me with your shopping list. Got a pen?'

'All right, I will write your number down,' she finally agrees. 'And you'd better take mine. In case you decide … in case you can't come. But I can give you the list right away. I always have it written out, ready.'

'Perfect.' I take the slip of paper from her. There are only about a dozen or so items on it. 'Is this all?' I say gently. 'Don't you need more meat than this? Some nice fruit?'

'That stewing steak and that mince will last me all week, so does a big cabbage and a few carrots. There's apples on the list. Can't afford fancy stuff. And I'm not used to eating big meals. You don't get hungry at my age.'

'OK.' I slip the list in my pocket and head for the door. 'I'll see you on Friday, then. Thank you again, Mrs Jackman – for the tea, and the cake. And the chat.'

'Oh, call me Stella, for God's sake,' she says a little impatiently. Then she stops, looking thoughtful, and goes on quietly, as if she's talking to herself: 'I can't remember when anyone last called me by my Christian name.'

'Then I shall,' I say, feeling a lump in my throat at this revelation: that she has no one, family or friends, close enough to call her by her name. 'Thank you, Stella.'

The wind's howling across Hawbury Top as I make my way down her garden path and head across the frosty ground towards the track. I stand for a while, looking back at the cottage, and mentally considering the short distance between its ancient walls and the dangerous cliff edge, before staring down at the angry grey sea below. Waves are crashing against the cliffs, spume flying high into the air, making a sound like the cracking of a furious giant's whip. The force of nature, at times like this, is so awe-inspiring; it's easy to imagine the damage it can do to human life and our sad little civilisations. I'm aware, standing up here, of how small and vulnerable we are, and I quickly step back from the edge of the cliff before I start to feel dizzy. I wonder if Mrs

Jackman – Stella – ever feels afraid when she looks out to sea on days like this. I think I would.

As I'm standing here, watching a cheeky little robin hopping from branch to branch of the tangled bare hawthorn, a large tabby cat suddenly comes running out from a clump of gorse at the edge of the cliff, chasing the wind, her tail held high, her fur rippling in the breeze. So this must be Peggy, Stella's third cat. I smile and bend down, trying to entice her to come closer for a stroke, but she looks at me disdainfully, turning away from me with a flick of her tail and strolling back off into the undergrowth.

'Fair enough,' I say to myself, watching her go. 'You can't force friendship on someone who doesn't want it.'

But perhaps, if I tread carefully, it might be that Stella actually *does* want a friend. And it's not as if my own life is exactly overflowing with them either, is it?

6

Stella

I feel strange after she's gone. Unsettled. I'm not used to talking to people about myself – my life. Well, I suppose I'm not used to talking to people at all, these days. What must she have thought, when I said that about nobody calling me by my Christian name? She'll be thinking I'm a sad old bat, that's what. And she'd be right.

It was nice of her to offer to get my shopping, though – a complete surprise. But I felt embarrassed, still do, thinking about her carrying my cabbage and potatoes and whatnot up here. Perhaps I'm being a fool: once a journalist, always a journalist; she's probably just trying to soften me up, saying all that about my memories being personal so she won't write about them. She's probably gone straight home to type it all up on her computer. She'll be thinking she'll get my permission later, when I've finished the whole story.

Well, at least she liked the cats. And they seemed to like her, too. That must be a good sign.

This time, on Friday, she comes in the afternoon. She's got two shopping bags in each hand and she's obviously struggled, coming up the track. She's breathing hard, wheezing, as she comes through the door.

'It's freezing out there,' she says by way of explanation. She can hardly speak. She takes an asthma inhaler out of her pocket and takes a couple of puffs from it.

'Sit down, for God's sake,' I tell her. 'I didn't know you had a bad chest. I'd never have let you carry the shopping—'

'I'm all right,' she protests as she sits on one of the kitchen chairs. 'It's just – coming inside – after the cold air—'

She can only say a couple of words at a time. I look at her anxiously.

'Will a cup of hot tea help?' I've got no experience of asthma or anything like that. Never really had anything much wrong with me, myself.

'Lovely. Thanks.' Her breathing seems to be settling. She smiles. 'Sorry. It's a nuisance, but I'm fine. It's just the cold.'

'You shouldn't have carried these,' I say, nodding at the bags. 'What on earth have you got there, anyway? That must be more than I asked for.'

'Oh, I just got a couple of extras,' she says, a bit awkwardly. 'Some nice chocolate biscuits – for us to share with our tea. Let me put the meat and the butter in the fridge for you.'

'No. Sit still. I'll do that.' The kettle's boiling; I fill the teapot and put the cosy on, then lift the bags onto the worktop, one at a time. They're heavy. God knows how she carried them up here. I unpack them, and, stupidly, feel tears coming to my eyes when I see what she's brought.

'Jam,' I say, turning to look at her. '*Nice* jam. It wasn't on the list – I'd never buy expensive ones like this.' Especially not in a set of six jars, each one in a different flavour. Really extravagant.

'I know. I hope you don't mind – it's just a kind of little thank you gift, for inviting me back again. I thought of you when I saw them in the shop – because of your story. The bread and jam your great-uncle brought you on your first night. How much you enjoyed the jam.'

'I've always loved it; got a sweet tooth,' I admit. 'Thank you. But I'll have to pay you for the biscuits. They're posh ones!'

'If you don't want them, I'll take them home with me,' she says. 'I don't want you to pay me for them. I get a bit carried away sometimes, when I'm shopping. Sorry.' She pauses, then adds quietly: 'It was the same when I used to do my gran's shopping. I could never resist getting some little extras for her.'

I suppose she's thinking of me as a new grandmother. I suppose one old woman is much the same as another to a young girl like her. Although I can't deny it feels ... kind of nice ... to have someone thinking of me as family. Then I suddenly remember what I found out a few weeks ago, and I correct my own thoughts, with a little shock of surprise. Perhaps I *have* got family. How strange that feels, even though I'm not really even ready to believe it yet.

There's something else in the shopping bag too, that I didn't ask for. A pack of two croissants: to go with the jam, she says. I can't think whether I've ever even eaten a croissant before, but the thought of them makes my mouth water. What a treat.

'You really shouldn't have done all this.' I'm trying to sound cross, but it's difficult because there's a lump in my throat and my eyes are still stinging, because of the jam, the fancy biscuits and everything else she carried up the hill. The kindness. 'It's all ... luxuries. Things I can't really afford—'

'It wasn't much,' she says. 'I'll give you the bill for the things you asked me for, but please let me just give you these few little treats.' She smiles again. 'You've been kind to me. I appreciate it.'

I don't know what to say. All she seems to want in return is for me to carry on talking about my old wartime memories. And to be honest, I don't really mind, after all.

'I'll pour out the tea,' I say. 'Are you feeling OK now? Are you sure you're all right with the cats – they don't make you wheeze, do they?' She's stroking Gracie, and Vera's already on her lap.

'No!' She laughs. 'I'm fine with cats. Let's open those chocolate biscuits, shall we?

'Lovely. But go through into the living room, it's comfier. I'll put the fire on,' I add, and she grins back at me, like we're sharing a secret. 'I'm glad to see you've put a nice warm jumper on today, at least.' It's a red one, with a polo neck – far more sensible than the silly thin blouse she wore last time. 'I suppose you'd like to hear some more of my daft ramblings about my childhood.'

'They're not daft.' She sits in one of the armchairs and pats her lap for Vera. 'And yes, I would – if you're happy to talk about it? I've been wondering about the farm. Did your uncle own it?'

'No. It was his older brother Stan's. Jim and Nellie lived in the cottage on the edge of the farm, while Stan and his wife Flo lived in the farmhouse. It was much bigger, but then, they had four children, while Jim and Nellie didn't have any of their own. Just me.'

I stop for a minute, nodding to myself, remembering.

'Auntie Nellie was eaten up with jealousy about Uncle Stan being *the boss*, about him and Flo living in the big house *and* having children. Their eldest son would inherit the farm one day, you see. It was all about that – the farm – nothing to do with her wanting children. She'd have been a rotten mother.'

'Stan and Flo's children would have been your second cousins, then. They must have been company for you?' I suggest.

'No. They were all in their teens, so they pretty much ignored me. Although at first they took the mickey out of my accent and the fact that I didn't know one end of a cow from the other,' I add, laughing to myself. 'Uncle Jimmy used to tell me to take no notice when they teased me. "Sticks and stones may break my bones, but words can never hurt me," he'd say. And he was right. They soon got bored of it.'

'You said – the other day – that you had some good times there, on the farm. That the countryside suited you.' She smiles at me, encouraging me. Wanting me to tell her about the good times. Well, fair enough. It's true, it wasn't all gloom and misery during the war time. Human nature being what it is, we make our own happiness, wherever we find ourselves. So I settle myself more comfortably, take one of her chocolate biscuits, and have a sip of my tea. I must admit, it's cosy in here with the fire on, both of us snuggled down in my old armchairs drinking our tea together. I'm just about to launch into one of my happier childhood memories for her when she suddenly sits up straight, looking startled.

'Is that a cat crying outside?' she says. I can't hear it, but I get up and go to the window, staring out across the grass.

'There it is again!' Holly says, jumping up and coming to stand next to me. 'Is that one of your cats?'

Without stopping to answer her, I go to the front door, open it and listen – and she's quite right. I can hear her now. It's definitely Peggy, I'd know her voice anywhere, and she's crying out loudly in distress.

'Don't go out there without your coat on!' Holly's telling me before I've even stepped over the threshold. When I look round at her, she's already pulling her own coat on and winding her scarf round her mouth.

'Your asthma!' I warn her. I'm looking for my coat as I speak. 'Stay in the warm!'

We're still arguing with each other about who should be staying in the warm while we're both outside, crossing the frozen scrubby grass as the icy wind blows sleet into our faces. I can't move as fast as she can on her slim young legs but I'm following as quickly as I can – following the sound of my poor cat. Peggy's very independent, very streetwise. She wouldn't be screaming like that unless she's badly hurt or frightened. Holly stops at the edge of a patch of gorse and looks back at me, pointing into the middle of it.

'She's in there somewhere,' she says. 'Perhaps she's lost. If you call her, she'll probably find her way out to you, won't she?'

'No,' I tell her impatiently, 'the way she's crying, she must be hurt. Or stuck.' I pull my gardening gloves out of my pocket. The gorse is prickly. 'I'll have to go in and look for her.'

7

Holly

Sure enough, Peggy is making an almighty noise now that she can hear Stella's voice. I wonder if she's caught a paw, or something. But there's obviously no way I'm letting Stella go into that thicket of gorse!

'*I'm* going to look,' I tell her firmly. So firmly, that to my surprise, she doesn't argue – but she does hand me her gloves.

'Don't get yourself scratched to bits,' she says anxiously. 'Can you see where she is?'

I push myself deeper into the undergrowth.

'Peggy!' I call, but the cat's gone quiet now. She doesn't know my voice and she's probably scared.

I push myself through some more branches – and then, suddenly, I start to lose my footing. The ground seems to be giving way beneath me. I start slipping downwards, and just manage in the nick of time to grab one of the sturdier branches and hold on.

'*Shit*!' I gasp, as I try to pull myself back upright.

'Are you all right? What's happened?' Stella calls.

'I'm OK.' I've found a firm foothold now. 'But . . . there's a hole or something here.'

I force my way back out through the prickly gorse. 'I think Peggy may have fallen down there. I think I'm going to need to chop back some of the scrub so I can see—'

I glance up at Stella. She's gone quiet, staring out across the clifftop, looking puzzled and slightly annoyed. I follow her gaze. There's a man coming towards us – about my age, tall, good-looking in a casual kind of way, his dark-blond hair ruffled by the breeze, his face somehow managing to appear both earnest and friendly at the same time. As he comes closer, the weak winter sun suddenly breaks through the clouds, highlighting his face so that I can see he's smiling.

'Hello. Are you all right?' he asks. 'Have you lost something?'

'A cat,' I say, suddenly conscious that I'm staring at him. His eyes are the brightest blue I've ever seen.

'Can I help?' he offers.

'You're trespassing,' Stella snaps. 'I know the fence is broken, but this part of the clifftop is—'

'Actually, I came through the gate,' he says, sounding apologetic, 'from the track. I . . . really just came to look at the house. Cliff's End. Are you Mrs Jackman, by any chance?'

'Of course I am, since I'm the only one living here. And no doubt you're another ruddy busybody from the environmental department. Well, I don't need—'

'No.' He shuffles from one foot to another. 'I'm not. It's – look, I didn't intend to intrude . . . I only wanted to see the house. I was intrigued, you see, because I'm—'

'Well, now you've seen it—' Stella starts to retort, but just then Peggy lets out another loud wail of misery, and before either of us can stop him, the man pushes his way through the gorse in the same direction I've just been.

'The cat's in here somewhere!' he shouts back to us.

'Yes, we know – but there's a hole – be careful!' I yell.

'Oh yes. I see what you mean. Wait—'

There's silence for a moment. Stella and I exchange glances.

'He only seems to want to help,' I tell her quietly. But I'm just as puzzled as she is. Who is he? Why is he really here?

Then he suddenly calls back: 'Right. Actually, it's not so much a hole as a crack. A damn great big crack – wow. I'd say the land's properly destabilising just here, Mrs Jackman.' He suddenly bursts out of the scrub, a struggling Peggy in his arms. 'Got your cat out, anyway. Oops! Sorry!' He's pretty much had to drop her, she's now so desperate to get away from her rescuer. 'Bit ungrateful, aren't they, cats!'

'Thank you. How on earth did you reach her?' I ask, as Stella's now occupied with grabbing Peggy, before she runs off, and checking her all over to make sure she isn't hurt.

Then I look at his jeans – the knees now covered in red Devon soil – and look back up at the scratches on his face and bits of gorse in his hair.

'You crawled down there?'

'Just flattened myself on the ground and reached down. Oh—' He touches one of the scratches on his cheek and laughs. 'This was the cat – not the gorse. She was frightened, that's all. I'm used to cats. Got one myself.'

This seems to mollify Stella slightly. 'Well, thank you,' she says. 'Sorry she hurt you.'

'Yes, it was very good of you,' I say. 'But—' I want to ask him who he is, but even though it's a fairly reasonable question, it feels kind of rude, now that he's been so helpful. But Stella beats me to it, and despite her gratitude, she obviously doesn't have the same scruples as I do about sounding rude!

'So if you're not from the bloody environmental people, what are you doing here?' she demands. 'Selling something, are you? Or just being nosy?'

He smiles, and wipes a trickle of blood from one of his scratches.

'No, not selling anything,' he says. 'But I suppose you could say I'm being nosy. I . . . wasn't going to disturb you. I just wanted to see where you live. If you were still . . . here.'

I move closer to Stella, instinctively shielding her. Is he some kind of stalker? He seems far too nice, but you can't be too careful.

'What do you mean?' she demands.

'Well. That's why I wrote the letter,' he says. 'I'm Alec.'

Stella gives a little gasp.

I turn to look at her. Letter? What letter? She's actually gone pale. She looks like she might need to sit down.

'Stella? Are you all right? Shall we go inside—?' I've missed something, obviously. I've got absolutely no idea what's going on.

'I haven't come to hassle you, honestly,' he goes on quickly. 'If you don't want to – didn't want to – meet me, well, fair enough, but I couldn't resist having a look at the house. Now I've moved into the town myself, I've heard people talking about it – Cliff's End – so . . . ' He's gabbling now, looking anxiously from one of us to the other, but I still don't understand. And Stella's still looking like she's seen a ghost.

I grab hold of her arm. 'Come on, let's go inside, it's so cold,' I say. 'Please – come in, um – Alec. I'm Holly. I'm Stella's . . . Mrs Jackman's . . . well, I'm a friend.' Perhaps he, or Stella, will explain all this, when we're back in the warm.

I go to pick up the gardening gloves that I abandoned on the ground, but straight away he bends and grabs them for me, and follows us as I lead Stella back to the house.

'Sorry, Holly!' he calls after me. 'I ought to introduce myself. I wrote to Mrs Jackman and told her who I am, but she wasn't expecting me to turn up like this.'

I stop, turn to look at him, and he gives me that beautiful smile again.

'I'm Alec. I'm her grandson,' he says. 'Pleased to meet you.'

8

Stella

We're in my sitting room, all three of us. I've told Holly to turn on the other bar of the fire and it feels really warm in here now, but she still looks cold. To be honest I feel a bit shivery myself. I think it's the shock. Holly's made tea and coffee, and we're trying to have some semblance of a conversation. She's looking puzzled – worried, even. I suppose I could have told her about Alec's letter, when she asked me if I had any family, but I'm still only just getting to know her – and of course, I don't know *him* at all. It was enough of a shock, finding out I had a grandson, never mind taking in ... the rest of what he wrote.

'I'm sorry,' he says, as if he's reading my mind. 'This must have been a shock. It wasn't exactly how I'd hoped to meet you for the first time.'

'So—' Holly sits forward now, and I realise I haven't explained anything to her yet. And if I'm honest, I don't really want to. It feels too soon, and too personal. Despite how nice she's been to me and how I've come to like her, and despite telling her about my life as an evacuee and everything – meeting Alec like this, and thinking about what was in his letter, has brought it home to me: she still doesn't know me, and I realise I still know very little about her either. After a pause, Holly continues: '*Have* you got a family, then, Stella?'

I look down at the carpet. There's an awkward silence.

'Sorry,' I say. 'I don't want to talk about it.'

'That's OK. You don't have to tell me anything you don't want to.' She starts to get to her feet again. 'Look, I'll come back another day, shall I? This . . . should obviously be between the two of you, so—'

Out of the corner of my eye, I see Alec giving Holly a little look. I'm not sure if it's because he's surprised she doesn't know, or if he's just showing her some sympathy for the awkwardness of the situation. But either way, I like the kindness of that little look, and I feel my irritation, my reluctance, evaporate a little.

'It's all right,' I tell her. 'Stay for a bit. I don't want you going back down the track in this cold wind when you're still just warming up.' I turn to Alec and go on: 'I've only known Holly a few days, but she's been good to me, and I've been telling her a little bit about my life. I just hadn't got round to . . . this part . . . yet.' I take a deep breath and say, quietly, to Holly: 'I had a daughter: Susan. Alec's mum. But if you don't mind—'

'Absolutely, you don't want to talk about her; I get it, of course,' she's saying before I've even finished. 'It's true, Alec, I've only just met Stella. In fact, why don't I go and make you both some fresh tea while you chat together?'

She gets up and I smile my thanks to her as she heads for the kitchen.

'Well, I've known you for even less time!' Alec says. 'Only about half an hour so far, I think, and that includes the time I was in a hole in the ground with your cat!'

He's managed to lighten the mood, and I can't help giving him a smile. He's right, I don't know him at all, but somehow he's reminding me of Ernest, in ways I'm already noticing. He's much

46

fairer in colouring than Ernest, but he has the same height, the same blue eyes, the same smile, the same little inclination of his head when he speaks.

'I haven't thanked you for your letter,' I say, finally remembering my manners. 'I was going to reply. But I needed a while for it ... all of it ... to sink in.'

'I quite understand,' he says gently. 'And it hasn't helped – me turning up like this. I shouldn't have come, but my curiosity got the better of me. I honestly didn't intend to see you – just the house. He shrugged. 'Since I've been in the shop, I've kept hearing about the house from people, so—'

'Shop?' I query.

'Oh, didn't I say?' Alec looks from me to Holly, who's come back into the room to collect our cups from earlier, and I notice she looks down, blushing a bit. Well, he *is* very handsome. And he's about her age, I suppose. 'The bookshop in town,' he goes on. 'I took it over, just after Christmas.'

'You're running Hawbury Books now?' Holly says.

'Yes. I was assistant manager of a bookshop in Plymouth before, when I lived in Ivybridge. But I'd been looking for an opportunity to manage a shop of my own, so when this came up, it seemed perfect.'

'It's a nice shop,' she says, smiling back at him as she goes back to the kitchen again.

I'm watching them now – the interaction between the two of them.

'Are you married, Alec?' I ask him.

'Divorced,' he says. 'But amicably, three years ago. We've got a little boy, Alfie. He lives with his mum back in Ivybridge, but he spends every other weekend with me, and parts of the school holidays. We're lucky – it all seems to be going OK. He's a great kid. Doesn't seem to be fazed at all by us messing up.'

'So: you told me you're living in Hawbury Down now?'

'Yes. I love it here. The opportunity with the shop came up first, of course, and then I found the house. It's just—' he shakes his head, looking back at me as if he still can't quite believe it '—a mind-blowing coincidence, finding out that you live here too. That Mum's roots were here. It seemed almost meant to be. Not that I believe in that sort of thing, of course!' he finishes with an embarrassed little laugh.

The other two cats have wandered into the room while we've been talking. Gracie is looking at Alec very suspiciously, keeping her distance, but Vera – always the nosy one – has sidled up to him and is brushing herself against his legs. He leans down and strokes her.

'Lovely cats,' he says. 'I've only got the one: Billy. Very unoriginal name!'

'I love cats too,' Holly says wistfully. She's put the kettle on – I can hear it – but she's back again with a fresh plate of the chocolate biscuits. I have the distinct impression that, while she's trying to be polite and leave Alec and me to talk on our own, she's finding it hard to resist joining in. 'But I live in an upstairs flat, so it's difficult . . . and, well, you know, it'd be another mouth to feed.'

She goes back to the kitchen yet again, leaving Alec and me to talk – somewhat awkwardly – until she brings in the tea. It feels a bit more comfortable, somehow, with Holly in the room too. I'm already getting used to her being around, whereas he's still, really, a complete stranger. I notice Alec sneaking little glances at Holly and looking away quickly when she looks up – and her doing the same with him. It makes me smile. Even though it's been a shock to have him turn up like this, out of the blue, I can't get over the strange feeling it gives me, having to understand that I really do have a grandson! And he's actually sitting here in the room with me. Actually living in Hawbury Down, running a bookshop. It's all too much. I suddenly feel overwhelmed by it.

Holly turns to look at me. Maybe I gave a little sigh, or something, I don't know.

'Stella, this has all been a bit much for you, hasn't it?' she says sympathetically. 'I think perhaps we should leave you in peace now? Well, *I* should,' she corrects herself, giving Alec an apologetic smile. 'I've got a lot of work to get on with. But I'll wash up these cups and things first.'

I don't really want them to go – either of them. But on the other hand, I feel ridiculously exhausted. What with the worry about Peggy, to start with. I feel quite shaky inside.

'I'll go too,' Alec says. 'I need to get back to the shop.' He gets up, and turns to me again. 'It's been lovely to finally meet you,' he says, quietly. 'I was hoping you would reply to my letter eventually, of course I was. But if you hadn't – if you didn't want to meet me – well, I wasn't going to push it.'

'I'm glad you came,' I tell him. 'It might have taken me forever to reply to your letter.' I hesitate, then add: 'Come again, won't you.'

'Thanks, Stella.' Alec pauses, looking awkward. 'Sorry. Is it OK for me to be calling you *Stella*?'

I stare back at him. There's definitely something familiar about those blue eyes, that ready smile. Yes, he definitely has a look of Ernest about him.

'Of course it's OK.'

After all these years, I've now got *two* people calling me by my first name. And one of them is my grandson. How very strange life is.

9

Holly

I hardly know what to say to Stella after Alec's gone. I can see how tired she is, after all the emotional impact of that meeting, so after I've washed up, I remind her that I'm going to take my leave now.

'I'm sorry, Holly,' she says. 'But I can't ... I don't really feel up to talking to you about ... all of that, today. I didn't even know I had a grandson until he sent the letter, so it's all been a bit—'

'Don't be silly,' I reassure her. 'As I've said, you don't have to tell me anything. I'm going to leave you to rest now. And anyway, it must be nearly time for—' I quickly look at my watch – and jump to my feet, gasping.

'Oh, God! Oh, I'm so sorry, Stella, but I have to go right now! I'm late, already—' I grab my coat, thrust my arms into the sleeves and start heading for the door, apologising all the way. 'I'll come again, if that's OK—'

'All right.' She gets to her feet, starts to follow me, her knees obviously stiff from sitting. 'Got another appointment, have you?'

'No ... well, not an appointment, as such – it's the school. My daughter. I'll just about make it if I dash. Sorry.'

'Oh.' She's staring at me. 'I didn't realise you had – but never mind, off you go, don't be late, then. Thank you again. For the shopping, and all the extras.'

I thank her too and tell her goodbye, opening the front door and running down the path as she closes it behind me. The wind's fierce and icy in my face and I have to stop twice to use my asthma inhaler. When I finally reach my car, the engine's cold and it takes two attempts to start it. By the time I reach the school, the last few children are already coming out of Maisie's classroom. Maisie is standing alone with the teaching assistant, staring out of the window. I grab her hand as she comes running towards me, and gabble my apologies to both of them.

'You were *late*, Mummy,' Maisie says accusingly.

'I'm really sorry, sweetheart. You knew I'd soon be here, though, didn't you? The car didn't want to start.'

I don't bother trying to tell her where I've been. It feels like such a lot to try to explain She's used to me going to see people for features. We often talk about the local authors, artists, or musicians I interview. She's only seven, but she understands that this is part of my job. In fact she once wrote in her school 'news' book that I liked chatting to famous people, resulting in her teacher, at the next parents' evening, asking curiously and only half-jokingly, whether I was a celebrity-stalker. But I'm aware that Stella Jackman might never give me permission to write her story, so I don't really know why I'm starting to make a habit of going to see her. And it might seem quite odd, even to Maisie, that I'm doing Stella's shopping and worrying about whether she's lonely, or cold, up in that house on the edge of the cliff which everyone's been urging her to leave for years.

To make it up to Maisie for being late, we stop off at the corner shop on the way home and, deciding against the more expensive treats when I remember my bank balance, I just buy a packet of crumpets so that she can have one, hot, with butter and jam, for her after-school snack. Then she sits at the table with me while I hear her read from her new school book, before we watch some television together. My flat's so small, it warms up quickly as soon as the heating's on, but we still put a blanket over us while we're snuggled up on the sofa, just to be cosy. Outside, the wind's still howling, and there's sleet beginning to spatter against the window. I can't stop myself from wondering whether Stella's got her electric fire on and whether she's going to cook herself a hot meal. What the hell must it be like, up there, if it snows? How has she managed, up till now, to get down that track when it's covered in ice, to meet the Co-op delivery van? It's a wonder she hasn't fallen and broken her neck. I'm going to tell her I'll keep doing her shopping, at least while the weather's so bad. In a weird kind of way, I think I'm imagining how I'd feel if she were my gran and I didn't live close to her. And if nobody helped her or looked after her.

The next morning, Maisie wakes me up, shouting with excitement. It's been snowing in the night and there's a light dusting on the ground – not a common sight at all here on the South Devon coast.

'Can we go out and build a snowman?' she shrieks.

She's got her welly boots in her hands and a scarf on, even though she's still in her PJs. I try to explain that there isn't enough snow for that, but there's no calming her down so I laugh and say that once we're both dressed, we'll give it a try.

It's freezing cold outside and my gloves are soaked through almost as soon as we start trying to scrape some of the meagre scattering of snow from the ground into some kind of shape. I can't feel my fingers any more, my nose is going numb and I'm surprised Maisie is still jumping around, laughing with excitement, her little cheeks pink from the cold and her eyes sparkling.

'Sorry, Mais, I don't think we've even got enough for a snowball, never mind a snowman,' I tell her eventually. 'Come on, let's go back inside before we freeze.'

'Oh, but Mummy—' she starts to protest, standing still and scowling at me. I remind her that we've got the rest of the crumpets to finish off for breakfast and her mood changes abruptly. 'Race you back indoors!' she shouts, as if it's a hundred metre sprint rather than just a few paces to the door of our flats.

To be fair, she can sprint up the stairs a lot faster than I'd be able to do, even without my boots on. I remember feeling so grateful once she was old enough to climb the stairs herself. There's no lift, because these aren't purpose-built modern flats. They're what I think people used to call maisonettes: an old house converted into two flats. Carrying shopping *and* helping a toddler up here wasn't much fun, even though we're only one floor up. I was certainly thankful, back then, for the lobby downstairs where I could leave the pushchair. The couple downstairs haven't got children and they're out at work all the time. I hardly ever see them, and, when I do, they're always in a hurry. But at least they're not the type to complain about us making a noise when we're in the garden, or about the inevitable crying when Maisie was younger.

Once we've shed our coats, boots, hats and gloves, I toast the remaining crumpets and make a big pot of hot chocolate for us to share.

'This is my favourite breakfast *ever*,' Maisie says, as we enjoy our little feast together. She's wearing an old jumper she loves, in her favourite colour – purple – with a picture of a snowman on it. It's really far too small for her now, but I haven't got the heart to suggest getting rid of it, however ridiculous it looks, and, anyway, I can't help hoping it will last her for the rest of this winter. It was expensive enough having to buy a new school uniform for her in September because she'd outgrown the previous year's. 'It's been the best *morning* ever,' she goes on excitedly. 'I hope it keeps snowing!'

But by the time we've finished our crumpets and chocolate, the snow has pretty much gone. Maisie's disappointed, of course, but I get out her paints, cover the kitchen table with sheets of paper and set her to work painting snowmen and she's soon happily occupied while I do some washing and housework. And all the time, I'm wondering about Stella – whether she's warm enough, whether she's even got her fire on, whether the windows in that old house let a cold draught in. Should I call her? Check up on her?

I'm worrying in exactly the way I used to worry about Gran, but at least Gran was family; I could nag her as much as I wanted (in the nicest sense of the word) and go round there as often as I liked to make sure she was OK. She was family ... my only family, really, apart from Maisie, of course. And now she's gone, and I'm – what? Trying to make another elderly woman, who's still not much more than a stranger, into some kind of grandmother substitute? What exactly *am* I doing this for, probing into her life, getting her shopping, buying her treats like I did for Gran? Asking for her stories, her memories, unless I'm actually going to write something for the magazine? And if I'm not going to do that, I need to be writing something else or I'll lose my best client.

OK, I'm not going to call her. I'm in danger of becoming a nuisance – especially now she's discovered she's got a grandson – a *real* member of family to keep an eye on her. I wonder again about the daughter, Susan – as I've been doing constantly, ever since Stella mentioned her. 'I *had* a daughter,' was how she phrased it. And she doesn't want to talk about her; so it seems fairly obvious, sadly, that Susan's either no longer with us, or perhaps that Stella's fallen out with her, so badly that she doesn't even acknowledge her as a daughter anymore. That would be just as sad – but then, I know all about fractured family relationships myself. Nothing would shock me.

Anyway, I've decided that I'll go back on Monday and broach

the subject, again, of the feature for *Devon Today*. If Stella won't agree to it, I need to have an honest talk to myself about whether I really need an eighty-three-year-old friend, or substitute gran. Or more to the point: whether she needs me. But even as I'm telling myself this, I'm adding, in the back of my mind, that whatever I decide, I can at least still do her shopping for her, unless Alec wants to do it now. I picture him taking bags of shopping and little treats up to the house for her, like I did yesterday, and find myself smiling. He seems a nice guy. Lovely smile. I hope he'll be good to her.

10

Stella

TWO DAYS LATER

She's back. I presume it's her – Holly – anyway, as hardly anyone else ever came to my door until Alec turned up the other day, and I don't suppose he'll be back again yet. I don't want to start expecting it, looking forward to it, in case he doesn't. Apart from him and Holly, my only other visitors in recent years have been the busybodies from the council who come round to tell me how fast the cliff's eroding and try to talk me into moving out. Where exactly do they think I'm going to move out to? They're not offering me their spare bedrooms, or a nice little cottage down in the town. They want me to move into an old people's home, that's what they're getting at. Well, I'm not going anywhere. This is my home. It's not going to fall into the sea yet, I tell them; it'll last till I'm gone. If it was toppling over the edge, I'd be the first to know about it. My cats wouldn't come indoors. They've got a sixth sense, cats have – they won't walk into danger.

Holly's shivering as she comes in. The wind hasn't let up since Friday – sleet and even snow beating against the windows over the weekend. She's got her asthma thing in her hand, and I make her sit down and take some puffs of it while I put the kettle on.

'You shouldn't come out in the cold, with your bad chest,' I tell her.

She chuckles. She's trying to speak, but her breathing isn't right yet.

'Don't worry about *me*,' she says eventually. 'It's you I've been . . . thinking about. Are you managing to keep warm enough?'

'Course I am.' I tut. Why do young people always think we get dafter as we get older? I've got the fire on, not that I like using it during the day, but needs must. And anyway: 'I'm wearing my thermals,' I tell her. 'And two jumpers.'

'Good.' She goes quiet now, bending down to stroke Vera, who's already rubbing herself against her legs. I make the tea, leave it to draw, and put the rest of the biscuits she got me on a plate. 'And I hope you're OK after . . . all the excitement,' she says now. 'On Friday.'

'Course I am,' I say quickly. 'It was . . . just a surprise, that's all. A nice surprise, but still, he might be my grandson but I don't even know him. He might not even come again, for all I know.'

'I'm sure he will,' she says. 'He seemed very nice.'

'Mm. Handsome too, wasn't he?' I say, smiling at her, and I can see she's trying to take no notice, trying not to blush. I shouldn't tease her. 'I'm glad you've come,' I say instead – because I am. I don't want her to think she shouldn't come now, just because I've suddenly got a grandson. 'I'd have made another cake if I knew.'

'I don't want you to go to that sort of trouble.' She looks a bit uncomfortable, as if she's not sure how to go on. 'I don't want to . . . become a nuisance.'

Ah, I see. So perhaps she *does* feel like her nose is out of joint. Either that, or she's getting fed up with this, already – coming up here in the cold – and who can blame her? I feel stupid now. Embarrassed. I'd started to think, what with her getting my shopping, and buying me extra treats like she did, that she was ... I don't know ... perhaps wanting to be my friend. Perhaps actually interested in me, and in my silly old memories, rather than just being polite because she was still hoping to write something about me in her magazine. More fool me.

'You don't have to keep coming,' I say, a bit more sharply than I mean to. 'It's no skin off my nose, you can suit yourself.'

'Oh.' She looks mortified now. 'No, I ... I'm happy to come. I just don't want to *intrude*. But if you'd rather I didn't, well, look, I'll still get your shopping on Fridays.'

She tails off, looking down at the cat again. I've gone and upset her now. Damn it, have I got it all wrong? I'm not used to dealing with people these days, that's my trouble.

'You're not intruding,' I tell her. Well, I might as well be honest. 'I like you coming – as long as you want to. It's nice to have your company.'

She's nodding to herself, still looking unsure. Oh, what the hell? If the story's what she's really after, is it the end of the world? I suppose you could say it's a fair exchange: her company, and doing my shopping, in return for writing something about how long I've lived here and why I won't move. Or why they call me a witch, I suppose. Is that what people really want to read about?

'You can write your story, if you want,' I say – and she looks up in surprise. I'd almost say she's looking guilty, as if she feels bad that I've guessed right. 'You can call me "The Witch of Cliff's End", if it makes you happy.'

'It doesn't!' she retorts. 'That's just people being stupid. And I don't even know whether I want to write it at all, any more.' She looks shocked, for a moment, as if she hadn't known the words were going to come out of her mouth. 'It's just ... I need to write *something*,' she goes on more quietly. 'Or I won't get paid, obviously. And I can't think about anything else, quite honestly, since you started telling me your story. I just want to hear what happened next. Why you stayed in Devon. How things were, back then – during the war, and afterwards.'

'And you're a writer, and you need to write this story, you need to pay your bills.' I say gently. 'You've got a little girl – you don't look old enough!'

She laughs. 'I'm twenty-eight! And yes, I do need to pay my bills, and it isn't easy. But I'm not entirely reliant on my writing. Three afternoons a week, I do a cleaning job for an agency in the town.'

'I see.' I nod. Good for her, she's a worker. Trying to juggle two jobs, with a child at school. I remember all too well how it feels to be short of money; it was like that when I was young, working on the farm, having nothing to spend on the things I wanted.

And she's twenty-eight! She still looks like a teenager to me, with her long dark hair and tight jeans. Two jobs or not, with a little girl to fend for no doubt she's struggling, like most young parents. She hasn't said whether there's a man on the scene, but she's got no ring on her finger, so I'd hazard a guess she's a single mum. And she's buying *me* little luxuries! I tut to myself. I should be the one helping her! I've got my pension, after all, and my own house. I'm not so badly off. Suddenly, I make up my mind. New grandson or not, and unexpected though that is, I'd still like a friend. I can't remember when I last had one, and I haven't thought about it for years, but now the need is suddenly so strong it almost takes my breath away. I like this girl. I like her coming to see me, I like the way she seems to care about me, I even like telling her my life story. I don't want it to stop.

'Don't stop coming,' I say, putting down the teapot just as I was about to pour the tea. 'I'm enjoying your visits. I'm a bit lonely sometimes, I suppose, and I've got no idea whether my ... whether *Alec* is going to want to be part of my life yet. He might have just been curious. Wanted to see what I'm like. No, it's true,' I insist, as she starts to protest. 'I'm being realistic. He might come again, he might not! But meanwhile, maybe you and I can help each other.'

'I don't need help,' she says, smiling.

'Yes, you do. You need a story for the magazine. Well, you don't have to write about me, necessarily, if it makes you feel uncomfortable. But you can do something with what I'm telling you – about the war, and being an evacuee here – can't you? Hillside Farm's still here, after all. People might be interested to know what it was like here back then – when Hawbury Down was just a little village. When the school was just that old building, where the nursery school is now—'

'Yes. Maisie went there – that's my daughter. She's in the new building next door to it now, of course.' Holly's brightened up. She gives me a smile. 'That's such a good idea, Stella. I *did* feel uncomfortable at the thought of writing about you. It felt like ... taking advantage of our friendship. That's if we're going to be friends, of course?'

'Don't be daft. We're friends already, aren't we?' I say, trying to sound deliberately off-hand, so she doesn't know how much I'm smiling inside of me. 'Now then. I'm pouring out this tea. Take that plate of biscuits through to the sitting room and tell me what you want to hear about next.'

She jumps up, takes the plate through, and is already back for the tea tray by the time I've finished pouring.

'The only thing is,' I say, trying to keep my voice even, 'I don't want to ... talk about my daughter – Alec's mother. Not yet. I will tell you. But I'd like to build up to it slowly, if that's OK.'

'Of course. Just talk to me about whatever you want. What

you remember, from living on the farm as a child, being an evacuee,' she says.

'All right,' I agree. 'I'll tell you about when I started school, shall I? That's a really clear memory. I'd only been living on the farm for a week or so, and it was the first time I'd walked into the village on my own.'

'On your own?' she repeats, looking scandalised. 'At five years old?'

'Yes, we all went around on our own. There was no traffic, see, apart from the odd tractor. And the village was Hawbury Down, of course. That's all it was back then, a little village. Hard to imagine now, isn't it?'

SEPTEMBER 1940

Auntie Nellie stood back to run a critical eye over Stella's appearance.

'Pull your socks up. You want to look smart for your first day. Got your gas mask?'

'Yes.' Stella wasn't sure why she had to take it. She'd never had to use it. Uncle Jim had told her the Germans had never used the poison gas that everyone was frightened they were going to drop out of their planes to choke everyone. No, they just dropped bombs – and that didn't often happen in the countryside, just in the big towns. But if Auntie Nellie said she had to take the bag with the gas mask, she'd take it. She'd already realised it paid to just do exactly as she was told.

It felt strange, setting off alone for the first time, the bag with the gas mask hanging on her back, bumping her bottom as she walked. It was a nice morning, and she was happy enough, thinking about the friends Uncle Jim said she was going to make at school. It would be more fun than helping her uncle in the fields, or her aunt in the kitchen. When she arrived at her classroom, though, she hesitated, unsure what to expect,but the teacher, Miss Jordan, introduced her to another evacuee from London, who was starting in the class that same day.

'You'll be friends for each other,' she said, smiling at Stella and the other girl, Ruby. 'You may sit together, as long as you're both good.'

Stella was definitely going to be good. She was too frightened to be anything else.

'I'm going to show you both your pegs in the cloakroom,' Miss Jordan went on. 'They have labels with your name on. I want you to look very carefully at the labels and try to remember what your names look like.'

'Please, miss, I can already read my name,' Stella said eagerly. 'My uncle showed me. When can I start reading some books?'

Miss Jordan smiled. 'After you've learned your alphabet.'

'I know A, B, and C already and I can write them.'

'That ain't so hard,' said Ruby. 'I done D and E too.'

'Well, I'm *very* pleased to hear you've both already started learning your alphabet,' Miss Jordan said.

Stella looked at Ruby, and Ruby looked back at Stella. They grinned at each other. And Stella knew, right away, that she'd not only got a friend, she'd also got a rival. She was desperate to learn to read books. And she was going to learn to write D and E as quickly as possible, to catch up with Ruby!

Stella settled quickly into school life. Ruby was a tough, spirited girl who stood up to the inevitable teasing in the playground from the local children about the two girls' cockney accents, telling them cheerfully where to get off. She'd sling an arm around Stella's shoulders and they'd walk away together, heads held high, and giggle about it afterwards. It wasn't long before the teasing stopped.

It soon became clear that Ruby and Stella were among the fastest learners in their class. They practised their alphabet and their times tables together, chanting them out loud while they played skipping games in the playground, instead of the usual *Salt, Mustard, Vinegar, Pepper.* Before long Miss Jordan had given them both their first reading book.

'Can you come back to play at my place after school on Thursday?' Ruby asked Stella one day at playtime. 'It's my birthday and Auntie Lil said I could have a friend back for tea.'

Ruby often talked about her Auntie Lil – who wasn't an auntie at all, of course, but the lady who'd taken her in as an evacuee. Stella felt envious listening to Ruby's stories about Auntie Lil, who made nice pies and cakes for tea and let Ruby play in their garden with her own younger children instead of making her work all the time. Her heart leapt at the thought of going back to their house in the village instead of trudging home to the farm to do chores and eat stewed rabbit.

Stella ran all the way back down the lane that afternoon, her fingers crossed inside her gloves. It was December now, freezing cold, and there was sleet in the air.

'Auntie Nellie, please may I—' she began as soon as she arrived home – being especially careful with her grammar and her manners.

'You can fetch some more firewood in, before you do anything else.'

'Yes, I will, but please, may I go to Ruby's house on Thursday after school? It's her birthday and her auntie says I can go to play and have my tea there.'

'Does she, now.' Auntie Nellie turned round to give Stella a hard look. 'And who does her auntie think is going to help with my chores that afternoon, while you're *playing* and *having your tea*, like a lady of leisure? And you'd be expected to take her a birthday present, you realise that? What do you imagine you're going to take her? Eh?'

'I don't know,' Stella said, looking at the floor. Then she brightened up. 'One of my books! I can give Ruby one of my books, she'd love that. I'll still have the other one. And my school readers.'

'Books!' scoffed Auntie Nellie. 'They'll be wanting more than books. They've got twin boys; they'll be wanting something off the farm, you mark my words. Like we're not struggling ourselves. There's a war on, girl, there's no money for luxuries like books. You'll come home here and help out as usual on Thursday, and be grateful you've got a safe home, away from those murdering Nazis and their bombs.'

Stella swallowed back tears. 'I *am* grateful,' she said. 'But can't I just—'

'No, you can't! Now do as you're told and get that firewood in. Your uncle will be back from the fields soon, it's nearly dark and there's no fire lit yet.'

Stella turned and went outside. She'd just started to fill the wood basket with firewood from the stack in the woodshed when she heard her uncle whistling as he walked back from the fields. Seeing the shed door open, he peered inside and gave her a little wave.

'Hello, my lovely. Want a hand with that?'

She sniffed back her tears. 'Thank you.'

'What's up?' he gave her a sideways look as he helped pile wood into the basket. 'Hurt yourself?'

'No.' She hesitated, then went on in a rush: 'Ruby asked me to go and play and have my tea at her place on Thursday 'cos it's her birthday, but I've got to come home to do the chores and anyway we can't afford to give her anything off the farm 'cos there's a war on.'

'I see.' Uncle Jim looked at her solemnly for a moment. 'Well, that's a dilemma, and no mistake, isn't it?'

'Yes, and I really wanted to go, and I could give her one of my books, but that won't do, because her auntie's got other kids and they need stuff and . . . ' She paused again. 'Couldn't we give them some of my meat coupons? I don't like meat much anyway. And we *have* got lots of spuds and cabbages on the farm. And rabbits,' she added, pulling a face. Although she had to eat them, she'd never really got used to the fact that her uncle shot rabbits for their dinners.

He laughed. 'No, love, we can't give them our rations. We need them ourselves. We don't grow everything we need! But leave it with me. I'll have a think.'

She brightened up. If her uncle was going to have a think, she was sure he'd find a way round it. A way round Auntie Nellie, perhaps – although that was probably going to put her in an even worse mood with Stella. But she trusted him. He'd always been kind to her.

And so it was that, despite the pinched look of disapproval on her great-aunt's face, Stella set off for school that Thursday carrying a net shopping bag. Inside it was a home-made birthday card; her Peter Rabbit book wrapped up with brown paper and string; and a cabbage and two pounds of carrots.

Holly

Stella's stroking Gracie and smiling to herself. It's nice to know she's got some happy memories of her time as an evacuee, after all.

'I'm glad you made a friend at school,' I tell her. 'Ruby sounds lovely.'

'Yes.' She nods. 'We were company for each other. The only two kids from London in the village. There were other evacuees, of course, in fact the school was crowded with them. But they were mostly from nearby towns – Exeter or Plymouth – so they didn't have our *funny accent.*'

'Did having a friend make up for having to live with that horrible auntie, though?'

She laughs. 'Ah, well, like I told you before, I got used to Auntie Nellie. And she *never* stopped reminding me what a favour they were doing me, keeping me away from London, the bombs, all the danger.' There's quite a long pause, before she adds: 'As it turned out, she was quite right.'

I wonder what she means; what she's going on to tell me about next. But I'm conscious that I've been here quite a while already, and time's getting on, so I suppose I'll find out more another time. We chat for a little while about other things: how cold the weather is; how her cats love to snuggle indoors on the cushions; and whether she's cooking herself good hot meals. Then I check my watch again and say:

'Sorry, Stella, but I'd better be going. I've got to work this after-noon – cleaning one of the big houses up on The Avenue.'

'Oh, very nice too. I had a friend who used to live in one of those. I'll tell you about it another time.'

'Yes, please do!' I say with a smile. 'Look, it's brightened up a little bit outside now. I expect it's still cold, though. Keep the fire on, Stella.'

'All right, all right, don't nag!' she says, even though she's smil-ing back at me.

I go home to make myself some lunch, but then, as I'm early enough, instead of driving straight to the house on The Avenue, I head for the lane that leads to Hillside Farm. It's on the out-skirts of town and although I knew where it was, I wouldn't have remembered that the road's actually called Hillside Lane. I drive slowly up the lane, watching my mileage on the dashboard. It's well over a mile from the centre of town, where the school is, to Hillside Farm Cottage, which must be the house where Stella lived with her great-aunt and uncle. I stop in the gateway of the farm itself, another quarter of a mile further on – the road runs out here anyway – thinking about Stella, as a five year old, walking all that way to school on her own. Although Maisie's seven now, there's no way I'd consider her even doing the ten-minute walk from our flat to school without me. She'll probably be eleven before I let her go anywhere on her own, and even then, I'm sure I'll be worried sick. I suppose, as Stella pointed out, there wasn't much traffic around when she was young. That isn't the only danger to our kids, obviously, but perhaps in those days, the other horrible things we parents imagine happening just weren't reported so widely. As she's said: no television, and no social media.

I drive back down the lane even more slowly, looking more carefully around me. Hillside Farm Cottage looks like any traditional picture-postcard old country cottage, with crooked cream walls, a red roof, and a nice garden, fenced all the way round, with a child's swing prominent at the side. Perhaps the cottage doesn't even belong to the farm anymore. I haven't asked Stella whether any of her second cousins or their families still own the farm, but surely if they did, they'd be looking after her now? Didn't she say nobody ever called her by her first name these days? I start wondering what happened to those second cousins – her Uncle Stan's children – but then I realise that they'd probably all have passed away by now.

There's a small modern housing development halfway down the lane, a group of neat little grey stone houses in a cul-de-sac curving around a tiny green. Probably built around the nineteen-eighties or nineties. Other than this, the countryside around here might not have changed too much since Stella used to run back up this lane to avoid being late home for her chores.

I'm finding myself feeling strangely nostalgic – if it's even possible to feel nostalgic for something that wasn't my own life, but somebody else's. I need, tomorrow, to start writing up some of what Stella's told me about already, leaving out the personal detail, as I promised. I need to have something to send Frosty Fran before too long. I can use Stella's descriptions of life on Hillside Farm during the war, and what the village school was like. And whatever comes next.

It's a nicer day next time I go to see Stella. Still cold, but bright and sunny. She tells me she's been outside and had a wander around the garden, just to get some fresh air.

'I don't do anything much out there nowadays,' she says. 'Apart from hanging out a bit of washing if it's windy enough. Not until the daffodils come out, anyway – then I like to pick some to put indoors; they brighten the place up.'

'I think you told me you used to grow your own veg,' I say.

'Yes. All sorts of veg. Had chickens too, for a few years – four of 'em. I suppose it came from living on the farm all that time. It got into my blood.'

'It must have been nice, growing your own food, and getting your own eggs,' I say. I turn to look at her, feeling a bit embarrassed. 'I drove down Hillside Lane the other day,' I go on, watching her reaction. 'Just ... wanted to see the farm, and your cottage. So that I could picture you living there.'

'Oh.' She sounds surprised, but not displeased. 'I haven't been there for years.'

'I presume the farm doesn't belong to anyone in your family now? Or the cottage?'

'No. Geoffrey – my Uncle Stan and Auntie Flo's younger son – inherited the farm after they died. But he never married, never had any children. He sold the farm in the end.'

'Really? Why was that? Didn't any of the other siblings want to take it on?'

'No. The eldest son, Stanley Junior, had died in the war, see. And the girls weren't interested in farming; they got married and moved away. One went to Cornwall, the other one somewhere up-country.' She shrugged. 'Geoffrey was getting on in years and of course by then my Uncle Jim and Auntie Nellie had passed away too—'

'But what about you?' I ask her. 'Surely the farm cottage was still your home! Was that sold too?'

'Yes, it was sold as part of the estate. But it wasn't my home any more, by then. I'd moved out. I was living here at Cliff's End,' she says, suddenly looking away from me.

'I see. So . . . how did that come about?'

'Well, we're getting ahead of ourselves, aren't we?' she says. 'I'll come to that, in due course.'

'Yes, of course. Sorry.'

'Anyway, I have some news too.' She's smiling now. 'Guess who called on me again yesterday?'

From the look of pleasure on her face, I don't think it would take a genius to guess.

'Alec?' I reply, smiling back.

'Yes. And we had a bit more of a chat this time, because it wasn't such a shock to see him.'

'Ah, that's nice. I bet you're really enjoying getting to know him at last. How lovely for you.'

'To be honest, Holly, I still can't get over it. It's so sudden. First you, now my grandson. *Two* new people in my life, after God knows how long I've been up here on my own, talking to the cats, never seeing a living soul apart from the nosy parkers telling me my house is falling down—'

'Well, I'm pleased for you, I really am.'

'Alec's given me his phone number and says I've got to call him if I ever need anything. He did ask about my shopping, and I explained you've started doing it. But it might help if he does it sometimes, Holly? If it's heavy. Or if your asthma's bad. He said he'd talk to you about it.'

'Did he?' I feel suddenly a bit flustered. Stella's grinning at me as if she's said something funny. I hope she didn't notice how attractive I found her grandson when he was here last week; I feel embarrassed at the very thought of her knowing.

'Yes,' she goes on. 'I said I'd ask you if it's all right to give him your phone number.' She's chuckling to herself now. I bet she can see how awkward I feel. 'But if you'd rather I didn't—'

'No, no, that's fine, of course; give him my number by all means.

71

We'll discuss the shopping but I'm happy to do it,' I say, trying to make it sound like I couldn't care less one way or the other. I just want to change the subject. I do *not* want to start thinking like this about Alec, especially if I might bump into him any time I'm up here visiting Stella. I promised myself years ago I wouldn't have these sort of thoughts about a man, ever again. 'Let me take the tea tray into the living room for you,' I tell Stella, to distract her from the matter of her grandson. 'And perhaps you've got another little story to tell me today? About your childhood?'

'Right, let me think,' she says, following me into the living room. 'Well, I could tell you about when I first saw the sea.'

'When you first –?' I look at her in surprise. 'You'd never seen the sea before?'

'No. If there hadn't been a war on, of course, my mum might have taken me to Southend on a Bank Holiday, back when I lived in the East End. That's what people around there used to do for a day trip. But from what I've heard since, Southend was in the exclusion zone during the war so nobody could go there unless they lived there. Anyway, until Ruby told me, I didn't even know Hawbury Down was on the coast. When I found out the sea was only a bit further down the road from my school, I begged my auntie and uncle to take me to see it.'

'And I suppose your aunt said no?'

'Of course. In her view, there was no time for such things as looking at the sea, when there was work to be done!' I chuckled. 'But one day Uncle Jim took me there, when we were supposed to be going to see someone about buying some new chickens.'

'And how was that? When you saw it?'

'Well, you can imagine. Like most kids, I suppose, I couldn't believe how huge it was. I would have still been in my first year at school, then. Probably the spring of forty-one. I'd still only have been six, so I don't remember it terribly well, although obviously we couldn't go on the beach – the beaches were all fenced off with barbed wire.' Then I laugh, something else coming back to me. 'But I've got a much clearer memory of another time I went down there. With Ruby!'

'Oh, tell me about that, then!' I say eagerly, taking a sip of my tea.

'Well, it was maybe a year or two later. And a winter day, much like this, actually. Ruby and I used to hang about together after school for as long as I dared, before I had to run all the way home so I wouldn't get told off for being late ...' She pauses. 'It must have been March, actually. I realise why I remember it so well. It was the same day—'

Stella has suddenly stopped, her cup halfway to her mouth, frozen in mid-sentence, staring into space.

'Are you OK?' I ask her.

'Yes. Sorry. I'm all right. It's just—' She shakes her head. 'Nothing. So, like I was saying, it was all because of Ruby, of course. We went down to see the sea on our own, on a cold, windy day in March. Trust Ruby!' she adds with a little laugh. 'It was typical of her.'

I wonder what association this memory has brought back to her. Whatever it is, I don't think it could be such a happy memory as her visit to the sea with Ruby seems to have been. I wonder if she'll even want to tell me about it.

12

MARCH 1943

It had been a good day at school. Stella and Ruby had both moved on to the next reading book. And Ruby had scored a rounder during outdoor games, which they were still expected to do, wearing little more than their underwear despite the freezing conditions, the reasoning being that they'd move around a whole lot faster, to warm up, so it wouldn't do them any harm. They were both in a cheerful mood as they lingered in the playground after school, playing hopscotch on a court someone had chalked up during playtime.

'Home time, children,' one of the teachers yelled at them after a few minutes, and they strolled out of the school gate, arms linked, heading for the corner of the lane where they would have to separate and head in different directions.

'I don't want to go home,' Stella admitted.

'Me neither.' Ruby turned and grinned at her friend. 'I know! Let's go to the beach!'

'The beach?' Stella stared at Ruby as if she'd just suggested taking a trip to the moon. Neither of the girls had ever seen the sea until they came to live in Hawbury Down, and because of the dangers there now, it was far from being a place for happy family outings. *Going to the beach* was a phrase they only encountered in books, where they saw pictures of people paddling in the sea, in the days before the war.

'Come on,' Ruby encouraged Stella, grabbing her hand. 'Let's have an adventure.'

'But we can't go *on* the beach, Rube. It's all fenced off.'

'I know. We can just have a look, though, can't we? On our own? I 'ain't been down there for ages.'

'Me neither.' Stella shrugged, laughing. 'All right. I better not be long, though. My auntie will go mad if I'm late.'

She put her arm through Ruby's again and the two of them set off, giggling, in the opposite direction from that she should have been taking.

It wasn't far. In fact, it was only five minutes or so before the sea came into view. Stella and Ruby stopped a little way short of the barbed wire at the edge of the beach, watching the towering waves, listening to the crash of them against the shingle.

'Ain't it *noisy*,' Stella shouted above the sound of the wind and the waves.

'Yeah.' Ruby was looking a bit less sure of herself now. 'I don't think I like it so much when it's like this. Let's go back. It's cold down 'ere.'

'Yeah, we'd better,' Stella agreed. 'Look at them notices. "Keep off",' she read out loud. '"*DANGER*".'

'Yeah, that's 'cos of the mines,' Ruby reminded her. 'To kill the Germans, if they come. I hope they don't.'

''Specially not right now,' Stella agreed. 'While we're standing here, eh?'

'Would you be scared?' Ruby grinned at her. 'I wouldn't. I'd punch them right on the nose, kick them in the legs—'

'They're not coming. My uncle says they're not, he says we're going to win the war.'

'Course we will,' Ruby agreed.

'Come on, then, let's hurry up back, or I'm gonna be in such bad trouble.'

Despite her anxiety about being late, Stella couldn't help giving a little skip and a jump as she walked back up the lane towards Hillside Farm. It had been lovely that she and Ruby had had their own little secret adventure. She'd remember this day for ever!

When she walked into the cottage – the front door was never locked unless everyone was out – she found both her aunt and uncle in the kitchen, waiting for her. Her first thought was that she was in for a serious telling off. The fire was already built up and lit, so they must have given up waiting for her and done it themselves.

'I'm sorry I'm late,' she said, looking from one of them to the other. She tried to think of an excuse, but she wasn't very good at lying.

'Sit down, Stella,' said Uncle Jim. His voice was soft, but he wasn't smiling. Nor was Auntie Nellie. 'We've got something to tell you.'

'What?' she asked, wondering if somehow they'd found out where she'd been.

'It's ... something's happened, child,' Uncle Jim said. 'Something very sad.' He ran a hand over his face, sighing.

'Is one of the sheep dead?' she asked. The previous spring, one of the new baby lambs had died. It was her first close-up experience of death. When she'd asked if the lamb had gone to heaven, Uncle Jim had laughed and said maybe, but the fox that got it could definitely go to hell.

'Not a sheep,' he said now.

'Oh, for God's sake, Jimmy, just tell her,' Auntie Nellie interrupted impatiently. 'She needs to know. It's no good pussyfooting around it.' She turned to Stella, putting one of her big, red hands on her shoulder. 'It's your mother, child. We got told today. She's dead. And your nan too.'

'What?' Stella shook her head, confused. 'No, they ain't dead. My mum ain't dead, she wrote me a letter last week, didn't she? I read it all myself.'

'It's happened since the letter, child,' Uncle Jim said. His face had gone grey, and his voice sounded funny. Stella was frightened. She didn't understand. 'They were killed by a bomb. A direct hit. A very bad hit,' he went on quietly. 'Lots of people ... women and children ...'

'No.' Stella knew the Germans were dropping bombs on London – but her mum always wrote in her letters that she would be safe. 'Mum said she wouldn't get hit by the bombs!' she said, pushing Auntie Nellie's hand off her. 'Her and my nan go down the Tube station to stay safe from the bombs. That's what she said!'

'But it was the station that got hit,' Uncle Jim said. 'That's why they died, Stella. They wouldn't have known anything about it,' he added, glancing at Auntie Nellie, who nodded her head in agreement. 'It ... would've been quick, child. They'd have gone quick.'

'To heaven?' she said, looking from one of them to the other. 'They've gone quick to heaven?'

'Yes. Course.' He turned away, but not before she'd seen the glint of tears in his eyes. Even Auntie Nellie looked upset. But to Stella, it just didn't feel real. Even though she liked getting the letters from her mum every couple of weeks, she couldn't remember her very well now. She didn't have any photos, so try as she might, she was finding it harder and harder to think what she looked like. The idea of her mother and grandmother being dead, like the lamb was dead, or like she'd been taught at school, the previous Easter, about Jesus dying on the cross, was too momentous to take on board. She knew she should be glad they were in heaven, but that was even more impossible to imagine.

'It's all right if you want to have a little cry,' Uncle Jim said in his funny different voice.

'Thank you,' she said. 'But I don't think I will.'

'You don't have to do your chores tonight,' Auntie Nellie said.

Stella stared at her in surprise. 'Oh. Well, I've got to practise my twelve times table.'

But, even more surprisingly, when she went to school the next day, her teacher called her 'poor child', and kept giving her sad little smiles all day. And Ruby was very quiet, holding her hand under their desk, and putting her arm round her while they were in the playground.

So, although Stella knew that the news about her mum and her nan was a very sad thing, and a very hard thing to understand or believe, the worst thing about that day was that she couldn't talk to anyone about going down to the beach with her friend on their own.

It was two whole years before she – or anyone else – found out what had really happened at Bethnal Green tube station. And by then, her mum and her nan were just names from her past. That was what made it *really* sad.

13

Holly

'I wasn't going to tell you all that,' Stella says, looking up at me apologetically. She's been staring at the electric fire, talking quietly, almost to herself, but now she's come to an abrupt stop. 'Didn't want to upset you.'

I shake my head at her. 'No, it must be upsetting for *you*, surely – remembering it, and talking about it.'

'Well, what you have to remember is, lots of children lost their parents during the war. My father died too, of course. He was shot down, about a year after my mum died.'

'So then you were an orphan.'

'I was. I suppose it does sound horrible, put like that.' To my surprise, she shrugs. 'But don't forget, I didn't know my dad at all. He'd been away in the air force since I was very little. And as I said, eventually it was hard to remember my mum too.'

'You said you found out the truth later – about what happened at the tube station. Was it *not* a bomb, then?'

'No, it wasn't. That was just the story the government put about. It was an accident really, a terrible accident. There were so many people rushing to shelter in the Underground because they heard the air raid sirens – someone tripped, pulled someone else down with them, and the people at the top just kept pushing … falling on top of each other—'

'Oh, God. Like the Hillsborough disaster?'

'Worse than that. A hundred and seventy-five people got crushed to death, most of them women and children. And everyone was told it was a bomb. Afterwards, the government explained it had to be covered up in case the Germans heard what happened and tried to cause more panics like that, to kill more people.'

'So there weren't really any bombs there at all that night?' I ask, a bit confused.

Stella shakes her head. 'No. The bangs they heard weren't bombs. They were actually anti-aircraft rockets being fired by *our* side. They were new. Nobody was used to hearing them.'

'But how on earth did the government keep the truth quiet?'

'Easy, in those days: censorship. And there wasn't any television, or Twittering or whatever you call it. Even the nurses and doctors who looked after the wounded that night, and certified the dead, weren't allowed to tell anyone what had really happened. It must have been a terrible thing to live with.'

'It wouldn't work now,' I retort. 'It's not right, is it? People need to know the truth.'

'Yes – and we *were* told, eventually.' She gives me a gentle smile. 'Everything's different when there's a war on, Holly. Secrets have to be kept from the enemy. Anyway, I've heard there's a memorial at Bethnal Green station now, to everyone who died that night. Some of the relatives fought for it to be built. Nice idea.'

'Have you been to see it?'

She looks astonished. 'Me? No. Why would I want to go all the way up to London?'

'You've got no family left up there at all now?'

She shakes her head. 'Not that I know of. Auntie Nellie and Uncle Jim were my family, really. They brought me up.'

'So that's why you stayed here, after the war. You had nobody to go home to,' I realise.

'But like I said, I was happy here, anyway. It *was* my home. Despite everything. It was all I knew, see? All I can remember.'

'Yes, I get that, now.' I get up, stretching, moving the cats from around my feet.

'Do you want another cup of tea?' Stella asks me.

'No – thanks, but I'd better get going.' I've got work to do, now: I need to type up everything Stella's told me, before I forget anything. I pause for a moment, then add: 'I've been looking at your cardigan, Stella. And the one you wore the other day, too. They look so nice and warm. Did you knit them yourself?'

'Yes.' She smiles. 'Auntie Nellie taught me how to knit when I was a little girl, and I still enjoy it. I reckon it's kept my fingers from seizing up with arthritis the way my knees have – spending all my evenings sitting here doing my knitting.'

'I wish I'd learned. It's come back into fashion, you know.'

'Never knew it went out,' she says with a shrug, and I laugh.

'My gran tried to teach me.' I bend down, give Vera a little stroke and add: 'I think I'm too impatient, unfortunately – and I don't have much spare time. What else do you knit?'

'Oh, not much, these days. Mostly squares, to make into blankets, see. I used to do them for the Cats Protection place. I volunteered there, after I retired. It's where these three came from.' She nods at Vera and Gracie – both fast asleep. Peggy's outside, as usual.

'Oh. How lovely! I didn't realise you did that.'

'Well, I can't do it now, can I? Too old, too bloody useless.' She sighs. 'Sorry. I don't mean to sound cross, but that's just how it makes me feel sometimes. Everyone tells you about the aches and pains, the loneliness, the general miseries of old age, but it's this feeling of redundancy that sometimes hurts the most. I know I'm lucky my brain still works all right, but I haven't got anything to use it for.'

'I don't think you're useless at all,' I protest. 'You can do things I'd have no idea how to do. Where do you get your wool, for your knitting?'

She points to a bag by her side. 'Got a stock of it here. Unravelled jumpers, most of it.'

'Unravelled?' I stare at her. 'Why would you unravel your jumpers?'

'Ah, well, they weren't all mine.' She looks away and changes the subject quickly. 'Anyway, you can make all sorts of things with knitted squares. Years ago I made a blanket that's big enough for the bed.'

'How clever you are,' I say with a sigh. 'I wish I'd persevered with learning to knit, so I could make Maisie some proper home-made jumpers. She grows so fast, I can't keep up with her.'

'Your little girl? Want me to knit her one?'

'Oh, no – I wasn't hinting!' I say, embarrassed now.

'No, I didn't think that. But it'd give me something to do. You'll have to choose a pattern, though. I've only got old ones. Old-fashioned. And you'll have to buy me the wool.'

'How much would you need? Sorry, I've really got no idea.'

'Get the pattern first,' she says. 'From the wool shop on Fore Street? Then check your daughter's measurements and look at the amount of wool it gives on the pattern, for her size. They'll help you in the shop, if you ask them.'

'And you'd really like to do it? You're not just being kind?'

'I'm not being kind at all. I'm asking you to pay for my little hobby. My entertainment,' she says with a chuckle.

'Well, in that case, I think I'll take you up on it!' I'm really excited by the idea. 'Thank you!'

'Don't thank me till you see how it turns out.' She laughs. 'I might drop all the stitches and make a pig's ear out of it.'

But I think, really, she seems pleased at the thought of it. And I'm glad. Perhaps it'll give her something different to do on these cold evenings.

A couple of days later I get a phone call from an unknown number while I'm trying to work on a story for the local paper. It's tricky because it's about a dispute between the head teacher of the primary school and the local education department, and because of Maisie being at the school I've got my own opinions, which I need to keep to myself. I answer the call distractedly, a bit irritated, expecting it to be a cold call.

'Um . . . hello?' says a friendly but rather apprehensive-sounding voice. 'Is that Holly?'

'Yes – who's calling?' I start – but even as the words leave my mouth, I think I know. I turn away from my laptop, suddenly more alert.

'It's Alec here – um, Stella's grandson? We met a few days ago—'

'Yes, of course – sorry, Alec, I didn't recognise your voice at first.' This isn't strictly true. It's a nice voice, actually; the kind of voice you could listen to for hours.

'Stella gave me your number,' he says. 'I hope that was OK. I understand you've been doing her shopping for her—'

'Well, I've only just started, actually. I haven't known Stella long.'

'Neither have I!' he says. 'But I can tell already that she thinks a lot of you, and she's very grateful for your help. So I just wanted to say, I don't want to do anything to interfere with your relationship with her, or what you're doing for her, but I'm more than happy to help too. If I can . . . lighten the load, so to speak? Get some of the heavy items? Or take over if ever you're busy?'

'That's good of you,' I say. And it is. He seems to have a knack for offering in a nice way, without trying to take over. 'She actually doesn't seem to want very much at all at the moment, so I'm happy to carry on for now. But if ever I can't manage it, well, thank you, I'll definitely bear it in mind.'

'OK, cool. Well, you've got my number now, so just let me know if I can help any time. Or you can call on me at the shop if you're in town.'

'Thanks, Alec.'

'And maybe I'll see you again one day up at Cliff's End.'

I'm smiling as we say goodbye. Only because I'm glad Stella seems to have a nice guy for a grandson. That's all.

14

Stella

Holly calls on me again this morning. I was expecting her tomorrow – Friday – with my shopping so I'm surprised to see her on the doorstep today as well. She seems to be coming quite often. Don't get me wrong, I'm enjoying her visits, but I'm worried she'll get behind with her work.

'I just like to check you're keeping warm,' she says, when I say this to her. She turns her back suddenly, as if she's looking for something behind her . . . or as if she doesn't want to face me while she goes on quickly: 'Alec called me yesterday.'

'Oh yes?' I say, smiling.

'We've agreed he'll help if ever you want anything heavy from the shop, or if ever I can't do it. We'll sort it out between us.'

'That's nice, then. You're both being very good to me. I'm being spoilt.'

'So you should be! You've earned a little bit of spoiling, haven't you?' she goes on, turning back to face me now. 'After all those years of hard work.'

She sits down. I've already made the tea and put the electric fire on.

'Well, since I'm here, have you got time to tell me a little bit more of your memories?' she asks. 'I've started writing some of them up. And I've been wondering where you went to school when you were older – after you left the village school. Was that where you met the friend who lived in The Avenue? At senior school?'

Back to the history bit. Fair enough, it's what I promised her, and it explains why she wanted to come back again so quickly. She needs to get her feature written, to earn some money. Good for her.

'I already knew Elizabeth at primary school,' I explain. 'But it was because of going up to grammar school together that we became closer friends. I passed the eleven-plus, you see, and got a place at the girls' grammar school in Torquay.'

'Yes, of course, I suppose they still had the eleven-plus back then.'

'Still had it?' I laugh. 'It was quite a new thing. Started during the war, in fact: in nineteen-forty-four, when the government decided all children should have free education from the ages of five to fifteen. And we all took the exam in the last year of junior school to see if we'd be going to a grammar school or a second-ary modern.'

'So I guess you and Ruby both passed for the grammar school,' she says, smiling.

I don't smile back. She hasn't realised yet.

'Ruby wasn't here then,' I explain. 'It was nineteen-forty-six when we took the eleven-plus. The war was over. She'd gone back to London, to her family.'

'Oh!' Holly sits up straight with surprise. 'Oh, so you got separated from your friend? Did you still see each other – in the holidays, maybe?'

'Huh! Chance would have been a fine thing! We wrote to each other, though, for a few years. Long letters, every week, all about our new schools, our teachers, our new friends.' I pause, memories

86

flooding back to me. 'We gave up in the end. Lost touch. That's what happens, isn't it? But I was upset when she left. I begged and pleaded to go up to London with her. It coincided with when we were celebrating the end of the war.'

'VE Day?' she says.

'Yes, that's right, the eighth of May, nineteen-forty-five. Churchill made it a public holiday. And of course, after six years of war, everyone had been ready to celebrate for ages. As soon as people knew the war in Europe was coming to an end, there were plans being made for parties,' I tell her.

'I'd love to hear about that,' Holly's saying.

'Well, I'm sorry to say my memories are mostly about the foul mood I was in!' I laugh. 'I can't honestly say, looking back, that I remember much about the village party, apart from the fuss my aunt and uncle made about it. But I certainly remember Ruby leaving.'

8 MAY 1945

Hawbury Down may have been just a tiny village back then, but everyone was just as eager to get together and enjoy the occasion as they were in the big cities. Stella's Uncle Jim and Auntie Nellie even took a day off from the farm. Everyone put their Sunday clothes on and went into the village to join in the fun. There were tables out in the street, women were bringing sandwiches and home-made cakes out, there were banners up and everyone was waving Union Jacks, dancing and singing.

Stella knew she should have been happy and excited. But she wasn't. She was sulking. Her best friend had gone back to London two days before, and, at the age of ten, this was a tragedy that overpowered all other emotions.

Ruby's mum had been with the two girls on their final day together. She'd come down to Hawbury Down from London to collect Ruby and take her home.

'This is Stella, she's my best friend,' Ruby had introduced her, and Ruby's mum had given her a smile and said she was very pleased to meet her.

Stella had thought she was lovely. She was chatty and funny, and wore a nice pink-and-white striped dress with a little collar, that she'd told Stella she'd made herself on her sewing machine. Stella had wished Ruby's mother could have been her own mum too, now that she didn't have one.

'Would you like to come with us on the bus, Stella, when we go to the station?' she'd asked her, 'so that you two girls can say goodbye? Only if your aunt says you may, of course.'

To Stella's surprise, Auntie Nellie had agreed. She'd been in a good mood because of Germany surrendering, and had been making fairy cakes for the village Victory Day party.

'You'll have to come back from Torquay on the bus on your own, mind,' she'd reminded Stella. 'I'll give you your bus fare. Just watch you get the right bus.'

Stella wasn't stupid by any means, but it would be the first time she'd ever caught the bus home on her own. She'd been so excited about this aspect of the outing that she'd almost overlooked how upset she was going to feel, after she'd waved to the departing train that was carrying her best friend back to London.

While they'd waited on the platform for the train to arrive, Ruby's mum had told them all about the amazing celebrations that were being planned for the big day in London. Of course, Hawbury Down being so small, it could never match the crowds that would be gathering in the capital. Ruby had become so excited – because of being back with her mum, of course, and because she was going home, and seeing other members of her family, people she'd almost forgotten about while she'd been living in Devon. As she'd listened to the mother and daughter eagerly discussing their new life together, Stella had become more and more despondent. Of course, she had no family left in London. Nobody she could go back to. But at the age of ten, she was too young, really, to make sense of her own emotions. She hadn't been exactly sure what she was upset about. All she'd seen was that

Ruby was going back to London, happy and excited, even though she was leaving Stella behind.

By the time she'd got home, she was crying, and she'd taken it out on her aunt and uncle.

'I want to go to *London* for the victory celebrations,' she'd kept saying – while her uncle had tried to cheer her up with talk of the street party planned for the village, and Auntie Nellie had become increasingly impatient with her bad mood.

It had probably been quite obvious to them both why she'd been so upset, but the view, back then, tended to be along the lines of 'Least said, soonest mended'.

'You can't go to London, and that's that. And it's no good crying, girl,' Auntie Nellie had said. 'You have to move on and get over these things.'

And, of course, eventually, she did. Back at school on the day after the Victory Day party, Stella walked into her classroom to find another girl sitting in Ruby's seat at their shared desk.

'I've suggested Elizabeth moves next to you, Stella,' said their teacher. 'As she didn't have a partner before.'

Although they were the same age, and had been in the same class throughout their five years at the school together, Elizabeth hadn't been one of Stella's particular friends. Stella thought her posh. She didn't speak the way the other village children spoke, nor, obviously, like Stella herself – although Stella's cockney accent had faded a lot and she now had some Devon inflections, a process which would continue over the years until eventually she was speaking entirely in the accent of her adopted county. Elizabeth dressed differently from the rest of the children, too. Her shoes were shiny, her socks new and white, and her dresses were always the right length. All the other girls wore one dress constantly while it became shorter and shorter, patched and repaired, until eventually it was necessary for their mothers to buy material to make a new one – which would be too long, to allow for a year's growth – or spend precious clothing coupons on a ready-made dress. Stella knew that on some occasions, Auntie Nellie had unpicked the seams of a dress of her own, and cut it down to make a desperately needed one for her growing foster daughter. And nobody expected anything to change much in that respect, now the war was over; rationing was predicted to remain in place for years yet.

During the course of the first few days of sitting next to Elizabeth, though, and sharing their textbooks, Stella began to have an understanding of why the teacher had paired them up. Apart from Ruby, Elizabeth was the only child in the class who'd sometimes come ahead of Stella in tests. Her naturally competitive nature meant that she was now working harder than ever in class, to keep up with Elizabeth. She was writing better compositions, reading more difficult books and dealing with more tricky arithmetic problems – and this took up so much of her concentration that it was only after school that she missed Ruby so badly. The long letters they wrote each other didn't always help; they just intensified the pain of their separation.

But over time, Stella and Elizabeth became real friends, and Stella was surprised to find there was a lot more to the 'posh' girl of the class than she'd suspected. Away from the classroom, Elizabeth wasn't the quiet, studious, well-behaved girl everyone supposed her to be, at all. She loved to tuck her dress into her knickers to climb trees, and often went home with grazed knees and dirty socks just like the other children. Auntie Nellie, though, was pleased Stella's new friend was ostensibly a good influence, and reacted uncharacteristically well the first time Elizabeth invited Stella home for tea.

'I don't see why not,' she said. 'As long as you watch your Ps and Qs with her family, mind. Don't forget your manners. They live up on The Avenue, you know,' she added, looking suitably impressed.

Stella couldn't have cared less where they lived. One of the attractions – apart from the sheer pleasure of going home with a friend instead of back to the farm to pull up cabbages and peel potatoes – was that Elizabeth's family had a dog and two cats. There was a cat on Hillside Farm – Betsy – but she wasn't a pet; she was a working cat, whose job was to keep down the population of mice and rats. She was fed outside, slept in the barn, never came into the cottage and didn't take kindly to being stroked or picked up. She'd once given birth to kittens, but Stella had been upset that these were all given away. Or so she was told. She was a lot older before she wondered what might have really happened to them, and by then she didn't want to think about it. But Elizabeth's cats, Tigger and Mittens, were lovely, friendly cats, who lay passively in Elizabeth's arms and let her push them around the garden in her doll's pram. Stella promised herself that one day she'd have her own cats, and they'd be pampered pets like these two.

Elizabeth's parents, while very posh and proper, were kind, and happy for Stella to come to play with Elizabeth, who, like Stella, was an only child. Stella was impressed by all the space in the house. There was a separate dining room, with a polished wood table and fancy sideboard, unlike any of the usual utility furniture most people had in their homes. And in their sitting room, as well as a comfy settee and two armchairs, they had a piano, which Elizabeth had been learning to play since she was six.

From then on, Stella and Elizabeth became inseparable, and when, the following summer, they found out they'd both passed the eleven-plus and would be going to the Torquay girls' grammar school together, both their families, and the girls themselves, were delighted. Their school days were busy and structured, with new lessons like French, Latin, Algebra and Geometry to get to grips with, but they relished the challenges.

By now, schools were benefiting from an influx of male teachers who'd had to leave the profession to their female counterparts while they were at war. Stella and Elizabeth were in their third year at the school when a new young music teacher joined the staff. He'd apparently been badly injured in the war, walked with a limp and had a scar running down one cheek – which only added, in the minds of the impressionable young ladies he'd come to teach, to his attraction. The hint of war hero about him, together with his thick brown hair, bright-blue eyes and youthful sense of humour, was enough to turn him into an idol for them to gaze at longingly as he tried to explain *crescendo* or *ritardando* to them during singing lessons.

Stella and Elizabeth, like all their friends, giggled and swooned together over their favourite teacher on the way home from school.

'I've heard he's going to do private lessons,' Elizabeth said one day.

'Singing lessons?' Stella asked.

'No. Violin. My parents won't let me learn because I already have piano lessons and they say it'll cost too much. They always say that about everything,' she added with a pout. 'Even though Daddy earns pots of money.'

Elizabeth's father worked for a bank. He went to work wearing a suit and tie and a bowler hat, and had recently become one of the first people in Hawbury Down to own a car.

'You've got more chance of talking your Auntie Nellie into letting *you* have violin lessons,' Elizabeth went on crossly.

'Now you *are* being funny,' Stella retorted.

'Oh well,' Elizabeth said with a sigh, 'we'll just have to love him from afar.'

'Not so far. Just across the music room.'

And they linked arms and giggled together, happy to compare the merits of the gawky, spotty lads from the boys' grammar school on their bus ride home, while they waited for their chance to gaze at their idol during their next music lesson.

15

Holly

Stella's smiling to herself, and so am I.

'I can just imagine all the girls swooning over him!' I laugh. 'What was his name – can you remember?'

'Oh, I can certainly remember,' she says, with an odd little chuckle. She looks up at me, lifting her eyebrows with a strange, ironic expression on her face. 'It was Mr Jackman.'

'Oh, how funny – the same surname as you!' I say, but she shakes her head and corrects me quickly:

'No. I was still Stella Price back then.'

'But you became—' I'm looking at her in surprise. How has it not even come up in conversation between us, even now I know she has – or had – a daughter? I glance at the gold band on her ring finger and the penny drops. 'You became Mrs Jackman,' I say softly. '*Oh my God*, Stella. Did you actually marry the dishy music teacher?'

She gives a fleeting little smile. 'Yes, I did. Not till I was old enough, of course!' Her smile drops, and she's shaking her head sadly. 'Ernest was nine years older than me, Holly. And he developed dementia when he was in his seventies.'

'Oh. I'm so sorry. Is he—'

'Passed away now, of course,' she says abruptly. 'Fifteen years ago. He'd had to go into a care home eventually with his dementia, not that I wanted him to, but it … got too difficult. Didn't have any choice.'

'I'm sure you didn't.' Without even stopping to think, to remind myself again that she's not my gran, I get up, go over to her and take hold of her hand. She doesn't say anything. She's looking down at the floor.

'It must have been horrible having to make that decision,' I add gently. 'And you've been on your own ever since?'

'Yes, well, you get used to things,' she says with her character-istic brusqueness. 'Ernest wouldn't have wanted me to mope. You just have to get on with it.'

'Of course.' I nod. 'You're an inspiration.'

'No, I'm not!' She shoots me a look of exasperation. 'I'm no ruddy *inspiration*! I didn't have to fight in a war and get wounded, like he did, or get shot down, like my father. I didn't even have to struggle with feeding a child when the rationing was on, like my Auntie Nellie had to. My generation didn't have it so bad. And as for *yours*—'

'We've had it even easier. I know. I realise that, and I feel guilty all the time, just listening to your stories, and the stories my gran used to tell me. We've had everything easy, and we don't appreciate it – I *know* that, Stella!'

I didn't intend to raise my voice – or to drop her hand at the same time – but she's looking up at me now, concern in her eyes, making me regret my self-centred little outburst straight away.

'Sorry,' I mumble. 'I didn't mean—'

'No, *I'm* sorry.' Stella reaches to take my hand back, and gives it a little squeeze. 'I shouldn't have … well, there was no need to bring your generation into it. You can't help being young!' She gives me a quick smile now. 'Truth is I'm glad – glad your generation haven't got to live through a war. Glad life's being kinder to you. That's what all those boys were fighting for, in both the world wars – risking their lives, for a better world for us. And there's no reason you should feel guilty about it. That's silly.'

'Thank you. I know.'

I want to ask her more, of course – about her marriage, how she got together with Ernest – Mr Jackman – whether they were happy, and what's happened to the daughter, Alec's mother. But I can't, now. It's all got too emotional, and I think we need to leave it there, for now.

'You will come again, won't you?' she says as I put my coat on. There's just a trace of anxiety to her tone. It's unlike her. She thinks she's upset me, put me off.

'Of course I will!' I smile, to show it's all OK. 'I'll come tomorrow, with your shopping again. Have you got your list?'

'I'll get it. If you're sure? I don't think there's anything too heavy on it, but call Alec if you need to. Or want to,' she adds, with a little grin that I try to ignore. She finds the scrap of paper, behind the clock on the mantlepiece. 'You're a good girl,' she says softly as she hands it to me. 'I am grateful.'

'It's no problem. I'll see you tomorrow, Stella.'

You're a good girl. It's what Gran used to say to me. I have to blink back the tears as I'm walking back down the track to my car. There's a woodpecker hammering away at the trunk of the big holly tree halfway down, and I try to concentrate on listening to him, and looking at the glistening red berries among the dark leaves, to distract myself from my thoughts of Gran. It can all go in my next column for the nature magazine.

Later, while I'm waiting outside the school for Maisie, I think about the big, posh detached house up on The Avenue, the one

I clean every week. I'm thinking about the young Stella playing with Elizabeth in one of those big houses: running around outside with the dog and the two cats, in a garden probably just like the one there. Every week I polish the piano in the front room of that family's home, and I can't help thinking about the coincidence of Elizabeth's family having one in *their* front room. I suppose it was more common then, when families might have gathered around the piano for a sing-song instead of watching TV.

Stella's right, I don't know how well off I am; even if, to be honest, sometimes I don't feel like I am. But yes, I'm lucky to have my cleaning job, as well as the writing money, when I get any. But right now, I need to stop daydreaming and be ready to greet Maisie when she comes rushing out of her classroom! That's when I appreciate how very lucky I really am.

This evening, after Maisie's in bed, I open my laptop and try to add some more to my half-written feature for *Devon Today*. But I'm finding it difficult to separate the factual information Stella's giving me, from the personal stuff, especially now I know about her husband. Ernest – her teacher! I can't wait to hear how that came about. I wonder if she'll be OK to tell me, or whether it's too painful for her to talk about. How sad, that she had to put him into a home, and that he died there. That must have been so difficult for her, whatever she says. I think of Gran again. She lost my grandad at quite a young age, from a heart attack. I was only quite little at the time so I can only really remember her being on her own.

Except she hadn't been on her own, of course. She'd had me.

16

Stella

I shouldn't have said that, about her generation, implying she's got it easy. Silly old bat. No wonder she took offence, I can't blame her. She's a nice young thing, and, let's face it, I don't even know if it's true, at all, that her life is any easier than mine, or anyone else's. I've been making assumptions, without even trying to find out anything about her. I only know she lives in a flat, does a cleaning job on top of this journalism lark, and she's got a little girl. I don't suppose she's got it easy at all, and yet she's good enough to do my shopping for me, and I don't *think*, any more, that it's just so she can write her feature. To be honest, even if it is, that's fair enough, isn't it?

It was because of talking about Ernest, obviously – that's what did it. Not that it hurts any more. It's been fifteen years, after all. No matter what people think, you *do* get used to things. You have to. You can't just give up, turn up your toes and die. It's just that it's been so long since I've talked to anyone about him – or about anything, of course. Saying his name out loud – it felt almost like a shock, but now I've got over that, I'll be OK. I'll tell her what happened. I know she wants to hear about it, and ... in a funny kind of way, now, I'm quite looking forward to telling our story, after all this time. Well, there's one part I'm going to find difficult, but perhaps it'll be a good thing – good for me – to say *that* out loud, as well.

But first, I need to put something right, don't I? I need to get to know Holly a bit better, find out a little bit more about her, instead of just talking about myself every time she comes round. I know that's what she wants, but it's not good enough. If we're really going to be friends …

Are we really friends? Is this more than just a business arrangement – my random ancient memories in exchange for her getting my shopping? Well, let's be honest – I hope it *is* more. I'm looking forward to tomorrow's visit already.

She comes with the shopping in the morning this Friday, instead of the afternoon. I'm glad; I was worried when she was nearly late to pick up her daughter last week. She's loaded up with bags again, even though I tried not to make the list too long, and made her promise not to go silly with all the treats again.

'They're not heavy,' she insists as she carries them through to the kitchen. 'It's just that there were some special offers – three packs of those biscuit assortments you like, for the price of two. Butter reduced—' she pulls two packs of butter out of the bag '—so it seemed daft to only get one. I know you use it for your cakes. And the cat food was fifty pence off, so I got an extra box. It'll keep you going, won't it?' She glances at me quickly and adds: 'You can pay me for the extra stuff another time—'

'Don't be silly.' I'm smiling as we unpack the bags together. 'I see you're a canny shopper, like me. Like I *was*, when I could still carry it all. Old age is a bugger, Holly. There are things nobody warns you about, and one of them is losing the strength of your arms. When I think of all the digging I used to do in the garden when I was younger—'

'Doesn't seem fair, does it?' she sympathises. She's wheezing a bit. It's still cold out, and windy, and she's probably out of breath too, whatever she says, from carrying those bags up the track. She stops to take some puffs of her inhaler and I let her get on with it while I put the kettle on. I mustn't fuss over her. I'm not her mother – or grandmother.

'Come on,' I say when the tea's ready. 'The fire's on in the other room.'

She picks up the tea tray. We've got our own little routine now. I made another cake yesterday, a fruit loaf. I've cut some slices and put them on a plate and I can see her eyeing them already. I'm glad. I bet she never normally eats home-made cake, or maybe not cake of any sort, by the look of her. 'Take a piece,' I encourage her as we sit down in the sitting room.

'Lovely, thank you, I will. I love fruit cake.' She smiles at me. 'My gran used to make one – a tea loaf. She gave me the recipe, but Maisie and I mostly have chocolate cupcakes. She likes helping me make them.'

I've got her wrong, then. Just shows, I shouldn't make assumptions, should I? I suppose she's naturally slim. I was like it myself once; we all were, years ago. Life was hard work, and we had to walk everywhere, that's why. Didn't have to go to the bother of joining a what-d'you-call-it – gym – to get our exercise, that's for sure.

'The cake's lovely,' she says, wiping crumbs from her mouth. 'Did your Auntie Nellie teach you to cook?'

'Yes, she did. To be honest I've got a lot to be grateful to her for, in that respect. By the time I left the village school, I knew how to cook and clean, look after a house – and myself! – as well as how to grow my own crops and keep chickens.'

Once we're settled in the sitting room with the usual two cats on our laps, the fire on, and one of my knitted blankets hanging over the back of her armchair in case she wants it – in case she's still chilly and doesn't like to say so – I ask her:

'Have you always lived around here, Holly? I might know your parents. I might actually have taught them – or even you! Did I tell you I used to teach? I worked at the village school. Did you go there?'

There's a strange expression on her face. She'd been about to take a mouthful of her tea, but she puts the cup down on the saucer, a bit unsteadily, and hesitates for a moment, as if she's trying to compose herself before she answers.

'Yes, I did,' she says eventually, 'from the age of eight, when I moved here from Exeter. I don't remember you being there, though.'

'I taught in the infant section. I retired in two-thousand.' I think about her age, try to do the sums. 'If you were eight when you came here, I suppose you'd have gone straight into the juniors. Did you go on to the comprehensive here when you turned eleven?'

It wasn't even built in my day, of course. All the village children were bused out to one of the bigger towns like Torquay for their secondary education. I keep forgetting Hawbury Down isn't a village anymore.

'Yes, I did. I didn't know you were a teacher,' she says. 'You hadn't got to that part of your story yet. But as far as my parents are concerned, no, you wouldn't have taught them. You wouldn't have known them.' There's another pause, then she goes on, all in a rush: 'In fact, I never even knew my father myself.'

'Oh, I'm so sorry.' Oh dear. As soon as I've started asking her about her own life, I seem to have put my foot straight in it.

'It's fine,' she reassures me quickly, although her tone is definitely telling me otherwise. 'I don't care. What you've never had, you've never missed.'

'What about your mum?' I ask, watching her face carefully. 'Does she live in the village?'

'No.' The same slightly abrupt tone. Perhaps I shouldn't ask any more, after all. But she finally takes her mouthful of tea before going on: 'She lives in Australia.'

'Oh!' I can't hide my surprise. 'Does she come home often?'

'No.' Holly gives a little ironic laugh. 'Never. Says it all, really, doesn't it? She couldn't have gone much further away. Shows how much she cared about us.'

'Us?'

She shrugs. 'My sister and me. Half-sister, actually. Hannah was born in wedlock. I came along eleven years later and broke up her parents' marriage. I don't think she ever forgave me,' she adds, with a funny little smile. Trying to make me think she's joking.

I'm taking a moment to work this out.

'So your father was . . . a new boyfriend of your mother's?'

'Not exactly a boyfriend. She had an affair, possibly just a one-night stand by the sound of it, and her husband – Hannah's father – found out about it, worked out from the timings that I must be the lover's child and not his – and promptly walked out. Divorced her. I don't think Mum really liked either of us – my sister or me – very much, but I must have been the biggest nuisance. She obviously hadn't wanted a second child at all. I suppose I'm lucky she didn't just . . . get rid of me. Her career was all that really mattered to her.'

'What was her career?' I ask. It seems, now she's started, that she wants to tell me all of it. She's sounding angry. Whatever she says, it's obviously affected her whole life, and I'm not surprised. I wonder if she bottles this all up. Hopefully she talks to the sister.

'She was a director of a fashion manufacturing company,' Holly says. 'They were expanding, at the time, and she was eventually offered the chance to run a new branch of the company in Sydney. Apparently she jumped at it. I mean, would you *do* that – if you had an eight year old?' she demands. 'And not even consider taking your child with you?'

I shake my head. No, I wouldn't.

'My sister told me all this, of course, years ago,' she goes on. 'I hadn't had much idea what was going on, at the time, as I was so much younger. When Mum went to Australia, Hannah was nineteen, nearly twenty, and living her own life. It still must have hurt, but at least she saw her dad at weekends.'

She gives another of those little laughs that don't fool me at all, before adding: 'Obviously, he didn't want anything to do with *me* – his wife's illegitimate daughter. Not that I blame him for that.'

'So who looked after you, Holly, if you were only eight years old when your mother left? Who were you living with?'

She smiles now, a genuine, proper smile this time. 'My gran, of course. She'd always looked after both of us – me and Hannah – while Mum was working, anyway. We lived in Exeter, and Gran used to drive up from Hawbury Down every single day to take care of us. From when I was a baby. She'd collect Hannah from school, give us our dinner and stay with us till Mum got home late in the evening. And when Mum went to Australia, I moved in with Gran permanently. Went to school here.' She continues so quietly now that I have to strain to hear her: 'Gran was the only parent I ever had, that's the truth of it. She was the only person who loved me.'

I don't know what to say. She sounds quite matter-of-fact about it, considering she experienced such ... abandonment ... by both her parents. Thank goodness she had her gran, anyway.

'So did your gran live here in Hawbury Down all her life?'

'Yes; and my grandad lived here from the time they got married. He died when I was about three, though, so I didn't really know him.' She gives herself a little shake, and starts stroking Gracie, as if she's only just remembered the cat's on her lap. 'Anyway: enough about me!' She laughs. 'I want to hear the rest of *your* story! I've been dying to hear how you got together with your music teacher. How romantic that you ended up marrying him!'

I'd been going to ask her more about her gran and grandad. Surely I must have known them, if they'd lived in Hawbury Down all that time. But she obviously doesn't want to talk any more, and I don't want her getting upset. She's giving me an anxious look now as she adds:

'Were you happy together – you and Ernest?'

'Oh yes, we were,' I reassure her. I can feel the smile stretching my face. 'Very happy. He was the love of my life, Holly. I never loved anyone else.'

And now I wish I'd kept my stupid mouth shut. I think I might've upset her again. I'm just going to get on with the story and pretend I didn't see those tears she just wiped away.

JANUARY 1949

Stella could hardly sit still all morning at school. All through history, double needlework and games, she could think of nothing but the lunch break, when she'd be having her first violin lesson.

She could still hardly believe how things had worked out. When she'd got home, that day towards the end of the previous term, with a letter from the school about private music lessons, she'd fully expected her aunt to give her a lecture on the facts of economic life, to say nothing of possible ridicule for giving herself airs and graces for even daring to dream of such a thing. 'Not for the likes of us' was one of Auntie Nellie's favourite expressions. But to her complete astonishment, the next morning, her aunt had announced that she and Uncle Jim had talked it over together.

'We wouldn't have normally considered it,' she'd added, 'but for the bit on the end of the letter, here—' she'd held up the typewritten document, jabbing the final paragraph with her finger '— which says: *Any girls who have never had the opportunity to learn a musical instrument can apply for a half term of free tuition during their lunch hour, borrowing a school violin.*' She shrugged. 'If you're any good, no doubt the music teacher will hassle you to carry on with his private lessons. But your uncle and I thought maybe you should give the free ones a try. If you're no good at it, we're no worse off.'

She'd managed to make it sound like it was a foregone conclusion that Stella wouldn't be any good at it. But Stella hadn't cared; if she was accepted for the free lessons, she'd have a whole half term of spending one lunch hour a week with Mr Jackman. She had no idea whether she'd like learning the violin, but she was just coming up to fourteen, and she was in the throes of her first crush.

She hadn't needed to think any further; she'd rushed at Auntie Nellie and had thrown her arms around her.

'Thank you, auntie – thank you so much!' she'd said, as Nellie had blinked in surprise at this unusual show of affection.

'All right, all right, let's just see how it goes before we get too carried away,' she'd said. 'Now, how about getting those plates warmed up for the stew? And the table isn't going to set itself, is it?'

Later that evening, sitting at the kitchen table concentrating on her homework, Stella had overheard her aunt and uncle talking in the sitting room.

'She seems really keen,' Auntie Nellie had said. 'Right excited, she was. D'you think she's got some kind of musical what-d'you-call-it – talent?'

'Maybe she has,' Uncle Jim had agreed. 'She's a bright girl, Nell; she's doing well at that posh school. I think her dad liked music, didn't he? Perhaps it's inherited.'

'Her dad liked singing down the pub at night, from what I hear.' Nellie had laughed. 'He had a talent for boozing, that's what he had.'

'Yes, well, that's as maybe. I reckon I'd be right proud, though, if our girl turned out to be talented, Nell. Right proud.'

Our girl. Stella had closed her eyes, feeling a flood of warmth. She'd never heard him refer to her that way before.

Would it really make them proud if she learnt to play the violin? In that case, she'd thought, she was going to try hard. She owed them that, at least.

'I'm nervous,' she admitted to Elizabeth that day as their class was dismissed for the lunch hour. 'I mean, I don't think I'll know what to say to him.'

'You've been swooning over him all this time,' Elizabeth teased her, 'and now you're nervous.'

Stella knew Elizabeth was jealous, of course, although she'd never admit it. It was an unusual situation, for Elizabeth to be jealous of her. Elizabeth had everything – nice parents, a lovely house, two cats, a dog and a piano. Stella had never begrudged her friend any of her good fortune, but she was just quite pleased that, for once, she was the one to land a bit of luck.

'Just talk to him like he's a normal teacher,' Elizabeth suggested more gently. 'Try to forget how handsome he is, or you'll never be able to concentrate on the violin lesson.'

With this sound advice in her mind, Stella knocked on the door of the music room at one o'clock and went in for her first lesson. She needn't have worried. Mr Jackman was so kind, chatting to her in a friendly way while he helped her to get the hang of which string was which and showing her how to place her fingers.

'You won't use the bow to begin with,' he explained. 'To start with, we'll just get you plucking the strings, learning where the notes are. I presume you've never played a musical instrument before?'

'No, although my best friend has a piano and she's taking her exams on it. I've had a go on it, but I don't have much idea what I'm doing; I just copy what she shows me to do.'

'Is that Elizabeth Ashworth? I noticed in class that she's quite advanced in reading music.' He gave Stella a smile and added: 'But you're a bright girl too; you can soon be just as good on the violin as she is on the piano, if you practise hard enough. Will your parents allow you to practise at home?'

'They're my aunt and uncle. But I think they will. I think they're quite pleased that I'm learning.'

'Good.'

He really did have a lovely smile. And a nice, warm way with him. Stella picked up the violin again, determined to show him how quickly she could learn where to pluck the different notes on the strings. And because it was her determination to please her aunt and uncle, and make them proud of her, that was pushing her on even more than her desire to please the handsome music teacher, she'd already forgotten to feel nervous and awkward around him.

By the time the half term of free tuition was coming to an end, Stella was using the bow confidently and progressing well with reading the music. She'd tackled some scales and exercises and a couple of simple tunes. It was gratifying how Uncle Jim, and even Auntie Nellie, would sit with her in the evenings, listening while she practised everything over and over. They never seemed to tire of it, however often Stella made horrible screeching noises with her bow or played the wrong notes.

'We've never had anyone musical in our family before,' Auntie Nellie said, with such pride in her voice that Stella felt even more fired up to keep working hard at it. Especially as Mr Jackman seemed so pleased with her progress too.

'I hope you're going to continue after half term,' he said at the end of the last lesson in February. 'You're doing really well.'

Stella had almost forgotten that the free lessons were finishing. She hadn't discussed with her aunt and uncle what was going to happen now, but she had a sinking feeling about it.

'I don't think my ... family ... will be able to afford private lessons,' she said sadly. 'Or to buy a violin.'

He nodded thoughtfully. 'Well, I don't think it would be a problem to borrow one of the school ones for a little while longer. But unfortunately, I have a list of girls waiting for the opportunity of the introductory lunchtime lessons.'

'I'll talk to my aunt and uncle,' she said.

'Would you like me to talk to them?' he offered.

'Thank you, but I think I should ask them myself.'

Stella knew things were still tough, financially – not just for her aunt and uncle but for most families. The economy was taking time to pick up after the war. And on the farm, Uncle Stan and Uncle Jim were both getting older, struggling with arthritis and other physical effects of a lifetime of manual labour in the fields. Geoffrey, Stan's remaining son, was now doing much of the work.

'I'm going to try and get a job,' Stella announced over dinner that evening. 'At weekends. I'll ask in the village shop if I can help there on Saturdays.'

Auntie Nellie dropped her fork in surprise. 'You're going to do what? No, you're not, young lady. You're needed to help out here, in the kitchen and on the farm. Isn't it enough that we give you all the time you need for your homework, and your violin practice? Do you think it's fair that your cousins do everything, while you enjoy your books and your music like a lady of leisure?'

'I thought you said you were proud of me?' Stella shot back, hurt and disappointed. 'Proud of how I'm at the grammar school, and playing the violin? If I want to keep having violin lessons, I've got to start paying for them after half term.'

'We are proud, love,' her uncle soothed her. He gave her aunt a look. 'We'll talk about it, Stella. We'll try to think of a way round it.'

*

The following day, Uncle Jim announced that they'd made a decision. Instead of trying to find a Saturday job, Stella was to continue with her work at home but her aunt and uncle would pay her some pocket money every week, which she could save up.

'Thanks,' she said, a little begrudgingly. 'But I bet it won't be enough to pay the violin teacher.'

'Probably not. But maybe you can save for a second-hand violin. If you haven't got a violin to play, there's no point paying for lessons, is there?'

'I s'pose not,' she admitted.

'And when you leave school next year—'

Stella looked up in shock. 'Next year? But I want to stay on and take my School Certificate!'

'No, Stella.' Her uncle looked unusually stern. 'We've done what we can for you. Paid out for that uniform, encouraged you to get a good education. Most girls leave at fourteen, and yes, we agreed you could stay on till fifteen as the school seems to expect it—'

'The school expects us all to stay on till *sixteen* and take the exam! Some of them are staying on for the sixth form to take the Higher Certificate. All my friends will be doing it. I'll be the only one leaving at fifteen!'

'I very much doubt it, love. People need their children to go out to work. We need you to either work here full-time or get a job in a—'

'Don't say a job in a factory! I will *not*! I want to be a teacher. What's the point in me having this education if all I'm going to do is leave at fifteen and work in a factory? Or skivvy on the farm like I've been doing since I was five years old?'

'That's enough, Stella. I'm sorry we're not wealthy like your friend Elizabeth's family, but if you get a job and work hard, you can still make something of yourself. There are better times coming; women are working in all sorts of jobs now. You'll have plenty of opportunities. But we can't afford to keep you at school – or send you to college to be a teacher. That's that.'

Stella screwed up her eyes, trying not to cry, as her uncle walked away.

'My life is ruined,' she told Elizabeth melodramatically the next morning on the bus. 'I might as well leave school this summer. What's the point in doing another year if I can't even take the School Certificate? I might as well get a job in a factory straight away.'

'My dad says education is never wasted,' Elizabeth said, putting a sympathetic arm around her friend. 'Stay at school for next year; you never know, your aunt and uncle might change their minds by then and let you go on to the fifth form after all. And you'll still be able to see Mr Jackman in music lessons!'

Stella tried to smile. 'I suppose so.'

It wouldn't be the same, of course, as having her violin lesson with him every week. But then, nothing was going to be the same now she knew she wouldn't be staying on at school for the exam – or training to be a teacher.

17

Holly

'So how come you *did* get to be a teacher?' I ask, as Stella seems to have come to a stop. 'And I presume you did go back to learning the violin, after all?'

How else would she have got together with her lovely teacher?

She smiles. 'Oh, it was some years before I went to college. Not until after we were married. But yes, I ended up going back to Ernest for violin lessons. After I left school.'

'At fifteen?'

'Yes. I had to come to terms with that. And my uncle was right – there were other girls leaving school at the same time as me. Elizabeth didn't, of course. She stayed on till she was eighteen, and went on to medical school.'

'Wow. That must have been pretty unusual in those days? For a woman?'

'Not so common as it is now, of course. But girls were beginning to get more ambitious for careers. Going into professions, like men. Elizabeth eventually became a paediatrician, in fact. We were still in touch then, but gradually we lost touch—'

'It's sad that you lost touch with both of your school friends – Ruby and Elizabeth.'

Stella gives one of her snorts of derision. 'Oh, that's just life, isn't it? Some friends you keep, others you lose track of, especially if your lives go in different directions.' She shrugs. 'She was working in a hospital up north somewhere. I still saw her parents around the town. Of course, they've gone now. Elizabeth too, maybe.'

She's right, of course – I should know. I haven't kept in touch with any of my friends, either – and partly for the same reason: life going in different directions. Well, that's my excuse, anyway.

'So you left school at fifteen and – what? Worked in a factory?'

'No. In fact Uncle Jim had lined up a job for me in a hotel in Torquay. Receptionist. But I only worked there for a year. Soon after I turned sixteen, my auntie had a stroke.'

I gasp, but Stella goes on quickly: 'She recovered, to some extent. But she was never quite the same. So Uncle Jim needed me at home, of course – to look after her, and to run the home for him.' She chuckles. 'He wasn't doing as much of the manual work on the farm as he used to, by then, but he wouldn't have coped with cooking or cleaning. Men in those days were clueless about all that. Not like today, where everyone shares everything – and much nicer it is, too.'

'So you couldn't even go out and earn your own money anymore?'

'No. But I'd saved up. Women couldn't open a bank account in our own names back then, but my uncle had set one up for me, and from the time he started giving me pocket money every week for doing the work at home, I'd saved almost every penny. When I worked at the hotel, I had a uniform, so I didn't even have to spend much on clothes. So I still saved as much as I could. There was a second-hand shop in Torquay and one day I found a violin in there. It was in good condition, so I told my uncle I wanted some money out of my account to buy it. It must have been December, because to my amazement, he went into Torquay himself on the bus and bought it for me for Christmas instead.'

'Ah, that was nice, then!'

'Yes. I used to try to play it at home, but of course I couldn't make any progress on my own. And then, one Sunday, after church, Uncle Jim and I went for a walk. It was September – a lovely sunny day. This was after Auntie Nellie had her stroke, but one of my cousins used to sit with her sometimes while we went to church, so we knew she'd be all right for a bit longer. We walked all the way up the track—'

'Up here – to Hawbury Top?'

'Yes.' Stella smiles. 'Of course, I'd had no idea where Mr Jackman lived. I'd never even seen him since I left school. But he was here, outside, working in the garden.'

'He actually lived in this house?' I can't keep the surprise out of my voice.

She nods. 'I couldn't believe it either – it felt like fate! I gave him a wave, and he stared at me, just as surprised as I was. I was sixteen then, coming up for seventeen, so I probably looked a whole lot different from the scruffy little girl he used to teach.'

'I'd love to see what you looked like then,' I tell her. 'Have you got any photos – of you, or Ernest?'

'Ernest used to take pictures, but I'm not sure where they all are. Probably in the attic. I have got a couple of our wedding day, though. I'll find them for you next time, if you like.'

'Yes, please. And . . . is that how you fell in love with each other? Gazing at each other across the garden—'

'Not quite.' Stella laughs. 'But I *did* tell him I'd got a violin, and on the way home, I asked my uncle if I could use some of my own money to pay for lessons. I still had to ask him, you see, for money out of my account. That's how it was, back then. And . . . well, it went from there. Ernest was as lovely as I'd remembered. And he was different with me then, of course – as I was a bit older, and not at school any more. I think I realised straight away that he . . . liked me. But I didn't say anything to my uncle. He'd have stopped me going for lessons!'

'So did you go out with him, then?' I'm finding it quite shocking, really. I mean, I know she wasn't at school any more, but he *was* her violin teacher! And she was nine years younger than him.

'No!' She laughs again, shaking her head. 'We were still just teacher and pupil. But it gradually developed into a kind of . . . *friendship*, really. He'd talk to me about the war, his injuries, and his recovery, in hospital. That kind of thing. And I'd talk to him about being an evacuee, and how I had to do everything at home because of Auntie Stella's stroke.'

'And all the time you were hoping he'd ask you out?'

'Oh, I never really thought it would happen. I thought it was just – well, a silly, childish infatuation.'

'So what changed?' I'm aware that I'm asking about her personal life instead of concentrating on the social history, and what life was like in Hawbury Down, as I promised. But I'm so intrigued by this love story. I won't write about any of this in my feature, obviously, but Stella seems quite happy to tell me about it, now that she's started. 'Did he just suddenly tell you one day that he loved you?'

'No! Of course not. It all changed, in fact, on my eighteenth birthday.' Stella takes her glasses off and rubs her eyes. 'But I'll tell you about that next time you come, shall I? I'm getting a bit tired of talking, now.'

'Of course – sorry, Stella. The time's gone so quickly, again. I'll come back one day next week, shall I?' She looks exhausted, actually. I hope going over these old memories of Ernest isn't upsetting for her. I get to my feet, lifting the sleeping cat gently from my lap to the floor. 'Don't come to the door – I can see myself out. Bye.'

I lean and give her a quick kiss on the cheek as I pass her chair. I know she's not my gran – and she can't be a replacement – but I really care about her now. I didn't expect that, when this all started.

As I walk away from Cliff's End, I turn back and stare at the house, looking at it differently, somehow, now I know that Stella's and Ernest's romance began here. I wonder how long Ernest had lived here before he met Stella; whether the house had been in his family for generations. Suddenly, I have a flash of understanding of how Stella must feel about the house. There must be so many memories there for her ... and not only that, so much of Ernest himself about the house. It must almost feel, to her, as if his soul is there, within the very fabric of the walls. No wonder she doesn't want to leave. I wonder if she's got any old photographs of the house? I'd love to see whether it's changed much since the 1950s, or since whenever Ernest's family first lived there. How awful it would be if she *did* have to move, and had no pictures to remind herself of Cliff's End.

Maisie's in a thoughtful mood when she comes out of school this afternoon. Normally on Fridays she comes rushing out, full of excitement about the weekend ahead, but she seems quiet and preoccupied.

'Everything all right, pickle?' I ask her, squeezing her warm little hand.

'Yes. But Mummy,' she adds solemnly, 'we're doing the war for our next topic. Was the war when you were a little girl?'

'World War Two?' I ask her, and she nods a little uncertainly – but I've seen this term's curriculum so I'm pretty sure. 'No,' I tell her. 'It was a long time before I was born, Mais. It was over just after Gran was born—'

I swallow. It's always hard to talk about Gran to Maisie. She was so distressed by her loss – the first loss she's had to cope with.

Gran was such a huge influence on her little life; they loved each other so much. And of course, I never had to refer to her as 'Great Gran' to Maisie, as there was no actual grandmother in her life to differentiate from.

'So even she wouldn't have been able to tell you anything about it,' I finish, giving her hand another squeeze and forcing a smile. And the thought comes to me: But I know someone who could.

18

Stella

TUESDAY 30 JANUARY

I'm finding myself thinking about Holly a lot, in between her visits. What a sad start to life that poor girl had. She must have been so close to that gran of hers, who brought her up. And now it seems she's on her own with a little daughter. But then, she never talks about any friends, or cousins, or even the sister – *half*-sister. She's only mentioned her once. I definitely get the impression she's lonely. She doesn't seem particularly happy – and she should be, at that age. If you're not happy in your twenties, when you're in your prime, and looking nice and slim and pretty like she does, God help you when you get to my age! Not that I'm not grateful for living as long as I have. I've had a good life, despite ... everything. It's outliving everyone else that's hard.

Holly gave me a call yesterday afternoon. She wanted to know if it would be all right to bring the little girl with her one day. Apparently she's learning a bit about World War Two at school, and her teacher said there weren't many people still alive now who would remember it. So Holly told the child about me, and now she wants to come and see me. Probably can't believe how ancient I am!

I told her she might as well bring her daughter next time she comes; so she'll be here this afternoon, after school. I'm looking forward to meeting her. But it's been a long while since I had anything to do with children, and I'm not quite sure what to expect, today's children probably being so different from those I was used to. I decide to make some little chocolate cakes. I remember Holly saying they sometimes make them together, so they must be a favourite. And no doubt she'll be hungry after her day at school. I make some chocolate buttercream, and when the cakes have cooled, I cut a slice off the top of each, spread the buttercream on the cakes, then cut the slices in half and arrange them on top of the cakes like butterfly wings. The first time I ever had butterfly cakes myself was at Elizabeth's house. Her mother used to make things I'd never dreamed of before. We had trifle one day. I can still remember the first taste of that delicious combination of sponge, fruit, jelly and custard. It wasn't the sort of thing Auntie Nellie would have done. She did make lovely bread pudding, though.

I'm feeling quite jittery with anticipation when the doorbell rings at a quarter to four. Holly's obviously come straight from picking up the little one from school.

'Hello,' I say as I open the door. I stoop slightly to greet the child as she comes in. 'You must be Maisie. I'm Stella.'

I'd expected her to be shy, but to my surprise she responds in a confident and chirpy little voice:

'Hello. Why is your house right on top of the cliff? It's a long way to walk from the car! Shall I take my shoes off?'

Even as she's asking this, she's squatting down by my feet and unbuckling her shiny black shoes. It's so nice to see such good manners, I don't want to tell her she doesn't have to bother.

'Mummy says you've got three cats,' she goes on as she stands up, places the shoes neatly together against the wall and starts to wriggle out of her coat. 'Can I see them? Am I allowed to stroke them? What are their names? Where shall I put my coat?'

'Maisie!' Holly stops her, laughing. 'One question at a time, please! Sorry, Stella.' She gives me a kiss on the cheek. We seem to be on kissing terms now. I quite like it, but I feel a little awkward. I didn't grow up with cheek-kissing from friends. 'Are you OK?'

'Yes, I'm fine.' I'm laughing too. It's amazing the difference the presence of a child can make to a house. It suddenly feels warmer, more alive. Who'd have thought I'd be entertaining a young woman like Holly here, to say nothing of a seven year old, after all the years of being alone? Let alone suddenly having a grandson, who I still have difficulty believing is really mine, even though – like Holly – he's taken to calling me every couple of days to make sure I'm warm, fed, and haven't turned up my toes yet.

We go through to the sitting room so that I can show Maisie the cats. Vera's curled up in front of the fire, making the most of it because I always put it on now while Holly's here, so that we can be nice and cosy while we sit chatting together. Gracie's just woken up, standing up and stretching herself in a long yawn, the way cats do. I tell the child their names, and she sits straight down on the carpet and begins to talk to Gracie as she strokes her tentatively on the head.

'She likes to be stroked,' I reassure her. 'They both do. They won't mind.'

'Where's the other one? Mummy said you had three.'

'Peggy mostly only comes indoors when she's hungry. She likes to be outside,' I explain.

'I wish we had a cat. Mummy says it's another mouth to feed,' she says with a pout, reminding me so much of myself when I was a girl and couldn't get my own way, that I have to smother a laugh.

'Your mummy is right. Their food costs money. So does food for little girls!' I add with a smile. 'Speaking of which, I've made some cakes. I don't suppose you like chocolate cakes, do you?' I tease her.

'Yum!' She jumps to her feet, startling Gracie, who makes a bolt for the door. My cats aren't used to small humans with quick movements. 'I *love* chocolate cakes! They're my favourite!' She glances at her mum, evidently remembering her manners, and says: 'Please may I have one?'

'Of course. I'm going to bring them in.' I stop, halfway back to the kitchen, a sudden thought occurring to me. 'What would you like to drink? I'm afraid I don't have things like orange juice or lemonade—'

'She can just have a glass of water, thank you, Stella,' Holly says firmly.

'Right.' I look at Maisie's face and add: 'Or milk? If you like it?'

'Yes, please!' she says at once. 'I love milk. Mummy makes me chocolate milk—'

'Just milk, today, Maisie,' Holly warns her. 'Why don't you go into the kitchen with Stella and see if you can help bring something in.'

The child skips after me. I notice the cats' hairs on her navy school trousers. I'll have to apologise to her mum. I notice too that it's a sensible uniform at the school these days: a warm navy jumper in that fleecy material, over what looks like a short-sleeved white T-shirt, the type with a collar. And thank goodness, it seems the girls can wear trousers. No chapped red bare legs like we used to have in the winter! I give her the cake tin and tell her to take it back to the other room and come back for the three little plates, in case it'd be too much for her to carry. I'm waiting for the tea to draw when Holly comes out to carry in the tray.

'Maisie's sitting by the cake tin, waiting for the OK to open the lid,' she laughs.

'She's a lovely little girl. Very polite. You've brought her up nicely,' I tell her.

'She's on her best behaviour! She can be a bit full-on at times. But thank you. I try my best.'

'It can't be easy,' I sympathise. 'On your own.' I stop, correcting myself quickly: 'I mean, I presume ... you've never mentioned a partner, or a husband ... I haven't liked to ask.'

'You're right on both counts. Maisie and I are on our own. And it isn't easy.' She gives a rueful smile and adds quietly: 'But it's better than being with the wrong man.'

'I'm sure that's true,' I agree.

I pour out the tea and she picks up the tray. I think the subject's closed. And why spoil a nice afternoon by talking about a man who obviously wasn't the right one? She'll tell me eventually if she wants to.

'They're butterflies!' Maisie gasps in delight as she's finally told she can open the cake tin. I couldn't have hoped for a better reaction, and once again I remember how it felt to be her age, when everything was either the best thing that ever happened, or the worst. I'm glad she didn't think they were rabbits or cats! She takes a cake and turns it around in her hands. 'Can we make some like this next time, Mummy?'

'We'll give it a go!' Holly agrees. 'You shouldn't have gone to all this trouble, Stella.'

'No trouble. I like baking. What else am I going to do?' I laugh. 'I've got all the time in the world.'

'Mummy says you remember the war,' Holly says through a mouthful of cake.

'Well, only just,' I tell her. 'I was a little girl then, you see, about your age, so I don't remember very much.' I glance at Holly, wondering how much she might have told Maisie already, or what she's been told at school. 'I lived in London when it started, but I came to live here instead, because it was quieter, and safer. Did you know, all the beaches were fenced off? We couldn't go on them. It was dangerous.'

'Because you might have got blown up? That's what my teacher said.'

'Yes. And there were lots of things we couldn't have, because they were in short supply. We had to have coupons to buy things, and once we'd used our coupons, that was it – we had to go without.'

'Did you have cakes?'

'Only if we had enough flour and eggs to make them.'

'Did you have any toys?'

'Not many! I just had my teddy bear, and two books, when I arrived here.'

She stuffs the rest of her cake into her mouth, seemingly shocked into silence by this. She looks at me, her head on one side, and then asks:

'What were you like when you were a little girl?'

'I might have a picture,' I say. 'I promised Mummy I'd show her the pictures of my wedding, too. Wait a minute, I'll go and look.'

The picture of Ernest and me on our wedding day is on my bedside table. I think there's another one in my memory box at the bottom of the wardrobe, with my school pictures. That's what Maisie will want to see. I rummage for the box. It's not heavy, I haven't put anything in it for years, haven't even looked in it for a long time. I can't remember what's in there now, apart from the photos. I carry the box back to the sitting room, with the framed wedding picture, which I hand over to Holly while I sit back down, open the box and start thumbing through the contents.

'There you are,' I say to Maisie, holding out a couple of

dog-eared black-and-white pictures. 'That's my class at school – the school you go to – when I was probably about ten. Round about the time the war ended. That's me at the end of the middle row, there – see? And this one would have been taken at my other school, when I was a bit older.'

I stop. I'd been rummaging in the box with my free hand, while Maisie took the photos from me. I really *had* forgotten what I'd put in here. Some theatre programmes from so long ago they've gone faded and brown. Tickets that have long since lost their significance. At the bottom, tied up together with pink ribbon, are my mother's letters to me when I was first evacuated here, still in their envelopes, her neat loopy writing in royal blue ink and the postage stamps with the old king's head, making something twist in my heart. But it's the card that really makes my eyes sting. It's the one Ernest gave me on my eighteenth birthday: the very point where I left our story the last time Holly came. And it takes me right back there, the memories as unforgettable as ever.

JANUARY 1953

As the new year heralded in 1953, Stella was coming up for eighteen. There was nothing special, back then, about an eighteenth birthday. Twenty-one was the age of majority, the age people could vote for the first time, and generally be considered adults. As Stella's eighteenth birthday approached, she was still living on Hillside Farm, caring for her disabled aunt and keeping house for her and her uncle. And going once a week to Cliff's End for an hour of violin tuition – and chat, and laughter – with Ernest Jackman.

By now, Stella was finding her violin lessons much harder.

'I'll *never* be able to play really well – like you do,' she sighed after Ernest had played her one of the tunes she'd been struggling with, to show her how it should sound.

'Maybe not,' he conceded, giving her a gentle smile. 'But as long as it gives you pleasure—'

She smiled back. The pleasure came mostly from being in Ernest's company, of course – he'd encouraged her, now that she wasn't a schoolgirl any more, to call him by his first name – and she absolutely loved her visits to the old house on the top of the cliff. Sometimes Ernest would take up his own violin and play to her, to show her how it ought to be done. He'd stand in the bay window of the room he used as a music room, which overlooked the garden that stretched right down to the edge of the cliff. She'd watch the clouds scudding across the wild winter sky, the seabirds swooping and diving or the sunlight slanting through a gap in the clouds as she listened to his masterful rendition of the music she'd been struggling with. Sometimes they'd take a rest from the violin altogether and he'd play her one of his favourite classical records on the wind-up gramophone that had belonged to his late parents, from whom he'd inherited the house. She'd watch his expression as he sat across the room from her, his eyes half closed in concentration, his foot tapping to the rhythm of the music, and ask herself whether the yearning, the almost physical ache she felt in her heart at times like this, was really just a crush, or something altogether different.

'See you next Friday, then,' he said at the end of one of these lessons, as she was putting her violin away in its case and her coat on, ready to leave.

'Yes.' She smiled up at him. 'It's my birthday that day.'

She didn't know why she told him. She hadn't been expecting him to do anything about it; it had just come out, without her thinking. But he stood for a moment in the hallway, looking back at her, smiling.

'Will you be wanting to go out with your friends instead, then?' he said. 'Or with your uncle, perhaps? Unless this weather's too cold for him?'

Stella hardly ever went out anywhere, with anyone. She and Elizabeth occasionally went to the pictures, at the new 'picture palace' in Torquay, but Elizabeth was now in her final year at school and studying hard for her A-levels, the new exam that had replaced the Higher School Certificate. She also now had a boyfriend, who inevitably took up a lot of her free time. And the only place Stella ever went with her uncle was church on a Sunday – and then only if one of the cousins was able to sit with her aunt.

'No, I won't be going out,' she said. 'It'll just be an ordinary day.'

'That's a shame. A birthday should be a thing to celebrate,' he said seriously. 'We're all lucky to be alive, aren't we?'

She knew he was referring to his own brush with death during the war. She nodded.

'Yes, you're right. Well, I suppose I could ask my friend if she wants to—'

'Unless you'd like to come to a concert with me?' he said, looking down at her intently, his clear blue eyes gazing into hers. 'Would your aunt and uncle allow that?'

'I don't know,' she said, trying to ignore the involuntary racing of her heart. 'I could ask them.'

But, already, she knew perfectly well that she wouldn't. She wouldn't ask, because she was afraid it might not be allowed. She'd tell them she was going out with Elizabeth.

'Let me know, then.' He smiled at her as he opened the front door. 'Then I'll get the tickets, and I'll meet you at the bus stop in Fore Street. I hope you'll be able to come. You deserve a treat for your eighteenth birthday.'

Of course, she told herself as she ran back down the track, heedless of the icy patches on the ground and the sleet blowing into her face: he wouldn't have had to guess her age; he'd known her when she was at school, knew which class she'd been in. But it was gratifying that he'd remembered. She didn't know exactly how old *he* was, but she guessed he must be at least twenty-five. And she was pretty sure she knew what her uncle would think about that!

'So who are you really going out with?'

Stella had called at Elizabeth's house the next morning, a Saturday, while she was out doing the shopping in the village, and asked if they could have a private chat in her bedroom. Elizabeth's eyes were out on stalks at the suggestion of her friend needing cover for a secret assignment.

'Promise you won't tell a soul?' Stella urged her. The two girls were sprawled across Elizabeth's bed, trying to avoid the temptation to pick at the threads of her candlewick bedspread. Elizabeth reached over to the table next to her bed and turned up the volume on the brand-new *record-player* – not just a gramophone! – that she'd recently been given by her parents for her birthday. The sound of Al Martino's 'Here in My Heart' blared out across the room and they could talk without fear of being overheard.

'You have to promise,' Stella repeated. 'You can't even tell Frank.'

Elizabeth's boyfriend, Frank, was in the same school year as the two girls, at the nearby boys' grammar school. Stella remembered him, from their days of mingling with the boys on the school bus, as being a serious, rather pale, thin boy who played chess and liked train spotting, but she was sure that, like all of them, he'd improved with age. Stella had had to come to terms with the fact that Elizabeth was now going to the picture palace with Frank more often than with herself. And she'd also had to try to ignore the occasional patronising comments from Elizabeth, implying that Stella, despite having left school three years before her, was somehow less sophisticated, worldly wise and mature since she didn't have the experience of being courted by a spotty teenage boy.

'Of course I won't tell anyone. Not even Frank. Cross my heart and hope to die,' Elizabeth assured her, making the appropriate gesture.

'Well, it's *him*,' Stella whispered excitedly. 'Ernest. Mr Jackman.'

'Mr *Jackman*? The music teacher?' Elizabeth's face was a picture.

'Yes. But I mean – I'm sure it's not a date, or anything like that, he just wants to take me to a concert, so it's probably sort of educational, it'll be a violin concerto or—'

'So why not tell your uncle?'

Stella fell silent. She could feel her face reddening.

'You still like him, don't you?' Elizabeth said. 'Oh, Stella, don't go making a fool of yourself over him, will you? I don't want you to get hurt. He's a lot older than you—'

'I know. I do know that! I'm not making a fool of myself, I promise. It's nothing like that, but my uncle might read something into it. Please just say you'll pretend you're coming into Torquay with me.'

'Of course I will,' her friend soothed her. 'I'll be going into town myself on Friday evening anyway, to meet Frank, so I'll tell my parents we're both going out with you as it's your birthday. In case they speak to your uncle. OK?'

'Thanks.' Stella smiled. She *was* grateful. It might have been nice, of course, if Elizabeth *had* offered to go out with her just this once – for her birthday – instead of it having to be a pretence. But on the other hand, she wanted to go out with Ernest even more than with Elizabeth. And definitely more than she wanted to go out with Elizabeth and Frank together!

Ernest had a phone at Cliff's End, which was still quite unusual, especially in country areas, and he'd given Stella the number in case she ever had to cancel her violin lesson. She used the telephone box outside the post office in Fore Street to call him.

'I can come to the concert!' she told him, her voice coming out squeaky with excitement. She didn't, of course, tell him about the alibi she'd arranged or the lie she'd told her uncle.

'That's marvellous,' he said. 'I'll get the tickets.'

*

On the evening of her birthday, she put on her 'good' dress, the one she normally wore for church and for her outings to the picture palace with Elizabeth. It was dark green with tiny white spots, and had a mid-calf-length skirt, a white collar, and a white belt to pull in the waist. The dress had short sleeves so, as it was cold out, with an icy wind, she wore one of her aunt's hand-knitted cardigans on top, and reluctantly added her shabby black coat. By the time she met Ernest at the bus stop, her heart was beating so furiously she could hardly speak to him. She'd been looking around her, hoping nobody who knew her aunt and uncle would see them out together, but as soon as she saw him waiting for her, smiling as she walked towards him, all her worries evaporated.

'I hope you've had a nice birthday,' he said as they sat together on the bus.

'Not very different from other days.' She laughed. 'Although my uncle did buy me some chocolate. He'd saved up their rations.'

'That was nice of him,' he said. 'By the way, I've heard rationing on chocolate will be finishing in a few weeks' time. Last time they tried to end it – about three or four years ago – do you remember? – they had to put it back on ration again, because people bought so much the manufacturers couldn't keep up with the demand.'

'Yes, I remember. I hope it works this time! I love chocolate. Twelve ounces a month doesn't go very far when you have a sweet tooth,' she admitted.

He laughed. 'Well, I have a surprise for you.' He pulled a small wrapped package from his jacket pocket, together with an envelope. 'Happy birthday, Stella. I hope you enjoy it.'

'Oh! Thank you, I will!' she said, blushing with pleasure. She opened the envelope first. It was a simple birthday card with a picture of flowers on the front and a quite plain message, signed just 'Ernest' – but she already knew she'd be keeping it for ever. Then she unwrapped the precious small bar of Cadbury's chocolate. 'You have to share it with me,' she told him. 'I can't eat it on my own.'

By the time the bus arrived in Torquay, they'd polished off the chocolate together. It felt strangely intimate, breaking off a square at a time, passing the bar between them.

'Where are we actually going?' she asked as they left the bus.

'To the Pavilion. There's an orchestra playing. I hope you'll enjoy it.'

Stella was quite sure she'd have enjoyed that evening, no matter where they went. The grandeur of the Pavilion, combined with the splendour of the music, made it even more special. Sitting next to Ernest, stealing glimpses at his face during the performance, she almost had to pinch herself to believe this was really happening. And when they walked back to the bus stop at the end of the evening, and he took her hand when she nearly tripped crossing the road – and didn't immediately let go of it – she thought she must actually have died and gone to heaven.

It was cold and dark as they waited at the bus stop, and nobody else was around. Ernest took her hand again and pulled her closer.

'If I were to kiss you,' he said, leaning down towards her and sounding almost as shaky as she was feeling herself, 'would you slap my face?'

'No,' she whispered. 'But I might think I must be dreaming.'

'In that case,' he responded as he leaned down towards her, his beautiful blue eyes gazing intently into hers, 'I must be having the same dream. And I don't ever want to wake up.'

19

Holly

Stella stops talking abruptly and looks around the room. I guess she's suddenly remembered about Maisie being here, and worries whether she's said too much about her romantic encounter with Ernest in front of her.

'It's all right,' I say quietly. 'She's busy playing with the cats.'

I think Maisie lost interest when Stella started drifting off into that dreamy state she got into while she was describing her birthday outing.

'It all sounds so romantic,' I say a little wistfully. 'The bus ride together, the chocolate, the concert at the Pavilion—'

'Oh, it was, Holly,' she says, sighing. 'He was such a *gentleman*. I'm not sure men are like that anymore. It seems to have gone out of fashion.'

'You're right there!' I laugh. Then I add, carefully: 'But . . . was it a bit shocking? I mean, because of the age gap. You were still only eighteen, after all, and he was your music teacher.'

I can just imagine what my gran would have had to say about something like that when I was a teenager!

'Well, as it happens, he wasn't my music teacher any more after that,' she says, giving me a funny little smile.

'Oh. Did you stop coming up here for lessons, then?' I want to ask if the kiss had put her off – had it been that bad? – but I'm not sure she'd realise I'm teasing.

'I stopped coming for lessons, yes.' She nods, and to my surprise, gives me a little wink. 'But I still kept coming up here.'

'Oh!' I say again, laughing. 'You cheeky thing! You pretended to your uncle . . . you kept coming on Fridays, bringing your violin –?'

'But it didn't come out of its case!' She laughs too. 'Oh, it wasn't quite as wicked as it sounds, Holly. They were different times, much more proper. We'd sit together on the sofa and listen to music. We'd chat – we never seemed to run out of things to talk about – and we'd have a little kiss and cuddle. But he treated me with respect. We were *courting* – not jumping straight into bed with each other.' She pauses, then adds with another little grin, 'Not right away, at least.'

'Oh!'

It seems to be all I can say. It's me, this time, that's giving Maisie an anxious glance; I think we'd better keep the rest of this story for another time, when she's not here. As it happens, she seems to have tired of playing with Vera and Gracie now. She gets up off the carpet, brushing the cat hairs off herself, and is looking around the room with a puzzled expression.

'Where's your TV?' she asks Stella. 'Is it in a different room?'

'No, poppet.' Stella smiles at her. 'In fact it's in the shed.'

Maisie frowns. 'Do you go out to your shed to watch the TV?'

'No. I haven't watched it for a long time. Partly because it stopped working – that's why I put it out in the shed—'

'Oh, perhaps I can take it to someone in town and see if I can get it fixed for you?' I interrupt, but Stella's laughing now as she goes on:

'—and partly because the shed fell into the sea!'

I stare at her, my mouth open. 'Oh yes!' I remember. 'Of course it did! And your TV was in there?'

'It was, yes, but don't look so worried. It had been in the shed for about twenty years. It was very old; we'd never bothered much with it, much less with getting a new-fangled one with all those fancy channels on it. BBC was always good enough for Ernest and me. And after he went into the care home – well, I couldn't even be bothered with that. I have my wireless.' She points to her ancient-looking transistor radio on the sideboard. 'I can listen to the news every day, and listen to a play, or have some music on, when I want to.'

'Yes, you like listening to your classical music, don't you?' I remember. 'You told me about the *Little Night Music*, the first time I came here.'

'Oh, I like all sorts of music. But yes—' she gives a little smile '—*Eine kleine Nachtmusik* will always be my favourite, Holly. Ernest used to play some of the movements from it so beautifully. And ... it was actually one of the things the orchestra played that night – at the Torquay Pavilion.'

'On your eighteenth birthday? Oh, Stella.' I stare at her, suddenly feeling quite choked. 'No wonder it's your favourite.'

'Yes, well.' She shrugs, looking embarrassed now. 'Anyway, my radio's enough for me. From what I read in my paper on Fridays, all everyone cares about seeing on television these days is celebrities. Celebrities doing ballroom dancing, celebrities going on about themselves, and as for celebrity chefs – I ask you! – since when was a cook a celebrity? How does knocking up a sponge cake make you famous?'

I'm laughing, but at the same time, I can't help thinking she's got a good point.

'I like watching cartoons,' Maisie informs her. 'Why did your shed fall in the sea?'

Stella glances at me; I suspect she doesn't want to give Maisie nightmares about the situation of the house.

'It was a bit old, Mais,' I answer for her, seizing on a convenient presumption. 'Remember that little shed Gran used to let you play in, in her garden? Like that. Falling down.'

'Falling *right* down,' Stella agrees, chuckling.

She seems so completely unfussed by the loss of her shed – to say nothing of a chunk of her land. And I'm seeing such a sense of humour from her today. It's been quite an eye-opener. I wonder if it's talking about the beginning of her romance with Ernest that's perked her up. The more I get to know her, the better I like her. And the more she reminds me of Gran, after all. I'd never have thought it, when I first met her.

'Have you got an Alexa?' Maisie's asking now, still looking around the room with a critical eye, hands on her hips.

'Who's Alexa?' Stella says, sounding genuinely interested.

'Maisie, I think that's enough questions now,' I tell her, glancing at the clock. 'We ought to be getting home for dinner.'

'Oh, but I just wanted to ask one more thing,' Maisie says, giving me a look that's so surprisingly panicked, I nod consent.

She turns to Stella. 'Where's your toilet?'

Stella laughs. 'It's on the other side of the hall, sweetheart. Next to my bedroom.'

'I'll come with you,' I tell Maisie, taking her hand. I don't want her wandering around Stella's house, being nosy, looking for an Amazon Echo that quite obviously won't be here.

The bathroom's quite big, with half-tiled walls and a greenish-coloured bathroom suite – I remember my gran saying it was called *avocado* and was very fashionable around the nineteen-seventies. I take Maisie inside and wait for her to finish.

'Is this a house or a flat?' she asks me curiously as she washes her hands.

'It's a house, Mais.'

'But houses have an upstairs,' she points out. 'Where's the upstairs here?'

'There isn't any upstairs. It's called a bungalow. Everything is downstairs.'

'Oh. That's funny.' I pass her the towel and she frowns to herself as she dries her hands. 'So Stella's house is all downstairs, and our flat is all upstairs. If we put them together, we'd have a whole house.'

You have to admire kids' logic sometimes. Personally, I'm glad Stella hasn't got an upstairs. With her bad knees, she'd probably have had no choice but to move out by now, coastal erosion or not.

'Come on, Maisie,' I encourage her. 'We need to get our coats on and head home. It's dark already, and we've got to walk back down the track, remember.'

'Can I hold your phone, with the torch on?' she asks excitedly.

'Yes, if you're careful not to drop it.'

I usher her out of the bathroom. The door to the next room is wide open. I presume it's Stella's bedroom and I don't mean to glance into it as we pass, but I do, and there on the bed is the blanket she told me about: the one she made out of her knitted squares. It looks like a real work of art. There seem to be pictures embroidered onto some of the squares. I must remember to ask her about it next time I come. Then I remember, too, that Stella offered to knit a jumper for Maisie, and that I was going to look for a pattern and some wool.

'I'll see you on Friday, with your shopping, Stella,' I tell her as I kiss her goodbye. She doesn't look quite so shocked by the kisses now. 'I've got your list. Call me if you think of anything else.'

'Thank you, love; but don't forget, Alec is happy to do it if you can't. He mentions it every time he calls me. Or maybe,' she adds with a little grin, 'he just likes asking after you.'

I try to ignore this, She's teasing me, I know, and she's probably in the mood for inventing some romance, after telling me about her date with Ernest! She struggles to her feet and hands me the tin with the remaining butterfly cakes. 'Here, take these home. You and Maisie can finish them off after your dinner.'

Maisie's eyes are like saucers.

'Are you sure you don't want them?' I ask.

'No. I can't eat too much cake on one day! I'm not a big eater these days. I'll make another walnut cake tomorrow, though. We can start on it on Friday.'

'Thank you, Stella,' Maisie says. 'I *love* your butterfly cakes, they're totally yummy.'

We leave Stella smiling to herself as she sits back in her armchair.

It's even colder than before, the wind whipping the hair around Maisie's face as we start to walk down from Hawbury Top, and almost drowning out the distant sound of a fox crying for a mate. It's an eerie, plaintive sound that makes me shiver and wrap my scarf tighter around my neck.

'Put your hood up, Mais,' I tell her. 'Where's your hat?'

'I think I left it at school. Sorry, Mummy. Is your breathing bad?' she adds. She hates it when I have an asthma attack, and is always listening anxiously for any wheezes.

'It's only the cold wind making me a bit breathless. I'm fine, don't worry. Let's hurry back to the car and get the heater on.'

I take some puffs of my inhaler while she's walking ahead of me with the torch. It's OK, I know it's just the weather, but my chest does feel a bit tight. I'll be fine when I'm home, with the heating turned up. I just hope Stella leaves that fire on this evening.

21

Stella

THREE DAYS LATER

It feels a little less cold when I wake up. It's February now, not exactly my favourite month. Although it's the shortest month of the year, I always feel it drags. I can't wait for the spring, the longer days, the daffodils, feeling some warmth in the sunshine. I've fed the cats, had some breakfast and I'm just putting some washing in my machine when the phone rings. I don't get many calls. Alec only called yesterday, so I don't think it'll be him again, and Holly's got no reason to call as she's due to come with my shopping today. No, it's either going to be the doctor's surgery down in the town, nagging me about some check-up I'm supposed to have, or it's one of those cold calls. So I probably sound a bit snappy when I answer, especially when the person on the other end of the line sounds like they're talking through a mouthful of peas. I'm just about to hang up when they go into a terrible spasm of coughing and splutter out my name:

'Stella! It's me, Holly.'

'Oh. Holly, it didn't sound like you. Are you all right?'

'No. I'm not well.' I can hear the wheeze in her voice now. 'I'm ... so sorry ... I won't be able to ... bring your shopping.'

There's another spasm of coughing. She sounds awful.

'For God's sake, don't worry about my shopping. Get yourself to the doctor's. Or—' I don't know much about these things, but you read terrible stories in the paper sometimes about asthma attacks. I feel a bit panicked and out of my depth. 'Or do you need to go to hospital? Should I call you an ambulance?'

'No. It's ... OK. I've got a ... chest infection. The doctor's ... given me tablets ... it'll settle down. But ... he says I need to ... stay in the warm.'

It sounds like the effort of getting the words out is exhausting her.

'Of course you've got to stay in the warm. Don't you dare start fussing about my shopping. Alec will get it for me – I told you, he keeps offering.'

'But I've ... already got it.' Another bout of coughing and a gasp before she can go on. 'I got it this morning ... on the way to the doctor.'

I feel so cross, I want to shout at her, but I know it's just because I'm so worried.

'Why on earth did you worry about *that*—'

'I had time to kill. Between ... taking Maisie to school ... and the doctor's appointment. So ... what I'm going to do ...' She starts coughing and wheezing again.

'You're not going to do anything,' I tell her firmly. 'You take yourself to bed right now, and—'

'But I'm going ... to call a taxi ... and they'll bring up your shopping ... OK?'

'No!' I say. '*I'll* call the taxi, and send it round to you for the shopping.' But I won't really, of course. I know exactly who I'm going to call! 'What's your address? Let me get a pen.'

Victoria Road. I know where that is. I know the maisonettes she lives in. Knew them before they were converted from the original houses. I'm putting on my boots even before I've hung up from her, and as I'm putting on my coat, I'm dialling Alec's number. If it's not convenient, of course I'll have to call the taxi company instead. I've used them often enough, if I have to go into town these days for the doctor or the dentist, now that I can't walk all the way anymore. Not that I go if I can help it. So the taxi drivers are used to me, used to allowing me time to walk down the track to meet them. I wasn't going to tell Holly I'm planning to turn up at her place, of course. She'd have got upset with me. But whether she likes it or not, and whether Alec can take me or not, I'm on my way.

'Absolutely,' Alec says immediately when he answers the phone and I explain what's happened, and what I need. 'My assistant can manage the shop for a little while, no problem. I'll be straight round. *Don't* walk down to meet me, Stella – I'll come up to the house and walk down with you, OK?'

It's strange walking down to the car with Alec. He's holding my arm, treating me like I'm an invalid, or made of glass or something. At first I have to curb my irritation, stop myself from shaking him off, but I know he means well, and after a few minutes I find to my surprise that, actually, I quite like it. It's been so long since I've had a man take my arm, and the realisation of this makes my eyes suddenly sting with tears, remembering how Ernest used to look after me so protectively, so tenderly – until the tables were turned and it was me looking after him.

'Are you all right, Gran?' Alec says. He asked me, last time he called to see me, whether I'd mind if he started to call me *Gran*. I was so overcome, I thought I might cry – just at the unexpected pleasure, the realisation that I'm actually somebody's grandmother.

I probably answered a bit brusquely, to stop myself from blubbing, telling him that of course he could call me *Gran*, that was what I was, after all! And it's the same today: I have to blink quickly and tell him I'm fine, I'm just worried about Holly, because that's true – I am; I can't wait to get to her, to see how she is.

'I could have driven round there myself to see how she is,' he says, 'and reported back to you. To save you the trouble.'

'It isn't any trouble,' I tell him firmly. 'She's my friend, she's been good to me, I want to try to help her. And anyway, it wouldn't be proper for you to go on your own, while she's not well. She might be in bed.'

He doesn't seem to know how to respond to this, and I find myself smiling a little at his discomfiture. He's a nice young man. Holly could do worse. But then I stop the train of thoughts abruptly. She's barely even met him yet, and anyway, I've got no business fantasising about matchmaking for her. And from the little she's told me, I gather she's had a bad experience with Maisie's father, and probably has no interest in finding another man – despite those little furtive looks and blushes I noticed.

It doesn't take long in the car to get into town and I tell Alec where to turn into Holly's road. He hasn't lived here long enough yet to know all the little side turnings. We pull up outside her building, and I look up at the windows of the upstairs flat. The stairs are going to be the hard bit, but it's not like I've got to hurry. I tell myself it'll be good exercise for the knees. I let Alec take my arm again and this time I'm grateful for the help. When we finally make it to Holly's door, I have to lean against it for a minute, take a few breaths and get myself together – otherwise there'll be two of us coughing and wheezing.

I ring the doorbell, hoping she's not already asleep in bed, but a minute later I can hear her coughing inside, coming towards the door. When she opens it, we both take a step back in shock. She looks dreadful. She's in baggy fleece trousers and a big jumper, with no make-up, and her hair just pulled back off her face. She's holding her arms around herself, as if she's shivering. And she's staring at me as if she's seeing a ghost.

'What ...? Stella?' She glances at Alec, and then back at me. 'What on earth ...?'

'Well, let me come inside, so you can shut this door, and I'll tell you.'

She does as she's told, coughing, her chest rattling, and I'm hit straight away by the warmth in here. She's obviously got her central heating on at full blast. Fair enough, I reckon she needs it. I'm not used to it, though, and I'm already having to undo my coat. Alec is standing stock-still just inside the front door, staring at her in alarm. He clearly doesn't know quite what to say. 'Were you in bed?' I ask her. 'Did we wake you?'

'No. Just lying on the sofa.'

'Well, go back and lie down again. I'll just take this off – and my boots—'

'Don't worry about that,' she croaks. 'Floor needs a wash anyway.'

The floors are all wooden, with just rugs everywhere. Funny, isn't it. When we were young, we had lino on all the floors, and if we were lucky and could afford it, just a square of carpet in the middle of the room. When fitted carpets came in, we thought it was wonderful. No more cold feet from walking across the lino. It felt like luxury. Now it seems like we've gone backwards again, if you ask me, and from what I see from pictures in the paper. Even the so-called celebrities, showing off their mansions: all polished wood floors, or worse, tiles, or even stone. Stone, indoors! Are they mad?

'Well, you don't want to be doing any cleaning at the moment,' I say as I follow her into her sitting room, Alec trailing behind me, still silent.

'Couldn't if I tried,' she responds, sitting down with a sigh of exhaustion. Then she looks up at us both and adds: 'You still haven't told me . . . what you're doing here.'

'What d'you think? I called Alec, instead of calling the taxi, to see if he was free to give me a lift.' I give her a smile. 'Did you really think I'd just send a taxi to you to pick up my shopping? I wanted to come here myself. To see how you are.'

She shakes her head at me. 'You shouldn't have done that. I'm all right.'

'No, you're quite obviously not,' I reply as she goes into another spasm of coughing.

'You look awful,' Alec agrees, finally finding his voice. He's standing staring at Holly, frowning with concern, like he's never seen anyone poorly before. To be fair, he's right. She does look awful, but I'm cross with him for saying so. Men are so hopeless sometimes, even the nice ones! I shoot him a furious look and he gives a start of understanding and adds, awkwardly, 'I mean, you look fine but I'm sure you *feel* awful.'

'Well, thanks!' she says, trying to laugh but not managing it. Poor thing, she immediately starts trying to smooth her hair, looking down at her comfy clothes and sighing. It must be embarrassing for her that he's seeing her at her worst. Perhaps I shouldn't have let him come in. 'But I'll be OK,' she goes on. 'I've . . . got antibiotics . . . for the infection. And steroids.' She stops for breath, clutching her chest. 'To get the asthma under control. I'll be . . . fine.'

'Good. And in the meantime, you need looking after,' I tell her.

'Oh, Stella!' She looks like she's about to cry. 'No, I don't. You shouldn't have come . . . it's sweet of you but . . . I can manage.'

'What about picking Maisie up from school? The doctor said you have to stay in the warm.'

'Her little friend's mum . . . down the road . . . she's my nominated person . . . to pick up Maisie if I can't. I've already called her.'

'Good. I'd have gone myself otherwise.' I see the look on her face and laugh. 'I'm not so decrepit I couldn't walk from here to the school and back.'

'*I* could have picked her up,' Alec retorts. 'Rather than you, Stella.'

Holly's trying to laugh again, but it's a tired, pathetic attempt. 'Well, don't argue over it, please!' she croaks. 'The thing is … the teacher wouldn't let you … we have to have a … nominated person … to pick up our children if we can't.'

'Of course,' Alec says, nodding. 'I realise – it's the same with Alfie, of course.'

'But thank you. Both of you,' Holly goes on. 'You're … so kind.' Her eyes actually do fill up with tears now. 'Sorry,' she says. 'I'm just … feeling low …'

'Of course you are!' I look at my watch. 'Now then. I'm going to make you a hot drink. Want a coffee or something, Alec?' I glance at him. He's still standing there, looking awkward, his eyes clouding with concern every time he glances at Holly. 'Or do you need to get back to the shop?' I add.

'Well – is there anything I can do?' he asks, sounding quite wretched. 'I mean, I don't want to just … leave you to it. Abandon you. If I can help at all?'

'I don't think so,' I say. 'It was good of you to bring me, Alec, but—' Frankly, I don't think he's going to be of any use. Men rarely are, in my experience, when it comes to illness.

'Well, I'll come back for you when you're ready to go home,' he says at once. 'Just call me. It doesn't matter what time.'

'Thank you. I will, if you're sure.'

'Thanks, Alec,' Holly says, closing her eyes, like talking is tiring her out. He's still staring at her.

'Will she be all right?' he whispers to me as he heads for the door.

'I'm not a doctor!' I tell him. 'But she's seen one, so we have to presume she's on the right treatment.'

'She looks . . . ' he tails off, shaking his head. 'Well, look, call me if . . . she gets worse or anything. If she needs – I don't know – to go back to the doctor. Or to hospital. Or whatever.'

'I will. Thank you.'

'Tea?' I ask Holly, when he's gone. 'Or something else?'

'Tea, please, Stella. Are you sure . . . you don't mind?' She doesn't wait for an answer. I think she's given in; accepted me looking after her. She's too tired to argue, poor girl. 'The kitchen's . . . just through there,' she adds, waving a hand to a door behind the sofa where we're sitting. 'Tea bags . . . in the cupboard . . . '

'I'll find everything, don't worry.'

She hasn't got any proper tea in the cupboard, of course, just tea bags. And when I open the box I see they're not tea at all, they're 'lemon and ginger'. I catch myself sniffing with disgust, but then shrug instead. Well, perhaps lemon and ginger will do more for her poor chest than normal tea. I don't really fancy one myself, but on the other hand if you never try something, you'll never know, will you? I look for cups and saucers but there's only mugs, big ones, some of them with silly slogans on. I choose a couple of plain blue ones, make the so-called tea and carry them into the sitting room. She's propped herself on the sofa with a couple of cushions.

'Drink it while it's hot,' I tell her. 'Now, then. Do you need me to call anyone for you? What about your cleaning job?'

'I don't work on Fridays,' she says. 'Monday, Tuesday, Wednesday. I'll . . . be all right . . . by Monday.'

'Hmm.' Well, I hope she will, of course. Let's hope the tablets work fast.

'There is one thing, though,' she goes on, pulling herself up a bit more and suddenly looking anxious. 'I've got . . . to send an email. I promised . . . '

'Well, it can't be that urgent, can it?' Emails, and mobile phones, and Twittering or whatever they call it – apparently her generation can't live without them. Even when they're ill, so it seems. 'Wait till you feel better.'

'No. My editor ... at the magazine ... she wants my story submitted today. It's ... finished. I just ... want to read it through again ... then it's got to go off. Before five o'clock.'

Ah. Well, this is obviously important for her. Her work.

'Where is it, Holly?' I ask her. 'I'll bring it to you and you can sit and read it through while you drink your drink.'

'Oh, it's ... OK. It's on my laptop. But I can read it ... on my phone.'

I have no idea what she's talking about. How she can read a story on her phone is beyond me. So I just say that's all right, then, and I'll keep quiet so she can concentrate. I take a sip of the ginger drink. To be fair, I've tasted worse. It's definitely not tea, though.

'Well, actually ... ' Holly says. She's holding her mobile phone. It's in a pink leather cover with a picture of a unicorn on it. More appropriate for Maisie, I'd have thought, but what do I know? 'Actually ... I was wondering. Would you like to read it for me?'

Turns out it isn't a *story* as such. It's the article she's been writing about the things I've told her. Life in Hawbury Down in the nineteen-forties. I feel a bit taken aback. I mean, I knew she was writing it, of course. I've tried to tell her some things that might be helpful, although I must admit I've kept on drifting into my personal life story. Difficult not to, really. But I didn't expect to read it, not even when it's published in the magazine, let alone now, before she's even sent it off to her editor. What if I don't like it? What if I find mistakes in it? Will she be offended?

'Well, I don't think I'd be able to read it on that,' I say, pointing to her phone. My glasses are quite strong, but the print must be tiny, to fit on that thing.

'I'll get the laptop. It'll be ... easier.'

'Sit still. Tell me where it is. And what it looks like,' I add, as I have no idea.

'It's in my bedroom. At the end of the hall. On the ... table in there. It's silver. About this size,' she says, holding out her hands to demonstrate.

The bedroom's just as hot as the living room. I wouldn't like a hot bedroom. Not what I'm used to. Even in here there's polished floorboards and rugs. And blinds at the windows instead of proper curtains. Not very cosy-looking. There's not much furniture in here, apart from her bed against one wall, a small wardrobe and ... ah. A little table, with a chair, a lamp, some papers stacked up on one side, and the silver thing she referred to. Laptop. It's a kind of computer, I know that much – I'm not completely clueless – but I wouldn't hazard a guess about how it works. I carry it in to Holly and she sits up, opens the lid and taps a few keys before handing it back to me. The print on the screen is quite a decent size. She shows me which button to press to go down the page, and I settle down and start to read it. I can tell straight away that she's a good writer. If she'd been one of my pupils when I was teaching, I'd have had high hopes for her. And she's remembered everything I told her: about the village (as it was then), the farm, the school, the rationing, the barbed wire on the beach – everything, so well described, almost better than I could have done myself.

'I kept ... your personal memories ... out of it, like I promised,' she says, giving me an anxious look as I finish reading. 'I hope it's OK?'

'It's better than OK,' I tell her. 'It's really very good. I hope your editor agrees.'

'Oh, thank you. So do I. She hinted ... at a double-page spread. But I have to send it today.'

'OK. Well, while you do that, I'll make us some lunch. Don't give me that look,' I add as she pulls a face. 'You may not be hungry, but you need nourishment. No, sit still, I'll find something in your kitchen.'

I'm hoping she's got soup – and she has, two tins. I stare at the labels. Butternut squash? I don't think so. Carrot and coriander? Well, that sounds quite nice, I suppose, although I don't know what was wrong with the old favourites like chicken, or cream of tomato. I open the tin and find a saucepan in another cupboard. She's got a microwave but its controls look too complicated. Her cooker is gas. I haven't got gas at home so I haven't used it since I was a girl, on the farm, but it lights easily enough and while the soup is heating, I find some bread in her breadbin and put it on a plate. It's all ready within a few minutes and she's got a couple of trays in the cupboard where I found the saucepan. I carry in one at a time and sit down on the other end of the sofa.

'Eat up,' I say. 'Sent your story off, have you?'

She nods, and takes a spoonful of soup. 'Yes.'

We eat in silence for a while. I'm pleased to see she finishes most of hers, before putting her tray down on the floor and lying back against the cushions again.

'Have a little sleep,' I suggest. 'I'll wash up.'

'No,' she says, giving me a smile. She doesn't look quite as bad as she did when I arrived. Bit of colour in her cheeks now. 'Leave that for a minute ... It's so nice you being here. I'd rather listen to you talk ... if you don't mind? Tell me a bit more. About you and Ernest ... unless you need to get back home?'

'Course I don't. Nothing to rush for. All right, then; now, where did I get up to? Ah, yes, of course.' I nod. 'Nineteen-fifty-three.'

That was certainly a year to remember. I'm not even sure how much I ought to tell her ... or how much I *want* to.

1953

'Coronation Day is going to be a holiday,' Ernest told Stella one Friday evening when she was at Cliff's End with him, as usual. 'Tuesday the second of June. The queen wants everyone to celebrate. There's going to be a party in the village square.'

Stella's face lit up with pleasure. For young people like her, the war was already almost forgotten. Life was slowly improving, people were feeling more optimistic in general, and they were going to have a new young Queen Elizabeth, who seemed to represent a new, youthful, and forward-looking era for Britain. 'Oh, just like VE Day all over again!' she said. 'That'll be nice.'

'And have you heard?' he went on enthusiastically. 'It's going to be televised.'

'What is? The village party?'

'No, silly! The coronation ceremony, at Westminster Abbey. Apparently, though, Mr Churchill doesn't think it's fitting for such a solemn occasion to be televised. He thinks the queen should refuse. But Her Majesty wants it to go ahead, so that as many people as possible can watch it.'

'Yes, as many *rich* people as possible!' Stella retorted. 'How many people around here have got television sets?'

'Ah, but they can be rented, you know,' he said thoughtfully. 'I've been thinking about it. Wouldn't it be wonderful to watch the whole thing – the procession, the crowning – just as if we were there, up in London?'

'Yes, I suppose it would,' Stella agreed. 'But I think I'd prefer to go to the party.'

'The party will be afterwards. We could do both.'

'Well, I don't know.' Stella frowned. 'I don't think there's any possibility of Uncle Jim renting a television. He'd think I was mad if I even suggested it.'

Jim and Nellie were getting on by now, of course. Jim would be seventy the following year, and no longer able to do more than the lightest of tasks on the farm, and Nellie – who since her stroke had been unable to walk without assistance, and whose speech had never recovered properly, so that only Jim and Stella were able to understand her – was sixty-seven.

'But you could come and watch it with me here, if I got a set,' Ernest said.

Stella laughed, leaning her head against Ernest's shoulder. 'I'm not sure how we'd explain that to my aunt and uncle!'

'Just tell them the truth: that your violin teacher is getting a television set for the occasion of the coronation and has invited you to watch it with him. I can't see why they would object to that.'

'No, but they might, if they knew how we really spend our so-called violin lessons!' She reached up and gave him a quick kiss. 'They'd think you were leading me astray!'

'Yes, well . . .' he said, pretending to try helplessly to fend off her kisses. 'I'd tell them I'm just the innocent victim here!' He looked at her thoughtfully for a moment. 'Do you still practise the violin at home, by the way? Does the poor instrument ever come out of its case these days?'

'Yes!' She grinned. 'But only to keep up the pretence.'

'They must wonder why you haven't made any progress for months now,' he teased.

'Oh, I doubt they'd notice. They think it's wonderful that I can get so much as a note out of it.' Her smile dropped as she added quietly: 'I do feel a bit guilty, Ernest. For deceiving them. They've been good to me, when all's said and done. They'd be hurt if they knew. To say nothing of flipping furious!'

'You're good to them, too, don't forget. You've cared for your aunt for years now. You've given up your own life, really, to keep house for them and help on the farm. It's a shame. You should have been looking forward to going to college now, to train to be a teacher.'

'But they gave up a lot for me, too. Auntie Nellie never wanted children, and she found me a great irritation when I was little. But they both love me in their ways.' She shrugged. 'Anyway, I might still be able to go to college one day.'

'When they're both gone?'

'I suppose so. If I'm not too old to consider it then.'

'You might be married by then, and have children!'

'Married!' she exclaimed, laughing. 'Oh, that'll be a long way off. If ever.'

Stella looked away, trying to calm the beating of her heart. There was only one person she could ever imagine wanting to marry, but she could hardly tell him that. He was sitting right beside her, stroking her hair so tenderly it was driving her crazy with desire. She loved Ernest desperately, but she suspected that, for him, she was simply an amusing diversion.

'Well, look, your aunt and uncle don't seem to have a problem with you coming here,' he said. 'So why don't you ask them about Coronation Day? I'll rent a set, if you can come and watch it with me. Then we can go down to the village together for the party.'

It was tempting, of course. 'All right, I'll ask them,' she agreed.

'A television set?' Uncle Jim's eyebrows had shot up to the top of his bald head. 'He must be doing all right, on his teacher's salary, that young man.'

'He's going to rent one, uncle. Isn't it exciting? And isn't it kind of him to invite me to watch the coronation with him?'

'It certainly is. Will he be inviting all his other violin pupils too?'

'Um ...' Stella hadn't anticipated this question. 'Well, maybe. But of course, most of them are only children. I'm probably one of the oldest ones he teaches. But yes,' she went on quickly, 'I expect there will be others there.'

Jim nodded slowly. 'Then I think it might be very nice for you. It's a historical occasion, after all, and seeing it on the television would be a wonderful memory for you to take through your life with you. Don't you agree, Nell?'

Auntie Nellie was still always properly consulted on matters concerning the home and family. She gave a grunt and a nod now in response, and Jim turned back to Stella with a smile.

'Tell Mr Jackman we're very grateful for his invitation.' Jim looked down at the floor for a moment, blinking, and added quietly: 'You deserve a treat, Stella, love – and a day off, a holiday from the farm. It'll be something for you to look forward to, what with the party and all.'

Stella gave him a hug. 'Thank you, uncle! Thank you, auntie!' she added to Nellie. 'I really *am* looking forward to it.'

If only they knew how much, and why, she thought to herself with a little pang of guilt. But she was eighteen, she was in love, and the guilt only lasted for as long as it took to run to her bedroom, throw herself on her bed and hug herself with excitement.

Stella still got together with Elizabeth from time to time, when her friend could spare her an evening away from Frank. On one such occasion, they were chatting in Elizabeth's bedroom together when she suddenly burst out:

'Oh, I've been meaning to tell you, Stella: Daddy's getting us a television set! We'll be able to watch the coronation on it, just as it's happening, in London. Isn't it exciting?! I'm going to ask Mummy and Daddy if you can come and watch it with us. Frank's coming round too, with his parents.'

'Oh.' Stella bit her lip. 'Actually, I've already got plans.'

Elizabeth's face dropped and she sucked in her breath with disapproval.

'With *him*? But this is Coronation Day, Stella. It's special. Wouldn't you like to watch it on television?'

'I'm going to. He's renting a set. My aunt and uncle have even agreed to it.'

'Only because they don't know what's going on!' Elizabeth shot back. 'You are taking *such* a chance, Stella. I mean ...' she dropped her voice, and added more gently, 'from what you've told me, things are getting a bit – you know – near the mark.'

Stella blushed. 'So what? He won't take it any further than I want to. He cares about me. He respects me.'

'But he's going to want to go further, sooner or later. He's older than us, he's bound to have ... had some experience. And you're so gone on him, one day you're going to get carried away and go too far.' Elizabeth put her hand on her friend's arm. 'I'm only saying it because I'm worried about you. You're so infatuated with him, you're not thinking straight. You ought to find yourself a boyfriend of your own age.'

'Like Frank, you mean?'

Stella didn't mean to say it quite the way it came out, but it was understandable that Elizabeth took offence.

'There's nothing wrong with Frank. He's a nice, kind boy and I happen to be very fond of him.'

'Good, I'm pleased for you, I really am. But—' Stella sighed '— being *very fond* is never going to be enough for me now, after the way I feel about Ernest. I love him. I'm crazy about him. I'd die if I couldn't be with him.'

'You read too many of those romance stories, that's your trouble,' Elizabeth said with a sniff. Then she shrugged and relented. 'Don't worry, I won't tell anyone. I've never breathed a word, you know that. But please be careful, Stella.'

'All right, fusspot! I will.' Stella laughed. 'Anyway, tell me how the swotting for the exams is coming along,' she added, to change the subject. 'I bet you'll be glad when they're over.'

Now that her uncle had virtually retired from the farm and was living on his pension, Stella's allowance was being paid by her second cousin Geoffrey, who was now running the business. Although most of her time was spent working in the cottage she shared with Auntie Nellie and Uncle Jim, she also helped on the land, and with the animals, as much as she could, and Geoffrey did at least recognise that she was part of the workforce as well as part of the family. Without much else to spend her allowance on apart from contributing to the household provisions and bills, Stella had saved up enough to buy a dress from a smart new shop in Torquay. It was blue, with a tight waist and full skirt, and after years of having only one good dress, and wearing old slacks, an overall and a scarf around her head during her days at the farm, Stella was quite stunned by her own reflection in the mirror of the shop's changing cubicle. Her morale boosted, and with a few pounds still in her purse, she then visited a hairstylist for the first time in her life and asked for her long dark hair to be cut off, in favour of one of the new, shorter bouffant styles.

She felt grown-up and glamorous as she dressed on the day of the coronation, and strangely shy when she arrived at Cliff's End Cottage. It was a cool, cloudy day – a disappointment after the beautiful weather they'd been enjoying throughout May – and she'd put a cardigan around her shoulders for the walk up to Hawbury Top.

'Wow,' Ernest said as he opened the door to her. 'You look . . . so different.'

'Different in a nice way, or not?' she teased him, taking off her cardigan and doing a twirl.

'Definitely in a nice way.' He took hold of her for a kiss. 'That's how nice,' he finished with a grin when they finally broke apart.

The television set had arrived the previous week and was a matter of pride for Ernest, and complete mystery to Stella. She was surprised at how small the screen was, considering the large size of its wooden casing, and to be honest, a little disappointed at the grainy black-and-white picture. But still, it *was* wonderful to be able to watch the entire coronation ceremony from the sofa, feeling almost as if they were there, in London, with the crowds cheering and waving flags outside Westminster Abbey despite the gloom and the threat of rain.

'Shall I make us a cup of tea to celebrate?' Stella suggested when it was all over. Tea rationing had now come to an end, thank goodness, and Stella couldn't get enough of it.

'I can think of other ways to celebrate,' Ernest said, taking hold of her again as she stood up and smoothed down her dress. 'You look so beautiful today,' he added as he started to kiss her again.

By the time Hawbury Down's street party was beginning down

in the village, Stella's new blue dress was lying in an inelegant heap on the floor. And Stella was lying in Ernest's bed.

'It'll be all right,' he tried to reassure her for the umpteenth time as they finally strolled, hand-in-hand, down to the village. 'I'm sure it will. I ... think I managed to, um ... be careful.'

'And it was only my first time,' Stella agreed. 'I've heard nobody ever falls, the first time.'

'I promise I'll get something – things to use – next time,' Ernest said awkwardly, looking down at his shoes, and then added quickly: 'If there is a next time, I mean. If you want to. I should have ... the thing is, I didn't expect ... I wasn't planning ...'

'I know. I wasn't planning to, either,' Stella said. She was quite amazed by how little she was worried about the risk she'd taken, or the damage she might have done to her reputation, to say nothing of what her aunt and uncle might think if, God forbid, they ever found out. She was far too overcome by the things Ernest had said, the endearments he'd whispered in her ear as he made love to her. He'd told her he loved her; that he'd love her for ever and never want anyone else. She repeated it over and over inside her head as they joined the crowd in the village square. The sun had finally broken through; women were serving the children with sandwiches, jelly and cake at tables set out on the green; men were standing outside the White Lamb pub, pint glasses in hand, laughing and joking together, while teenage girls giggled and flirted with the boys. It was like VE Day, only even better, the intervening years having brought a little more prosperity, the horrible wartime memories dimmed.

'Would you like a glass of cider?' Ernest suggested. 'I'm going to get one for myself.'

'Oh. I've never tried it!' she said, unsure.

'Well, there's a first time for everything,' he said, squeezing her around the waist and winking as he gave her a quick kiss.

She giggled and blushed. 'All right. Yes, please. As long as nobody tells my uncle.'

But of course, there were worse things than a glass of cider for her uncle to find out about. And unfortunately for Stella, the moment to have been careful about that had just passed: the moment when Ernest had squeezed her waist and kissed her.

They'd been spotted.

22

Holly

'Oh my God!' I've sat up on the sofa, almost knocking my empty mug onto the floor. Stella's story has certainly taken my mind off my illness. It's romantic, and shocking, and enthralling all at the same time. 'Who saw you? Did they tell your uncle? What happened?'

But just as Stella opens her mouth to go on, there's a ring at the doorbell. I glance at my watch. It's three-thirty, and this will be Maisie, home from school already. Where has the time gone?

'I'll get it,' Stella says, stopping me as I begin to struggle to my feet.

I sit back again, and I hear her open the door and thank Maisie's friend's mum, Karen, for bringing her home.

'I'm a friend of Holly's,' Stella's explaining. 'I just popped in to see how she was.'

'Thank you, Karen!' I call out hoarsely, and immediately go into a coughing fit, unable to respond when she calls back to ask how I am.

Maisie comes charging into the sitting room, stopping short in surprise when she sees me propped up on the sofa.

'Are you still feeling poorly, Mummy?'

'A bit, darling. But I'll soon ... be better,' I manage to gasp. 'Come and sit up here with me, and tell me about your day.'

'Is Stella staying for tea?'

I smile up at Stella as she comes into the room. 'I think ... it might be nice ... if you call her Auntie Stella,' I suggest to Maisie.

I don't want to add, 'Because of her age, and the fact that she's a bit old-fashioned.'

But Stella's smiling now as she looks down at Maisie and says: 'Do you know, Maisie, I'd love to be called auntie. I've never been an auntie to anyone before.'

'Will you be my auntie, then?' Maisie says, looking pleased about it. 'I've only got one auntie and we never see her, do we, Mummy?'

'No,' I mutter, looking away. Stella's giving me a puzzled look, and no wonder. I've told her I've got a sister. I'll let her assume that Hannah lives too far away for us to visit, rather than knowing the truth: that, as far as I know, she still lives in Exeter, but we don't speak to each other.

'You're welcome to stay for dinner,' I croak to Stella.

'No. I won't intrude. But I'll get something ready for you and Maisie. Then, as long as you think you'll be all right, I'll call Alec to take me back – as he insisted! – and leave you in peace.'

'I'll be fine. I feel ... a bit better in myself, already. And my breathing's settling. It's just the cough.' I guess resting today has done me good. 'You've been so kind,' I add.

'Nonsense. What are friends for? Now then, Maisie why don't you come into the kitchen with me and show me what you normally have when you come home from school. A drink and biscuit, is it? And I'll make Mummy another drink too. Then we can decide what you might like for dinner.'

'Then can I read my reading book to you, please, Auntie Stella?'

I smile to myself. She seems to be enjoying saying that.

'I would *love* to hear you reading, Maisie,' Stella tells her.

I watch them going off into my kitchen together. The rest of Stella's story will have to wait, now, of course, and whatever is still to come from it, I'm trying to reassure myself that it must have all ended well. She did marry Ernest, after all, and she says they were happy.

I've been half asleep, listening to Maisie's little voice as she reads a chapter of her school book, and Stella's encouragement and occasional help over a difficult word. I sip my tea, and then I must have dozed off completely because the next thing I'm aware of is Stella putting a tray down next to me.

'It's only a little bit of chicken and some mashed potato,' she says. 'I haven't given you too much, but try to eat it, won't you? Maisie's having hers up at the kitchen table. I'll keep her company.'

I can hear her chatting to Maisie while I eat. I'm not hungry but the chicken's nice, the mash is smooth and creamy, and she's made a gravy to go with it. I'm making an effort to eat it, to please her, as if I'm a child.

'Auntie Stella,' I hear Maisie say. 'Mummy said you're going to make me a jumper. Can I have a purple one, please? It's my favourite colour.'

'Let's see what Mummy says about that, shall we?' Stella replies, laughing.

In fact, I've already bought the purple wool, and the pattern for the jumper. The lady in the wool shop helped me choose. I forgot to take it to Stella's on Tuesday. I tell her this when she comes back into the room, Maisie skipping behind her.

'Well, that's good,' she says. 'I'll take them home with me now. I'll be glad to have some knitting to work on again. Now then: Maisie's asked if she can watch something on the television. Is that allowed?'

'Yes. There are some programmes for children that she likes.' I smile at Maisie. 'You can turn it on and find the one you want, can't you, Maisie? Thank you for the dinner, Stella.' I point to the tray. 'I've eaten nearly all of it.'

'Good. Let me just rinse that plate, then. I've washed up everything else and tidied it all away. Maisie showed me where everything goes. And I've just called Alec. Are you sure you'll be all right getting Maisie to bed?'

'Yes, we'll be fine now, and you should get yourself home. Don't forget to take your shopping with you. Some of it's in the fridge, in a bag . . . Oh! But you won't be able to carry it up the track from the car. There's a lot, and some of it's heavy.'

'Don't worry,' she says. 'I imagine Alec's going to escort me up the track again. Coming down this morning, you'd have thought I was made of china, the way he hung onto me!'

'That's nice. I'm glad he's looking after you, Stella.'

'Hmm, not that I need it. Two of you now, fussing over me like a pair of old hens! And you're the one who needs help.'

'Not for long, though,' I point out.

'I hope not. Now, I've left the money for the shopping on the side, where you put the bill. Thank you for getting it for me, especially while you're not well, you silly girl. And I'll come back tomorrow. It's Saturday, isn't it, so there won't be any school to worry about. I'll come about the same time as today – I'll get a taxi if Alec's busy in the shop—'

'Actually, I really think I'll be OK. I'll have an early night. And I'll take it easy again.'

She looks at me doubtfully. 'Well, I'll call you in the morning. I'd be happy to come if you need me. Promise you'll tell me if you do?'

'I promise.'

To my surprise, she bends down and gives me a kiss on the cheek.

'I hope you're feeling much better tomorrow, then,' she says.

I feel a bit tearful, with all this pampering. I'm not used to it . . . not anymore.

'Thank you, Gran,' I say.

It's not until she's closed the front door that I realise what I called her.

23

Stella

I've got to be honest, the walk back up the track from where Alec parks the car feels longer and steeper than ever, even hanging onto Alec's arm. He's insisted on carrying all the shopping, only letting me hold the small bag containing the knitting wool and the pattern, which obviously isn't heavy. But it's been a tiring day. I'm not used to going out much, now, and it's surprising how a little one like Maisie can tire you out – just listening to her chattering away, lovely though it was to hear it.

So yes, I'm shattered. But at the same time, I haven't felt more alive in years. It was just so nice to feel useful again. To be helping someone, feeling needed, feeling ... as if it was worth me being here: being alive, I mean. Instead of just being a nuisance, hanging on to life when I'm past my sell-by date, hanging on in a house everybody thinks I should have moved out of. I had a purpose, today, and I've realised that's what's been missing from my life. Not that I was happy to see poor Holly so unwell, of course. It worried me when I saw her this morning, but I think she does look a little bit better already. As long as she keeps resting now.

Gran. She called me 'Gran' by mistake when we were saying

goodbye. She was sleepy, and she didn't even realise, so I wasn't going to correct her. But it would have been her gran, of course, looking after her like that if she was ill, before. The gran only died last year, and she seems to have been the only person Holly was really close to. Holly and I have talked about her a bit, and she told me her name, but I don't remember her, hard as I've tried to think who she might have been. She'd have been quite a few years below me at school, of course. And apparently the grandad, who died when Holly was quite young, didn't live around here at all until he met Holly's gran and married her.

But as to whether Holly thinks of me as a replacement for her gran – I don't know. Probably not consciously. And anyway, does it really matter?

I must admit, it was nice spending time with little Maisie. I'd forgotten how much I used to enjoy the company of children. Not just those I used to teach at the infant school, but those who came to the house for their music lessons when Ernest was still here, when he was still teaching the violin, as well. I got to know them all.

When I finally get back to Cliff's End, the cats are all meowing frantically around my legs for their food. Even Peggy's feigning affection, the way even the most stand-offish cat will do when they're hungry.

'All right, all right, my lovelies. Let me just get my coat off—'

Thank the Lord for my cats. I can't imagine life without them now: I'd be lonely. Like most dotty old cat-ladies, I talk to them all the time, and the two who spend more time indoors will always fight to sit on my lap. They're such a comfort.

'I can stay for a while, if you'd like me to? Help you with anything?' Alec says. 'Cook you something?'

He sounds a bit helpless, a bit out of his depth, like he's desperate to be useful but isn't sure how.

'It's OK, love. You've done quite enough to help me. I just want to sit quietly now, if you don't mind,' I tell him, and he seems reassured, happy to leave, but not without pressing me again – for about the sixth time – to let him know how Holly is tomorrow, and whether he can help again.

After he's gone, I turn on the wireless while I do myself a couple of scrambled eggs on toast. I'm too tired to bother with cooking a proper dinner, but unusually for me, I'm so hungry, I clear the plate, washing it down afterwards with two cups of tea.

I've been so out of my usual routine today that it's hard to relax this evening. I get the knitting pattern for Maisie's jumper out of the bag and have a look at it. It's not a complicated pattern. Within a few minutes I've found the right sized needles and started casting on the stitches with the purple yarn. I sit back in the chair to allow space on my lap for Vera, who's been pushing her head against my leg, waiting for her chance to jump up. Once she's settled down, I can hold the needles over the top of her head. I've had years of experience at this! With a Radio 3 classical music programme playing on the wireless, I'm now settled happily myself. I'm doing something useful. Knitting for someone else. I smile to myself in contentment.

I call Holly the next morning, as promised, and I'm pleased to hear her sounding brighter, more like herself. She's still coughing a lot, but she says she does feel a bit better and the asthma has settled. That's a relief. I offer to go back today and help her with Maisie, but she says the friend down the road – Karen – has already invited Maisie round to play with the other child.

'That's nice,' I say. 'I'm glad you've got a friend close by.'

'Oh, she's not really a friend. Her daughter, Flora, is Maisie's little friend, but we only know each other because of school. I just didn't know who to put down as my emergency contact – you know, for picking up from school if I was ill or whatever – and Karen offered.' She pauses, and then goes on: 'It was always Gran, you see. Before.'

'Of course. Well, Karen seems a nice woman, doesn't she? You could be friends, couldn't you?'

'I presume she has her own friends,' Holly says. 'Everyone does.'

I don't know quite how to respond to this. It seems odd, really, almost as if Holly doesn't even want to attempt to make friends with the other school mums. From what I've seen in the past, some of the best friendships between women seemed to be made during the years at the school gates.

'Well, as long as you're OK,' I say, not wanting to show this has concerned me. 'You're sure you don't need any help today?'

'Thanks, Stella, but no, I was really grateful for yesterday, but I'll be all right now, just resting.'

I mustn't be disappointed – even though, in one way, I'd have quite enjoyed going down there again, looking after her, making sure she gets better. But I suspect she thinks it was a bit much for me yesterday. And in a way, of course, she'd be right. Anyway, the important thing is that she's feeling better, and I'm so relieved about that. 'You will take it easy today, won't you?'

'Yes, I will, I promise. And tomorrow too. I'm not planning on doing anything.'

I feel at a loss after I hang up, which is ridiculous, really, as today isn't going to be any different from any other Saturday of any other week or any other month. I find myself going over the conversation in my head, wondering about Holly and her apparent lack of friends. Perhaps, now Alec's around, he might be able to fill that gap in her life a little? If I keep encouraging them to 'bump into each other' when they visit me here? He could be a friend for her, couldn't he – even if she's not interested in a romance.

But no, I shouldn't interfere. I shouldn't be *plotting* like this! I need to keep myself busy, distract myself. I'll do a bit of washing, hang it out on the line if it stays breezy like it is now, cook my meals, feed the cats, maybe make a cake or a pie for later in the week. Maybe just sit in the chair by the window and re-read one of my old books again, or get on with the knitting.

In fact, after I've done what I needed to do, and had my lunch, I do end up sitting in the chair by the window, but I'm not reading, or knitting: I'm just staring out at the garden and reminiscing.

This used to be the music room. I made it my sitting room after Ernest had to go into care, partly because it was always my favourite room, and partly because I had no use for a music room any more, and I needed to make some changes, to make everything feel different, less painful for me, without him here. This is the window where Ernest used to stand and play his violin – with the light behind him – and where I'd watch him, never tiring of seeing the concentration on his face, the dexterity of his fingers on the frets, the tenderness with which he held the bow. When, finally, the dementia stopped him from playing, because his brain refused to co-operate anymore, it was terrible to see his frustration. More than once he shouted in rage, pushed over the music stand and stomped off into the other room. More than once he actually threw down the bow, and once even the violin. And once – only once – he actually pushed *me* over. He didn't mean it. He couldn't help it. But I knew then that I was getting to the point where I wouldn't be able to keep him at home for much longer.

I give myself a little shake. It's not a memory I really want to keep going over.

I call Holly again the next day, and again on Monday. She says she'll be all right to do her cleaning job in the afternoons, but she'll take it easy in the mornings. So I don't see her again until she visits on Thursday. I'm pleased to say she's looking much better by then.

'I've almost finished the back of Maisie's jumper,' I say as I'm making our tea.

'Wow, that was quick!'

'Not really. I've had all week, and nothing else to do.' In fact, I have had another visit from Alec during the week – to say nothing of how many times he's called me to ask how I am, and also asking, almost as if it's an afterthought (but I'm not daft!), how Holly is.

'Sorry I haven't seen you,' she says. 'I've missed you.'

'You should have said. I did offer to come down again—'

'It's hardly fair to expect you to come all the way into town, just to keep me company, is it!' she laughs.

It's good to see her back to her old cheerful self. But she's missed the point.

'I like the company too,' I tell her. 'And anyway, Alec would have brought me down again. He's been asking after you, by the way,' I add, giving her a little grin. 'Every day.'

'Oh, that's nice of him,' she says, looking the other way quickly. 'Well, you'd have been welcome to take him up on the offer, if he wanted to bring you again. But I *was* all right, really.'

'Good. And I'd have come if I thought you needed me, but I wouldn't want to be a nuisance.'

She comes over to me and puts an arm around my shoulders, almost making me drop the tea cosy.

'You wouldn't be a nuisance. Don't ever think that.' We meet each other's eyes and she smiles. 'We're company for each other, aren't we? Perhaps we both needed someone to chat to. I think I did, anyway. I just didn't realise it.'

'Me neither,' I admit. But suddenly this whole conversation makes me feel a bit awkward – self-conscious – and I change the subject abruptly. 'Anyway, did you hear back from your editor?'

'Oh – yes.' She beams happily. 'She loves the story! But ... she needs photos to go with it. I know it's a lot to ask, but you wouldn't happen to have anything suitable, would you? Not personal photos, obviously. But if you had any pictures of the town – I mean, the village, as it was then – of the farm, or the school ... ?'

I think about this for a minute. I don't think there's anything else in my memory box. But would there be anything in the attic? I'm sure Ernest used to have some photo albums. He certainly used to take pictures. He loved his camera.

'I might have,' I tell her. 'How urgently do you need them?'

'Well, I don't want to be a pain. But really, as soon as possible.'

'In that case: how do you feel about going up into my attic?'

24

Holly

I'm halfway through the hatch into Stella's attic and she's standing in her hallway at the bottom of the loft-ladder, holding onto it, not that it's wobbly or unsafe in the slightest, and telling me to please be careful. I lever myself up so that I'm sitting on the attic floor with my legs dangling over the hatch.

'There's a light, up there,' she says. 'Or there used to be – I don't know if it still works. I haven't been up there for years. Ernest wired it up. He was clever with things like that.'

Hmm. I certainly hope he *was* clever with it – I'm not overly excited by the thought of switching on a light wired up by a do-it-yourselfer, God knows how many years ago, that hasn't been used or tested for almost as long. I fumble around in the gaps between the rafters and manage to find the switch. Well, it works, at least, and doesn't immediately blow the place up or trip a fuse or anything. And hooray, the attic is partly boarded. And surprisingly big. I'm just about to get onto my feet and start having a proper look around, when Stella's doorbell sounds.

'Oh, bother – who on earth can that be? Stay there, Holly,' she instructs me. 'Don't start moving around up there till I come back.'

I do as I'm told, although quite honestly it's debatable whether she'd be able to help if I got into any kind of difficulties up here! I hear her open the front door and say, sounding surprised and pleased:

'Oh, Alec! Hello, how nice to see you again.'

Alec. Really? Right now, while I'm on all fours up here on the floor of Stella's attic? Not that I care in the slightest what he thinks of me, of course, why should I?

'Come in,' Stella's telling him. 'I'm glad you're here, you can help Holly in the attic.'

I hear him following her down the hallway. I try to sit myself up and straighten my clothes a bit, and the next minute, his head appears through the loft-hatch. He doesn't look pleased.

'Do you really think you should be doing things like this when you've just been so ill?' he says, sounding worried. 'Stella, why didn't you call me to do this for you?'

'I'm actually up here for my own benefit,' I explain quickly. 'Not Stella's. She's helping me. Lending me some photos, I hope.'

'Oh, right. Sorry.' He looks down, presumably at Stella, and then back up at me. 'Well, look, now I'm here, please let me help? It's probably dusty up there, Holly. With your asthma, and just getting over a chest infection—'

'Oh, Holly, I didn't think of that!' Stella's voice floats up to me. 'Alec's quite right! Come down, quickly, before you breathe in all that dust—'

I try not to laugh. 'I haven't even touched anything yet to disturb any dust! And I was doing my cleaning job yesterday, dust and all!' But nevertheless, I give in gracefully, backing down the ladder and brushing my jeans down carefully before I look up at Alec and say, 'Thank you. It's old photos of Hawbury Down I'm looking for. From the nineteen-forties, if possible.'

'It's no trouble,' he says, smiling. 'I'm glad I decided to call round today, now. It's my lunch break. I wanted to pick up your shopping list, Gran, for tomorrow. I don't want Holly to be doing it, while she's still recuperating.'

My instinct is to retort that I'm absolutely fine now and a little bit of shopping won't hurt me, but then I look at the expression on his face and I'm suddenly hit by a strange feeling. He simply looks concerned. I hardly know him, but he's concerned about me. So's Stella – she's got her hand to her mouth, looking guilty for letting me go up into the dusty attic. I feel the threat of tears behind my eyes, and have to look away quickly before muttering:

'OK. Thanks. I expect Stella's got her list all ready.'

'But I'll go up and look for your photos first,' he insists – and I don't argue.

'It's very tidy up here,' he calls down to Stella a few moments later, as I wait with her at the foot of the ladder.

'Yes, Ernest was very organised. Everything was always in boxes, and labelled. Can you see what's written on any of the labels? It's been so long since I was up there, I can't remember.'

'There's a label on this first box. *ASSOCIATED BOARD RSM GRADES ONE TO FOUR,*' he calls back. 'What does that mean?'

'Oh, they must be old violin exam music books,' she says. 'RSM is Royal Schools of Music. I ought to get rid of them. What else can you see?'

'Another box – the same but it's grades five to eight.' This could be a long job. 'Do you want me to bring these down for you, Stella? So you can throw them out, or give them away, or whatever?'

'Not today, love – thank you. Just look for the photos. You don't want to be up there all day.'

'Right. The next box says: *CLASSICAL A – M*. More music?'

'I suppose so. Oh dear. I didn't realise he had all those up here; he had lots down here, too. I've already turned out most of it. Can you see what's on the other side of the attic? Anything that says "Photos" or "Albums"?'

'Hang on.' We hear him treading over to the other side.

'More boxes,' he calls down. 'Some are full of books, by the look of their labels. 'And this one says "COINS AND STAMPS". It seems he was a bit of a collector, as well as everything else! Here's another one labelled "BRIC-A-BRAC".'

'Are you OK?' Stella calls, as it's gone a bit quiet up there now.

'Yes!' he shouts back. 'Stella, I'd be happy to help you sort all this lot out one day, if you'd like me to. There might be some valuable things up here, you know.'

'Maybe,' she says, not sounding at all enthusiastic. 'No photos, though?'

'Wait – there's some more boxes in the corner, here. Aha! "PHOTO ALBUMS nineteen-seventy to nineteen-ninety"!' he calls down. 'Now, then – does that mean the next box is ... yes! "PHOTO ALBUMS nineteen-forty to nineteen-seventy". Wow. He really was organised, wasn't he, Stella?!'

'Yes, he was,' she says, with a smile in her voice. 'Very efficient.'

I wonder what happened to nineteen-ninety onwards. Perhaps he gave up taking photos after that – or perhaps he just didn't get around to putting his later pictures into albums, and they've been lost over time. Alec's backing down the ladder now, pulling a cardboard box behind him and lifting it down and onto the floor. It's sealed up with Sellotape, but the tape's come unstuck over the years so it's going to be easy enough to pull it open.

'Bring it into the sitting room for me, could you, Alec?' Stella asks him.

He picks it up and follows us into the room, putting it down on her little table. It's really dusty; he looks at the dust on his hands from carrying it and asks:

'Can I get a damp cloth from the kitchen, Gran, to wipe it with?'

He gives me a little smile, and adds, 'I don't want to spread dust all over Gran's table, or to start you coughing again.'

Again, the concern in his voice. Again, I get that strange feeling; a kind of tickle behind my eyes, that's nothing to do with the dust.

'I'll get you a cloth,' Stella says. 'And I'll put the kettle on, and we can sit and look through the box together with a cup of tea.'

Of course, we don't just have a cup of tea, we also have home-made shortbread. I'm sure Stella's trying to fatten me up. She looks as excited as I feel, as Alec wipes the box carefully all over, before tearing it open, taking out the first album and showing it to us.

'Oh, I haven't seen these albums for *years*!' she says.

This first one has a red cover that's faded and battered with age, and it's labelled '*1940*'. Some of the pages inside have come loose, and there are black-and-white photos falling out, where the little holders on their corners have come unstuck. The captions, written on the thick black paper pages in white ink, are just as neat as the labels on the boxes. I'm glad Ernest was such a perfectionist!

I sit next to Stella on the sofa so that I can look over her shoulder as she turns the pages, while Alec's dusting the next album.

'He'd have been fourteen in nineteen-forty,' she muses, holding the album on her lap. 'I doubt many people would have had a camera then, but he would have been the type of boy who'd have wanted one.'

'It was wartime, though, wasn't it? Surely a fourteen-year-old boy wouldn't have been given luxuries like a camera?'

'No. I'd imagine it was his father's. He used to tell me his father was a very clever man – into everything mechanical and such.' She smiles at me. 'What you youngsters might call a *deek* now, I think.'

'Geek!' I correct her, smiling back. Where does she hear this kind of modern terminology, without having a TV or any social interaction? From her weekly newspaper, I suppose. 'So you think his father might have had a camera before a lot of other people did? And let Ernest use it?'

'Probably.' She opens the album, carefully tucking in the loose photos. 'Anyway, Ernest joined up in nineteen forty-two.'

'But ... you're saying he'd only have been sixteen then?' Alec says, looking up from his album-dusting and frowning.

'Yes.' She nods. 'Conscription was only for those over eighteen, but lots of boys joined up voluntarily at sixteen, or even younger. Nobody stopped them.'

'How awful, though. Imagine being the mother of a fifteen or sixteen year old, and waving him off to war,' I comment.

'But war *is* awful, Holly. It just is.' Stella shrugs as she looks down at the first page of the album. 'Well, I don't know who any of these people are,' she says a bit sadly. 'I guess these must be Ernest's parents. They'd both died before I met him. Oh!' She's turned the page now and is looking excited. 'It's Cliff's End, Holly. Oh my goodness,' she adds, her smile dropping.

I can see exactly what she's exclaiming about. The house – amazingly – has barely changed from the image of it in this slightly wonky, dog-eared black-and-white picture. But the real shock is the second photo, taken from the back of the house and looking towards the sea. Beyond where Stella's land ends now, there's a stretch of lawn in this picture that doesn't exist anymore. There's a child's swing. There's a large area of rose beds. There's a garden bench, set beneath a willow tree. I can see the spot – a flowerbed in this picture – where Stella's shed, obviously a more recent addition, stood until it fell into the sea earlier this winter. But there's so much, even beyond that. It's shocking to see exactly how much has disappeared over the years. I can see Stella's even more shocked than I am, but I'm not sure what to say so I just put a hand over hers and wait.

'Well, it was certainly a big garden back then,' she says eventually, nodding to herself, sounding more philosophical about it than I suspect she really feels.

'Yes.' I look at her anxiously. I don't think now is the time for a discussion about the cliff erosion and its inevitable long-term consequences for the house. She's been told enough times, and this picture must have said more on the subject than I, or anyone else, ever could. Alec has come to look over our shoulders, and when I glance up at him, he's raising his eyebrows at me. I suspect he's thinking the same as me, but to my surprise he changes the subject abruptly.

'I've dusted all the albums, Holly,' he says. 'I'm sorry, but I really need to get going now, Gran, but I'll come back tomorrow with your shopping. Have you got your list handy?'

'It's on the mantlepiece there, behind the clock,' I answer for her, as she's turning the pages of the album now, and seems engrossed in the photos. 'I'll see you out, Alec,' I add, and follow him to the front door once he's got the list and kissed Stella goodbye.

'It's a worry – about the house. The erosion,' I say very quietly as he opens the door. 'But she won't talk about it. And she won't let the environmental people anywhere near. Chases them away! Calls them busybodies!' I pause and smile. 'But then, she's pretty scathing about everyone from the town who comes up here, being nosy. I can't blame her; half of them say she's a witch and talk about hearing "ghostly noises" up here at night.'

'I gathered that.' He lowers his voice further. 'I'll try to have a good look around outside next time I come. See if there are any more danger signs. Not that I'm an expert, or anything—'

'*More* danger signs?' I query.

'Well, there's at least one crack, isn't there – the one Peggy fell into.'

Stella looks up at me with interest as I come back into the sitting room.

'Saw him off, did you?' she asks, with a cheeky expression on her face.

I give her a look, and she just smiles to herself. But it occurs to me that I don't really mind her teasing now. And also, that I don't feel so flustered anymore around Alec. Not because I don't find him attractive – because, I have to be honest, I do. But because the concern on his face today made me feel . . . safe with him. Like he's going to be kind to me, good to me – a friend – whatever happens. Or whatever *doesn't* happen, of course, I add to myself quickly.

'Do you know how long the house was in Ernest's family?' I ask Stella, sitting back beside her and seeing she's turned back to the pictures of Cliff's End.

'His grandparents bought it, apparently. His grandfather was a wealthy industrialist of some sort up in the Midlands, and decided to move down here for the coast and the countryside.'

'How wonderful for Ernest to have grown up here, and then brought you here to live with him,' I say. It seems so romantic. Not at all the sort of thing that happens these days.

'Yes. It was a good life, Holly. We were very happy here.'

She sighs and turns the page, but the image of the child's swing, in the picture of the garden as it once was, has got me wondering. Of course, Ernest would have been a child then, but did Stella and Ernest's daughter – Alec's mother – also play in the garden here – perhaps long after the swing itself, and the land it was on, had gone into the sea? I presume she grew up here, but Stella still never mentions her, and hasn't shown me any photos of her. If she's no longer alive, she obviously must have survived beyond childhood, long enough to have Alec! But it's obviously a painful subject – one that Stella's already warned me she wasn't ready to talk about – so I wouldn't dream of pressing her on it.

'Here are some pictures of the village, look,' she's saying now. 'Are these any good for you? One of the church; it hasn't changed at all. And the school – look, before the new building, of course. Ernest must have walked around taking pictures, to practise his photography. And the shop – now, that's completely different, it's the Co-op now, of course. Oh, I remember it well, when it was like this: look at the produce on the tables outside! There were only three shops in the village back then: this was the general store and post office; they sold fruit and veg too. Next door was the baker's – you can just see it there on the edge of the picture – and the butcher's was down the alley in the middle of Fore Street. Where the hairdresser's is now.'

'I'd love to borrow those pictures, please, Stella, if that's all right? I'll scan them, and bring them back to you tomorrow. They'll be perfect for the magazine. Thank you so much.'

She takes them carefully out of their remaining photo-corners, still smiling at her memories as she hands them to me. 'Nineteen-forty. This was the year I arrived in the village, of course. I was only five.' She gives herself a little shake. 'Shall we look through the rest of the album? Oh, look, here's a picture of Ernest himself,' she exclaims as she turns the page. 'I suppose his father must have taken it.'

'Oh.' I stare at the grainy image of the slim, dark-haired, serious-looking boy who's gazing straight at the camera as he poses awkwardly, one hand in the pocket of his trousers, the other on his hip. 'He was a good-looking boy.' *Like his grandson*, I find myself thinking.

'Even better-looking when he was older,' Stella says with a twinkle in her eye. 'The scar on his face didn't spoil his looks at all. It made him more interesting.'

'You were so in love with him, weren't you?' I say softly. I sit back on the sofa. 'Tell me what happened, Stella. That day – the day of the coronation party. You were saying somebody saw you together. Did your uncle find out?'

She nods. 'Yes, he did, unfortunately. We must have been mad to think he wouldn't, in a small village like Hawbury Down was back then, where everyone knew everyone.'

'So how did you manage to keep on seeing each other – and get married?'

'Well, that didn't happen straight away,' she says. 'There was a lot happened in between.' She pauses, and then adds quietly: 'And not all of it good.'

25

2 JUNE 1953

Stella was floating on air as she finally walked home to Hillside Farm that evening. The street party had been fun; she'd had her first glass of cider, danced in the square with everyone and joined in the singing. And she'd spent more time with Ernest – albeit they were trying not to make it obvious that they were together – than ever before. The memory of being with him at Cliff's End, in his bed, earlier in the day, kept flooding her mind and making her heart race. She knew they'd taken a stupid risk, but he'd assured her it should be all right. They loved each other, that was all that mattered.

When she arrived home, it was to find her uncle sitting in his usual chair in the sitting room, with a very serious look on his face. Her aunt, propped up in her usual position opposite him, looked even sterner. Although it was always hard, now, to read her expression, as one side of her face didn't work properly, Stella knew quite well when she wasn't happy.

'What's up?' she asked them. 'Are you both all right? Has something happened?' She had a sudden awful memory of the day when, as a child, she'd come home from school to be told her mother and grandmother had died. As her aunt and uncle both continued to stare at her crossly, she added: 'I'm not late, am I? I came back as soon as the party finished—'

'You may not be late—' Uncle Jim began, and his tone made her actually take a step backwards in surprise. He'd hardly ever spoken harshly to her before, but he sounded really cross now. '—but you are in trouble, young lady,' he continued. 'What's going on between you and the music teacher?'

'Um – nothing!' she squawked, in panic. What on earth did they know? How had they found out? 'I told you I was going to his house to watch the coronation, didn't I? And we walked down to the party together—'

'Where your cousin Geoffrey saw you brazenly hanging on his arm, giggling together like ... like ... *sweethearts* ... and that ... that *bounder* ... grabbing you around the waist and kissing you.' He paused for a moment, red in the face with anger. 'Tell me it isn't true, Stella. Tell me, if you can, that Geoffrey got it wrong, because he swears to God he wasn't mistaken. Tell me you're not making a disgrace of yourself with that man, and I promise you, if I find out you're lying to me, you'll leave this house and you won't come back.'

Stella shuddered, on the verge of tears.

'Geoffrey's a horrible sneak!' she said, before she could stop herself. She should have simply lied; pretended Geoffrey must have drunk too much cider, pretended he'd made it up; anything rather than admit it was true. But her uncle's threat – to banish her from the house if he found out she was lying – was terrifying.

'I was with Ernest, yes,' she admitted, her voice trembling. 'And he did kiss me, but—'

'But nothing!' Uncle Jim roared, getting to his feet. 'He's twice your age – and he's your *teacher*!'

'He's only twenty-seven,' Stella said, crying properly now. 'And actually, he isn't my teacher any more. He hasn't been for months.'

There was a horrible silence. Auntie Nellie's face had turned as red as Uncle Jim's, and she was spluttering, trying to get some words out, spittle trickling down her chin.

'He's not teaching you the violin anymore?' Uncle Jim said, more quietly, but with a deadly edge to his voice now. 'But you've been going up there to his house, every Friday, taking your violin, pretending to us – letting us believe you were still having lessons? Letting us trust you? We *trusted* you, Stella!' he said, shaking his head at her as if he was completely bewildered. 'We trusted *him* with *you*. What's going on? Just tell me. *Tell* me!' he added more fiercely.

'I'm sorry.' Stella wiped her tears with the back of her hand. 'I'm sorry, Uncle – I'm sorry, Auntie. I really am. But I knew you wouldn't agree to me seeing him. And I had to see him. I'm in love with Ernest – and he loves me!'

'No, Stella, he doesn't. Listen to me. You're a child—'

'I'm not! I'm eighteen!'

'You're a child compared with him,' he repeated slowly. 'He – he's grown man. He's got no *business* messing with you. Telling you he loves you! He's only after one thing, Stella – you mark my words. He's an experienced man, he's been to war, he's probably been with more women than you can even imagine. Do you think he's going to content himself with kissing you? You have no idea what you've got yourself into.' He sighed, his shoulders slumping. 'I suppose it's partly our fault. You've been stuck up here, on the farm, with your aunt and me, instead of mixing with other young people, meeting boys of your own age—'

'I don't want a boy of my own age! I've been in love with Ernest ever since I was fourteen.'

Uncle Jim raised his eyebrows, sighed again and shook his head. He glanced at Auntie Nellie, who was almost apoplectic now with the effort of letting Stella know – from her limited range of grunts and scowls – exactly what she thought of the situation, and he stretched out a hand to pat her on the shoulder.

'All right. Let's all calm down, shall we? Let's just thank goodness we've been alerted to what's going on while it was still only at the kissing stage.'

Stella looked down at her feet.

'We'll say no more on the subject after today,' her uncle went on. 'But—' and here his voice changed tone abruptly '—there'll be no more visits up to Cliff's End, you hear me? No more pretence at violin lessons, no more secrets, no more contact with that man. If I was another sort of fellow, I'd be on my way up there already to knock his block off. You understand me, Stella? He's lucky I'm a gentleman. Which is more than I can say for him.'

'But—' Fresh tears had sprung to Stella's eyes. 'I need to see him! You can't stop me. I'm not a child!'

'You're under twenty-one, and while you're living under my roof, you'll do as I tell you. It seems I can't trust you anymore, and I'm disappointed about that, but perhaps I've been an old fool. In future you don't go anywhere without either me or your cousin.'

'That's not fair! You can't keep me a prisoner here! I'm not going *anywhere* with Geoffrey, I hate him, he's—'

'That's enough,' her uncle said firmly. 'You're not a prisoner, you're in a good home, which perhaps you could be a bit more grateful for.'

'I am! You know I am. I've always been grateful for how you took me in, I know I've got a good home, but I'm eighteen, I can't be treated like a baby, not allowed out. I can't be separated from Ernest—'

'You'll realise eventually that it's for your own good. In the meantime, if you want to see your friend Elizabeth some evenings, I'll walk you to her house, make sure it's all right with her parents, and I'll come back later to walk you home. Don't push me, Stella!' he added sharply as she began to protest. 'That's more than you deserve, the way you've behaved.'

Stella sat down, her head in her hands. It felt as if the world had come to an end. She was upset enough that her uncle was so angry with her. But not to be able to see Ernest – how was she going to endure it? She knew her uncle must be shocked, and hurt that she'd deceived him, but surely he'd calm down eventually and relent? If he saw how devastated she was, how much she loved Ernest, he couldn't be cruel enough to keep them separated for long, could he? She decided her best plan would be to go along with his demands for now, pretend to be contrite, behave perfectly, and bide her time until he changed his mind. It would be unbearable, but there didn't seem to be any other option.

'All right,' she said quietly, wiping her eyes. 'I'm sorry I went behind your back. I'm sorry I disappointed you both. I'll make it up to you.'

'No need for that,' Uncle Jim said gruffly. 'You do enough for us already, we're well aware of that. But that's no excuse for—'

'I know.' She looked up and met his eyes. 'Can I please, at least, just talk to Ernest on the phone?'

There was a moment of hesitation before he replied.

'Well, he needs to be told you won't be seeing him. And perhaps it's better that it comes from you. I don't like losing my temper, and I don't think I'd be able to help myself if I had to speak to him.'

'Thank you,' Stella said.

'Just this once, mind you,' he added. 'You needn't think you'll be calling him again. I'll walk down to the village with you in the morning, and wait while you're in the phone box. Now then: make yourself a cup of tea and go to bed. I think we've said all we need to say to each other tonight, don't you?' He swallowed hard, and continued more gently: 'Tomorrow's another day.'

Tomorrow's another day. The phrase he'd always used to calm her in her childhood. For a fleeting moment, she wanted to throw herself into his arms, as she'd done countless times when she needed comfort from a tummy ache, a grazed knee, or a trivial dispute with a school friend.

But this time, she didn't. There wasn't anything he could do for a broken heart.

The next morning, they walked in silence to the phone box outside the village shop.

'Two minutes,' Uncle Jim said as she pulled the kiosk door open and went inside. 'I'll wait here.'

He turned his back, but she was aware that he'd be able to hear every word unless she kept her voice very low. She put in her money and dialled, praying that Ernest would be home. To her relief, he answered almost straight away and sounded so delighted at hearing her voice, she had to swallow back more tears. This had to be done quickly – there was no time for crying.

'Ernest, something's happened – something terrible,' she started.

'What? Are you all right, darling? Is it your aunt? Not your uncle?'

'We're all OK. Well, sort of. My cousin saw us together at the party yesterday. He saw you kissing me.'

'Oh God.' There was a pause. 'He told your uncle? You're in trouble?'

'More than trouble. I'm not allowed to see you again. Oh, Ernie!' She gave up the attempt to refrain from crying. 'He'll throw me out if I try to see you. I can't even speak to you again after this. He's waiting outside the phone box,' she added in a hoarse whisper.

'He hasn't – he hasn't hurt you, has he? Hit you, or—'

'No. He's not like that. But I've never seen him so angry. He means it. I can't go out unless I'm with him. It's going to be awful!'

'He doesn't know ... you didn't tell him about ... *yesterday*, did you?'

'Ssh! No, of course not. But he's furious that I've been going behind his back. And that you're ... older than me. He doesn't understand.'

'Let me speak to him, Stella. It might help. I can reassure him that I'm—'

'No. You can't. He says you're lucky he isn't coming up there to knock your block off. He won't speak to you. It's no good, I'm going to have to wait for him to calm down—'

'I won't be able to bear it. Not seeing you – not even speaking to you! *Will* he calm down? If you do what he says for a couple of weeks?'

'I don't know,' she said hoarsely. 'I can't bear it either. I'll have to find a way, if he doesn't change his mind.' She dropped her voice to a whisper. 'He's going to let me go to Elizabeth's, but only if her parents are there. I can trust Elizabeth, but if Uncle tells her parents I'm not allowed out ...'

'Oh, Lord. I'm so sorry, darling. I should have been more careful, shouldn't have kissed you in public. I didn't think anyone saw. I was just – so happy—'

'Me too,' she said, her voice breaking. 'Oh no – the pips! The time's up! He won't let me talk any more – he's knocking on the glass—'

'Don't cry! I'll work something out, I promise. I love you!'

'I love you too,' she sobbed. But the phone line was already buzzing in her ear; they'd been disconnected. Her uncle had opened the door of the kiosk and watched her as she hung up the phone, a strange expression on his face.

'Wipe your eyes,' he said quietly, passing her his handkerchief. 'Blow your nose.'

He waited for her silently, and when she'd managed to compose herself a little, took her hand, and kept hold of it while they walked back out of the village.

'I know you won't believe me at present,' he said after a while, 'but you'll get over this, Stella. You'll get over it, and in time you'll meet someone else.'

'I won't! Not ever!' she retorted, trying to snatch her hand away, but he held onto it firmly.

'You probably won't believe this either,' he went on, 'but I'm sorry I've had to hurt you like this. Your aunt and I love you, whatever you might think. We love you just the same as if you'd been born to us.'

'But I wasn't, was I?!' she spat back. 'You're not my father, Auntie Nellie's not my mother, and you've got *no idea* how to be proper parents, or you wouldn't be so cruel to me! I'll never forgive you for this – either of you! I hate you! And I hate her too! She's *never* loved me like a mother would.'

And, finally breaking free of his hand, she marched ahead of him, drenched in hopeless misery. She knew her words had been spiteful and unfair, but at the time, of course, she'd meant every one of them. How could she have known how soon she'd regret saying them? Less than a week later, and perhaps – she'd always wonder – because of the stress of the family argument, her aunt had another severe stroke, and passed away where she sat in her chair.

'I didn't mean what I said,' she mumbled miserably to her uncle as they stood, heads bowed in sorrow, watching the undertakers carrying out her lifeless body. 'I *did* love her. And I know she loved me. But—'

'No *buts*, Stella,' Uncle Jim said quietly. 'It doesn't need to be said.'

Because sadly, for Auntie Nellie, tomorrow wasn't going to be another day.

26

Holly

Stella's stopped talking. She's stroking Gracie's soft fur as she lies purring on her lap. It's fairly obvious she doesn't want to go on. Not today, anyway.

'Shall I make us another cup of tea?' I suggest. I wish I could think of something less inane to suggest. But Stella immediately gives herself a little shake, looks up at me as if she'd forgotten I was here, and agrees:

'That'd be nice. If you've got time?'

I check my watch. 'Just enough time. Are you all right?' I add gently as I pass her on my way to the kitchen. 'That was all a bit upsetting for you to remember, wasn't it?'

She shrugs. 'It was upsetting at the time, yes. But sometimes when you look back on things, and compare them with other things that happen, they don't seem quite so terrible.'

'How do you mean?'

'Well, I was only eighteen. Being separated from the man I loved felt like the end of the world, of course. But now, when I think about my parents' generation – yes, and my aunt and uncle's, too – and how they were separated from *their* loved ones by years of

189

terrible world wars . . . ' She pauses, before going on more quietly: 'Not only separated during the wars themselves, but in many cases separated forever, because so many people were killed—'

'Yes. That does bring everything into perspective,' I say. 'But still, it must have been so hard for you.'

'Of course it was. But life *is* hard,' she says with a shrug.

She picks up the nineteen-forty photo album again and flicks through its pages, but I don't think she's really looking at the photos. She's just distracting herself from her thoughts. I go into the kitchen and make the tea. It hasn't taken me long to get used to this procedure again: warming the pot, measuring out the tea, leaving it to draw. I had to do the same for my gran, after all. I'm even getting a taste for it. Perhaps it's true, perhaps it's nicer than my fruit teas. More . . . comforting, somehow. Maybe that has more to do with the ritual of making it than the actual taste, though.

'I'll just drink this, then I'd better go,' I say as I carry the tray into the sitting room. 'But I'll be back tomorrow with your shopping.'

'No, you won't,' she reminds me, giving me that saucy smile I'm starting to get used to. 'Alec's doing it. Unless you want to come back and see him again.'

I'm not getting drawn into this. And no, I'm not coming straight back tomorrow, now she's reminded me. I don't want Alec – or Stella herself! – getting ideas.

'Well, I could come Saturday instead of tomorrow?' I suggest instead. 'I'll have to bring Maisie with me, though.'

She brightens up instantly. 'Oh, yes, I'd love to see Maisie again. And I can check her arm measurements. For the knitting!' she adds, seeing my puzzled look, and I laugh. Of course, the knitting!

'That's decided, then.' I sip my tea. 'I'll tell her. She'll be excited. She's talked about you, and your house, all the time since we last saw you.'

'I suspect it's the cats that are the attraction,' Stella says with a smile.

'Well, yes, perhaps that could have something to do with it!'

I've allowed myself time, at home, to scan the old photos of Hawbury Down and email them to Frosty Fran. She must have been sitting at her desk just waiting for something to happen, because she mails me back almost instantly saying they're 'perfect', adding a 'well done' – almost as if I'd gone back in time and taken the pictures myself. Still, praise from Fran is rare, and I'm chuffed that she seems so pleased with them, as well as with the feature itself. I've also finished my column for the nature magazine, so I get that mailed off too, and if I'm not going to see Stella tomorrow that'll give me time to start working on something else. I need to contact a few Devon celebrities to see if anyone will agree to an interview. And perhaps think about doing some book reviews. Or visit some of the tourist attractions along the coast – yet again – and write about what's new there. I wish I could feel more enthusiastic about any of these ideas, but the truth is, the only story burning a hole in my brain at the moment is Stella's. I've kept my word; although I've credited her for the information she's provided, and for the photographs, there's nothing about her personal life in the feature I've written for *Devon Today*. But it's her personal story that's so enthralling. I'm desperate to find out what happened next – after she was stopped from seeing Ernest. They obviously must have got around her uncle's ban somehow, to end up getting married, and having had a daughter.

'We're going up to Hawbury Top again on Saturday, to see Auntie Stella,' I tell Maisie when she comes skipping out of her classroom. 'She wants to measure your arms.'

Maisie stops and gives me a comical look. 'My *arms*?' she squawks. 'What for?'

I laugh. 'For the purple jumper she's making you.'

'Oh, good! Will she make butterfly cakes again?'

'I don't know, Mais. It's a bit rude to expect her to make us cakes, isn't it? Perhaps *we* should make some this time, and take them to her.'

'Yes!' she shrieks with delight. 'Can we do them when we get home? Can they be chocolate ones? Can I lick the bowl?'

'I've got to buy some flour and eggs first. And if we make them now, they won't be fresh for Saturday, will they?' I reason. 'So let's do something else today instead.'

'I want to draw a picture for Auntie Stella,' she says immediately. 'I'll draw her cats, shall I?'

'I think she'd love that. Do your reading, and your spellings, first, though, OK?'

It's never too hard to get Maisie to do her homework. She's doing well at school. She seems to be one of those lucky children who are good all-rounders – equally comfortable with PE as she is with English, maths, and art. And equally good at being friends with the other children. I've worked hard at encouraging this, of course, partly because she's an only child, but also because I wanted so much to avoid her being as miserable at school as I sometimes was. At primary school, I felt different and awkward when the other children talked about their mothers, or their fathers, or their siblings – none of which I had, in any recognisable way. And at the senior school it was worse; the popular kids were those who excelled on the sports field, or those who were arty, or musical, or those who were really clever with computers. Being mediocre at everything except for writing good essays and understanding the finer points of grammar, on top of being quiet and shy, meant nobody took much notice of me. It could have been worse. I wasn't bullied, I wasn't teased or ridiculed – I was just ignored most of the time. And when I did finally make friends, later, at uni ... I ended up losing them again. But that's another story. Suffice to say, I'm glad Maisie doesn't seem to be taking after me. She loves school, and she gets lots of invitations to her schoolfriends' birthday parties, or for play dates, which of course we reciprocate. Maisie's the most important thing in my life, and keeping her happy is all I care about.

The next day, after I've dropped Maisie at school, I do my grocery shopping then go home to knuckle down to some writing. I stare out of the window, looking over our little garden, trying to get some inspiration from somewhere, but, again, the only thing buzzing inside my head is Stella's life story – or what I know of it, so far, and what I'm waiting to find out happens next.

Suddenly, I make a decision. I open a new document, head it simply *Stella's Story*, and start typing. It won't be for publication; it's just for me. But until I get it down in writing, it's going to take up so much room in my head that I've got no chance of writing anything else half-decent.

By the time I have to pick up Maisie from school, I've got as far as I can with the story until Stella tells me more. It's only a rough draft; it's just the bare bones of Stella's life, and still needs details to be filled in, but I can go back and work on that when I've got more time to spare. Reading it through afterwards, I'm aware that, if Stella wasn't a friend, and I hadn't promised her I wouldn't do it, this could be the sort of story I could offer to a national magazine – something like a Sunday supplement – and they could snap it up and pay me well.

But she is a friend, and I have promised. So that's not going to happen.

27

Stella

It's Saturday; Holly and Maisie are coming this afternoon and, this time, having got a new bag of flour – a large one – from Alec when he brought my shopping yesterday, I've made scones. I hope they like them. I'd forgotten how much nicer it is, making things like this, when you can share them with somebody. I haven't always been a lonely old woman. I used to have friends here for tea: we used to have such fun! During the summer holidays, when Ernest and I were still teaching, we'd both invite colleagues from our respective schools to dinner parties, or picnics in our garden here. They were wonderful days, lovely memories. I still used to invite those friends after Ernest started showing the first signs of his dementia, but I think some of them found it embarrassing; he lost his filter, didn't always behave the way people would expect, in company. Gradually, we stopped hosting people, until – after I retired – I lost touch with them. It's only to be expected, in the circumstances. Perhaps I should have tried harder, after he moved into the care home, to get back in touch with them, but I didn't. I volunteered with Cats Protection, and made some new friends through that, instead – and a new purpose in life, while I was fit enough to do it.

It's windy again today. Holly and Maisie almost get blown through the door when they arrive. Maisie's carrying a tin, which she places in my arms, her little face beaming.

'*We* made butterfly cakes this time!' she announces. 'They're chocolate ones!'

'Oh, how lovely! Thank you very much for bringing them.'

'*And*—' she goes on eagerly, pulling a slightly crumpled piece of folded paper out of her coat pocket '—I done you a drawing.'

'*Did* a drawing, Maisie,' Holly corrects her gently.

'I *did* you a drawing,' she repeats obediently, 'of your cats. I done it with paints.'

Holly raises her eyebrows at me but doesn't correct her this time.

'So in fact it's a *painting*, then,' I say with a smile as I allow her to place it on top of the cake tin for me.

'It's a drawing *and* a painting. 'Cos I drawed it first, then I painted it.'

'*Drew* it, Maisie!' Holly says, shaking her head despairingly.

'She's excited,' I whisper to Holly. It's easy to slip up with your grammar when you're excited, everybody knows that! 'Maisie, it's a beautiful painting. I'm going to put it on my mantlepiece so that I can look at it all the time while I'm sitting in my chair.'

She beams as I prop the picture up. And her eyes are like saucers when I've made the tea and bring both the scones and the chocolate butterfly cakes into the sitting room.

'Am I allowed both?' she asks her mum.

'Well . . . just this once, perhaps,' Holly says. 'If you eat them nicely and don't make any mess.'

We sit in companionable silence for a while, eating nicely, not making any mess. Maisie's watching Vera, curled up in front of the electric fire, and when Gracie wanders in from the kitchen and sits down by my feet, washing her face, she smiles and asks me, between mouthfuls of scone:

'How old are your cats, Auntie Stella?'

'Well now,' I tell her, 'that's a tricky question. They all came from Cats Protection, you see. That's a place where cats are looked after if they don't have a home—'

'Why don't they have a home?'

'All sorts of reasons. Perhaps their owner has had to move abroad.' I don't want to mention the other all-too-common reasons. I'm not sure which Maisie would find harder to hear about: the unexpected deaths of owners, or the cruelty and abandonment that sometimes goes on. I move quickly on to explain: 'Cats Protection looks after them until somebody else comes along and adopts them, and gives them a good home.'

Maisie nods thoughtfully. 'So *you* went along and adopted them.'

'Yes. In fact I was working there, then. Helping out, looking after the homeless cats. And I'd already adopted one cat from them, but he had . . . sadly . . . got very old and died. So I decided to adopt these three, because they'd lived together before and were used to each other. But nobody was quite sure how old they are.'

Maisie seems to accept this. She's finished eating now and asks if she's allowed to get down on the floor and play with the cats.

'Their previous owner had Alzheimer's,' I explain more quietly to Holly. 'She kept forgetting she even had the cats, forgetting to feed them. So, of course, there was no way to tell how long she'd had them.'

'I see. Poor thing. Poor cats.' Holly smiles. 'But thanks to you, they've now got a lovely life, however long or short that may be.'

'Oh, believe me, it isn't all one-sided. They've given me back just as much, in terms of companionship and love.'

'You said you'd always wanted cats. After playing with Elizabeth's, when you were children?'

'Yes. But it had to wait. Unfortunately, Ernest was allergic to them. And I wanted to live with Ernest even more than I wanted cats!' I add with a laugh. 'In fact, I chose my first cat, Caspar, the week after Ernest had to go into care.'

'I can understand that. You must have felt so alone,' she says sympathetically.

'To be honest, I'd been feeling alone for quite some time. Living with someone with dementia – you can feel just as lonely as if they weren't there at all. They're not, in many ways.'

'Yes. I can understand that too.'

'Well, it's just the way things are.' I give a little shrug, as if it doesn't still hurt, even now. 'I drove to the Cats Protection place,' I go on, 'straight from visiting him at the home one day. I was feeling quite wretched; but when I walked into the centre, it lifted my spirits.' I pause, thinking back to that day, remembering the impact the place had had on me, coming directly from the sadness of seeing my poor, confused husband, bewildered by his new environment. Not that it wasn't a good care home: it was, and the staff were lovely too. The sadness was all my own. 'By the time I'd been shown around the centre, I'd made up my mind: I was not only going to choose a cat to adopt, but I would volunteer to help there myself.'

'Ah, I'm sure that was a really good decision. It must have been helpful for you, in your situation.'

'It was. It became an important part of my life. Not *just* because of the pleasure of looking after the cats,' I try to explain, 'but the atmosphere of optimism there. As volunteers, we were caring for all sorts of cats, and some of the cases were, well, heartbreaking, you know? But we were nursing them back to health, and moving them forwards to a new, happy life. It was ... the opposite of what was going to happen in Ernest's case. No matter how lovely the care staff were at that home, he wasn't going to get better, or have a new life.'

I can't go on. I've said more than I intended to, anyway. Holly's looking at me with tears in her eyes. I hope the child hasn't been listening – or hopefully, if she has, it's gone over her head.

'Anyway!' I say, as brightly as I can manage. 'No good going on about all that. It's in the past. Life goes on, and life is good, no matter what.'

'You're amazing,' Holly says softly.

'No, I'm not,' I retort. 'I'm just surviving, like we all have to. Now then, young Maisie,' I say, raising my voice. 'How about you come and stand here next to me and let me check some measurements for this jumper.' I reach into my knitting bag, by the side of my chair, and pull out the part that's finished. 'How do you like it so far?'

'Ooh, nice!' she says, getting up and coming to stand by my knees. 'My favourite colour.'

'I know. Mummy chose the wool. Now, hold out one of your arms – that's right. And I'll get my tape measure.'

She giggles as I run the tape measure from her armpit to her wrist, and I give her a deliberate tickle when I've finished. It's so nice to hear that giggle. She smiles at me and says, in her polite little voice:

'Thank you very much for making me a purple jumper, Auntie Stella.'

'You're very welcome, dear. I'm enjoying making it. It's nice to have a little girl to knit for.'

'Haven't you got any little girls of your own?' she asks. 'Are they grown up now?'

I should have anticipated this question.

'No,' I say, with a smile. 'Sadly, I've never had any little girls – or little boys – of my own.'

Holly's looking at me strangely, and it's obvious why. She knows I had a daughter. I told her I did, and she knows my daughter had a son – but now I seem to be denying it all.

'Why not?' Maisie asks.

'Maisie!' Holly rebukes her quickly. 'That's enough of the questions.'

'It's all right,' I tell her. 'Maisie, I just wasn't lucky enough, that's all. Sometimes that's the way it goes. But I *was* lucky enough to be a teacher. Did Mummy tell you that? I was a teacher at the very same school you go to now. I taught the youngest children there. So that made up a little bit for not having children of my own.'

She nods thoughtfully. 'Did you used to knit jumpers for those children at the school?'

Holly and I both laugh.

'Sorry, Stella,' Holly apologises.

'Don't be silly. How can children learn anything, if they don't ask questions? I didn't knit them jumpers, Maisie, because I didn't have as much spare time then, as I do now. But I *did* love teaching them to read and write, and do their sums.'

'I think *I* might like to be a teacher,' Maisie says. 'Can I, Mummy?'

'You can be anything you like, sweetheart, if you work hard at school,' Holly says, smiling at her. 'Isn't that right, Stella?'

'Of course.'

We all like to believe that, anyway, don't we? But sometimes, unfortunately, working hard doesn't make any difference. The one thing I wanted to be more than anything else was a mother. To have children with Ernest, to raise a family of our own. But there it is: life doesn't give you everything you want. No point moaning about it, is there?

28

Holly

It's the half-term holiday this week. I don't have the childcare worries that some parents have, fortunately, as I'm self-employed, and the cleaning agency knows I don't work for them during the school holidays. They have plenty of people on their books, and some of the others are grateful for the extra sessions when I'm not doing my regular houses, like the big one on The Avenue. I wish I didn't have to do the cleaning job at all, but my freelance writing doesn't pay enough to cover the rent and the bills, never mind everything else. I'd do more sessions – and sometimes I do – if the agency makes them available to me, just to keep from having to rely on the Universal Credit to top up my income. But – with the little bit I get from Maisie's father towards her upkeep – I manage. And this way, at least I don't have to pay for expensive childcare.

Maisie and I have got a whole lot of plans for this week. As an only child, she does need some stimulation during the school holidays, so we tend to decide on a programme of free or cheap activities – something for each day, that we can do together – well in advance. I trawl the local websites and Facebook pages for what's on. This week, we've signed up for a parent and child book club in the library, a Fun Day at the swimming pool in Torquay, a craft session at a garden centre, a bake-your-own-bread afternoon at one of the local cafés, and a nature trail (weather permitting) in the park. The thought of fitting all these in around my writing commitments is a bit exhausting, but I'll be fitting in some work when Maisie's in bed every night, and hopefully I can catch up some more on the afternoon Maisie's been invited to play at her friend Flora's again.

I've had to tell Stella I probably won't have time to see her this week, but I call once or twice to make sure she's OK. By the time Monday comes around again and Maisie's putting on her uniform ready to go back to school, I'm looking forward to catching up with Stella again.

Luckily the weather wasn't bad during the holiday, but over the weekend it was really windy yet again, with bouts of heavy rain. I was thinking constantly about how it must feel up there on Hawbury Top. At least down in the town here we're a bit sheltered, but Cliff's End is so exposed; Stella's very vulnerable up there in bad weather. It's calmer today, with a blue sky that cheers me up despite the cold, so I call Stella to say I'm going up there straight from dropping Maisie at school.

'There's no need, I'm fine,' she says. As always.

'Well, actually, I'd like to come, as long as it's OK with you? I'm itching to hear the next part of your story,' I admit. Stella, understandably, didn't refer to it at all while I was there with Maisie the previous Saturday. 'But only if you're sure you don't mind talking about it – whatever came next.'

'No, I don't mind at all, as it happens,' she says. 'It's strange; I haven't talked about these things for so long. But it hasn't been as hard as I thought it might. In some ways, it's been ... quite useful, revisiting what happened. Thinking about how it all panned out.'

'Therapeutic?' I suggest.

'If you say so.' I hear her give one of her dismissive sniffs. 'Not that I need therapy.'

About an hour later, I'm standing on the cliff, looking down, when a voice behind me makes me jump almost out of my skin – not a good thing when you're this close to a drop of over a hundred metres.

'What are you doing out here?' she demands.

I manage to turn without losing my balance.

'Stella! You made me jump. I've only just got here. I was about to come to the door.'

'You've been standing there for five minutes or more. I've been watching you from the window. I thought maybe you were thinking about throwing yourself off.'

She chuckles to show she's joking, but it's not really funny. There was a case of a suicide here, a couple of years ago. The body was down below on the rocks for about a week before it was found. It must have been horrible for Stella, happening so close to her house, with police all over the place up here, and the rescue helicopters.

'I just wanted to have a look. After the storms over the weekend,' I tell her.

And now I wish I *hadn't* looked, because sure enough, another piece of clifftop has dislodged and has slid down towards the sea.

'Satisfied, now you've had a look, are you?' she challenges me.

I'm a bit taken aback by her tone. But then I look at her face more closely. She's afraid – that's what it is, I can see it in her eyes. I'm not sure whether her fear is about her land slowly disintegrating – a fact she's well aware of – or whether she's worried I'll report this latest collapse to somebody, or try, myself, to nag her into moving.

'You should have stayed indoors, in the warm,' I say gently, taking her arm and leading her away from the cliff edge. 'Come on, I'll put the kettle on, shall I?'

'I might be old, but I'm not ruddy feeble,' she protests, shaking off my hand. 'I've already been out here and looked, this morning. I know there's a bit more land gone. It's not much. There was already a crack there.'

'All right.'

I'm not arguing with her about it. From what little I understand about coastal erosion, there's actually no *immediate* danger to her house. The people who have tried, in the past, to persuade her to leave, have obviously been concerned about her long-term future. Whether that's necessary in the case of someone of eighty-three is debatable. But perhaps I've only seen it that way since I've got to know her.

'I do understand, Stella,' I say gently as we're taking off our coats in her hallway. 'I know why you love this house; why you don't want to leave it.'

'Well, then,' she says grudgingly. 'There's no need to look, is there?'

'I just like looking down at the sea,' I excuse myself. 'Always have done.'

Finally, she gives me a smile. 'Me too. Ever since the first time I saw the sea, back during the war. Always loved it, no matter what mood it's in.'

'Like we love our kids,' I joke – and then stop abruptly, shaking my head. I still don't know what's happened, regarding her daughter, but by now it's pretty obvious it isn't a happy situation. 'Sorry, what a stupid thing to say.'

'It's all right. I do know what it's like to love a child. Well, I can imagine, anyway. Come on, let's leave the tea to draw for a minute and get the fire on, shall we?'

*

Once we're finally settled, with the fire warming up, the tea poured out and biscuits arranged prettily on the plate, she sits herself up straighter in her chair and makes a strange kind of announcement.

'Right. I'm going to tell you the next bit of my story, then, since you wanted to hear it. Like I said, I haven't talked about this for years. In fact, I've hardly ever told anyone. I don't intend to get silly and emotional about it, but if I do, I don't want any fuss – understand?'

'Oh, Stella!' I protest. 'I'm not sure you should go on with this, if it's going to upset you.'

'I told you, didn't I? I *want* to talk about it, now. I think I need to, but please don't give me any of that – what-d'you-call it? – psychological claptrap. All right? Let me finish the story. So that you'll know, and it won't be … sitting there, between us, unsaid … if we're going to be friends.'

'I *am* your friend, already, I hope.'

'Yes, you are. And friends are supposed to know what's-what, aren't they, about each other.'

I nod, looking down at my feet. I'm conscious of the things she doesn't yet know about *me*. Things I didn't see any need to tell her. She's never struck me as being someone who demanded full-on honest self-revelation. Far from it, I'd have said she was quite a private person, unused to talking about herself. If what she's going to tell me now is so deeply important for her that she's determined to talk about it, the least I can do is respect her feelings, and do as she says.

'OK. I promise. No *psychological claptrap*.' I smile. 'I'll just listen. I'll try not to react.'

'Good. Thank you. Well: as you know, there I was, eighteen years old and in love with a man of twenty-seven, and forbidden to see him.' She sighs, then shrugs and squares her shoulders again. 'So this is what happened.'

29

SEPTEMBER 1953

Stella's life seemed to have narrowed to a dull, colourless existence of household chores, helping on the farm, cooking meals for herself and her uncle, and going to bed in a state of misery and despair. So far, all she'd been able to look forward to were the occasional evenings with Elizabeth – delivered there and brought back by her uncle, and supervised with, she felt, at least a degree of sympathy, by Elizabeth's parents. Elizabeth herself was irritating in her all-too-obvious disapproval of Stella's situation, her all-too-often repetitions of her opinion that Stella should have known it would 'all end in tears', and should have found herself a nice boyfriend of her own age, like Frank. But at least their evenings together in Elizabeth's bedroom, listening to records, singing along to songs by Dean Martin and Perry Como, were a break from the routine at home. Now, though, Elizabeth was about to go off to start studying for her medical degree in London. Elizabeth's parents, John and Doris, had kindly told Stella she'd be welcome at their house any time she wanted a change of scenery, but Stella felt awkward about the idea of going there while their daughter was away.

The last weekend before Elizabeth was due to leave, Stella was invited to have Sunday dinner with the family. Since the debacle over Ernest, and the loss of her aunt, Stella had given up going to church with her uncle and cousin Geoffrey on Sundays, but she had to wait for Uncle Jim to return after the service, to be accompanied to The Avenue and handed into the care of John and Doris, as if she were four years old. On this occasion, Frank was there for dinner too, and as it would be one of the last meals he had with his girlfriend until her medical school's half-term recession, he took priority over Stella for Elizabeth's attention. All of which added to Stella's frustration and anxiety; because she really, badly, needed to talk to her friend before she left for London.

By the time Frank had gone home, and the two girls were free to shut themselves away in Elizabeth's bedroom, Stella was almost beside herself with the urgency of the conversation she needed to have.

'What on earth's eating you?' Elizabeth demanded as she closed the bedroom door behind them. 'You're so jumpy today—'

'Liz, I don't know what to do. I'm worried sick. I haven't told anyone else, there's nobody I can tell. I'm in a terrible fix.' Stella started to cry.

'Hey, all right, don't get all worked up.' Elizabeth put her arm around her friend and pulled her down to sit beside her on the bed. 'It can't be that bad.'

'It is! It's the worst thing ever! It couldn't be any worse.'

'Spit it out, then. I can't help unless you tell me.'

Stella took a deep breath and then, lowering her voice, admitted: 'I think ... well, I'm quite sure, really ... I'm pregnant.'

'*What*?!' Elizabeth stared at her, her mouth dropping open. 'You can't be! You didn't go all the way with him, did you? I presume it *was* him – Ernest?'

'Of course it was him!' Stella retorted. 'I haven't been with anyone else! And it was only that once. My first time.'

'Oh, golly, he didn't use *that* old line on you, did he? That you can't fall the first time? Of course you can, Stella!'

'I know that *now*, don't I?! But he said he'd been careful – you know – so that I wouldn't get pregnant. He seemed so sure about it. And anyway,' she added indignantly, 'he didn't use a *line* on me. I wanted to do it, just as much as he did.'

'We all *want* to do it!' Elizabeth shot back. 'You're not unique, you know, you're not the only one who's been in love, but some of us have more self-control—'

Stella grabbed her handbag from the bed and jumped to her feet.

'I'm sorry I told you now. I should have known you'd just lecture me like this, miss goody-two-shoes. I'd have been better off telling my *uncle*—'

'Wait.' Elizabeth grabbed her arm to stop her leaving. 'Don't go. I'm sorry. Honestly, I am. I was just … shocked. You didn't tell me you'd gone the whole way with him.' She hung her head and admitted. 'Perhaps I'm just jealous.'

'Well, there's nothing to be jealous about, now, is there? I'm pregnant and I'm not even allowed to see him, and I've got no idea what I'm going to do. My uncle will throw me out.'

'Are you absolutely sure you're pregnant?'

'Yes. I've missed two monthlies. I'm never late. And … I just know, Liz. I feel different.'

'Oh gosh.' Both girls sank back down on the bed. 'Well, you'd better tell *him*, hadn't you? Or have you already – as you've been sneaking letters to each other?'

Elizabeth was the only person who knew about the letters. Stella had had to tell her, because they could only write to each other if she'd agreed to act as their 'post office'. She'd been a bit reluctant at first, when Stella asked her to post a letter to Ernest, and he sent his first reply back, care of her house. But when Stella told Elizabeth she was the only person in the world she could trust, and the best friend anyone could ever have, she'd given in. The weekly exchange of letters was the only thing that had been keeping Stella from complete despair – and it was going to have to end this week, when Elizabeth went to London.

'I don't know,' she said now. 'I'm scared to tell him, Liz. What if he doesn't want anything to do with me once he knows about it?'

'What *are* you talking about?' Elizabeth stared at her. 'It's his fault! How can he say he doesn't want anything to do with you? He'll have to marry you, and that's all there is to it.'

'But what if he won't?'

'Then he's not worth knowing, is he? Face it, Stella, he either loves you or he doesn't. If he does, he'll say straight away that he'll marry you.'

'I suppose that's why I'm scared of telling him. I think he does love me. He *says* he loves me. But if he doesn't—'

Elizabeth looked at her friend with sympathy. It was a terrible thing, for any girl, to be in that situation if the man refused to marry her. She couldn't think of anything to say that would be helpful.

'You've just got to tell him. The sooner the better,' she said more gently. 'Write the letter now, and I'll post it for you. You have to find out, one way or the other, and if he's as wonderful as you say, I'm sure he *will* marry you.'

Stella nodded agreement. The letter was written, and Elizabeth promised to post it first thing in the morning when she went to the shops.

'You've reminded him I'm going to London on Wednesday,

haven't you?' she said. 'He has to reply straight away, otherwise I won't be here to pass it on to you. My mum already thinks it's strange that I keep getting letters with a local postmark. I've had to pretend it's one of our friends from school, who just likes writing letters.'

Stella sighed. If only all she had to worry about was a mother wondering about letters!

'Please can I go and say goodbye to Elizabeth?' Stella asked her uncle on the Tuesday morning. 'She leaves for London tomorrow.'

'I thought you said your goodbyes on Sunday?' He glanced at her, and relented. 'Oh, all right, of course, she's your best friend, and you're going to miss her, aren't you? It's a nice day; we'll have a walk into the village after breakfast and I'll go and see Old Bob while I wait for you.'

Old Bob, one of Hawbury Down's most senior residents, lived with his ancient collie dog in a cottage on the corner of The Avenue. All the villagers liked to call on him from time to time for a chat and to make sure he was all right.

'I haven't got long,' Stella gasped after she and Elizabeth had rushed upstairs to the privacy of Elizabeth's bedroom. 'Has it come? Ernest's reply?'

'Yes, in this morning's post.' Elizabeth pulled the envelope out of her pocket, and turned away, busying herself with her packing for London, while Stella sat on the bed to read it.

'Well?' she asked eventually, as Stella was still sitting staring at the letter. 'What does he say?'

Stella looked up at her, relief evident on her face. 'He's going to marry me. He says he was shocked and upset about the baby – but he says, only because he knew how worried I must be. He wants us to be married and live together with the baby at Cliff's End.

Oh, Liz!' She dropped the letter and rushed to hug her friend. 'He does love me – he says it over and over. I'm so happy! It's all going to be so wonderful—'

Elizabeth returned the hug, but Stella thought she looked less than ecstatic.

'What about your uncle?' Elizabeth said gently.

'Oh – Ernest says he's going to come and tell him. Tonight. Then we can get married as soon as possible. You will come back for the wedding, won't you, Liz? I want you to be my bridesmaid. Can you believe it? I'm getting married!' She glanced at her friend. 'What's the matter? You *are* happy for me, aren't you?'

'Of course I am, silly. I'm just worried you're getting too excited, too soon. Your uncle . . . has to give his permission.'

'But he will, won't he?! He'll be shocked, obviously. But he won't want me to be—' she dropped her voice to a whisper to utter the shameful words '—an unmarried mother.'

'I hope you're right, Stell.' Elizabeth smiled, but Stella still thought it looked a bit forced. Was her friend actually feeling peeved that the attention was being diverted from her own excitement about medical school? Surely not.

'Well, I'll have to write to you and tell you,' she said. 'You're leaving first thing in the morning, aren't you?'

'Yes. You've got my student address, haven't you?'

She said the word *student* so proudly, Stella had to smile. She was proud of Elizabeth too.

'Yes. Oh, I'm going to miss you, Liz! But you'll have a fantastic time, and you'll make new friends. You'll soon forget about everyone back here.'

'No, I won't. Don't be daft. I'll be waiting for that wedding invitation.'

The two friends hugged again and Stella, having tucked the precious letter from Ernest into the pocket of her skirt, set off to meet her uncle on the corner as arranged. It was only when she was walking home with him that she began to feel nervous. How was she going to tell him that Ernest was coming to see him this evening? How could she explain the fact that they'd been secretly keeping in touch – let alone tell him about the baby? She couldn't! It was all too much, and however relieved he'd be that Ernest was going to marry her, he'd be furious about her going behind his back – again. She decided the only course of action, if the most cowardly, was to say nothing until Ernest actually appeared on the doorstep. Then it would all come out at once, and they'd face the music together.

She was too nervous to eat her dinner that evening, pretending she didn't feel well. In fact, she'd been feeling a bit queasy from time to time ever since she'd missed her first period, and Uncle Jim had asked her a couple of times if she was sickening for something – a difficult question to answer, in the circumstances. When the knock on the door came at seven o'clock, he looked up from his library book in surprise.

'I'll get it!' Stella jumped up and ran to the door, her heart beating wildly.

'Come in,' she whispered.

Ernest looked as nervous as she felt herself, but he gripped her hand, stood up straight and gave her a shaky smile.

'Leave this to me,' he whispered back, and they walked into the sitting room together, hand in hand.

Uncle Jim looked up, surprise turning to outrage when he saw who the visitor was.

'You!' he said, getting to his feet, dropping his book. His voice was shaking with anger. 'How dare you! How *dare* you walk into my house? Let go of my niece's hand this minute! I've forbidden her from seeing you, as you know perfectly well—'

'I'm sorry, sir. Believe me, the last thing I want to do is to cause any upset between you and your niece—'

'Then get the hell out of my house!'

'Mr Thorogood, please allow me to say what I've come to say.' Stella heard Ernest take a deep breath before going quickly on: 'I love Stella and I want to marry her. We want to be married. As soon as possible.'

There was a moment of horrible silence.

Then Uncle Jim spoke, much more quietly than before, but in a tone Stella knew didn't bode well:

'You do, do you? You want to be married *as soon as possible*. And might I ask what exactly the rush is? Because if it's what I think—'

Ernest coughed, glanced at Stella, but before he could answer, she burst out herself:

'Yes, I'm having a baby, uncle. And I'm sorry, I know it's not what you'd want to hear. But we'll get married – we wanted to anyway, even if it wasn't for the baby. We love each other. Ernest's a good man, he'll look after me and the baby, we'll live together at Cliff's End—'

'No,' Uncle Jim said, his tone icy. 'You won't.' He took a step closer to Ernest, and jabbed the air in front of his face. 'You're a bounder, young man, that's what you are. You've forced yourself on an innocent young girl, half your age—'

'He didn't *force* me, uncle! And I'm not half his age!'

'Be quiet, Stella,' he snapped. 'I'm talking to this . . . this *rat* you call a *good man*. You have the temerity,' he went on to Ernest in the same deadly tone, 'to come to my house and tell me you've got my niece into trouble, and you expect me to agree to you *marrying* her? You want me to give my permission to her tying herself for life to a milksop of a music teacher, a *cripple,* who's never done a proper day's work, who *pretends* to teach little girls the violin while he seduces them in his own home—'

'Uncle!' Stella gasped. 'You can't say those things about Ernest — you don't even know him! He's not a cripple, he got his injuries fighting in the war, fighting for people like us. And he's never *seduced* anyone! He's a good, decent—'

'It's all right, Stella,' Ernest said quietly, laying a hand on her arm. 'Your uncle's shocked, and angry. It's understandable.'

'I don't want your bloody understanding!' Uncle Jim roared. 'I want you out of my house, and out of my niece's life. I *do not* give you permission to marry her. Or to see her — ever again! Do *you* understand *that*?'

Stella was crying uncontrollably now, but Ernest stood firm, although Stella could feel him trembling next to her.

'Would you prefer, sir, that your niece endures the shame of being an unmarried mother?' he asked quietly.

'That,' Uncle Jim retorted, squaring up to Ernest and jabbing his finger so close to his nose this time that Stella was afraid he was going to poke him in the eye, 'is not going to happen either. Now get out of my house — before I have to call the police to have you *thrown* out.'

'I'm sorry, darling,' Ernest whispered to Stella. 'Let's give him some time . . .'

Without stopping to see how much this comment had further enraged her uncle, Stella followed Ernest to the front door, clinging to his arm, crying.

'I won't give up,' he assured her, stroking her hair and kissing her quickly. 'I'll come back again, whatever he says, and keep on asking until he changes his mind.'

'Oh, Ernie! What if he doesn't?'

'He won't want you to live in shame. He'll come around. I love you!'

'Is he still here?' roared Uncle Jim from the sitting room.

'I love you too,' Stella sobbed as Ernest finally stepped outside.

She watched until he was out of sight. And then she ran upstairs to her room, where she stayed until the next morning, crying into her pillow.

30

Holly

I'm trying not to cry, myself. Trying not to, because I promised not to react, but also because – although Stella's story is so sad, so shocking, at least in the context of what would pass for normal behaviour today – despite this, Stella herself is actually smiling to herself slightly as she recounts it.

'It must be so upsetting for you, remembering all this now?' I suggest, when I've managed to compose myself. 'What happened? What on earth did your uncle mean, when he said you weren't going to become an unmarried mother *or* marry Ernest?'

I want to add: *and what happened to the baby?* But I don't like to ask, because the answer is beginning to feel fairly obvious.

'Upsetting?' she says, giving me a surprised look, almost like she'd forgotten I was here. 'Well, it's strange, really. I thought it would be. I thought I'd find it hard to talk about, after all this time. But do you know what? I'm actually smiling to myself as I look back on it all. How foolish we were to think the world was coming to an end because we weren't allowed to marry. What a hypocritical generation we grew up in.'

'I don't understand.'

'Well, your generation wouldn't handle it like that at all, would they? You're so much more honest about things. You'd just go off somewhere and live together. Or you'd just *be* an unmarried mother—' She stops abruptly, looking at me guiltily. 'Oh. I didn't mean anything personal, Holly.'

'It's OK.' I smile. 'You're right, it's perfectly acceptable today, and yes, I am an unmarried mum and nobody minds. Except me.' I pause, then go on quickly: 'But it's not me we're talking about here. I can see what you mean. Those were the times you grew up in, though, and everything was different. Your uncle had different values, obviously, and so did the rest of society. He was your legal guardian, so you needed his permission to marry, until you were over twenty-one. And you *couldn't* just live together, could you?'

'No. The entire population of Hawbury Down would have collapsed and died from the shock of it!' Stella laughs – actually laughs out loud! – while I'm sitting here nearly crying! She never fails to surprise me. Then she suddenly stops, gives me a long look, nodding to herself, before she adds: 'But as for what my uncle meant – what he had in mind for me – well now, that *is* the difficult part to tell you about.'

'Do you want to wait till next time I come?' I suggest.

'Not unless you're going to be late for your work?' she says. 'Your cleaning job is this afternoon, isn't it?'

We both look at the clock.

'Well ...' I begin, 'I ought to go before *too* long. But ...' I tail off. How can I tell her that although I'm unsure how I feel about hearing what she describes as *the difficult part* – as if I didn't find the last part sad enough! – I also won't be able to concentrate on anything else until I know the answer to the most important question. I take a deep breath. 'If it's not too painful for you,' I say very carefully, 'I am wondering, obviously, about the baby.'

'Yes. The baby,' she says. She stops, closes her eyes for a minute, and then – just as I'm about to tell her not to worry, she doesn't have to talk about it if she doesn't want to – she goes on: "I had a baby girl. She was born on March the first, nineteen-fifty-four. She was perfect. She looked like her father: bright-blue eyes and wisps of dark hair. She weighed seven pounds, six ounces. I only held her once. She was taken away from me.'

For a moment, we're both so quiet, so still, it's almost as if the room itself has been stunned into silence. Then I'm having to brush away the tears, despite my resolve not to. This time, I can't help myself.

'You had to give up your little girl,' I say softly. 'For adoption? And – I presume this was Alec's mother?'

'Yes. This was Susan.'

'Oh, Stella, that was so cruel! So ...' I hesitate for a moment, unsure if she's going to like me probing any further. But how can I not ask – now I've met Alec? Now that I know Susan was his mother. 'So did you stay in touch with her at all?'

'No. I didn't. It ... was considered the best thing to do. For the child's sake. Let her start a new life, with her adoptive parents, without being confused by the complication of ... another mother. They'd wanted a baby for years, apparently. They'd give her everything, make her happy.' Finally, she looks up at me, and forces a smile. 'And I know they did that. Alec's told me. He says his mum always spoke about the lovely time she had growing up with his grandparents – *adoptive* grandparents – how much she loved them, what wonderful parents they'd been—'

'But *you* could have done that – given her a good life – you and Ernest, her *real* parents!' I protest.

'Yes. Oh, don't imagine I didn't often think, over the years, what a fool I was not to fight it. But I was powerless, you see. Without a husband – and I didn't marry Ernest until I was twenty-one; my uncle never backed down and gave permission – there was nowhere for me to go, with a child, on my own. It wasn't that my uncle didn't love me – he did. He was actually quite kind and compassionate to me about the whole thing, once he'd calmed down after that awful confrontation. He saw me as the victim,' she added with a little chuckle. 'He refused to believe I'd consented to sex with Ernest. He thought I was just trying to protect him. He truly believed he was helping me by arranging the adoption. Saving me from ruining my life. Ironic, isn't it? Ironic that, in fact, *not* keeping my baby could have ruined my life.'

'Could have?' I say.

'Yes,' she answers firmly. 'Could have, but it didn't, because I still had Ernest. Because we did end up marrying, as soon as I was twenty-one, and we had each other. It was tragic for both of us that we never had any more children. But if I hadn't had *him* – as well as not having had children – then yes, I think my life would have been ruined.'

She's so matter-of-fact about it, I can't do anything other than stare at her and shake my head.

'We have to count our blessings in this life, Holly,' she tells me, seeing the look on my face. 'I did *want* to keep Susan—'

'Did her adoptive parents keep the name you gave her?' I wonder aloud.

'Yes, apparently they liked the name, so they did,' she says quickly, brushing this aside. 'But you see, I followed protocol. It was what was expected, in those days. Nobody brought up a child without having a husband – well, without at least starting off with one. They just ... didn't.'

'And you never tried to find her? Not even later, when ... things, people's views ... started to change?'

'No!' I'm surprised by the vehemence in her tone now. 'No, I wouldn't do that. We didn't think it was fair. Wherever Susan was, we decided she didn't need the disruption to her life of a mother turning up out of the blue – a mother who'd given her up at birth. Ernest and I agreed on that. We gave her up. We had no right to suddenly want her back.'

I can see she feels strongly about it. It's not for me to disagree. If I'd been Susan, and suddenly found out I had a mother like Stella, I'd have been over the moon. But then, my own mother's so rubbish, I'd probably jump at anyone else prepared to take me on.

We're both silent for a while. I'm still trying to take it all in – make sense of it.

'I don't quite understand, Stella,' I begin again finally, a little hesitatingly. 'Now that Alec has obviously found you, somehow, and written to you, and you're getting along so well together, why are you still not seeing Susan herself? Don't you want to? Or does she not want to see you? Is that it?' I add, giving her a sympathetic look.

'Oh, if she'd found me, if she'd wanted to, I'd love to have met her,' she says. 'Even though I never tried to find her, I always wondered, of course – all the time – about her. I'd wonder if she was happy. Whether *she* wondered about *me*. Whether she hated me for giving her up, or if her adoptive parents explained it to her in a way that helped her to forgive me. Every year on her birthday, I'd say a silent little prayer for her, even though I'm not even completely sure about God anymore. It would have been her birthday in a couple of weeks, as it happens.'

'Would have been?' I look at her in surprise. 'What do you—' And then I understand. I put my mug down, almost slopping my tea over the edge. 'Oh. Stella, I'm sorry. I should have realised. You never tried to find Susan ... but when Alec got in touch with you – wrote to you, he must have told you—?'

'Yes.' she clears her throat, and then says it quite abruptly: 'Susan's dead.'

'Oh, *Stella*!' I don't even attempt to swallow back my tears now.

'No wonder you didn't tell me. You must have been ... absolutely distraught when you read that letter! Susan couldn't even have been very old.'

'Sixty-three. She'd have been sixty-four on the first of March. She died in December. Cancer.'

I shake my head. 'I don't know what to say. It seems so unfair.'

'Yes. But apparently she'd been ill for more than a year, so – well, you can imagine. Alec said that in the end, he felt it was ... a release. He said he grieved for her more when she first got the terminal diagnosis, than now, now she's at peace.' We're both quiet for a minute, before Stella coughs and goes on, quickly: 'Alec was clearing out her things, when he found an envelope, filed away – with his parents' marriage certificate and everything. He says his dad died when he was quite young. Anyway, in the envelope was Susan's certificate of adoption, with our names – Stella Price and Ernest Jackman – and this house as our address.'

'This house?' I ask, puzzled. 'For both you and Ernest? But you weren't living with him then.'

'No.' She smiles. 'I refused to put my address as the farm cottage, because I was so angry with my uncle, and so sure I'd be living up here, anyway, within a couple of years!'

I smile back. Good for Stella!

'Alec told me he didn't think there was much chance of finding me still living here, after all these years. But he decided to try. He said I deserved to know about his mum. He tried to get in touch with the adoption agency first – the one named on the certificate – but he couldn't find any trace of them now.'

'So he sent the letter,' I say. 'What a shock for you, though. I can understand why you didn't reply right away.'

'I was going to. As I told him, I just needed time for it to sink in. And then he just turned up here like that, out of the blue.' She gives a short little laugh. 'And ended up getting Peggy out of a hole in the ground … it's funny really, isn't it?' She shakes her head, trying to smile, but looking like it's an effort.

Funny. I smile back at Stella, but my face almost aches with the effort. She might say her life wasn't ruined, but honestly, she's had so much sadness, hasn't she? And still she can laugh. Whatever she says, I still think she's amazing.

Stella

31

Stella

Susan's dead. Finally, I managed to say the words I've been trying out, under my breath, over and over during the past few days, while I've been preparing to tell Holly. Trying them out, because I just couldn't quite imagine myself speaking them aloud. Even though Alec and I have talked almost obsessively together about Susan, of course, during the past few weeks – talked about her life with her adoptive parents, as well as *his* life growing up with his mum and dad, and talked, too, about her illness and her death – I haven't had to tell anyone else before – to actually say the words, *Susan's dead*. And now I've said it, and the world's still turning. I haven't collapsed in a heap, or keeled over dead myself. I'm more surprised about this than I was by Holly's reaction. Bless her, she's a sensitive soul, I knew she'd be upset to hear about it. But it's strange how relieved I feel, now that I've talked to Holly about Susan. It was the worst thing that ever happened to me – giving up my baby – sobbing as she was taken out of my arms, never seeing her again, always wondering how she grew up, what her life had turned out like. Ernest and I hardly told anyone about it, ever. It was too personal; in our day, people didn't endlessly discuss the ins and outs of their lives, going on about their emotional pain, like I read in the paper about these so-called celebrities doing. We just got on with things. Put them behind us. I suppose these days they'd say it isn't healthy, that we should have had counselling or whatever, but I've managed to cope pretty well, I think, without having to open my bleeding heart to anyone, professional or otherwise. Until today.

Why did I feel I needed to tell Holly? I didn't have to. I could have glossed over that chapter of my life, left it to her imagination. She says she's finding my story fascinating, but I don't think she enjoyed today's part. As usual, it upset her more than it did me. I suppose she's imagining how it would have felt to give up her own baby, little Maisie.

I'm smiling to myself even as I think about that child. She's changed some of my preconceptions about today's children. I know I'm old-fashioned, but even before I retired from teaching, it was getting more and more frustrating, with these parents who complain about the slightest word of correction being uttered to their offspring. Children were never spoilt in my day. Loved, but not spoilt – they're not the same thing. Still, I suppose people would argue that I don't know what I'm talking about, not having brought up any children of my own.

Holly seems to be bringing Maisie up nicely. She's sweet, but not precocious, and she's very polite. Seems bright, and confident, too. Perhaps child-rearing without a man to help isn't so hard, after all. What would I know?

When Holly comes again on Wednesday, I can tell she's been thinking over everything I've said, and is desperate to ask me more questions. We sit down with our tea and biscuits, she crosses her legs and fixes me with a frown.

'How did your uncle arrange the whole thing?' she asks. I think she's finding it hard to forgive my uncle. 'I mean: surely the adoption couldn't have been done locally, or you'd have known the couple who took the baby?'

'Oh, no. I was sent away,' I say. 'I should have explained. The very next day, after the big row with Ernest, my uncle told me he was making plans to send me to stay with my cousin Janet in Cornwall. She was one of his brother Stan's daughters – Geoffrey's sister – and she'd married a police sergeant called Harry who'd been stationed down near Truro. I was being sent there without further ado – any nosy neighbours who asked would be told I'd been ill and was being sent to a convalescent home. And Janet and Harry looked after me until the baby was born.'

'Sent away – like an evacuee all over again,' Holly comments sadly. 'Did anyone at least tell Ernest?'

'Not my uncle, obviously! But Janet, as it happened, was very sympathetic. She saw me as a victim too, but not in the same way as Uncle Jim did! She thought of Ernest and me as star-crossed lovers, and found the whole thing quite romantic. She let me write to him, and even talk to him on the phone sometimes – they had a phone in the house. But she drew the line about him coming to visit. She was too worried about going against my uncle.'

'She didn't stick up for you over keeping the baby?'

'Oh no. That would have been a step too far. As I said, Holly, it was what everyone expected, in those days. If you were a "fallen woman", you didn't keep the baby. Even though Ernest and I were still determined to get married, I couldn't expect Janet and Harry let me stay with them for another two years, with a baby, until I turned twenty-one.'

'Because their neighbours would have talked?'

'Not for that reason. I was supposedly a widow, you see, as far as the neighbours in Cornwall were concerned. My uncle had given me a brass ring to wear on my wedding finger, and I had to pretend my husband had passed away. For the sake of respectability – Janet's and Harry's, as well as mine. Whether anyone believed it or not, I don't know. It was fairly common practice. As I said, they were such hypocritical times! No, it wouldn't have been fair to impose myself on my cousin any longer. And anyway, my uncle expected me to come straight back to Hawbury Down after I'd recovered from the birth, and get back to a normal life.'

'A normal life of looking after him!' Holly says, sounding a bit disgusted.

'Yes, of course!' I sigh. 'And the irony is, Holly, he ended up dying from a heart attack two weeks before Ernest and I finally got married. He'd insisted all along that he wouldn't come to the wedding, but in the end, he never even got the satisfaction of staying away.' I pause, and add quietly: 'It was sad. I'd always hoped he'd change his mind and turn up on our wedding day. I missed him – despite everything. He was the closest thing I had to family at the time.'

Holly's quiet now, looking at me as if I'm some kind of puzzle she can't work out.

'I don't want to be rude, Stella,' she says eventually, 'but I just don't get it.'

'Get what?' I say.

'Well, I appreciate that you missed your uncle – that he and your aunt were your family – of course. But how can you still say you've had a happy life? Honestly? I mean, what you went through must be the worst thing any parent can imagine. Giving birth to a child and then losing them – no matter how – it must be unbearable.'

'Yes,' I agree. I sigh. I can see why, from her perspective, it's impossible to understand. 'Perhaps it's only with the advantage of old age,' I try to explain, 'that we can look back and actually balance one or two truly awful things that happened to us, against a lifetime of . . . underlying happiness. Yes, I lived through a war; I was orphaned; I grew up in hard times. I wasn't allowed to be with the man I loved when I wanted to; I had a baby who was adopted, and sadly couldn't have any more children—'

'And yet you've prevailed, haven't you. You're saying you've been happy.'

'Well, you see: despite all that, I had love, all my life. My parents loved me. My aunt and uncle – yes, I knew you'd pull that face, Holly, but they *did* love me, in their own way. My wonderful husband loved me, we had the most blissful life together, happily married until the day he died, and not a lot of people can say that.' I pause. I'd been counting things off on my fingers, but now I've stopped, and forgotten where I'd got to. 'Just as important,' I go on, 'I've had good health all my life too. And friends. I had a career I adored, and a lovely volunteering job after I retired. And on top of all that, I've been lucky enough to live in a beautiful part of the world, in a house I love too. Even if it *is* on the brink of falling into the sea,' I add mischievously, giving Holly a wink.

She's gone quiet. She looks down at Vera, purring on her lap, and strokes her ears. She's nodding to herself as if she's translating something, in her head, from a foreign language and gradually making sense of it.

'I think you should make that into a speech, or something, to be published in all the papers and shown on TV,' she says eventually. She sounds so earnest, her face is so serious, that I want to laugh. 'Seriously, Stella! If you were my age, you'd be putting it on all your social media, and you'd get thousands of *likes*. People all over the world would retweet it, and they'd be saying *This is amazing, this woman has the key to a happy life.*'

I actually am laughing out loud now, laughing so much I'm almost crying.

'Oh, Holly, there's nothing new in any of what I said! It's just about making the best of things. How else do you want to live? These people you think would want to read my ... ramblings ... on

Tweeter or whatever you call it – would they rather be miserable, is that what you're saying? Would they prefer to bleat on all the time about how unfair life's been to them?'

'Yes, quite honestly. I think that's what a lot of us are like. Maybe I'm like it myself.'

'No. You're not. Well, you don't seem like that to me. You've got your problems, like we all have, I'm sure, but you don't complain, do you?'

'Oh, I do, at times!' She looks down again. 'I do complain about my lot. I do think I've been unlucky. Sometimes it *is* hard to focus on the positives, Stella.'

'I know.' I stop laughing. She's right, of course. 'It's hard while you're going *through* the difficult times. As I said: it's easier to get everything into perspective when you're old enough to look back on it all. So, at my age, I have the advantage.'

'You see? You even manage to make a positive out of being elderly!' she exclaims.

'But it *is* a positive! Don't you see? How can I not be grateful for having lived to this age, when so many people are struck down much younger?'

'I give up!' She's laughing herself, now. 'You're just an incurable optimist.'

'I'll take that as a compliment,' I chuckle, 'being as how I'm an optimist.'

We both sit back in our chairs, smiling at each other.

'It's nice, having someone like you to talk to,' she says.

'Nice for me, too. There – you see! – we both have another positive, now.'

'True!' She picks up her tea and drains the cup. It must have been cold, now. I'm just about to ask if she wants another one when she goes on: 'Stella, there's a lot more I still want to ask you, but do you still feel up to it today?'

"Course I do,' I say. 'What do you want to know?'

'Well, I've been thinking – about what happened. When you got sent away to Cornwall, to live with that cousin until you had the baby. Did you keep in touch with Elizabeth then? She was at medical school, wasn't she? So was that the end of your friendship?'

'No, not at all. We wrote letters to each other. And she even came to see me, when she was home from London for her holidays. Janet was good like that; she let Elizabeth sleep overnight in my bedroom with me.'

'The two of you still got on all right together, then? Even though Elizabeth had been – well, a bit funny with you, really, about getting pregnant.'

I shrug. 'She'd only been taking the normal view of that time – that girls who *got themselves into trouble* had only themselves to blame.'

'That sounds incredible to me, now – to hear that! As if the man had nothing to do with it! Girls didn't get *themselves* into trouble, did they?!' Holly exclaims.

'Well, we were supposed to *resist*, you see,' I explain – chuckling at the indignant expression on her face. 'Seriously! We were taught that men couldn't be expected to help themselves, and it was up to us to keep things under control. There was no pill back then, remember. Not much in the way of birth control at all. And no legal abortions, either, not until a long while after this. Lots of women died from having illegal abortions. One way or another, it was always us women who ended up with our lives ruined, so it was in our own interests to say no!'

'I'm glad I didn't live then,' she says.

'Yes, I expect you are!' I smile. 'But Elizabeth wasn't being a bad friend, or unsupportive. She had a boyfriend herself, so she understood how hard it could be—'

'The insipid-sounding Frank?'

'No! She'd got a new one by then. Ah, let me tell you about Ashish! *This* will make you understand how much things have changed! The nineteen-fifties were like a different country, Holly. You wouldn't believe it.'

January 1954

Stella was seven months along in her pregnancy and beginning to feel tired of it. She missed Ernest; the pain of their separation was like a nagging toothache, hurting all the time even when she was doing something nice. And there *were* nice things, despite everything. Janet was kind, and sympathetic to her situation, and often suggested little outings to try to cheer Stella up. They talked about Ernest, and Janet suggested that having to endure this separation could be a test of their love for each other, and ultimately even prove to Uncle Jim that they were serious. Stella doubted that last bit! But she was young, and life had to go on, and she was convinced in her heart that everything would work out, in the end. She just had to try not to think about the baby, even when she felt it turning and twisting inside her, even when it kicked her so hard in the ribs that she flinched. She had to pretend it wasn't her baby at all, that she was just carrying it as a present for somebody else. That was the only way she could bear it.

Christmas had been as happy as it could be, in the circumstances. Uncle Jim had travelled down to Cornwall to join them, bringing presents, and a turkey from the farm, and everybody had been cheerful and amicable, all taking pains to ignore Stella's bump and avoid any mention of Ernest. As soon as her uncle had gone home again, of course, Stella was on the phone to Ernest for her permitted short weekly phone call. She was grateful to Janet and Harry for allowing this, but phone calls were expensive so she couldn't expect more.

On the first of January, Janet answered the phone and called out to Stella:

'It's your friend Elizabeth for you. She's asked if she can come down for a couple of days before she goes back to London.' She handed the receiver to Stella and added, 'I've told her it would be lovely to have her, of course.'

'I can't wait to see you,' Elizabeth told Stella excitedly. 'I'll come tomorrow. Dad will drive me down. I've got something exciting to tell you.'

Stella mulled this over as she helped Janet with the chores. She had a good idea what the exciting news might be. Elizabeth was probably getting engaged to Frank. She hadn't spoken about him much recently, but perhaps that was just because they didn't get together so often now. He was at Oxford University, doing a degree in physics, so they'd been having to commute by train to see each other.

When Elizabeth arrived, Janet left the two girls to talk together on their own.

'Come on, then,' Stella said, as soon as they'd got through the formalities of asking about each other's Christmases, carefully avoiding any mention of Stella's very obvious baby bump; 'I can tell you're absolutely bursting to tell me something. What is it?'

'I'm in love!' Elizabeth said, hugging herself and going pink.

'Well, yes, I think we knew that, didn't we?' Stella laughed. 'After all, you've been going out together now for – what? – a couple of years?'

'No, not with Frank!' Elizabeth said dismissively. 'I've finished

with him, Stell. I never felt like this with Frank. I just never knew –
never realised – it was possible to feel like this . . . '

'You're going out with somebody new?'

'Yep.' She hugged herself again, giggling. 'He's at med school
with me. We study together. His name's Ashish and he's—'

'*Ashish*?' Stella tried out the unfamiliar-sounding name. 'That's
unusual, isn't it?'

'His parents are Indian. But he was born in London,' she
added quickly.

'Oh.'

'Don't say "Oh" like that, Stella. He's British. And he's educated, and clever, and kind, and oh, *so* handsome! I couldn't believe
my luck when he asked me out. I hadn't been able to take my eyes
off him from the very first day I saw him. He's . . . just wonderful!'
She paused, looked at Stella carefully and said more quietly: 'You
don't disapprove, do you?'

'Of course I don't!' Stella retorted. The fact was, having lived
in the countryside virtually all her life, she'd never actually met
anyone yet who wasn't white and Anglo-Saxon, so she was finding
it, in all honesty, a bit difficult to process. But she wasn't going
to be the type of person who would disapprove of anyone being
together with the person they loved. How could she? She smiled
at her friend. 'I'm pleased for you, obviously, Liz – really I am. It's
lovely to see you so happy.'

'I sense a *but*.'

'Not at all. As long as . . . well, as long as it doesn't make things
difficult for you.'

Elizabeth sighed. 'That's what my parents said at first. Until
they met him.'

'You've brought him home? Wow! It must be serious. And they
approved?'

'Yes, completely.' She grinned. 'It would be impossible not to approve of him, Stell. He's just so ... perfect. Such a gentleman. So intelligent, so polite, so caring—'

'All right, I get that he's a complete dreamboat!' Stella laughed. 'But were your parents worried at first? Until they met him?'

Stella had always thought of Elizabeth's parents as unusually tolerant for their generation. But she doubted many parents would jump for joy at the prospect of a boyfriend who was ... so different. Not that Stella, herself, could see anything wrong with it, but older people always clung to more traditional views.

'A bit,' Elizabeth admitted, 'but only because – like you said – they thought we might get picked on, you know? For being seen out together. But they were so impressed with the way Ashish discussed it with them – so calmly, so sensibly. So intelligently—'

Stella laughed again. Elizabeth could hardly find enough effusive adjectives to describe this paragon of virtue!

'He said he completely understood why some people found it difficult to accept mixed relationships, because it's not what they're used to, and people get nervous about anything different. But that unless these attitudes are *challenged*, nothing will ever change, and people won't ever stop staring at us or making nasty comments—'

'So *do* they? Are they horrible to you, Liz?'

She shrugged. 'Some people. Occasionally. But not as much as you'd think – not in London. If it does happen, Ashish just takes my hand, and says to hold my head up and ignore them. He says we have to go through this, to come out the other side into a world where nobody cares what colour our skins are—'

'He really thinks that will ever happen?'

'Yes, he really does!' Elizabeth's eyes were shining. 'He's convinced couples like us can change the world.'

Stella gave her a hug. 'Well, I hope he's right, obviously. And I'm happy for you, Liz, I really am.' She paused. 'How did Frank take it?'

'Badly, at first. Called me a couple of names himself.' She shrugged. 'I suppose he was just hurt. He said he'd been planning to talk to me about getting engaged.'

'I did wonder if that's what your news was going to be,' Stella admitted.

'Really? No, I'd never have married him, Stell. I knew, really, that I didn't love him enough. I knew it, when I used to hear you saying how you felt about Ernest. It was never like that for me, but I didn't want to admit it. I was jealous. I wanted ... a grand passion, like you had. *Have*!' she corrected herself quickly. 'Anyway, I think Frank realised that too, once he'd calmed down. He phoned me, just before Christmas. Told me he's met someone new as well. I'm glad. We can stay friends now.'

The two girls sat in companionable silence for a while.

'Strange, isn't it?' Stella said eventually. 'We've both found our *grand passions* with someone who other people might think is unsuitable.'

'Yes. Oh, Stell, how are you, really? I didn't like to ask. It must be so awful for you. The baby—'

Stella rubbed her bump, and sighed. 'I just have to keep telling myself the baby isn't mine. It's the only way I can manage. Ernest gets upset about it when we talk on the phone. He says we should have found a way to be together; that we could have run away – gone to Gretna Green or somewhere, got married and kept the baby. I don't know, Liz. Did I give in too easily? *Should* I have just defied Uncle Jim, and gone to live in sin with Ernest?'

'You couldn't have,' Elizabeth said firmly. 'You'd have been outcasts. And the baby would be a bastard. You couldn't do that to a child.'

'But we'll get married as soon as I'm twenty-one, whether Uncle Jim likes it or not.'

'I know. But your uncle would have disowned you if you'd just lived together. And two years is a long time, Stella – a long time to have to put up with people calling you names, maybe even refusing to serve you in the shops.' She shrugged. 'Ashish and I might get that kind of thing ourselves, if we were to live down here in the West Country. But it's different in London. There are more ... people like him around. You might even have got away with living in sin, in London,' she added thoughtfully. 'Possibly.'

'Anyone would think it's a crime, to fall in love,' Stella complained bitterly.

'It's God's fault,' Elizabeth said. 'He made the rules.'

'Don't!' Stella raised her eyebrows. 'That's sacrilege, isn't it – insulting God?'

Elizabeth shrugged. 'I don't care. I don't even think I believe in him anymore.'

Stella shook her head, secretly shocked. Elizabeth had changed quite a lot, it seemed, in one short term at medical school. It must be from living in London. She was talking almost like a *radical*. Next thing they knew, she'd be turning into a beatnik, taking up smoking, and experimenting with strange pills. That's what she'd heard sometimes happened with students.

In fact, although neither of the girls could have predicted it then, Stella was partly right. Elizabeth never did come back to live in Devon. She and Ashish did go on to get married, but it was a quiet ceremony in a registry office, and Elizabeth didn't even wear a wedding dress or have any bridesmaids. They both became eminent doctors eventually – but during their student days they were best known for their outspoken views. They joined meetings protesting about almost everything. They were against nuclear weapons, all wars, all religions, discrimination of any kind, censorship of books and films, and any laws that seemed to restrict anybody's freedom. Their lives diverged so much from Stella's own, that eventually, over the years, they lost touch. But fortunately, that didn't happen until after Stella and Ernest's wedding. Just as Stella had always hoped, Elizabeth was her bridesmaid. And in view of Uncle Jim's sudden demise, Elizabeth's father gave her away. It was the start of another new phase of her life.

32

Holly

I've listened to this latest episode in complete silence – it was so fascinating. I suppose I hadn't thought before about the cultural changes Stella must have witnessed during her lifetime. How strange that it was so shocking to see a mixed-race couple out in public in Britain. And even stranger that it was still considered, in the mid-fifties, to be a *sin* to live together without being married – so much so, that people might call you names and refuse to serve you in shops! I suppose I've got a little more sympathy now for Stella's uncle's insistence that she couldn't be allowed to become an unmarried mother.

'Tell me about your wedding,' I ask her. 'Was it difficult, being so soon after your uncle passed away?'

'Yes, it was, rather. We had the funeral one week, and the wedding the next. We did think about postponing the wedding, out of respect to Uncle Jim. But the banns had already been called, the church was booked, and the cake was being made. And, well, we'd already waited so long to be married, hadn't we?!' She smiles at me. 'And I was quite surprised, really: at Uncle's funeral, everybody was telling us we should go ahead. Even my horrible cousin Geoffrey. Do you know what he told me that day?'

I shake my head. 'What? That he was sorry? For telling tales to your uncle about you and Ernest? Causing all that heartache?'

'No. Not quite. But he did say that he thought my uncle had died with regrets about what had happened. Even though he'd still insisted, right up till the day he died, that he wasn't going to come to the wedding, Geoffrey thought that was more about his pride than anything else. He thought Uncle might have come to realise that keeping Ernest and me apart hadn't done anything to lessen our love for each other.' Stella pauses for a moment, then goes on: 'If that was true, I just wish he could have brought himself to say it to me – before he died.'

'Yes. That's a shame.'

She gives herself a little shake, and smiles again. 'Oh, but our wedding day was wonderful, Holly. It was February – the twenty-eighth. It would have been our anniversary next week. And it was freezing cold like it is now, but the sky was blue, the sun was shining, and everyone seemed to be happy for us. It was such a surprise! I'd been living under the cloud of my uncle's disapproval for so long by then that I didn't realise most of the villagers knew that Ernest and I were sweethearts who'd been kept apart by Uncle Jim. Nobody else seemed too worried about our age difference at all. Of course, they didn't know about the baby. That might have altered a few opinions.'

'It must have been horrible for you when you came back to Hawbury Down from Cornwall, though,' I realise. 'At least while you were living with Janet, you could talk to Ernest on the phone.'

'Yes. But I had a new ally then!' Stella chuckles. 'Elizabeth's mum, Doris. I'd got chatting to her one day, soon after I came back, while I was waiting for Uncle Jim outside the post office. She and John were so different from my aunt and uncle. Much younger, of course. And better educated. I was asking after Elizabeth, as I hadn't heard from her for a while, and it was so nice to hear how supportive they were being about her relationship with Ashish. How sensible and tolerant they were, too, about some of Elizabeth's rather ... *avant-garde* ... views. "That's students, for you!" Doris said. "And that's as it should be. If the younger generation don't rebel and protest, nothing ever moves forward." I told her my uncle would never feel like that about the younger generation, and she touched my hand and said, very quietly, "Stella, if you ever need a change of company, you'll always be welcome in our house."'

'Ah. That was nice of her.'

'Yes. And my uncle trusted her and John, of course, because John was a professional – a bank manager – so in his view, he must have been a decent chap. Which was all very handy for me. And for Ernest.'

'Did they let you see him?' I say, sitting up straight. 'They let you go against your uncle?'

'Not exactly. They just turned a blind eye.' She's grinning to herself at the memory. 'I used to go and see them regularly, and they allowed me to call Ernie from their phone. They said they couldn't see the harm in that. And then, well, if Ernie just happened to come down to the village and have a walk along The Avenue, and I just happened to be at their house, looking out of the front room window, well of course, I'd open the window and we'd have a chat to each other.'

'Ha! Good for you!' I'm almost ridiculously pleased about this, as if it matters to me personally, about sixty years later, that the two young lovers managed to sneak some illicit meetings for themselves!

'So I became great friends with Doris and John. I think they enjoyed my company too, because of course, they missed their own daughter. Even after Ernest and I were married, I would often call in to chat to Doris when I came down to the village for shopping.'

'You were living up here by then, of course.'

'Of course, straight after the wedding. We didn't have a honeymoon. Couldn't afford it. We only had Ernest's teaching salary, plus the little extra he got for the violin lessons. I wasn't earning anything at all. My allowance had stopped from the time I was sent to Cornwall – Uncle Jim paid it to Janet instead, for my keep, which was fair enough, and he didn't give me anything when I came back, either. All I did, for those two years, was keep house and cook for him. I refused to work on the farm anymore.'

'But didn't you inherit anything from him when he died? You were legally his ward, weren't you?'

'I only got what little he'd put away in his post office account. The cottage belonged to Geoffrey – it was part of the farm. Uncle Jim had always paid rent, first to his brother Stan – who'd died years earlier – and then to Geoffrey. So even if I weren't getting married to Ernest, I'd have had to find somewhere else to live, after my uncle died.'

'Surely Geoffrey would have let you stay there? You were family, after all – his second cousin!'

'Maybe. But I'd have hated to be beholden to him. Anyway, I'd been living in that cottage since I was five years old. I couldn't wait to move out!'

'And you were happy up here?' I ask her, smiling.

She nods, enthusiastically. 'Oh, Holly, we were happier than I can tell you. I always loved this house, and for Ernie and me – being together at last – it was like heaven on earth. In the winter, we'd have roaring fires in the fireplace here, and shut ourselves away from the world. Then, in summer, we'd open up all the doors and windows and have picnics outside on the lawn. It *was* a lawn, then,' she adds ruefully, glancing out at the unkempt grass and rampant undergrowth surrounding her small, moss-covered patio area. 'We'd invite all our friends up here for parties, and sometimes in midsummer we'd bring the gramophone outside and dance – all of us – in the moonlight. There was so much laughter here, so much love and happiness, it almost breaks my heart to think of it.'

'You deserved that happiness,' I tell her gently. 'It must be lovely for you to look back on now.'

'It is.' She suddenly starts to get to her feet. 'Let me show you something. I meant to show you this before, when we talked about knitting. The blanket I keep on my bed – I made it when Ernie first started suffering from dementia.'

'Shall I get it for you?' I offer. 'Is it heavy?'

'All right – thank you. No, it's not really heavy.' She sits back again and I pop across the hallway to her bedroom. The knitted blanket's folded neatly across the foot of her bed. I've glanced at it before as I've passed the door, but never liked to be too nosy. Even now, I don't look at it properly until I've brought it back to the sitting room and passed it to Stella.

'Here,' she says, taking two corners of the blanket and spreading it across her lap and over the arms of her chair. 'Take hold of the other end.'

I gasp as the blanket unfolds. It's an absolute work of art. Almost every other square has a design embroidered onto it. There's a picture of a soldier; one of a violin; one of a child in – I think – school uniform. Then there's one of a farm, and one of a house – this house, I think, with the sea below it. And one of a Union Jack . . .

'VE Day?' I guess, pointing to it, and Stella smiles and nods. 'And this next one,' I say, 'a crown – that represents Coronation Day, of course. It's your history, isn't it. Yours and Ernest's.' I shake my head in amazement. 'This . . . is so beautiful, Stella. So romantic.'

'Not romantic at all, really. It was to help him remember. He was losing them all, so fast – all those precious memories. All our special times. We used to sit and look at the squares every night, and go through what they represented. The picture of the envelope there – see? And the one of the phone – they were to remember how we kept in touch, when my uncle wouldn't let us meet. And here's the church, and the cake: our wedding day.'

'And the couple, here, dancing – under the moon – just like you said . . .'

'Our little soirees,' she says, nodding happily.

'The books?' I point to another square.

'My studies. When I went to train as a teacher.' She looks up at me in surprise. 'I haven't told you about that yet.'

'I'll remind you, next time. And of course, this picture – a blackboard, for your teaching days . . .' Then I stop, looking at a pink square with a picture of a baby's cot on it. I point to it, wordlessly, a lump in my throat.

'The empty cot,' she says, looking away. 'Well. That's self-explanatory.'

'Sorry,' I whisper. I look at some more squares. A picture of a car. One of a brown-and-white Spaniel, trotting across his blue square, looking so realistic. I didn't know they used to have a dog. A camera – Ernest's hobby. A pair of knitting needles stuck into a ball of wool – Stella's hobby. 'What about this one?' I ask, pointing to a picture of a plane.

'Our first holiday abroad!' she laughs. 'We'd been married for twenty years. Nineteen-seventy-six. We went to Italy for a week. See – the next picture is a pizza. First time either of us had ever eaten one. Or spaghetti bolognese! We thought we were *so* European!'

I smile. 'Did you go on lots of foreign holidays after that?'

'A few. France, a couple of times – camping. Spain, once. One of the Greek islands – Corfu – I booked that as a surprise, for his sixtieth birthday.'

'And did Ernest take photos on all those holidays?'

'Of course. They'll be in some of those albums. We didn't finish looking at them, did we? Remind me next time, Holly. You'll need to get going soon, won't you?'

'Yes, I'd better.' I fold the blanket back up carefully. 'I think this is wonderful, Stella. I love it.' I wonder if she's going to hand it down to Alec, now that she's got him, her grandson, so that he can pass it down the family. If I had a memory blanket like this, I'd wrap it up and keep it safe for Maisie to show her children one day.

I tell Maisie all about it when she's home from school, and promise her that Stella will show her, next time she comes to Cliff's End with me.

'Can you make a blanket like that, Mummy?' she asks me wistfully. 'You could put a picture of me on it, couldn't you?'

'Yes, sweetheart, I could,' I say, giving her a hug. 'If only I could knit!'

'Auntie Stella can make us one, can't she? When she's finished my purple jumper?'

'Maybe,' I say, doubtfully.

But I'm trying to keep my face turned away from her so that she can't see my expression. Because what I can't help thinking is: What would be the point? Honestly, apart from Maisie, what nice memories have I got, that are worth putting on a blanket? I can't think of a solitary one.

33

Stella

It's been a cold, wet week, and it's a gloomy day today; but that suits my mood, to be honest. I know Holly's going to turn up soon; she's promised to bring my shopping today, because she's going to something special at Holly's school tomorrow. She and Alec seem to be taking it in turns now to do my shopping. I save the heavier items for when he does it. It's so good of them both to do this for me, I wouldn't dream of making life difficult for Holly by telling her today isn't a good day. But I don't know if I'll be much company. After all this time, I still find today's date difficult, no matter how hard I try to ignore it.

She arrives just as I'm trying to give the cats their worming tablets. I've got Vera wrapped in a towel, tucked under one arm, and I'm trying to force her little mouth open. I don't know why I chose today, of all days, to do the most difficult thing any cat owner ever has to do.

'Let me help,' Holly says as soon as she's through the door. I'm trying not to drop Vera or let her jump down before I've done the deed. 'Why don't you use those drops you put on the backs of their necks instead?' she adds as she grabs the cat out of my arms and holds her in a vice-like grip while I manage to administer the pill and hold her mouth shut until she's swallowed.

'They're more expensive,' I mutter. But I'm thinking: she's right. It's ridiculous putting myself through this struggle every time. 'Anyway, that's that, now. I've done the other two already.'

'Well done.' She gives me a look and asks: 'How are you, Stella?'

'All right. Why shouldn't I be?' I turn away. 'Thank you, for the shopping. Let me get my cheque book. How much do I owe you?'

'Stella,' she says again, more gently. 'I've brought you these. I thought you might be feeling . . . a bit down, today.'

She takes a bunch of flowers and a box of chocolates off the top of one of the shopping bags and holds them out to me.

'Just a little token,' she says, and as I take them from her – so surprised that I can't even utter a word of thanks for a moment – she envelops me in a hug, almost squashing the beautiful pink and yellow tulips. I have to turn away so that she doesn't notice I'm suddenly, stupidly, on the verge of tears.

'You remembered the date,' I say when I've managed to get myself together a bit.

'Susan's birthday. Of course I did. I called Alec, too; I realised it would be a difficult day for him – his mum's birthday—'

'His first one without her. Yes. He called me too, first thing this morning.'

As I'm telling her this, I realise how grateful I should be that these two young people have come into my life, sharing this difficult day with me. Making me feel less alone.

'It must be hard for you, every year – the memories,' Holly's saying.

I nod. 'It's silly, really. It's just a date. I manage, all year, not to dwell on it. It was easier when Ernest was alive; when it was our wedding anniversary just before – a happier occasion, see? – to take the edge off it. But now, every year on Susan's birthday, it ... suddenly feels too much to bear. The not knowing was always the hardest part. But now – this year – I do know. She's gone.' I give a little shrug. 'I never knew her beyond the first day of her life, so it feels odd to mourn her. And, well, now I know she had a good life. And she's at peace.' I feel the tears welling again and shake my head. 'Take no notice of me, I'll get over it. I'm sorry.'

She follows me into the kitchen as I go to look for a vase.

'Why on earth would you be sorry? It's only natural to feel upset today. Don't be so hard on yourself.'

I sigh. 'Well, I don't generally go in for moping. Getting all emotional about things. It doesn't help, that's my opinion. I prefer to just try and get on with life.'

'I know. And that's great. But every now and again, we all just need to give into it, Stella.' She looks down at the floor. 'You're so much stronger than me. I'm hopeless! I'm always crying over something or other.'

I turn round and stare at her. She looks as if she regrets saying that already. She's shaking her head. 'Sorry. This isn't about me.'

'Actually, I'd prefer it *was* about you, today.'

She's shocked me, to be honest, with this talk of crying over things. What is there to cry about, at her age? Then I quickly correct my thoughts. Of course – she's had a bad start in life. No father to speak of, and a mother who simply abandoned her and swanned off to Australia. And she misses her gran, I understand that, too. She does seem quite lonely. She never talks about friends. Or what happened with Maisie's father.

'All these times we spend together,' I say without looking at her, 'we talk about me. I know you say you find it interesting—'

'Yes! I do!'

'And you needed to write the thing for the magazine, fair enough. But you've never told me much about your own life. Not that you have to, of course. But sometimes I sense ... perhaps you *need* someone to talk to? Maybe more than I do. And today, I really don't feel like talking much, myself.' I pause in the middle of filling the flower vase with water, and turn to look at her. 'So now's your chance, if you want to tell me what it is that you cry about. I'll just sit and listen. I won't even say anything, if you'd rather I didn't.'

'But,' she says cautiously, 'I was supposed to be cheering *you* up today!'

'You have. Just by coming. And bringing me the flowers, and the chocolates. Shall we have a couple each of those now? Come on, come and sit down. Talk to me, seriously. It's ... ' I pause, trying to find the words for what I need to say. 'It's helped me, you coming to see me during the last few weeks. Giving me someone to talk to. Can't I return the favour?'

She's silent for a moment once we sit down. We choose a chocolate each, and she looks out of the window, as if she's trying to decide how to start.

'You said something once,' I prompt her gently, 'that made me think you're not ... on your own with Maisie ... through choice.'

'Choice? Well, I didn't feel as if I *had* any choice.'

'You broke up with her father?' I suggest, as she's come to a stop again.

'Walked out. Yes. I thought ... oh, I suppose like everyone, I thought I'd found The One. The one person who really loved me, who'd always stay with me. Like your Ernest.' She shakes her head sadly. 'But instead, I'd just found someone else – like my mum, like my dad – whoever he was – who didn't love me at all.'

'I'm sorry to hear that,' I say softly.

'I'm so lucky to have Maisie,' she adds, with a smile, as if to contradict my thoughts. 'But I've got to be careful not to smother her with love, to make up for . . . well, the fact I haven't got anyone else. I want *her* to have lots of friends, lots and lots of other lovely people in her life. I made the mistake of limiting myself to one person. Correction!' she adds with a shrug. '*He* limited me.'

'Oh.' I see. This sounds bad. 'So he was – what do they call it these days? Controlling?'

She nods. 'Yes. It's even a criminal offence: coercive control. Liam fitted the bill totally, but of course I didn't see it at the time. That's the nature of it. He wanted all of my attention, all of the time. Didn't like me seeing my friends, so in the end, I didn't have any. Didn't even like me seeing my gran.' She swallows. This must be so hard for her to say. 'So I only saw her in secret. He checked my emails. Looked at my phone. Insisted on seeing all my card receipts, and went through them, looking for any money I'd spent on myself, wanting to know why. Looking back, it was like being held prisoner, except that I allowed it. I thought I was a reasonably intelligent, educated woman, Stella – but I *enabled* him to treat me like that, because I'd convinced myself he loved me. How can that make sense? I've gone over and over it, since I finally left him, and I still can't understand how I could possibly have believed that it was love.'

I think it's fairly obvious how. What experience of love had she had, after all – apart from that of her gran? But I won't say that. It's brave enough that she's telling me about it.

'Well, thank goodness you left him, anyway,' I say.

'Yes. I had to, in the end, after I had Maisie, because unbelievably, he even resented me loving our own child. That was what opened my eyes to it – how wrong it was, how stupid I'd been to put up with it. He didn't even like me holding her! Not for any longer than it took to feed her and change her. Then it was: "Put her down, Holly. Don't keep rocking her, Holly. Leave her in her cot, Holly, you don't need to keep cuddling her." If I hadn't left him, she could have grown up without any affection or love or cuddles at all.'

'Repeating the pattern,' I suggest quietly, raising my eyebrows at her.

'Yes. Exactly. And perhaps she'd have gone on to be incapable of giving love, herself. That's what happens, apparently. Lives get ruined.'

'Ah, don't say that. That's just those ruddy psychology so-called experts talking again. That pattern can be broken, I'm sure of it. People change. People *want* to love someone, and be loved, and have a nice life. Don't they?'

'Yes. But it doesn't always work out, does it? It was all too late for me, really, by the time I woke up and walked away from Liam – too late to get my life back, the way it was. I had my baby girl, thank God for that, but I didn't have any friends, and couldn't seem to remember how to make new ones. Still can't. And worst of all, Stella, I don't even have my sister any more. I'd sabotaged our relationship. It's gone for good.'

I hardly like to ask her why. But I don't have to. She gives a short, harsh little laugh before she looks me in the eye and says:

'Liam was Hannah's boyfriend, you see. He was her boyfriend first. She's never forgiven me, and I can't really blame her, can I?'

34

Holly

I'm so annoyed with myself. What on earth was I thinking of, pouring all that out to Stella? It's the last thing she needed, especially today when she's so haunted by the memory of giving up her baby all those years ago. I feel embarrassed, silly, and – my default setting, really – ashamed. Shame is what I've lived with, ever since my sister found out I was seeing Liam. Ever since she called me, over and over again, day after day, shouting at me to give him up, and when I kept refusing, she finally gave *me* up.

I'm surprised Stella didn't look more shocked when I told her Liam was Hannah's boyfriend first. She's still just nodding to herself, seeming to think it all over. But finally, she looks up and asks me: 'And were they still together when you started going out with him?'

'No. That was why I didn't think she'd be so upset. She'd finished with him,' I explain.

Stella nods again. 'So why do you think she *was* upset?'

'I presumed she just didn't like the idea of me having him, after she'd given him up.'

'Not because she was trying to protect you? Because she knew what he was like?'

'Oh, that's what she *said,* of course. She kept telling me not to get involved, that he was bad news, but I couldn't see it. It didn't make sense. They'd been together for two years, and I'd always liked him. Well . . . more than liked him, if I'm honest. He was *very* attractive. Fit. And charming, *so* charming. He was nearer my age than Hannah's – she used to call him her toy boy when they first got together. He told me Hannah had finished with him because she'd decided she'd *grown out of him.* He looked hurt – and it made sense. Hannah was thirty by then, and he was only twenty-four. I thought she was probably looking for someone more mature, to have a more serious relationship with. And of course, he told me their split was all completely amicable and she wouldn't mind at all about us getting together.'

'But she told you a different story,' Stella says.

'Of course. And I refused to believe her. He seemed so honest, so open and caring and – well, I *chose* to believe him. That was the truth. I chose his version, over my sister's.'

'How old were you then?'

'Nineteen. I was at university at Exeter, doing an English degree, but at that time I'd come home to Gran's for the Easter holiday. He invited me out for a drink, and I knew Hannah had finished with him. She'd been upset. She hadn't seemed happy with him for some time. But she didn't go into details, just said she'd had enough.'

'And you were only nineteen. Flattered by his attention, I suppose? – an older, charming man. Hardly surprising. Hardly a crime!'

'That wasn't how Hannah saw it, though. She was furious. She bombarded me with calls, emails, messages, demanding I stop seeing him. I told Liam, and of course, he said it was just because she resented me having him. When I stopped responding to her calls and messages, she stormed over to my student house – I was back in Exeter by then, and she didn't live far away – and confronted me. We had a huge row.' I hang my head, remembering how I'd squared up to her, the sister I'd never been particularly close to anyway, and told her I didn't care what she thought, and asked her to butt out of my life and stop telling stupid lies about Liam. 'She's never spoken to me since,' I add quietly.

'Oh, Holly. That's so sad,' Stella says. 'So she doesn't even know you broke up with him?'

'I don't know. We don't follow each other on Facebook or anything like that. Gran might have told her – she stayed in touch with Hannah, of course, but she never talked about her to me. It was . . . like a no-go area. The elephant in the room. I think Gran did tell her when Maisie was born, but I never heard a word from her. No congratulations or anything, not that I expected otherwise. I already knew by then, of course, that Hannah had been telling the truth about Liam.'

'Did you try to get back in touch with her? After you realised that?'

'I couldn't, could I? Not while I was still with Liam. He monitored who I spoke to, who I called or emailed—'

'What about since you broke up with him?'

'No.' I sigh. 'What's the point? I was too ashamed to try to make up with her. She obviously hated me.'

'I'm sure she didn't *hate* you,' Stella says.

'Cutting me off? Never speaking to me again?' I retort.

'Don't you think she was probably just exasperated? Because she'd tried her best to warn you off him, and you wouldn't listen? She'd been hurt by him herself, after all, by the sound of it.' She pauses. 'He didn't come after you, did he? After you walked out with Maisie?'

'No, thank God. He had another girl waiting in the wings by then. That's the way he operated – as soon as one girl had had enough of him – or as soon as he got bored with one, as I think he was starting to get bored with me – he started smarming up to his next victim. He had no interest whatsoever in Maisie; I think that's why he wasn't too bothered about me going. He found me boring by then – not only had he succeeded in sapping all my spirit, but I'd got a baby that he frankly resented. So at least I didn't have to fight him for custody.'

'So you went back to live with your gran?'

'Yes. She let me and Maisie stay with her until Maisie started pre-school – then she helped me with the rent on my flat until I got on my feet. She looked after Maisie for me, too, while I was working,' I add quietly. 'I only had the cleaning work at first. The journalism took a while to build up, and of course, because of my experience with Liam – and after I left him, too – I was so lacking in confidence, I struggled to get clients, and to manage deadlines and so on. You're supposed to be quite tough to succeed in journalism, and he didn't encourage me in any way. I think he preferred to think of me just doing a little cleaning job. It wasn't exactly the life I'd hoped for.'

'Did you get your degree, at least? Before all this happened?'

'Yes. Only just. I'd got pregnant with Maisie during my third year. She was born a couple of weeks after my finals.' I stop, giving myself a little shake. 'Stella, I really didn't intend to bore you with all this stuff – today of all days!'

'I haven't been bored. Why would I? I feel sad for you, that's all. About your sister. I'd love to have had a sister—'

'We were only half-sisters. We were never that close.' I shrug. 'She always resented me. I told you – I broke up her parents' marriage.'

'No, you didn't,' Stella says surprisingly firmly. 'Your mother did that herself, when she had her affair with your father. You were an innocent victim, just as your sister was.'

I suppose I've never looked at it like that.

'Anyway,' I say, pretending flippancy, 'none of that matters anymore. I've got Maisie. She's all I need.'

Stella doesn't reply.

'And I *really* didn't mean to do this,' I say yet again. 'Going on and on about myself like this. I don't normally ... haven't ever ... talked about this stuff. To anyone.'

'Then it's good that you have,' she says firmly. There's a pause. 'We're the same, in a way, you and I. I hadn't talked to anyone properly for years, either. Didn't *want* to talk about my life, to be honest, when you first started coming to see me. But I'm glad I have. You said yourself, didn't you, that it's – what's that daft word? Therapeutic?'

'I suppose so.'

But there's a difference. In my case, the whole thing was my own fault. Putting a man before my sister, even if we weren't close in the first place, it was unforgivable. Well, I can't forgive *myself*, and whatever Stella says, I'm sure she probably thinks the same, really.

35

Stella

Holly's story has certainly stopped me brooding about it being Susan's birthday, anyway. Poor girl – carrying all that guilt around all this time, and why? It wasn't her fault. It was that nasty piece of work, the boyfriend, undermining her self-confidence, letting her blame herself for everything. Look at the damage he's done. Why do some men seem to get pleasure from destroying a woman? They don't have to knock them about, it's more subtle than that, more *cowardly*. I suppose the so-called therapists would say he has something wrong with him, that he had a difficult childhood, or he feels insecure or worthless himself. Load of rubbish. He's obviously just an obnoxious person. Let's hope he meets his match sooner or later, someone stands up to him, or gets him arrested – Holly says it's a crime now to behave like that.

I feel too cross on Holly's behalf to concentrate on much for the rest of the day. I wish I'd tried to persuade her to do something about the sister. Never too late to rebuild bridges, is it? Surely if she called her, or wrote and apologised, they could try to talk it through. The sister knows, after all, how easy it was to get taken in by that Liam. But I shouldn't interfere. Hopefully it might have helped her, just to talk about it, after all this time.

She turns up again on Monday morning. She looks a bit sheepish when she comes through the door, and starts apologising, all over again, for 'bending my ear' – odd expression! – about her 'silly nonsense'. It's impossible to get her to believe I was actually quite pleased to keep away from my own memories, for a change. And glad to have my ear bent, if it helped. I decide the best thing to do is talk about other things today. If she wants to bring up Liam and Hannah again, she will.

'Shall we look through some more of those photo albums?' I suggest as she carries the tea tray into the sitting room for me. 'I've left them on the sideboard here.'

'Oh, yes. That'd be nice.'

I take down the second album in the pile.

'This one starts in the nineteen-fifties,' I say as I open it. 'Look, the house has hardly changed from those nineteen-forties pictures!' Then I quickly turn the page, before Holly can point out what has, actually, changed all too obviously between the two sets of pictures. There's less land, already, in these later ones. Funny how, at the time, nobody seemed to mention it, or care about it. Nowadays, it feels like as soon as the smallest stone dislodges from the cliff, everyone rushes up here to talk about it and take photos. As if it matters to them personally. As if it matters to anyone – even me – that a bit more of my garden's gone.

'I was already coming up here every week then,' I muse, turning another page. 'For my violin lessons.'

'The *real* violin lessons,' Holly teases me, and I laugh, and agree:

'Yes, before we gave up on the violin and started pretending.'

'If that happened now – between a teenager and a teacher – he'd probably be in trouble,' she says thoughtfully.

'I'd left school long before we embarked on the pretence,' I retort. 'And there was nothing improper – we just used to chat. We didn't even kiss until I was eighteen!'

'I know. But things are different now. People would have suspected him of *grooming* you. Because of the age difference, and the fact that you were his pupil, to start with.'

'Well, that's what my uncle *did* think, didn't he? Right up till he died. But it wasn't like that at all.'

'I know. I realise that, from what you've told me. The way it happened, how you fell in love.'

We've turned a couple more pages now, and here's the first picture we've come to of me, sitting in this very room, when it was Ernest's music room. I'd have been about seventeen here, and I'm smiling straight at the camera – at Ernest – looking so young, so happy, that it makes me smile again, as if I'm back there, in that picture, feeling the way I did then.

Holly's sighing. 'I wish I could fall in love with someone, like that. And stay in love, like you and Ernest did.'

'Oh, Holly, you will! You're young, and you're lovely. Why on earth would you *not* meet someone nice and fall in love?'

'Because . . .' She frowns. 'I'm not very good at relationships, I suppose.'

'Perhaps you've given up trying?' I suggest gently. 'You had a bad experience, and it's put you off.'

'Yes. Maybe.'

She doesn't say any more, and I'm not going to push it.

'Look at these pictures,' I say, to change the subject. I brush some biscuit crumbs off the photo album and turn a few more pages. 'Here – see? Nineteen-fifty-seven. This is after we were married. I think I told you how Ernest and I used to invite all our friends up here during the summer?'

'Yes. It must have been lovely,' she says, smiling at the

black-and-white photos of our friends enjoying one of our picnics out on the clifftop.

'It was.' I smile back at her. 'It was a good life. We were together, at last, and so happy. There was only one thing spoiling it, of course – but we managed not to dwell on that too much, at first.'

'Not having any more children?'

I nod, but manage to go on smiling. 'Can't have everything in this life, can we, Holly? I had Ernest, and he had me. And of course, at first, we thought it was just a matter of time. I'd fallen pregnant all too easily before, so we assumed it'd happen again, sooner or later. And in the meantime, of course, I was busy enough. I was studying hard—'

'Oh yes, of course! Your teacher training. You never did tell me how that came about.'

'I was very lucky, you know. It probably sounds odd to you, but back then, married women were still mostly supposed to just stay at home and do the housework.'

'I thought the war might have changed all that?' she says.

'It did, up to a point. While the war was on, women were needed to fill all the gaps in the workplace, while the men were off fighting. And yes, they enjoyed being out at work, getting away from the house. But those of the men who came back, and were fit enough to work, needed jobs again, and men were always given preference. The whole emphasis, in the fifties, was on rebuilding society, with women being responsible for happy marriages and happy family life.'

'Sounds like a bit of a step back for women's rights, then.'

I smile. It must be so hard for her to imagine.

'Looking back, yes, I suppose it was. But you see, it was what most people wanted – after the deprivations and tragedies of war-time. Everyone was so grateful for the peace, they just wanted to build a stable society for their children.'

'But you persuaded Ernest to let you go to college?'

'Oh, it wasn't like that. I didn't have to persuade him. He was very forward-thinking, and he knew I'd always regretted having to leave school at fifteen. And don't forget, I'd had nothing *but* domesticity for most of my life, so keeping house wasn't going to be new and exciting for me, like it might have been for some young brides!' I laugh. 'And my good friend Doris – Elizabeth's mum – had talked to me at length about how I could enrol for adult education classes to catch up with my education, and get some O-levels.'

'And that's what you did? As soon as you got married?'

'I started *before* we married, actually – in the September before our wedding. Doris and John had talked to my uncle about it, and because he looked up to them, he gave in and agreed to me going to the classes, on condition that I still managed to look after his house, of course, and cook his meals. And stayed away from Ernest!'

'Well. I suppose that was something, then.'

'I was surprised, at the time, that he agreed. But he was probably sick of seeing my miserable, resentful face around the place.' I laugh again. 'And, you know, now I look back, I think my cousin Geoffrey was right, when he said at Uncle's funeral that he probably had regrets in the end. Perhaps that was his way of trying to make it up to me a little.'

'Did you enjoy the classes?'

'Very much! But I didn't think, even then, that it would lead to anything: a teaching career – my childhood ambition. I didn't really believe that was going to happen, because it was more important that I married Ernest, and ... had a family. But eventually, of course, we had to ask ourselves whether the family was ever going to happen.'

'That must have been tough.'

'Yes,' I agree. 'Yes, it was.'

APRIL 1958

The doctor looked at Stella over his glasses. 'I can't see any reason why you shouldn't be able to conceive. You have already had a child, after all.'

He knew Stella's history, of course, and his tone of disapproval was clear. Dr Martin had been Jim and Nellie's family doctor – and the family doctor of everyone in and around Hawbury Down – for decades. He must have been getting on for seventy by now, but showed no sign of retiring. Stella wished fervently that he would hurry up and do so, and hand over to someone younger and more helpful.

'But we've been married for over two years now,' she said. 'With no luck.'

She'd already subjected herself to the usual embarrassing examination, carried out without much gentleness or sympathy.

'Some people wait for much longer,' he said, writing in her notes, not looking up at her. 'You might need to relax more. You said you're taking classes – as well as being a housewife? Perhaps it's a simple matter that you're trying to do too much.'

Stella sighed, choosing to ignore this all-too-common view. 'Do you think my husband should have a check-up? He said he'd be quite happy to come and see you—'

'What would be the point of that?' Dr Martin looked up at her now, almost crossly. 'Your husband *was* the father of the illegitimate child you gave up for adoption, wasn't he? Or was that a … matter of pretence on your part?'

'What!' Stella gasped. 'Of course he was the father! What are you suggesting?'

'Some girls would marry anyone who asked them, to cover up for a … situation such as you found yourself in.'

'Well, I'm not *some girl*, and I've only ever slept with my husband! And only once before we were married! We'd have got married straight away if my uncle hadn't stopped us.'

'In that case,' the doctor said, leaning back in his chair, looking completely unperturbed by Stella's indignance, 'your husband obviously has nothing wrong with him. He fathered the illegitimate child, so—'

Stella wished he wouldn't keep referring to Susan like that. She felt tears threatening. Was she going to be shamed for ever, for that one mistake? Would nobody help her, now that she couldn't seem to have another baby? Was this her punishment?

'Well,' she said, sitting up straighter, 'I'd like to see a specialist.'

'There really isn't any point, Mrs Jackman—'

'Actually, my friend's a doctor and she says—'

Dr Martin gave Stella a superior half-smile. 'You're talking about Elizabeth Ashworth, I presume? She's not *quite* a doctor yet, is she? Still a student, I believe. But of course, if you think she's an expert on the subject, by all means do talk to your friend instead of me.'

Not for the first time, Stella wished she had a GP who didn't know everything about everyone in the village. But she was determined to stick to her guns, no matter how small he made her feel.

'Elizabeth says I'm entitled to ask for a second opinion,' she muttered. 'So that's what I'm doing – asking you. Please.'

He sighed deeply, looked out of the window, as if searching for patience, and finally threw his pen down on his desk.

'Very well. Since you seem to be so insistent, I shall refer you to a colleague of mine, Dr Milne, an eminent gynaecologist, a leader in his field—'

Stella hoped he wasn't of the same vintage as Dr Martin.

'—but I think you're going to find that he'll tell you exactly what I've told you. You need to relax and let nature take its course.' He gave her a wave of dismissal. 'You'll get an appointment in the post.'

Dr Milne, when Stella and Ernest finally got to see him, was indeed an old medical school friend of their GP. He was completely thrown by the fact that they'd turned up at the hospital together.

'It's normal, in the gynaecology department, to see women on their own,' he stuttered, as if the sight of a man in his consulting room was terrifying for him.

'Well, since we're both equally concerned in this situation,' Ernest said pleasantly, 'we felt it was important for us both to be here.'

'I see.' He rubbed at his beard. 'Well, you'll understand that I need to examine your wife intimately, sir?'

'Of course. And if you don't find any cause for concern in Stella, I'd like to see a specialist myself. To rule out any problems with me.'

'But . . .' Dr Milne fumbled with the notes in front of him, 'your GP intimated that you've already fathered a child.'

'Yes, indeed. And my wife conceived that child, and gave birth to her. But unfortunately, neither of us seem to be able to repeat the process.' He paused, and added in such a firm tone that the elderly gynaecologist actually flinched: 'I think it's important that you understand, neither of us wanted to give up our baby for adoption, Dr Milne. Our hands were forced.'

'Quite, quite,' Dr Milne said hurriedly. 'Well, I'll do my best to get to the bottom of your ... er ... difficulty, of course. There may be something that's quite easily rectified.'

But apparently there wasn't. Within a couple of months, both Stella and Ernest had had the few checks and tests available at the time, with nothing found in either of them to explain their failure to reproduce again. Stella felt like she'd reached the end of a line.

'Maybe we should just give up,' she said. 'There doesn't seem to be anything else we can do, so – let's just pretend we don't care. I don't want it to ruin our marriage.'

Ernest took her in his arms, stroking her hair.

'We could adopt?' he suggested quietly.

'No.' She shook her head. 'It wouldn't feel right. We gave up our own baby for adoption. It would feel like ... a double betrayal of her, to adopt someone else's.'

'But can you live with that, Stella? Honestly? Possibly never being able to bring up a child?'

'If that's ... God's plan for us.' She shrugged. She thought about Elizabeth, who'd shaken off the very idea of God being behind anything, good or bad. Was she right, after all? 'If it's really God, at all.'

'If it is, it's pretty mean and unfair of him,' Ernest said. He held her out at arm's-length, looking at her carefully. 'And I think, if we're going to give up on the quest to have a child, you're going to need something else. Another passion in your life, darling.'

She laughed. 'I have you!'

'But you should have a career, too. You've got your exams, now – you got good grades, too. You could train to be a teacher.

You have it in you, and it's what you always wanted. You should apply to the training college as a mature student.'

'Do you really think I'd be accepted?'

'I do. And I think you'll love it, thrive on it, and it'll make you happy. Even happier!' he added quickly, smiling. 'Do it, Stell. Send off your application today.'

'Thank you.' She reached up and kissed him. 'I will.'

She was accepted for the course beginning that September, and Ernest had been quite right: from the very first day, she thrived on college life. She loved everything about it – the studying, the friendships with the other students – of whom she was the oldest, amongst a group of school leavers – and the feeling that she was, at last, going to embark on something useful, something that had always been her dream. Despite missing out on years of schooling that would have got her ahead, she'd already recaptured her love of learning by studying for her O-level exams, and now there was nothing stopping her. She threw herself into her studies. At home, she and Ernest would talk endlessly and passionately about education, and when their friends came for dinner or for their soirees on the clifftop, the conversations would go on into the small hours.

Occasionally, Stella would lie awake at night, wondering what she'd do now if she were to suddenly, miraculously, find herself pregnant again. Could she give all this up, and settle for a life of domesticity again? But of course, she'd want to, if that happened. If there were to be a baby. She'd feel the familiar pain in her heart, along with the growing conviction that it was never going to happen. And she'd remind herself that it didn't matter, because she had Ernest, and she now also had a life of her own, and was going to be a career woman – a teacher.

By the time she'd qualified, and started work – exactly as she'd always dreamed, in the infants' school in her own village – the idea of having her own children had been pushed so far to the back of her mind that it didn't even trouble her too often. She enjoyed the little ones she taught, instead, and the lovely life she and Ernest had, with their occasional holidays and their wide circle of friends. They were now into a new decade – the nineteen-sixties – with its promise of good times ahead.

She mostly only got upset about her one disappointment in life, when that date came around every year. March the first. Reminding her of the one and only day in her life that she'd actually been a mother.

36

Holly

I find myself thinking a lot about how Stella came to terms with not having another child: while I'm playing with Maisie, or picking her up from school and hearing her excited chatter about what's happened in her day; or when I'm reading her a bedtime story and she's warm and sleepy in my arms. I didn't intend to become a mum at only twenty-one. I had plans for my life. I was going to be a top-notch journalist, not someone struggling to make ends meet with the odd bit of freelance writing, topped up by a cleaning job and the pathetic amount of child maintenance I get from Liam. Despite going through the Child Maintenance Service – because he was refusing to pay anything, on the grounds that 'it was my decision to leave' – he somehow managed to manipulate the figures to indicate he doesn't earn enough – as a qualified electrician – to pay me more than the absolute minimum. I could have argued the case further, but frankly I was so desperate to have nothing more to do with him that I gave in. I'd prefer to have nothing from him whatsoever, especially given his total lack of interest in Maisie. But she deserves to have what little he gives.

I suppose, if I'm honest, I'm so used to blaming Liam for

everything, that I tend to forget that I also had some degree of responsibility for what happened – at least, at first, before he took control of my life so completely that I couldn't even think for myself anymore. I could have made sure we were more careful when we started our relationship ... but then I wouldn't have had Maisie now. And I can't imagine life without her.

The day after Stella told me that last part of her story, I'm getting our evening meal ready when I get a phone call from Karen along the road.

'Holly,' she says, 'could you possibly do me a big favour and pick Flora up from school on Friday afternoon?'

'Of course I can.' We've covered for each other like this a few times before, usually when one or other of us hasn't been well, so I add, 'Is everything OK?' before wondering if that sounds too nosy. Although we chat a bit at the school gate, we're not really friends, and I'm worried that after so long without any close friends I've gone back to being the socially awkward child I once was, unsure how to make normal conversation.

'Yes, we're fine, thanks. It's just – I've got a job interview.'

'Oh. Good luck, then.' I realise with a stab of guilt that I don't even know what she does.

'Thank you,' she says, and then suddenly rushes on, as if she's too excited to keep it to herself: 'It's the first interview I've had for ages. As you know, I'm on my own with Flora – like you are with Maisie. And I've been out of work for nearly six months.'

How did I not pick up on this? I always assumed she was busy – too busy to chat. Or was I just being too lazy, or too scared of rejection, to be more friendly myself?

'I'm sorry to hear that,' I say. 'But glad you've got an interview now. Where is it?'

'At the bookshop in Fore Street. It's just a part-time assistant's role. But it'll fit in with school hours—'

'Oh, perfect!' I say, before I've even had time to remember about Alec – and then I can't help exclaiming: 'In fact I know the manager there.'

'Really?' Karen says, sounding pleased. 'He seemed quite nice when I handed him my application. Is he a friend of yours, then, Holly?'

'Well ... kind of,' I say, now suddenly overcome with embarrassment. 'I mean, I've only met him recently, but we ... well, I'm friends with his gran.'

'Oh, OK.' No wonder she sounds a bit puzzled.

'And you're right, he's really nice,' I go on. 'I hope the interview goes well.'

'Thank you. And I *should* be home from it in time for school, but just in case—'

'It's no problem, Karen. I'll bring Flora home with Maisie and keep her here until you're ready for her. You won't want to rush.' I pause, then add, a bit cautiously: 'You'd be welcome to stay and have a cup of tea or coffee when you come back for her. But only if you want to, of course, if you've got time, if you're not—'

'That would be really nice, Holly. Thank you. I'll probably see you at the school gate before then, anyway.'

'Yes, of course.'

I pick the pieces of the conversation to bits so many times after we've said goodbye and hung up, that I'm actually getting annoyed with myself. Why am I over-thinking it? Why can't I just be pleased that Karen seems happy to be friends? OK, so I felt a bit panicked at first; I've more or less forgotten the art of social chit-chat. And that was embarrassing, jumping in with the fact that I knew Alec, as if he and I were best buddies. But it'll get easier, won't it, if I make an effort? Because, let's face it, that's what I haven't done. I haven't tried, all this time, because I'd lost so much of the confidence I managed to find, years ago, when I was a student.

Despite being such a shy, introverted child, I kind of came into my own a little, when I went to uni. I met other students there who were like me – into reading and writing, quiet, a bit socially awkward. I made two particular friends there, Julia and Nousha, and the three of us started to go out together, to the student union bar, and pubs, and parties. We seemed to feed off each other, all of us gradually becoming more confident and outgoing. We all had the occasional dates, and then the other two both started more serious relationships, round about the same time. But they were good friends to me; they didn't drop me just because they had boyfriends. Unfortunately, it was me who did that to them – when I started going out with Liam. Even when Nousha broke up with her boyfriend, I didn't make time for her. Liam didn't even like me going to my lectures, never mind seeing my friends socially. I think he'd have preferred me to be shut at home all day. By the time I realised how stupid I'd been, I was pregnant, at twenty. My lifestyle was so different from theirs by then, we had nothing left in common. They'd be out partying, going to nightclubs, and celebrating when we got our degrees, like normal graduates do. I was at home, changing nappies, being . . . constantly criticised.

I tell Stella all this, when I'm next up at Cliff's End, after I've told her the latest about Karen.

'Have you never tried to get in touch with those two girls from uni,' she asks, 'since you broke up with Liam?'

'No. I felt too ashamed. It was horrible, the way I dropped them, back then. Besides, I don't know where they live now, or anything.'

I know I could try. Everyone says nobody is impossible to trace, these days, but I've never searched for either of them on Facebook or Twitter. They might even be married, changed their names. I . . . just haven't tried.

'Fair enough,' Stella says evenly. 'Life moves on, and some

friends get left behind along the way. That's how it goes. No point beating yourself up about it. But *now* ...' She gives me a very direct look. 'You've got another chance. With Karen.'

'The thing is I felt terrible, Stella – I didn't even know she was out of work – looking for a job. All this time we've known each other, the children have been friends and we've helped each other out occasionally, but I never even bothered to find out what her situation was. I didn't make the effort.'

'Well, now you've got the chance to make up for that. What's the worst that can happen?'

'I know, you're right,' I say. 'I expect you think I'm being silly. I don't know why I feel so nervous about it.'

'I'd say it's because that awful man took all your confidence away. Don't you think?'

I nod, and Stella reaches out and pats my hand.

'Funny,' she says after a moment. 'You never seemed shy or awkward to me. First time you came here to talk to me, you seemed very confident, I thought.'

'Ah, well, I had my *professional* hat on!' I say, laughing. 'I wasn't here to make friends with you, I'm sorry to say, Stella. That just happened without me trying!'

'No need to apologise,' she chuckles. 'I never thought I'd make friends with you, either. I thought you were going to be a pain in the neck, if I'm honest, the first time you came! But I soon changed my mind,' she adds quickly. 'I couldn't ask for a nicer friend. Never expected to make a new one, at my age.'

'Same here,' I say.

'Well then. About time we had another cup of tea, isn't it? Or are you in too much of a hurry to get back home and have one with your *new* friend, now?' I tease her.

'Ah, don't say that! Of course not!' I laugh.

'But I'm pleased for you. Really. You need friends of your own age, Holly. I hope Karen's just going to be the first one, and maybe through her you'll make lots more. You've got out of the habit, that's all.'

And I think, as usual, Stella's right. Because when Karen comes back on Friday afternoon – beaming with excitement to tell me she's got the job, and is starting straight away – it's only a matter of minutes before we're chatting together like long-lost pals. She's only lived in our street since last summer – since she split from her husband – and she tells me she lost her previous job within months of moving in, so she's had a really tough time. I haven't told her too much about myself yet. But I will. I don't think it'll be quite so hard, now that I've already told Stella about it. Karen's nice, and easy to talk to, and we've agreed that we really should spend more time together. The children are already best friends. How has it taken us so long?

But it doesn't matter. I'm learning that from Stella. Whatever happens, you can get over it, and move on, regardless of how old you are. And friendship is one of the things it's definitely worth making an effort for.

37

Stella

NEARLY TWO WEEKS LATER

Winters seem longer now I'm older. It's well past the middle of March now: yesterday was officially the first day of spring, but up here on Hawbury Top it still feels like midwinter. I'm tired of it, tired of putting on my coat and boots just to go outside and hang out the washing. I want to sit in my chair by the window and feel the sun beating through the glass, instead of wrapping myself up against the wind whistling through the gaps in the window frame. It's my own fault. I should have had some repairs done, while I still had the money, and the energy to organise it. I never expected old age to bring this lethargy with it.

At least when Holly comes, she brings a burst of springtime with her, a breath of fresh air. She's brought Maisie a couple more times too. It's a joy to have that child here, usually bringing me a picture she's drawn, or a piece of school homework she's proud of and wants me to look at. Last time, it was a poem she'd written about me.

> *My Auntie Stella lives on a cliff,*
> *She's very old and stiff.*
> *She makes nice scones.*
> *I can see her pointy bones.*

'Sorry,' Holly says. 'I didn't want her to bring it. They've been talking about people of different ages, at school, and most of the children have grandparents, but—'

'Don't be silly!' I'm almost crying with laughter. 'It's the best poem I've read for years! Well done, Maisie. You've summed me up perfectly. Now then, come and try this jumper on, would you? It's nearly finished.'

It's been lovely, too, to hear how Holly's friendship with Karen is coming along. She says Karen's admitted to being a bit shy as well, so they're good for each other. And apparently Karen chats to Holly about her boss – who happens to be Alec. Well, Hawbury Down is a small world, of course. Holly never meets my eyes when she mentions Alec. And if he happens to be here when she pops in, she goes a bit pink and stays rather quiet. She pretends she just doesn't want to intrude in my conversations with my grandson. But I'm not fooled.

'I've got something to show you,' she says the following Friday morning when she arrives with my shopping. She pulls an envelope out of one of her shopping bags. Inside is a copy of the magazine – *Devon Today*.

'It's the April edition. They send me an advance copy, but it'll be in the shops next week, before the end of March,' she explains. 'My feature's in it.'

'And are you pleased with how it looks?' I ask her.

'Yes. I am. But I'm hoping *you* will be, too.'

'Nothing to do with me,' I retort. I don't mean to sound quite so gruff. It's because I'm trying to hide my excitement. I know she hasn't put anything personal in it; she showed me what she'd written, didn't she, before she sent it off. But it's still going to have my name on it, as her *source*, as she puts it. And Ernest's photos.

She finds the right page and hands it to me. It fills the whole of two pages. *Memories of Hawbury Down*, she's called it.

'It looks good,' I say. 'The pictures came out all right, didn't they?'

'Yes. My editor said they were pretty high res, considering how long ago they were taken.'

I've got no idea what that means, of course, but I do know Ernest was a good photographer.

'You can keep the magazine,' Holly says, smiling, as I start reading through it. 'I'll get another copy.'

'Oh, are you sure?'

'Absolutely. It's thanks to you that this was published.'

We sit in silence for a moment. I'm going to read the article properly after she's gone.

'Shall I make the tea,' she suggests, 'while you unpack your shopping?'

I don't like to admit I've already forgotten about the shopping bags. She put them down in the hall and we came straight into the sitting room so that she could show me the magazine. I get more forgetful every day. When we go back out to the hall, Gracie's sitting inside one of the shopping bags, sniffing around. She can probably smell the cat food in it. Or my cheese!

'As long as she hasn't squashed anything!' Holly says – but no, no harm done.

It's not till we've sat back down again with our tea, that she asks about the violin. I didn't realise I'd left it out. Normally I'm so careful to put it away – because of the cats. I don't want it scratched, or the strings broken. I must have forgotten.

'I hope I'm not getting . . . you know. Like Ernest did,' I say to Holly, picking it up to put it in its case.

'I'm sure you're not,' she soothes me. 'We all forget to do things, don't we? Is it Ernest's violin, or your one?'

'His. It's a much better one, obviously, than that old second-hand thing I had. I gave that away a long time ago, to one of Ernest's pupils.'

'You didn't used to play together?' she says, sounding surprised. 'I imagined you both in here – the music room – playing duets.'

'Oh no, Holly. I wasn't good enough! I was *never* any good. He did his best, and I got to a certain standard through hard work – trying to please him – but no amount of tuition and practice make up for a complete lack of talent! Despite my aunt and uncle's great ambitions for me at the beginning!'

'But you still get his violin out and play it? Will you play something for me?'

'Not unless you want your eardrums burst!' I say, laughing again. 'I play around with it sometimes – try to remember some of the very easy tunes I first learnt, as a girl. But I've lost the knack. Not enough practice over the years . . . decades . . . since I stopped learning. I only do it in memory of Ernest. That's all.' I sigh, and then go on, smiling at her, 'Even the cats scream their heads off when I start trying to play it!'

Holly laughs with me. 'I'm sure that's not true.'

Then she stops, suddenly, giving me an odd look as if she's just realised something.

And maybe she has.

Maybe she's the first person, ever, to realise what's been going on up here for years. The thing so many daft people from the town have never managed to work out.

But Holly doesn't say anything. Good for her. If she's guessed, she's keeping it to herself. It can be our secret. One we don't even talk about together. The best type!

38

Holly

I'm actually giggling out loud to myself as I walk back down the track. Good old Stella! I think she's just solved a mystery for me. The legend of 'The Witch of Cliff's End'. It has nothing to do with witchcraft, of course. The *ghostly wailing noises* people talk about, coming from the house on summer evenings when they come up to Hawbury Top for a stroll, are just poor Stella trying to get a tune out of Ernest's old violin! And her three cats meowing in protest!

I didn't say anything to Stella, of course. I'm not sure whether she realises that this could be why people spread that stupid myth about her. But it wouldn't surprise me if she knows. It wouldn't even surprise me if she does it on purpose! I'm never going to mention it, though. I quite like the idea that it's a little secret between us – one that neither of us actually talk about.

I seem to suddenly become much busier with work over the next few days. Frosty Fran appears to have thawed slightly in my direction since accepting the piece about Hawbury Down – so much so, that she's commissioned me to write a similar piece about the history of another village, on the edge of Dartmoor, from where an elderly man has sent in a letter about his memories, with some intriguing photos. I've already arranged an interview with him. Meanwhile I've had a pitch to one of the national women's weeklies accepted, about how important it is for us all to write down our memories, and keep our photos labelled, for the sake of generations to come. And the editor of the nature magazine I write the monthly column for, has contacted me to say they're planning a new regular page for children, and would I be interested in contributing? I'm buzzing with ideas. I feel more enthusiastic than I've done for ages. Creativity feeds off itself, and the more I think, plan, and write, the more I want to. And in odd free moments in between the work projects, I'm still adding bits to my private documentation of Stella's life story.

'Don't worry about coming to see me, while you're so busy,' Stella says when I call her during the following week, to make sure she's all right. 'I'm glad you've got lots of work.'

'I'll be up on Friday,' I reassure her. 'Call me with your shopping list.'

'No, I've given it to Alec this week,' she says. 'He insisted, as soon as I told him how busy you were.'

'Oh, Stella, you shouldn't have done that. I thought it was my turn. And he's busy too – he's got a shop to manage!'

'Yes, but he's so impressed with his new assistant – your friend Karen – he says she's perfectly capable of managing while he comes up here in his lunch break. And he was very impressed to hear how well you're doing with your work.'

I feel a strange mixture of pleasure and embarrassment, imagining Alec listening to Stella talking about me. But there's something else about this conversation that makes me suddenly catch my breath. Karen's told me herself how well she's settling into her new job, and I'm really glad for her, and glad, too, to hear that Alec is pleased with her. But now I can't help wondering: *how* pleased? Karen's lovely: she's beautiful as well as having a really nice nature.

No doubt they get along well, working in the shop, spending all their days together.

Surely I'm not *jealous*?!

The thought is ridiculous, but it does stop me mid-sentence, so that Stella has to ask if I'm all right, if I'm still here.

'Yes, I'm fine, Stella – sorry. Look, I'll probably still pop up and see you on Friday, if that's OK?'

I don't have to go at the same time as Alec, after all.

Karen always comes straight to school from the shop for the afternoon pick-up, and we chat at the gates while we wait. As usual, we exchange news about our work, and – as usual – she mentions Alec, and today I just can't help myself. I jump straight in.

'You really like him – Alec – don't you?' I say carefully, watching her face.

'Yes, he's great. He's a pleasure to work for—' She sees my expression, and laughs. 'Oh, don't get me wrong. I don't like him in *that* way. Lovely though he is – he's not really my type. No, in fact – I ... haven't mentioned it yet, because it's early days, and we're taking it slowly – you know, because of Flora – but I've actually been seeing someone for a few weeks now.' She gives me a happy little smile. 'His name's Paolo. I *think* it might be the beginning of something, Holly.'

'Oh, I'm *so* pleased for you!' I give her a quick hug. 'I'll look forward to meeting him.'

'Of course. Hopefully soon. But meanwhile ... ' She's looking at me quite intently now. 'I know for a fact Alec isn't seeing anyone. And he really does seem a genuinely nice guy.'

'Yes, I think so too.' I smile, even while I'm trying to avoid her gaze. 'I'm glad for Stella's sake, obviously.'

No other reason!

*

In the event, on Friday, I'm at a good place to break from my work around lunchtime, and I decide to make a quick visit to Stella now, telling myself Alec will probably already have been and gone. In fact his car is at the start of the track when I park, and it turns out he's only just arrived at Cliff's End. He seems pleased to see me, chatting to me cheerfully while he unpacks Stella's shopping and I put the kettle on. Stella, uncharacteristically, leaves us to it, retreating to the living room to turn on the fire, and giving me a funny kind of sly look when I join her with the tea tray.

'Managed to finish your work, did you?' she asks, grinning at me.

'I reached a natural break,' I say, trying not to sound defensive. I know only too well what she's hinting at!

Fortunately Alec comes to sit with us then, and the conversation flows comfortably between the three of us. We ask Stella about her week, he asks me about my work, I talk to him about the book-shop, we both stroke the cats, and both say, once we've finished our cups of tea, that we really ought to get back to work.

'I'll come for a longer visit next week, once I've caught up,' I promise Stella.

Alec and I walk back down the track together to our cars, chatting, as we walk, about Stella and her determination to stay in Cliff's End Cottage. It's clear he's worried about her.

'I had a good look over the cliff, last time I was up there,' he says. 'It's pretty obvious there's been some serious erosion there recently. And I'm no expert, but the crack I rescued Peggy from, that first day I came, might indicate there's something worrying going on, closer to the house.'

'She's very touchy on the subject,' I remind him again. 'She's still determined she's never going to move out of that house. It holds all her memories. As you know, she's been living there since she married your grandad in fifty-six. But she knew the house well, even before that.'

'Yes.' He nods. 'I get that.'

'It's understandable really,' I go on. 'I don't think we can badger her into moving.'

I realise I'm sounding protective – not just of Stella herself, but of the memories she's shared with me over the last couple of months.

'No, I agree. No badgering,' he says, giving me his beautiful smile again.

I'll have to watch myself, where that smile's concerned. I've known this guy for – what? A couple of months? And didn't I swear, after Liam, that I'd never have those kinds of feelings again, without making damned sure first that the person responsible isn't some sort of head case?

He stops now, looking at me carefully, before going on: 'Holly, I promise I'm never going to badger Gran, about anything. But I think we do need to discuss these things, as we're both involved now, not ... in her *care*, exactly, because I know she'd resent the suggestion that she needs it—'

I laugh. 'She certainly would!'

'—but in, you know, keeping an eye on her. I do kind of feel like it's such a happy coincidence, me moving here, and then finding out that my birth-grandmother lives just the other end of town from me. And I'm enjoying building a relationship with her. But I worry about her, too.'

'I understand that, obviously,' I reassure him at once. 'And of course I'm happy that we're both involved now, Alec. We can share the worries, as well as the shopping and so on!'

'Exactly. A worry shared, and all that. And it isn't just the erosion of the cliff that worries me. I keep trying to check she's warm enough, and safe and well, and—' he shrugs, and smiles again '—well, just what you're doing too, I'm sure.'

'Yes.' I smile back at him. I can't help it. He seems so open, so kind and thoughtful. He couldn't be hiding any horrible character defects, could he? But then, didn't Liam seem just as charming as this, when I first met him? Will I ever be able to trust a man again?

I have to. The thought comes to me abruptly, just as we reach our cars and turn to say goodbye to each other. I have to trust *this* man. I already do, because he's Stella's grandson. He's been visiting her, in her home, and if I didn't trust him, I wouldn't have been letting that happen. I'm consumed by a sudden panic. Suppose he's *not* as charming as he seems? Should I have insisted on always being there when he visits her? Or would that have seemed ridiculously over-protective?

But, as if he can read my mind – or as if he's just, in fact, a really decent, thoughtful guy who understands exactly how I might be feeling – he says:

'I've got to dash, Holly, but I'll see you again very soon, I hope. I'm glad we've had this chance to chat – out of Gran's ridiculously sharp hearing! I've been wanting to give you some sort of assurance, I suppose, that you can trust me – but I realise it's a bit late in the day for that now. It all happened so suddenly at the beginning, didn't it?'

I laugh, remembering him emerging from the bushes with Peggy in his arms and twigs in his hair, but he goes on, sounding suddenly more sombre:

'I was feeling pretty desolate back then. My mum had passed away just before Christmas and although, as I've explained, it was frankly a release from her suffering, it was still –'

'Still the loss of your mum,' I say gently. 'Of course.'

'So finding Gran – finding her and getting to know her – has been such a perfect antidote for the sadness. For both of us, I hope. But I could understand completely if you were suspicious of me – turning up out of the blue like that, and suddenly starting to go up to the house to visit her. I just want you to know I'm not – well,

I'm not after anything from her. I just want to be around for her. And to help, if ever she needs it.'

'Yes, of course,' I say, feeling almost too choked by this little speech than I care to admit to myself. 'I completely get that. We're on the same page. That's how I feel about Stella too.'

And what I'm actually thinking is that I like him a little bit more with almost everything he says. And . . . it's starting to scare me.

—

39

Holly

Two weeks later

Since our recent conversation about Stella, Alec and I have started to visit her together more often, sometimes even sharing the weekly shopping and its delivery up to Hawbury Top. She's now completely adapted to his sudden arrival in her life, and seems to be filled with a new energy and enthusiasm. Her pride and excitement at finally accepting her grandson is such a joy to see, it has me on the edge of tears half the time.

'Silly thing!' she teases me, noticing on one occasion that I've had to wipe my eyes. 'I'm *happy*!' She squeezes my hand as I pass her on my way to the kitchen. 'I never expected to be so lucky, at this great age. Having two lovely young people come into my life: a best friend, and a grandson. It's more than I could have hoped for.' She looks over at Alec, smiling, and adds: 'I was a miserable old bugger when Holly first came to talk to me. I thought she was just going to be another interfering busybody. Like those ruddy environmentalists.'

Alec laughs, but then he and I exchange a glance. Neither of us have talked to Stella any further about the original crack in the ground, and since Peggy was rescued from that one, we suspect there might be more. Alec's told me he's had a chat with one of the *ruddy environmentalists*, having explained his relationship to Stella, and the guy told him that if there are big new cracks appearing close to the house, it could be a warning sign, but the most worrying thing would be new cracks appearing in the walls of the house. And they ought to come and investigate, if only Stella would let them.

She's repeated a lot of her stories to Alec by now, of course – about her childhood, about Ernest and her unplanned pregnancy with Alec's mother, and about the happy life she and Ernest enjoyed together, up here on top of the cliff. He understands why she can't bear the thought of leaving the house, just as much as I do, but we're both now increasingly anxious. April has brought some fine, milder weather, but we can't help wondering how much worse the apparent subsidence might become during another winter up here.

One beautiful Sunday afternoon, I bring Maisie with me to meet Alec and go up together to Cliff's End. She's a bit shy with him at first, but before long she's holding his hand, and giggling at his jokes.

'What's your little boy called?' she asks him. I've already filled her in on the fact that he's a daddy.

'Alfie,' he says, smiling at her. 'He's nine – a bit bigger than you.'

'Does he go to my school?'

'No,' Alec says. 'He lives with his mummy, in another town, so he goes to school there. But he comes to stay with me for weekends. He's coming next weekend. Perhaps your mum might bring you along to meet him?'

'No, thank you,' Maisie says politely. 'I don't like boys.'

Alec and I both burst out laughing. 'Wise girl,' he teases her. 'But you might change your mind sooner than you think!'

Another day, after he's listened to some more of Stella's stories, and been shown the memory blanket, he's unusually quiet as we walk back to the cars.

'I'd hate for all that history to be lost,' he says. He doesn't need to explain what he means. Stella might be pretty sprightly for eighty-three, but she obviously won't live forever.

'It won't be lost,' I tell him, swallowing back the lump that's come to my throat at this thought. 'I've written it all down.'

'You have?' he says, looking at me in surprise. 'Does Gran know?'

'No. I promised her, when I wrote the magazine feature, that there wouldn't be anything personal about her in it. But I felt the same as you do: her life story needed to be written down. I just did it for me. But I'll email it to you, of course, if you'd like me to.'

'I would. Thank you. And perhaps you *should* tell her. She might actually like to read it herself.'

'I suppose so,' I say, doubtfully. Perhaps he's right. But I'll have to read through it again myself. I'd hate her to think I hadn't done it justice.

Throughout all this time, I've been seeing a lot more of Karen. Now that we've become friends, we've moved on from our initial shyness and we tell each other ... almost ... everything. I haven't actually spelled out how I feel about Alec. I think she knows, and she's respecting my reticence. I'm still too nervous to admit it – even to myself. I don't suppose he'd ever feel the same about me, anyway. He's just being a really nice friend. Well, perhaps that's the best kind of relationship to have with a man, anyway.

On another glorious Sunday, towards the middle of May, Alec and I have arranged with Stella to have a picnic up on the clifftop. We take the children. It's Alfie's weekend with his dad, and Maisie has now met him a couple of times. She's coming round to the idea that some boys can be tolerable after all! We manage, between us, to carry a picnic hamper, a bottle of Prosecco and a fold-up chair for Stella up to Hawbury Top from Alec's car.

'Stella's garden chairs were all in the shed that went into the sea,' I explain as Alec pretends to huff and puff under the weight of the (very light!) canvas chair as we climb the track – the two children running ahead.

He shakes his head, looking worried, as he does every time we talk about the damage to the cliff.

'We can't keep on ignoring this situation,' he says. 'I don't want to upset her, but—'

'I know. The cracks.'

We looked around the outside of the house last week, while Stella was having a nap. It doesn't look good. Alec thinks the erosion to the base of the cliff might be reaching further in than anyone realises. But Stella's adamant about not letting any 'busybodies' come up to give a professional opinion.

Alec manages to raise the subject, obliquely, after we've enjoyed our picnic. The children are playing a card game in the shade of one of the trees, while we three sit back in the sunshine, sipping a glass of wine each.

'I can see why you don't ever want to leave this house, Gran,' he says, smiling at her. 'On days like this, it's certainly beautiful up here. And of course, all your memories of Grandad are wrapped up in the house.'

'It's not just that,' she replies. She doesn't sound as cross as she normally would, at any talk of leaving the house. Perhaps the wine, and the sunshine, have softened her a little – as well as being with her grandson, and great-grandson. 'I carry my memories in here, you know.' She taps her heart, nodding to herself. 'And anyway, some of the more recent memories weren't even good ones.'

'No?' Alec meets my eyes, looking surprised. 'In what way?'

'In the way . . . poor Ernie became,' she says softly. 'And the way he had to leave here. I've never really told you much about it, have I, Holly? It was a sad time.'

40

June 2000

The doctor looked across the desk at Stella, his eyes full of sympathy.

'You haven't been able to find another carer for him – since the last one left?'

'Not one who'll stay more than a couple of days.' Stella shrugged. 'It's tough for them.'

'I can see that. But I don't see how it's a viable option for you to give up work and look after him full-time yourself, either.' He shook his head at her. 'Sooner or later it'll be a broken wrist, or worse. The bruises are bad enough. So is the depression,' he added softly. 'This medication, Stella – it's not good for you to be on it long-term.'

'What else can I do?' she pleaded. 'He can't help it. He's not bad-tempered; he never has been.'

'I know. He's frightened, and confused. But how is it going to help him, if one day he grabs you so hard you end up in hospital? He'd *have* to go into care then.'

Stella bit her lip.

'And you can't leave him on his own all day,' the doctor went on.

'No. That's why I'm giving up work. I'm old enough to retire, anyway.'

'You've told me before that your job is what's keeping you sane.'

'It was. When I had someone I could trust, looking after Ernest. But now I'm worried sick all day at work. I can't concentrate properly on the children. It isn't right.'

'And with the turnover of carers you've been having now, he's in such a state when you get home, he grabs you so hard that you end up with all these bruises. Stella, it can't go on. I'll talk to Social Services.'

'No! How can I let him go into a home? He won't understand. He'll be terrified.' She held her head in her hands. In truth, she was at her wits' end. Dr Sutton had been so kind, all through Ernest's terrible descent into dementia, and she knew he had both their interests at heart, but she couldn't bear to take the next, final, step. It would break her heart, as well as Ernie's.

'There are good homes around, Stella, with caring, experienced staff – they're used to handling people with Ernest's condition—'

'*I'm* used to it!'

'But he's a big, strong, man, despite his age. Despite his bad leg. And you're sixty-five yourself, and what? Five-foot-one or -two? I'm afraid you *can't* handle him when he's going into one of his meltdowns. I have to think of you, as well as Ernest, and I'd be negligent in my duty to you if I didn't tell you this: I'm seriously concerned about your welfare, Stella, and your safety at home.'

'He doesn't mean to hurt me,' she said miserably, tears in her eyes.

'I know that. He's a lovely man. It's a cruel disease, and it started when he was still relatively young; it's not fair. You've looked after him so well. But now, you have to put his needs – and yours – first. He needs professional care. And you need to be … strong. For him.' He picked up his pen. 'I will give you another prescription. But I'd like it to be the last one. And I'm going to talk to Social Services. Why don't we arrange some respite care for Ernest, in the first instance? And we'll go from there.'

Stella nodded. To say *yes* out loud felt a step too far – as if she were becoming complicit in this dreadful plot to move her beloved Ernest from his lifelong home. She knew, in her heart, that Dr Sutton was right. But that didn't mean she had to like it.

The short-term respite care didn't go well. Stella visited Ernest every day, despite Dr Sutton's advice that this was defeating the object of giving her a rest, and he cried through each visit. The young carers at the home were lovely, and dealt with him proficiently but kindly, but once the week was up and he was home again, he threw himself at Stella, almost knocking her over, begging her – in his now limited vocabulary – not to send him away again. She knew she couldn't make that promise. It was soon July, the school holidays were approaching, and at least then she'd be able to stay at home with Ernest until September. The latest carer was doing his best, but Ernest didn't seem to like him and she doubted it would last long.

It was about a week before the end of term when things came to a head. In a fit of rage about something – he couldn't explain what, and Stella, for once, couldn't work it out – Ernest got out of his chair, pushing it over, and came at Stella, pushing her backwards. Stumbling to stay on her feet, she staggered backwards and eventually fell, hitting her head against the wall. She must have passed out for a moment, because when she came to, it was to find Ernest on his knees beside her, sobbing with fear.

'It's all right, it's all right, my darling,' she soothed him.

But of course, it wasn't, really, and finally she knew she had to accept that. She had a headache the next day so called in sick at school, and went to see Dr Sutton.

'You may have a mild concussion,' he told her. 'You should rest for a day or two. If that's even possible.' There was a pause, and he held her gaze, but before he could go on, Stella said, very quietly:

'And I know. I know it's time. I can't risk that happening again and . . . possibly not being here for him.'

She tried to explain it to Ernest, but it was beyond him. He'd shake his head, rock himself and say, over and over, 'Stay here, stay here'. It was heartbreaking, but Stella knew that, as Dr Sutton had said, she had to be the strong one now. The day he moved out was terrible. Dr Sutton, and a care worker from the home, came to help walk him down the track to a waiting car. He struggled, and cried, and lashed out, but they held him firmly, talking to him quietly about things he liked: music, films, his favourite food – all of which he'd get, as soon as he settled into his new home.

And, eventually, he *did* settle, up to a point. And Stella recovered, and began to accept that she'd done the best she could for him. But every time she went to see him, he'd look at her with the same bewildered expression. And – until, sadly, he lost the ability to communicate at all – he'd plead with her, over and over, 'Home now? Go home now?'

He lived for another three years. It wasn't much of a life for him, but he was safe, and cared for, and Stella didn't reproach herself, anymore, for allowing him to be moved. But she'd seen enough to convince her that, when she came to the end of her own life, she'd rather fall into the sea with her house than go the same way that Ernest had had to. And that was what she intended to do.

41

Stella

Well, I suppose I've ruined the party now. Everyone's gone quiet, except for the children, laughing together over their game.

'Sorry,' I say. 'Didn't mean to put a dampener on the picnic.'

'Don't be sorry.' Alec lays a hand on my arm. 'I needed to hear it – about Grandad. It was horrible for him. But I think it was worse for you, wasn't it?'

'Oh, I was all right,' I say a bit impatiently. 'Silly, getting all upset about these things.'

'No, it isn't, it's natural,' Holly says. 'But Stella, you mustn't talk like that – about going into the sea with the house! That isn't going to happen!'

'Isn't it?' I raise my eyebrows at her. 'It's what everyone's fussing about. I'm not blind, or deaf. I know what you've both been worrying about – the cracks. Well, I don't want you getting those buggering busybodies up here again, I'm telling you that. Because I know exactly what they want to do. Put me in a home. And I'm not going. I don't care if it's the best home in the world. Ernest's was one of the good ones, they did their best, they really did, but even so—'

'But Ernest had dementia! You don't *need* to be in a home, Stella!' she says.

'And what exactly do you think my options are, then, if they condemn this house, and tell me to get out of it? It's all I've got. It's not insured, they've refused to cover it for years now. Whether it falls into the sea or they knock it down, I'd have nowhere to go, and I've only got my pension. They won't give me a house – why should they? They need houses for young families, and that's as it should be. No, they'd want to put me in a home. And I wouldn't be able to take my cats. So I'm staying put here, till I die, or till it goes off the cliff. And that's the end of it.'

'But there must be other options, surely,' Alec says.

'There aren't.' I shrug.

'You have people to live for now, Stella,' Holly joins in. 'You've got your grandson, here – and your great-grandson! I could understand how you felt, if you were ill, and lonely – struggling, not enjoying life – but now, right now, your life is *better*, isn't it?'

I look away, out over the sea in the distance.

'Yes, of course it is,' I say quietly. 'I sound like an ungrateful old woman, don't I? But I'm not. I do know how much I've got to be grateful for. It's true, I haven't got dementia like Ernie, and I hope I never do. I'm not in too bad nick for eighty-three. I've got a lovely new friend who cares about me – and on top of all that, I find out I've got a grandson and great-grandson. I *do* appreciate you all, believe me. I thank God every night for what I've got. I've been lucky.' I pause, trying to find a way to explain it. 'I'm not talking about popping a few pills and saying goodbye – taking the easy way out. All I'm saying is, I don't want to leave my home, unless they take me out in a box. Is that too much to ask?'

'It wouldn't be, of course,' Alec says. 'If the house weren't tottering on the edge of a crumbling cliff.'

'*Tottering*!' I scoff. 'Look how far away it is!'

We all gaze across the grass to the edge of the cliff. Nobody speaks. Well, all right, perhaps it *isn't* quite as far as I'd like to think. Alec's put a bit of wire fencing round the place where the big crack is. It won't stop Peggy going in there – I've just got to hope she's learned her lesson – but it's keeping the kids away from it. I'm a bit anxious, the two of them being out here, in case there are more cracks that we haven't noticed. I suddenly feel hot with shame for talking about 'going over the edge with the house' so blithely. Supposing somebody else – one of the children – were to fall? Maybe they should be indoors – maybe we all should. I think back to those evenings, out here with our friends, around this time of year, dancing to Ernest's gramophone in the moonlight. Oh, to be able to go back, to relive just one day of those wonderful years! But I've got my memories, thank God. A lifetime of memories.

'Stella,' Holly says suddenly, interrupting me just as I realise I'm muttering out loud about my memories, like a prattling old fool, 'I've been meaning to tell you: about those memories of yours. I hope you don't mind, but I've been writing them down. It's – well, I suppose it's, like a biography, really. Your life story. I just did it for my own enjoyment; don't worry, it's not for publication in any shape or form—'

'As if I'd care!' I say, laughing. 'Not if it's after I'm dead, anyway. That's when memoirs are usually published, isn't it?'

'Stop talking about dying, can you?' she protests. 'We're supposed to be having a nice summer picnic—'

'Sorry. But of course I don't mind, Holly. Not that I can see why you think my life story is remotely interesting.'

'Oh, it is!' she says. 'But honestly, it's just for my personal enjoyment.'

'And mine,' says Alec. 'Holly's sent me a copy. And I can tell you it's very good. Not only interesting, but very well-written too.'

He smiles at her, and she smiles back. I've been watching those smiles. They remind me of . . . how it felt, to be young, and looking at somebody you love. I wonder. Is this what's happening, here? I've suspected it, of course, right from the start: all those little smiles and blushes. How lovely it would be.

'But I'd like *you* to read it, Stella,' Holly says. 'In case I've got anything wrong.'

'All right. I'll read it. Thank you.'

It'll be strange, reading about myself. Funny that she wanted to write it all down. But there you are – she's a writer, I suppose she can't help herself.

They leave soon after this. Holly says she can see I'm getting tired. There was a time I'd have scoffed at the very idea of having an afternoon nap. Now, unfortunately, I can't seem to get through the day unless I've closed my eyes for half an hour or so. Just another inconvenience of old age.

I go indoors, sit in my chair by the window, where the sun's the strongest, and put my feet up on the little stool. I shouldn't have talked the way I did, should I? Upsetting them both, letting them think I'm about to throw myself off the cliff. I wouldn't do that. Too horrible for the people you leave behind. Like everyone, I hope I'm just going to go in my sleep: perhaps one day, like this: sitting here, in my chair, looking out over what's left of my land, with one of the cats on my lap, and thinking about Ernest.

But I don't want it to happen just yet. I want to live long enough to see whether my grandson, and young Holly, are going to acknowledge what's becoming increasingly obvious to me. A happy ending for the two of them? I like to think she'd be able to round off my so-called life story nicely, then.

42

Holly

We're quiet this time as we walk back to the car. The kids are running ahead of us as usual, and to my surprise, while they're not looking, Alec takes hold of my hand and squeezes it. I think it's just a consoling thing – a friend to a friend thing, nothing else – because we're both still feeling a bit disturbed by the way Stella was talking today.

'There *are* other options for her,' he says. 'We just need to be careful how we ... guide her towards them.'

'Really? I can't think of any options, to be honest. As she says: she doesn't have any means of funding herself, and the council won't give her a house. It'll be, if she's lucky, some sort of sheltered accommodation for the elderly, and I don't know of any of those around here. Or at best a flat. She wouldn't like that.'

I sigh. It all just feels so sad, so unfair. She's lived this long life, working hard, but now all she has is her pension and a house that's got no market value.

'I'd have her come and live with me, if I had any room,' I go on. 'But I think she'd refuse – she's so independent. And anyway, being in an upstairs flat—'

'I know. But there *is* another alternative.' I can hear a slight smile in his voice. I look up at him in surprise, and he goes on: 'She could come and live with *me*.'

I blink in surprise. 'Would you really want that? You've only known her a few months. And would you have the room?'

I've never even been to his place yet. He's asked me, a couple of times, but I suppose I'm holding back, still nervous of taking another step closer to him, in case ... what? In case I fall any deeper than I already seem to be doing, and he turns out to be another Liam.

'Of course I'd want her to. She's my gran, however long it took me to find her. And—' He swallows and looks away '—we don't know how many years we might still have with her, do we? Hopefully lots, of course. But if not, well, I don't want to see her last few years being spent in some dire situation because suddenly she *has* to move out. If the house does literally start to collapse, God forbid, she won't have any choice, no matter what she says.'

'I know. And it's lovely that you want to have her live with you, Alec. But I doubt you'd be able to talk her into it.'

'I'm going to bring her over to see the house. Without saying why.' He smiles down at me now. 'But first, I want *you* to come and see it. I'd like your opinion, before I start trying to tackle Gran!'

I go the next day, at twelve o'clock, when Alec comes home for an early lunch break from the bookshop. It's lovely that Karen's settled in so well at the shop that he trusts her to be in charge whenever necessary. I take the car, so that I can make sure I'm not late going on up to The Avenue for my cleaning job afterwards, and I drive slowly down to Alec's road. I know where it is, but as it's a cul-de-sac, I've never actually turned into it before. I don't know what I'm expecting – perhaps a fairly modern semi with a neat little garden. That's exactly what the first few houses look like; but then the road turns a corner, back on itself towards the coast – and there, at the end of the close, is a house on its own, completely different from the others. It's detached, but not particularly big, and it has cream-coloured stone walls and a thatched roof. To say I'm surprised is an understatement. This is definitely Alec's house; the number on the door is quite clear. It just wasn't at all what I imagined.

'It's a proper cottage – not a house!' I say as soon as Alec opens the door to me.

'It's a bit of an anomaly, isn't it?!' He agrees. 'A country cottage, stuck at the end of an ordinary residential cul-de-sac. Come in, come in. The kettle's on and I know you can't stay long. Would you like a Stella-type cup of tea, or a mug with a teabag?'

I laugh as I follow him inside. 'You surely don't make Stella-style tea, do you?'

'I've bought a teapot. And loose tea, a tea strainer, and even a tea cosy,' he admits. 'I can't invite her here and give her a teabag, can I?!'

'Well, in that case, you'd better make me a Stella tea. You might need the practice!'

I follow him into the kitchen. I can see there's been a lot of modernisation inside the house, but it still retains its character. The kitchen's big enough for a wooden table and chairs, and there's a range cooker and a big fridge-freezer.

'Fortunately,' he says as he pours the boiling water into the teapot, 'there's a little utility room, built into the back of the garage – room for the washing machine and dryer. The garage was obviously an add-on. Have a seat, Holly, while the kettle boils. I'll show you the living room in a minute.'

I pull out a chair and we both sit, facing each other. The kitchen window overlooks a narrow stretch of lawn at the side of the house.

'That bit of garden gets the sun early in the mornings,' he says, seeing me looking. 'The back of the house faces south, though. It gets the sun all day, but there's lots of shade from the trees.'

'Sounds perfect,' I say. 'How on earth did you find this place? I never knew it was here, and I've lived here nearly all my life.'

'Property website, obviously!' He smiles. 'But, like you, I'd never have imagined a house like this being tucked away here. Apparently, the whole of the land that this road is built on, originally belonged to the house. At some point, most of the land was sold off, and those newer houses were built during the nineteen-seventies. But there's still a sizeable back garden here.'

'Come on, then, make the tea and leave it to draw while you show me the rest of the house!' I say. I feel – something like excitement. I don't know why. Like there's a surprise coming.

And . . . there is.

He goes ahead of me down the hallway and into the living room. And I just gasp, and stand there in the doorway like I've been struck dumb.

'Oh!' I finally manage to say. 'The sea!'

I should have worked it out, if I'd thought about it. The road turned in the direction of the coast, and Alec did say the rear of the house faced south. But I'd never have imagined this. The back garden is quite wide, and, as he's already said, bathed in sunlight, apart from the areas shaded by the trees. At the end of the garden is an ancient-looking wall, overgrown with climbing roses, and with a gate in its centre.

'That leads out onto the coast path,' he says, following my gaze. 'Come into the room, Holly. You are allowed!'

'I'm just . . . overwhelmed,' I admit, joining him at the patio doors across the other side of the room. 'It's so beautiful.'

He opens the doors and I can already hear the sea.

'How close is it?' I ask.

'Not as close as it looks,' Alec says with a smile. 'Don't worry.

I had a geological survey done. Not that I knew about Stella's house at the time, of course. Just what you have to do, these days, when you buy a coastal property. And – I'm obviously not a geologist – but apparently this area of the town is on the type of soil, or rock, or whatever, that doesn't erode. Well, not the way it does up on Hawbury Top, anyway. I think we might be OK for at least a thousand years, failing another ice age,' he jokes.

'Can we ... have you got time? ... I'd love to have a quick look outside.'

'Of course. But let's have our tea, first. Oh, and I've made sandwiches. Come on.'

'You shouldn't have gone to all that trouble!' I protest.

'I need lunch anyway,' he says. 'And so do you, if you're going on to work.'

I follow him back to the kitchen, and on the way, he shows me the other downstairs rooms. 'Study,' he says, opening one door. 'Not that I study anything. It's still full of boxes at the moment, from when I moved in. But it *could* be a study: that's what it was for the previous owners. Or it *could* be a downstairs bedroom.' He gives me a wink, and then pushes open another door, directly opposite this one. 'Downstairs bathroom,' he says. 'Nicely fitted out by the previous occupants.'

It's small, but perfect, with a shower in the corner, toilet and handbasin, all new modern fittings.

I'm following his meaning here, of course. Downstairs bedroom and bathroom. View over the sea.

'Are you *sure* you didn't have a premonition about finding your gran, when you bought this house?' I tease him.

He laughs. 'I just fell in love with it. I didn't even think it through particularly well. I'd imagined this room might be for Alfie, when he's here. But no, Alfie wanted one of the upstairs rooms.'

'How many of those are there?'

'Three. One large, two smaller. Come up and have a quick look. Mustn't let the tea get stewed!'

The house is definitely bigger than it looked from the outside. Upstairs there's a small landing, with three doors off it. The master bedroom is big, like the living room below it, and has an even better view over the sea. It's decorated in white and a pale green, giving it a lovely light, countryside feel, and there's a door on one side leading to a small en-suite bathroom.

'I'm very lucky. The previous owners had similar taste to mine!' Alec says. 'I'm not much of a do-it-yourselfer, but nothing here will need doing for a few years.'

The other two bedrooms were obviously used by the previous occupier's children. I can see straight away why Alfie likes his. The walls are plain: two cream, two a cheerful royal blue. But one of the blue walls has been partly fitted with cork tiles, where Alfie has already pinned up some of his favourite posters and photos. The other room, across the landing, has been treated in the same way, but with two walls painted a lilac colour instead of the blue. And both of the children's rooms have a small desk fitted under their window.

'Yes, I can see what you mean about the décor,' I say. 'It's perfect.'

As we go back downstairs, he tells me – without going into too much personal detail – that it was actually quite a big decision, buying this house. It was more expensive than he really wanted to spend, certainly more than his half of the proceeds of the marital home. But he'd been living in a quite small flat since the divorce, and desperately wanted more space for when Alfie stayed with him. A bedroom Alfie could call his own, and a nice garden.

'And I was just so smitten with this place,' he says. 'So was Alfie. But my mortgage here is . . . quite eye-watering.' He shrugs. 'The job pays more than my previous one, naturally – it's my first job as a manager. The guy who owns the business has another two shops so it's a good one to be in. But still . . . ' He tails off.

'It's tough. Tell me about it!' I laugh. 'And I'm only renting.'

'Yes.' He gives me a sympathetic look. 'I know, I'm lucky to have my own place. Really lucky. Well, here you go.' He hands me a plate with a neatly arranged sandwich, and I sit down at the table while he pours the tea. 'Sorry, it's not exactly cordon bleu, but I think you like ham and tomato – judging from what you brought to the picnic?'

'It looks lovely. Thank you.'

After our lunch, as promised, he takes me down to the end of the garden, through the gate and out onto the coast path. Sure enough, there's quite a wide stretch of grass and scrub sloping down from the path to the sea wall. The sea *isn't* as close as it looked from the windows. Because the house is only a little way above sea-level, there's no dizzying prospect of looking down at the waves, like there is up on Hawbury Top. Instead, it's a much gentler view over an expanse of sand-and-shingle beach, where the sea laps prettily at the tide line.

'Alfie must love it here!' I say.

'He does. But his home is back in Ivybridge,' he adds quickly, 'with his mum, and all his school friends. And that's as it should be.'

'So what do you think?' Alec asks me, a little anxiously, as we both prepare to go back to our cars.

'I think your house is absolutely perfect,' I tell him. 'I'd buy it myself if you were selling it. And if I had any money!' I add, laughing.

'But will Stella? Will she think it's perfect?' he says. 'You obviously realise what I have in mind. The downstairs bedroom.'

I turn to look back at the house. How could she not like it?

'But you'd have to take her cats, too,' I point out, suddenly remembering. 'And you said you already have one yourself. I didn't see him!'

'Old Billy is like Stella's Peggy: always out somewhere, exploring. He's fine with other cats; he was one of a six-cat household before he went for adoption.' He smiles at me. 'I'm fine with multiple cats too, obviously. They'd be welcome here.'

'Well, then: if you're *absolutely* sure you're happy to open your home to her, then of course, it would be wonderful if she agreed to it, Alec. But I just don't know. She's going to be a tough nut to crack.'

'I know. But I'm going to do my best,' he says. 'I just hope she *will* crack. Before Cliff's End does.'

43

Stella

The two of them – Alec and Holly – often come up here together now: sometimes at lunchtimes or on Sundays, when he's not working at the shop. I'm enjoying watching their friendship develop, the easy way they have of chatting and joking together, like they've known each other for years. I wonder why they haven't realised yet – or perhaps they have, but they're trying to ignore it? Those little glances, those secret smiles: it's not how two people who are just good friends look at each other. Still, what do I know? I'm past it. I've only got my memories, now, of how that used to feel, and maybe people are more careful, if they've already been hurt. I feel protective of Holly, and I'm sure she wouldn't rush into anything again, after what she went through with that Liam. But I know, already: Alec's different. And not just because he's my grandson. He's just a nice chap. I presume there are still some around.

It's been a beautiful day today: a Friday, towards the end of May. It's early evening – six o'clock, but still sunny and warm outside – and I'm waiting for them with my summer dress and my best cardi on. Apparently they've got a surprise for me, so they've waited till Alec's finished work, and Holly's left Maisie with Karen, so that they can just concentrate on me and not have to rush. They're taking me out in Alec's car. Not far, they said; they want to show me something. I'm intrigued, and quite excited.

When they arrive, Alec's carrying my Friday shopping, and I let them put it away for me before we set off. They know where everything goes now, but it makes me feel lazy: they're doing more and more for me. I managed all right on my own before, didn't I? But I do sometimes seem to feel quite tired these days. Just getting ruddy old and feeble, I suppose.

'Right, Gran, are you ready?' Alec says. He sounds a bit apprehensive, to me, for somebody just driving us out on a little trip. Maybe he's worried about me walking down the track. I want to tell him I've done it millions of times before – I'm not quite decrepit yet – but he takes my arm as we go out of the door, and I must admit, it feels nice, being on the arm of a strong young man again, after all these years. My grandson! I feel a glow of pride. Such an unexpected pleasure.

They put me in the front seat of the car. 'More room for you,' says Alec, which I find quite funny as I'm not very big and I've only got little legs. He drives into town, down to the other end of Fore Street, and turns off just before we would have come to the place where Hillside Lane leads off towards the farm where I grew up.

'Would you like me to take you up there first?' he asks when I mention this, 'to have a look?'

'No,' I retort. 'I can remember it all too well, thanks. Had enough of it, back then!' – and they both laugh.

He drives us down School Lane, and I'm immediately transported, as I look out of the window at the little playground on what used to be the infants' side – now part of the nursery school – to my happy days there as a teacher. It feels so long ago. Then, a little way before the end of the road, he turns off again, into a cul-de-sac I'd forgotten all about. It's nothing special. Post-war style houses – I vaguely remember them being built, probably around the mid-sixties or early seventies. Nice enough, but all identical, a bit boxy-looking. I can't imagine what they've brought me down here for. There's a bend in the road, and then I sit forward in surprise. The house at the end is distinctly different from the others. It's a thatched cottage! I've obviously never been to the end of this road before because I didn't know about this, at all. Quite a surprise.

'Is this what you brought me to see?' I ask Alec, as he pulls up outside the house.

I mean, it's nice, and yes, it's a surprise to me. But I didn't need to have put my best frock on.

'Well, yes,' he says – but he sounds so unsure of himself, that I just stare back at him, flummoxed. Well, maybe it's the home of someone he knows. Someone he'd like me to meet.

'Do you know who lives here?' I ask as he helps me out of the car.

'Yes!' is all he says. He takes my arm again and walks me up to the front door, Holly following behind us. And to my astonishment, instead of ringing the door bell, he puts a key in the door and ushers me inside.

'Oh!' I step inside, and look back at him, shaking my head. 'This is your house, Alec? Why didn't you say?'

'We promised you a surprise,' he says in a strangely casual way. 'Now then: it's still lovely and warm outside, and there's a comfy seat on the patio. So why don't you and Holly go and sit out there, and I'll bring you a nice drink. White wine, Holly? Or gin and tonic? And what about you, Gran? Would you prefer a cup of tea?'

'No, I'd prefer a gin and tonic, if it's on offer!' I retort. Can't remember the last time I had one of those. I laugh at the surprise on Alec's face. 'Better make it a small one,' I add on reflection. 'It might go to my head.'

He laughs. 'OK then. We don't want to be carrying you back up the track!'

Holly takes my arm and leads me out through the patio doors.

'Oh!' I say, standing still and staring ahead of me. 'Look at the view! I didn't expect—'

'That's just what I said, when I first came here,' she says. 'Isn't it lovely?'

'I'm just trying to work out whereabouts we are – along the coast,' I say. 'Is that the coast path, beyond the gate?'

'Yes. Do you want to have a look?'

The garden's wide, but not very long. She leads me down to the gate at the end, and we go through to the coast path. The sea wall is just across the grass there. I look left along the beach, and then right.

'It would have been just about there,' I say, nodding in that direction. 'A bit further along. I can see where School Lane ends, at the beach.'

'That's right,' Holly agrees, following my gaze. '*What* would have been just there, Stella?'

'The barbed wire. When I came down to the beach with Ruby, during the war.' I'm smiling at the memory. 'The first time we were down here on our own.'

'Oh yes.' Holly smiles back at me.

Neither of us mentions that it was also the day I found out my mum and nan had died at Bethnal Green. It's the memory of being at the beach with my friend – naughty though it was of us – that's so strong. Despite all the other happy times I've spent on the beach since then, over the years, with Ernie, and with friends. Despite all those fun years of the nineteen-sixties, when life was full of new things – new music, new fashions, new freedoms – and the seventies, when we were a bit more grown-up, when we went to different beaches, far away, overseas. Despite all those memories, it's the one of Ruby and me, when we were little kids like Maisie, coming down to look at that barbed wire, scared by the notice about the land mines, that's the strongest.

'Come on,' Holly's encouraging me, and I realise I've been standing here staring at the sea like a daft thing. 'Let's go back and see if Alec's poured out our drinks, shall we?'

As we walk back to the patio, Holly and I both notice, at the same time, the black and white cat curling himself around Alec's legs as he puts the drinks on a little table.

'Ah! So this is Billy!' Holly says, crouching to stroke him. 'Hello!'

'He's a lovely boy,' I say, smiling down at him.

'He's getting on a bit now,' Alec says. 'Nearly thirteen. But still going strong.'

We sip our drinks while we chat. I'm glad now, that I wore my frock, and my nice cardi. Apparently Alec's cooking us dinner too. What a treat! I feel like I'm being spoilt, pampered, and it's not even my birthday. After a while, he suggests we go inside so that he can show me around the house.

And it's just as nice inside as outside. I keep telling him he did well to find it – but then, I'm sure he knows that. Until the new houses were built, there was only a track here before, not a proper road, and we just never walked down it. I don't remember even wondering where it led to. Just to this house, it seems – and the beach. It's like finding a hidden treasure!

You've got a downstairs bathroom too!' I exclaim. It's all the thing now, apparently – not just one bathroom indoors, but two: one being actually part of the main bedroom. I have to laugh, when I think of my childhood at the farm. Just the kitchen sink, we had indoors, and a privy outside in the yard. Ripped up newspaper for toilet roll. A tin bath brought indoors and filled up in front of the fire. Uncle had a bathroom put in eventually, and we thought it was the height of luxury. Alec smiles now, when I tell him this.

'Well, yes, we don't know how lucky we are, these days, do we, Gran?'

'A box room down here too,' I say approvingly as he opens another door. 'Very useful.'

'I'm going to turn it into a bedroom, I think.'

'Really?' I wonder what he wants with four bedrooms. I haven't been upstairs yet – not sure my legs would carry me, after the gin and tonic – but he's told me there's three up there. He keeps one for Alfie, of course, and one is for himself, but two more spare ones? Still, it seems that's what people want now – lots of bedrooms, lots of bathrooms. Must be forever cleaning.

He's set the table in the kitchen. *Kitchen-diner*, he calls it. I get the feeling he's trying to impress me. He ought to know there's no need for that. We sit around the table, the three of us, and he serves us a chicken casserole, with salad *on the side*, as he calls it. He offers me a glass of wine, but I'm sticking to water now, or I'll fall asleep before I've finished. He's a good cook. He's even done a dessert – a crumble – and although I'm full up, I eat a little bit, to please him.

'This has been lovely,' I say after we've all finished and he's made us a cup of tea. Proper tea – I saw him warming the pot. We're sitting in the living room now. It's still not quite dark and I can see the silver-blue line of the sea beyond the garden wall. I feel strangely at peace. I don't think it's just the gin, or the big meal. I feel like . . . I'm part of a family here. It almost makes me want to cry, and I have to shake myself to stop from being so silly. 'It's been very kind of you.'

'It's not being kind,' he says. 'It's being your family, Stella.' And for a minute I think he must be able to read my thoughts – to have known how I'm feeling.

'Thank you,' I say. 'I do appreciate it. I can't believe how lucky I am, to have you. Both of you.'

'Then would you, perhaps, consider doing something for me, in return?' he says. That slightly nervous tone is back again. I look up at him in surprise.

'Of course I will. What is it? Whatever you need, Alec. Is it money? I haven't got much, but in my post office account there's—'

'No! For God's sake, I wouldn't dream of asking you for money!' He laughs, and then suddenly stops, seems to take a deep breath, and says, all in a rush: 'Would you consider moving into my box room, Stella? I'll make it into a lovely proper bedroom for you, and the whole house will be yours to share, of course. If you like it here – the house – and the garden, the outlook, then we think – Holly and I think – it could be the perfect solution for you. Whenever you're ready. No need to answer straight away. But we'd really like you to—'

He runs out of steam, and just sits there, looking at me, waiting, while Holly nods enthusiastically.

'It would be perfect, wouldn't it, Stella?' she prompts me.

I can't think what to say. I *want* to say: So this was your little plot. I want to say: You've bribed me with gin and tonic and chicken casserole, before dropping your bombshell. I want to say: No. But underneath all that, to my complete and utter surprise, I also – somehow – find myself wanting to say Yes.

'I can't go anywhere without my cats,' I say firmly. There. That's it, settled.

'The cats will be just as welcome as you are,' Alec replies immediately. 'Billy would love their company, too.'

I see he's already thought of everything. This has been planned. I'm finding it hard to take in.

'I think I'll need to ... go home and think it over,' I manage to get out, eventually.

'Absolutely. Of course,' Alec says.

'We didn't expect you to answer right away,' agrees Holly.

But they're giving each other hopeful looks, their eyebrows raised, little smiles exchanged. I'm cross with them, but full of love for them, at the same time. Tricking me like this! But I wouldn't have come, otherwise, would I? And they're concerned for me. I know, it's my own fault – all that nonsense I was saying the other week about falling in the sea with the house.

I don't want to leave my home. I've never wanted to, and I still don't.

But if I did, this *could* be somewhere I might be able to come, and – perhaps – be happy ... couldn't it?

44

Holly

It's dark as we walk Stella back up to Cliff's End, but the sky's clear and the moonlight's bright. Alec and I both turn on the torches on our phones anyway, to make sure the path is clearly lit for her. We're holding an arm each, and she's muttering about not being hopeless and helpless, but we're just laughing and ignoring her. We stay to get her settled inside the house before leaving.

'I will think about it,' she says. 'Your little plot. But—'

'It's not a *plot*, Stella,' I say gently.

'It's an offer,' Alec says. 'A ... way forward for you. And the point is,' he adds quickly, 'that I'd like it too. I'd *like* to have you close. After all these years of not knowing about each other, wouldn't that be nice?' He pauses, and then adds, quietly, 'Wouldn't Mum have been happy, to know we're together at last, you and I?'

It's so exactly the right thing to say, that I want to hug him for it. I can see Stella's moved by it, too. She doesn't reply, but we kiss her goodbye and leave her to think it all over.

'That was lovely,' I tell him as we walk back to the car. He's holding my hand again, and I find myself squeezing his, feeling something so deep and true and – just *wonderful* – about it, about him, that I can hardly restrain myself.'If anything can persuade Stella to leave Cliff's End, it will be that: knowing *you'd* like *her* company too.'

'Well, it's true, of course. I want to enjoy every moment of having my gran, now I've found her. As well as keeping her safe.'

'I know. I want that too.'

He drops me back at my place. Maisie's having a sleepover with Flora, and it feels strange knowing I'll be on my own in the flat. It's still not late, though, so I suggest Alec might like to come up for a coffee.

'That'd be nice,' he agrees – and my stomach does a strange lurch, making me feel fluttery with nerves.

We chat some more, over our coffee, about how well the evening went, and how much Stella seemed to enjoy herself.

'I didn't know you were such a good cook,' I tell him.

'Oh, I've got numerous hidden talents,' he says, laughing – and then he stops suddenly, looking alarmed, because he must be able to see I've blushed scarlet. 'Oh, I didn't mean anything suggestive! I wasn't being pervy!'

'I know.' I'm looking down at my feet now, but I manage to go on, because I need to, because sooner or later it's going to have to be said, and it really ought to be now, because I'm getting too carried away by my feelings and I don't want to frighten him off: 'Look, I know we're seeing a lot of each other, and, well, I think we seem to get on really well together? But don't worry, I'm not reading anything into it, Alec. I'd hate things to be awkward between us. I know we're just friends. I'm not . . . looking for anything, here – a relationship, or anything like that.'

He doesn't say anything for a moment. I look up at him and manage to meet his gaze.

'Oh,' he says.

I force a little laugh. 'What do you mean, "Oh"?'

'I suppose,' he says slowly, looking straight into my eyes, 'I'm a bit disappointed.'

I feel as if my heart's almost stopped. I don't know what to say. He's disappointed? But—

'You've never given me the impression you were interested . . .' I manage to stammer, 'in anything, apart from being friends.'

'I didn't want to push it,' he's saying quietly. 'I wanted to wait until you were ready. I know you've been hurt in the past, badly hurt, and I realised you wouldn't want to rush into anything. But perhaps I've been kidding myself all along. Why would you be interested in me? I'm sorry: perhaps I've misinterpreted something; got the wrong end of the stick—'

'No.' I'm hanging my head again now. 'You haven't. *I* have. I've misinterpreted you being kind, and patient, and considerate – waiting for me to feel ready and safe – as not being interested in me . . .'

But I have to stop again, and take a deep breath. Because I'm not really being honest, am I? I've seen the look in his eyes, sometimes. That look – it's reflecting exactly what he must, quite clearly, be able to see in mine. I've tried to hide it, tried to ignore it and deny it to myself, but we both know perfectly well there's something happening here. Something a lot more than friendship.

'I thought you could *see* I was interested,' he's protesting gently. 'I am interested. But I can wait, if there's a chance you might feel the same one day.'

'I do feel the same,' I whisper. Saying it actually makes me shiver. I feel like I've taken a step out of my safe little shell. Exposed my heart to something really, really scary. But if I'm not honest with him now, I might lose him – and the fear of that happening is suddenly even worse than the fear I've carried inside me ever since I got away from Liam. 'I've felt it ever since the day I met you. And more and more, every day. But the truth is, those feelings frighten me.'

'I understand that – I really do,' he says. He puts an arm around me, and it's not a gesture of possession, like it was with Liam. It's not threatening; it's just warm, and caring. 'But I'll never hurt you, I promise you that. I'll never, ever, treat you the way your ex did. We'll always be friends – first and foremost, whatever else we become – or I hope we become! That will always stay the same. I promise.'

And the way he kisses me now is exactly how I've been longing for him to kiss me. Gentle, tender, like everything he does. Why did I ever doubt that this is how it would be with him?

'Do you think we *could* be more than just friends? Even just a little bit more, perhaps, for now?' he asks softly when we finally break apart.

I'm smiling enough for him to know the answer. But all I need to say is 'Definitely!' for him to break into smiles himself. And the only thing I regret, now, is leaving it so long before opening my heart to him. But it's not a problem, is it? We've got all the rest of our lives – and I'm going to start looking forward now, instead of holding back.

45

Stella

TWO WEEKS LATER

They're laughing and teasing each other while they help me pack my stuff. Every now and then, when they think I'm not looking, one of them will lean over and give the other one a quick little kiss. So, it seems they're finally – what do they call it these days? *Walking out together* is old-fashioned, I suppose. I've heard Holly say her friend Karen is *seeing someone*. I'd say that's a strange term for doing a lot more than just *seeing* each other. Anyway, I'm pleased. Relieved, almost – I was beginning to think I'd have to give them a little shove to get them started. I know she's told him about Liam, but it's been clear as daylight, right from the first time we met him, that Alec's not like that. And he thinks the world of her.

They look round now, and catch me watching them together. Holly's blushing. I give them a smile.

'I'm wondering if I'm going to be in the way,' I say. I'm only half joking.

'How do you mean?' Holly says.

'I mean – moving in with you, Alec. I'm wondering if it should be Holly, not me.'

There's an awkward silence.

'Oops,' I mutter to myself. 'Foot in mouth, Stella.'

'We ... um ... haven't discussed that,' Alec says. 'Not yet.'

'It's a bit soon to be thinking about anything like that,' Holly agrees.

'Fair enough,' I say. 'Take no notice of me.'

I turn away and go back to my packing, but I know they're still looking at each other like that. Well, if things change, I can move straight back out again. Although we're already referring to it as *moving in*, the agreement we've actually come to is that I'm going to stay with Alec for a trial period. I suggested two weeks, but he says we should give it four, to have a clear picture of whether it's working out or not. Either way, I'm not taking much with me. A suitcase-full of my clothes – that's pretty much all I've got in the wardrobe anyway – and my own bedding. Plus the memory blanket, the memory box, a few other personal bits and bobs, and a couple of my favourite books. And of course, the cats' beds and food and things, and the contents of my fridge and food cupboard, so they don't go off. Everything else can stay here for now, and most of it can fall over the cliff, for all I care, if the house really does go one day.

'Don't you want to bring Ernest's violin?' Holly says, pointing to it. 'In case you want to play it?'

'No.' I laugh. 'Sell it, if you like. I've told you, I was never any ruddy good at it, and I've got worse as I've got older. Scares the life out of the poor cats. Don't want them running off in fright.'

As it is, we know we're going to need to keep them in for a week or two while they get used to the house. Alec and Holly have brought my cat carriers down from the attic for me, ready for the journey.

'How on earth have you managed, Gran, when any of them needed to see the vet?' Alec asks me.

'Normally for their vaccinations and so on, I give the Cats Protection people a call, and one of their volunteers comes and picks them up for me. They're very kind. I suppose it's because they all know I used to help out there, and adopted the cats from there,' I explain. 'But on the odd occasion when one of them's been poorly, the vet's paid a home visit.'

'Well, we can take care of all that for you from now on,' Holly says firmly – and I must admit, that will be a weight off my mind, knowing my little furry friends will be looked after . . . in the future.

I went back with Alec again yesterday to see the room – the room that's going to be mine, temporarily or otherwise. He's already cleared out all his stuff, and put a brand-new bed in there for me, plus a little wardrobe, and a small chest of drawers next to the bed. It's a pretty room. The walls are a pale-cream colour and the curtains are yellow – the colour of sunshine. I feel so grateful and humbled that he wants me there, but I'm nervous, too. I don't want it to spoil things – us being on top of each other all the time. And I don't want him trying to wait on me hand and foot, taking away my independence, treating me like a useless lump just sitting in a chair waiting to die. So I've said we'll have to see how it goes.

'It's fine, Gran,' he jokes when I worry about things like this. 'I'll find you plenty of jobs around the house. You can dig the garden over if you like.'

'That'd be one way to get rid of me,' I tease him back. Of course, he doesn't know – neither of them do – what the doctor warned me, a couple of years ago, about my heart. Not that I believe a word of it anyway. Look at me – strong as an ox. If I can still walk up and down this track without collapsing, there can't be a lot wrong with me, can there? I stuff the packet of heart tablets into a corner of my suitcase along with my toothbrush and towels and stuff. I do take the damned things most days, when I remember. But I don't want either of these two seeing them, and making a thing of it.

I feel a bit at a loss after we get to Alec's house, once they've helped me unpack and put everything away. The cats are completely disoriented, of course, and are making a fuss. Alec's not at all perturbed. He's put a litter tray out for them, and fed them, and says not to worry, they'll soon settle down. I'm not so sure that I will. I've never lived anywhere other than Cliff's End since I was twenty-one, apart from on holidays – and I haven't even had one of those for a long time. I don't quite know what to do with myself. Holly stays to have some lunch with us, and then she says she'd better go and collect Maisie from Karen's house – and it's just me and Alec, and I sit on my bed, feeling like I'm going to be in his way. I almost wish it wasn't a Sunday, so that he'd have to go to work and leave me on my own in the house. Much as I love him, I feel awkward. I've got out of the habit of living with another person.

'Come and sit in the garden, Gran,' he says, tapping on my door before peering round it and seeing me, presumably, looking a bit lost and pathetic. 'It's nice and warm out there. And I've got something for you to look at.'

It's a red cardboard folder, containing a thick bundle of type-written pages, bound together with some kind of metal clips to make them into a sort of book.

'It's what Holly's been writing,' he says with a smile, handing it to me. 'Your life story.'

'Oh! I'd forgotten about that.'

'She's saved it for you. She thought you might like something to do today – or over the next few days. She's really keen to hear what you think of it.'

I open up the folder. 'Stella Jackman: ONE WOMAN'S LIFE',

it says at the top of the first page. I rather like that. Nothing fancy or clever about it, just stating a fact: that's all it is – one woman's very ordinary life.

'I've got some paperwork to wade through before I go into the shop tomorrow,' he says. 'So I'm going to bring my laptop out here and sit in the shade with it, and leave you in peace. You can either start reading, or have a little doze if you like.' He smiles at me and adds: 'You can do whatever you want, Gran. I know it probably feels a bit strange at the moment, but I really want you to make yourself at home.'

'In that case,' I say, putting the folder down on the little patio table and getting to my feet, 'I'm going to make a cup of tea before I start reading. Want one?'

'I'll do it—' he begins, and then checks himself, and says instead: 'Of course. Help yourself – and yes, I'd love one, too. You know where everything is, don't you?'

I feel a bit better, being in the kitchen, making tea, tidying up a bit as I go. I'm going to have to persuade him to let me cook. Maybe every other day. And do my own washing – or his too, if he'll let me. I don't want to feel useless, or . . . like a guest.

'Thanks, Gran,' he says when I bring out his tea.

I sit back down in the sunshine, sipping from my own cup, and for a moment I just stare out over his lovely garden, and beyond, at the line of blue sea visible beyond the wall. I feel a shift within myself. I'm a bit more relaxed.

And I start reading my own story.

46

Holly

Alec and I are on our own in the living room. Maisie and Alfie are both sound asleep upstairs in their rooms, and Stella took herself off to bed too an hour or so ago; she gets pretty tired these days. We're a bit concerned about it, and I've suggested perhaps she should see the doctor. She says perhaps she will after Christmas, but knowing her, she'll keep putting it off. I do wonder if she's telling the truth about those tablets I found – she'd left them in the kitchen by mistake and swiped them away from me quickly before I could read the label, saying they were just Paracetamol, for a headache. They didn't look like Paracetamol to me.

I did worry a bit, when I first moved in here with Maisie, that she'd find it all too hectic and exhausting – four of us living together (five when Alfie's here). But as usual, I'd underestimated Stella. I think the hardest time for her was when she first came here herself, back in June – but once she'd got over that, she seemed to be ready for anything. She often said how much she enjoyed the weekends when Alfie visited; and as, gradually, Maisie and I started spending more and more time here, she actually seemed to thrive on the extra company – making endless pots of tea, baking cakes, playing games with the children. I know she missed Cliff's End at first, but she seemed to get over it surprisingly quickly. She's far more adaptable and resilient than either of us had given her credit for – and perhaps more than she'd realised herself. Unlike when she was up on Hawbury Top, she can now take herself for little strolls out onto the coast path, where the ground's flat and even. She likes to sit on the public bench just a little way along the path, watching the sea, no matter what the weather. She didn't have to think twice, when the four week 'trial' was up. She didn't even want to go back for any more of her belongings.

'You can get the house clearance people in, for all I care,' she said. 'Or just let it all fall into the sea.'

'Really?' I was staggered. I thought she'd want ... things that reminded her of Ernest. Those boxes in the attic: his stamp and coin collections, all the old sheet music and records. And all the furniture was his family's, after all. She'd often told me how she moved into Cliff's End with nothing. She'd been evacuated to Devon as a child with nothing, and acquired almost nothing over the intervening years. 'There could be some valuables: the coins, and the box labelled bric-a-brac?' I reminded her.

'No,' she said firmly. 'You and Alec can get things valued, if you want to. You're welcome to the money, if there's anything of any worth. But I've told you before: I've got my memories in my heart. I don't need any of that ugly old furniture, or that old-fashioned china tea set, to remind me of Ernest. Or his collections – they were his hobbies, not mine. I've got his photos, and, thanks to you, I've got our story written down now. That's all I need.'

I was almost moved to tears by how much she said she'd enjoyed my account of her life story.

'I've changed my mind,' she said, the first time I saw her after she'd read it, back in the summer.

'About what?'

'You can have it published. Before I die, if you want. Not because it's about me,' she added quickly, 'but because it's so good, Holly, and you ... you *deserve* it. You're a good writer, and you deserve to have more than just your bits and pieces in the magazines published. You've made my silly ... unimportant ... little life, into a proper story. An interesting story that people might like to read, whereas in reality, it's – just a life, like anyone else's. I don't even understand how you've done it.'

I couldn't answer for a moment. I'd been hoping, of course, that she'd like what I'd written, but I hadn't been prepared for such praise.

'It's nothing I've done,' I tried to assure her. 'Your story *is* interesting, and because you let me use a lot of Ernest's pictures, too, that really helps to bring it to life. But anyway, Stella, it isn't as easy as that – having a book published. Especially life stories, like this, however interesting they are. Too many people want to write their own stories. And it's really, really hard to get a publisher these days.'

'I didn't realise that,' she said. 'You could try, though, couldn't you? Not for me – for you. If you got a book published, you could give up that cleaning job, couldn't you?'

I talked to Alec about it later. This was before I moved in with him, but we were spending nearly all our free time together.

'She doesn't understand,' I said. 'She thinks having a book published means you earn pots of money. She only hears about the famous authors who *do* get rich, not all the others who never even earn out their advance, and never get a second contract.'

'You'd be surprised how many people think that,' he said. 'But it's nice that she's got such faith in you.'

'Yes, I'm really chuffed that she likes the way I've written it, enough to even suggest trying to get it published.'

He looked at me thoughtfully for a moment. 'There is an alternative, you know,' he said. 'Self-publishing.'

'Hmm. I'm not sure about that.'

'Seriously, it doesn't have that *second-best* reputation anymore. And to be honest, it might be a better option for a book like this. You're right in thinking a mainstream publisher probably wouldn't jump at a biography of an unknown woman. But a local bookshop would definitely stock a book by a local author, about a local character. With local interest.'

I stared back at him. 'You're only saying that because you happen to run the local bookshop!'

'And you happen to be the local author! Yes! But it also happens to be true, Holly. You must have noticed what's on the first shelf inside the door of my shop.'

I had, of course. It's the most prominent display, because the books it contains are so popular with people around here. They're all concerned, in one way or another, with the local area. Novels by local authors – some self-published, Alec says, but he's happy to stock them because they sell well here, even if nowhere else. Books about Devon. Some specifically about Hawbury Down. Books about the history of the area, books about myths and legends, about Devon recipes, famous Devon characters, even about the Devon dialect. We don't get as many holidaymakers here as they do down in Torquay, of course, but we do get quite a few day-trippers, especially during the high season, and Alec says they love books like that.

'I could talk to people for you,' he said, suddenly sounding excited. 'Other authors who've self-published. Find out the best way to do it, make sure you don't go with a company who take your money and don't provide any kind of service.'

'And you'd really stock it in the shop?' I said.

'Of course I would! And I'd organise events for you: author appearances, a book signing! What on earth are friends for?' he joked.

'*Friends*?' I joked back.

'Come on, we've already had that discussion, weeks ago, haven't we?' he teased, grabbing hold of me for a kiss. 'You don't have to sleep with your bookseller to show your gratitude. But of course, if you happened to want to . . .'

I might have been pleasantly surprised by how quickly Stella settled into her new home, but when we agreed that Maisie and I would move in too, I didn't really anticipate any problems with Maisie. She already loved Alec to bits, and had even begun to look upon Alfie as a kind of adopted big brother. But the fact that 'Auntie Stella' would be living with us too, was the icing on the cake for her.

'Can I still have Flora here for sleepovers?' she asked, on the day in September when we finally moved our things into the house. The lilac bedroom was of course going to be hers, and she was delighted, deciding it was a sort of purple – her favourite colour – like the beloved knitted jumper she wears so much that I have to almost prise it off her sometimes to put it in the wash.

'Well, I don't know, Mais. It might be a bit much—' I began. But Alec interrupted me straight away. 'It's your home too now, Holly. Yours and Maisie's. Of course you can invite friends here, and so can she. And as for sleepovers – Alfie's bedroom is free most of the time, but Maisie might prefer to have a mattress on the floor of her own room when Flora stays over. I'm sure that's more fun, isn't it, Mais?'

She jumped up and threw her arms around him.

'I think that's a *Yes*,' I said, laughing. 'Thank you.'

So here we are, looking forward to Christmas. I've been working my way through a list of self-publishing companies, taking my time to choose the right one, and I think I've made up my mind. I'm going ahead with them in the new year. Stella's almost more excited about it than I am.

'Are you ready to be a local celebrity?' I tease her, and she scoffs at the idea, saying it's me, as the author, who's going to be famous. I don't think she quite understands, even now, that it's probably only going to be people in Hawbury Down who'll be buying the book. Karen's already telling me she's going to point everyone who walks into the bookshop straight to the shelf where – hopefully – my book will be on display. And she wants to be the first person with a signed copy.

On Christmas Eve, Alec and I have stayed up late, having waited until Maisie's asleep so that we could leave her presents at the end of her bed. We're sitting together quietly, looking at the flickering lights on the Christmas tree, looking forward to the excitement of the morning, and to Boxing Day when Alfie's mum will bring him over to join us.

'Stella insisted on making the mince pies,' I say, smiling. 'She let Maisie help, though. It was so lovely to see them working together in the kitchen. It brought back memories of how she used to be with my gran.'

'I'm sorry I never met her,' Alec says quietly.

'Well, I do still miss her. Especially at times like this – Christmas. She was the only family I had, before Maisie was born.'

'I know.' He strokes my hand. 'Holly: I've been wanting to say this to you, but I'm afraid you might jump down my throat.'

'Oh. Well, thanks for the warning. Maybe not on Christmas Eve, then?'

'I think perhaps it *should* be now. Before I give you your Christmas present.'

I look at him, puzzled. 'What's it got to do with –?'

'You'll see.' He grins at me. 'But meanwhile, I'm going to say it anyway, whether you're cross with me or not.' There's a pause before he goes on: 'I think it would be nice if you tried to make up with your sister.'

'I *did* try!' I retort. I didn't expect *this*. 'I've told you! I tried loads of times, and she completely blanked me. And even when Gran told her I'd had Maisie, she didn't even send a card, or anything—'

'I know,' he says gently. 'And I understand how you feel. But that was eight years ago now.'

'And she still hasn't been in touch! For all I know, she could be married, and have kids herself—'

'Exactly. And you're missing out. You could have a niece, or a nephew. Maisie might have cousins she's never even met.'

I can't respond to that. It hurts, I admit, to think that I might be depriving Maisie of the pleasure of cousins.

'But it works both ways,' I say sulkily. 'She hasn't bothered, either, to find out how I am, what I'm doing, whether I'm even dead or alive—'

'Don't say that,' he chides me softly. 'All I'm saying, Holly, is that you could perhaps just try again. So long has passed now.'

'Exactly. She might have moved. She might have gone to bloody Australia to be with our so-called mother.'

'So look for her on Facebook or whatever. You've admitted you've never tried that. You could be the bigger person here, Holl. Be the one who's prepared to give it another shot. If she still doesn't respond, you haven't lost anything, have you? But if she does, then surely the two of you can try to build some bridges now? After all this time?' He pauses, looking at me sadly, and then goes on: 'It wasn't her fault. Liam damaged her, just as he did you.'

I know he's right. I've known it all along. What's been stopping me? Pride? Guilt? Perhaps a mixture of both.

'I'll think about it,' I say, a bit grudgingly.

'OK. See if she's on Facebook. Right after Christmas?' he presses.

'Perhaps.'

'And then,' he persists, 'if you find her, you can bring her up to date with everything, can't you. About living here. About you and me ...'

I smile at him, still puzzled by the whole conversation. 'What's brought all this on, Alec?'

'Well.' He puts his arms around me and tips my chin so that he's looking straight into my eyes. 'There's something I want to ask you, but I'm ... a bit nervous.'

'What – even more than you were about asking me to contact my sister?' I tease him.

'Yes,' he admits softly. 'But – as it's now just after midnight, I think I'm going to give you your present first, instead of waiting till the morning.' He pulls a small, wrapped box out of his pocket and hands it to me with a smile. 'Happy Christmas, babe. Open it, go on. I'm shaking with nerves, here.'

He watches me intently as I rip off the paper and open the box. It's a ring – quite obviously an engagement ring. A sapphire and tiny diamonds, set in white gold. It's beautiful – and so unexpected, I think I'm going to cry.

'Will you marry me, Holly?' he asks simply. 'Please?'

'Oh, Alec!' I can't get any more words out. My heart feels like it's about to burst with joy. I really wasn't expecting this – I'm completely stunned.

'Is it OK? If it needs resizing, it can be done,' he says, sounding slightly panicked. 'But I borrowed one of your rings to take to the jeweller's, so I'm hoping—'

'It fits perfectly,' I say, putting it on and showing him.

'So – are you saying . . . ?' He's just staring at me, looking like he's holding his breath, and I realise I haven't even given him an answer yet. The obvious answer, to the most important question I've ever been asked!

'I'm saying *Yes*, of course I am, what do you think?' I grab him around the neck, and kiss him until he starts to gasp for breath. 'I just didn't expect—' I say eventually. 'We haven't even discussed—'

'No. I was too scared to bring it up, in case you said no. So I thought – perhaps I'd just do it the old-fashioned way, and if you *did* say no, you could just keep the ring anyway, as a Christmas present, and maybe wear it on the other hand, or whatever, and—'

'Stop talking,' I say, softly, holding out my hand to admire the ring properly. 'Before I change my mind!'

'We can tell the kids? And Stella? Shall we do it soon?'

'Absolutely. As soon as you like. Why not?' I feel like I might actually be dreaming. This is all so sudden.

'So you'll invite your sister?' he persists with a grin.

I groan. 'Yes, OK, I'll try. And you'll invite your ex-wife?' I add wickedly.

'Yes. As long as you're happy for her to come, I would do anyway! I'm sure Alfie would like her to.'

'You're so civilised,' I tease him. 'But I love you for it.'

He laughs. 'Well, that's good, then. Because I'm thinking of chasing you up the stairs to bed.'

'Maybe we should wait, now, till we're married – since you're so keen on doing things the old-fashioned way, all of a sudden?'

'Nah!' he laughs. 'Not *that* old-fashioned. It's a bit too late for that!'

47

Stella

JUNE 2019

Sometimes, when I'm sitting quietly in the living room, or on my favourite bench along the coast path, looking at the sea, I feel like pinching myself, it's so hard to believe the way things have turned out. I'm glad – actually glad! – they persuaded me to leave Cliff's End. What a silly old woman everyone must have thought me, clinging on there for so long, living on my own, getting lonely without admitting it, and finding it harder and harder to walk up that track with my arthritis – just because I was so frightened I might have to go into a care home. That's what I *said*, anyway, but perhaps, really, I was just afraid of change. Now, I can see that change has done me good. It's invigorated me. My life now is better than ever, being with these lovely young people, and the children. I have company whenever I want it, but I can shut myself away in my own room if it gets too much. I know I'm getting increasingly tired. And yes, I know why, but I'm not having them worry about me, or fussing over me. I'm eighty-four now, and I can't live forever. Enough said.

I'm so glad, though – and feel so lucky – that I've lived long enough to see my two favourite people get married. The wedding was on the first Saturday of April, and it was wonderful. They looked so happy! Karen was Holly's bridesmaid, and her other half, Paolo, was Alec's best man. The four of them have become such good friends during the past year. Oh, and of course, Maisie was a bridesmaid too, and Alfie was a page boy. They loved it.

Holly didn't know for sure whether her sister was going to come to the wedding until a couple of weeks before. They'd been back in touch. Holly found her on Twit-Book, or whatever it's called, and then they started talking to each other on the phone. I know Holly found it all a bit upsetting at first; obviously they had to go over a lot of old ground, about Liam, and put a few things straight between them. But I was so glad they managed to sort it out. At the wedding, they hugged each other and both shed a tear or two. Hannah's about forty now, and married to a rather quiet chap called David, who was a divorcee with two children of his own when they met. Holly says she's so glad Hannah has a husband and children now – well, stepchildren, but apparently she loves them and treats them as her own. They even had a conversation about their mother. Hannah's still in touch with her, but understands why Holly doesn't feel ready yet – if she ever will – to make contact.

The other thing I'm glad I've lived to see, of course, is the publication of Holly's book. I don't really understand what they mean when they talk about self-publishing, but when Holly put a copy of the finished book in my hands, and I ran my hands over the title: *One Woman's Life: The Story of a Devon Evacuee* – I felt myself go hot all over with pride. Not pride in myself – I still can't see what all the fuss is about, my life has been so ordinary. But in Holly, I always knew she could do it – write a book, a lovely book that's on sale in the bookshop.

Alec organised a book launch for her at the shop. It was on the first Saturday in February, and we all went, the children too. I wore my good winter skirt and a blouse that Holly had given me for my birthday, and she did my hair nicely for me. They made me sit in a place of honour, next to Holly, with my name on a card on the table in front of us. Holly had a pile of the books to sign for customers, and some of them even wanted *me* to sign their copy too! Alec and Karen took photos of us, and the most unexpected thing was that a photographer from the local paper turned up, and we had our picture in the paper the following week. It was a lovely day, one I'll remember for ... as long as I live. I was so proud to tell people in the shop that Holly was going to be my granddaughter-in-law.

Since then, apparently the sales of the book have been so good that Alec's had to keep ordering more copies. His boss has been stocking it in the other two shops he owns, as well, and Holly says the company who she published it with have also brought it out as an e-book, whatever that is, and they're very pleased with those sales too.

My cats love living here. Gracie and Vera like having so much attention, with more laps to sit on, and Peggy seems to have made friends with Alec's cat, Billy. They're both getting on a bit, but still prefer to be outdoors. We see them prowling around the garden, one behind the other, and then lying down sheltering under the bushes together. It's a relief to know they'll all still be loved and cared for here, after I've gone.

I walked round to the doctor's one day, while Alec and Holly were both out. They didn't need to know. We had a nice chat, he listened to my old ticker and gave me some more of the ruddy pills. I warned him I'll probably keep forgetting to take them, and he smiled at me, a bit sadly, and said as long as I was comfortable, and happy, and not in any pain, he wasn't going to nag me. And I'm not in pain at all. Just getting very tired. But what can you expect at eighty-four, when you've had a long life and worked hard for most of it? Most of it's been good, and some of it not so good – like most people's, right? But all in all, I've got no complaints. As Holly says in the title of the book, it's just been *one woman's life*. And I wouldn't have changed any of it, good or bad. I'm at peace with it all. Completely at peace.

Epilogue

DEVON TODAY magazine: November 2019

'Cliff's End', Hawbury Down, finally destroyed by October's storm.

By Devon Today reporter

The house known as Cliff's End, on Hawbury Top, just outside the small Devon town of Hawbury Down, having been in a state of disrepair since its owner, the late Mrs Stella Jackman, moved out over a year ago, was dealt a final fatal blow by the storm which hit the area on 5th October. The remainder of the garden collapsed into the sea, taking with it part of the back wall of the house. The ruins of the building have now been scheduled for demolition. The council have cordoned off the area and warned people to stay away.

Cliff's End was built towards the end of the nineteenth century and had been owned by the family of Mrs Jackman's late husband Ernest for generations. Over the years, the land attached to the house had suffered numerous serious instances of erosion, eventually destabilising the house to the extent that it was considered unsafe for habitation.

Stella Jackman, who had moved out of Cliff's End in June of last year, passed away peacefully in her sleep on 2nd September, aged eighty-four, from a previously diagnosed heart condition. A funeral service was held on 16th September, attended by her family, together with many local people from the town.

Mrs Jackman had lived for the last year of her life with her grandson Alec Dean, 32, manager of Hawbury Down bookshop, and his wife Holly Brooks, 29, author of the best-selling book *One Woman's Life*, which tells the story of Mrs Jackman's life in Hawbury Down after being evacuated to the area as a child during World War Two.

Asked how he felt about the collapse of Mrs Jackman's previous home, grandson Alec said: 'It's exactly what my gran would have wanted. It waited for her to go first, and gave up soon afterwards.'

The book about Stella Jackman's life by Holly Brooks includes a humorous account of her attempts to play the violin which belonged to her late husband Ernest (a music teacher and accomplished violinist). It describes how, on Mrs Jackman's own admission, the noise was so awful that her three cats would howl in protest, leading to rumours among local people, of ghostly wails coming from Cliff's End at night.

'I often wondered,' Holly Brooks told our reporter this week, 'whether she was actually doing it on purpose to tease people. But I never asked her. I liked to think it was her little secret.

'She was probably the most interesting and remarkable woman I've ever met,' the author continued. 'But she always insisted her life had been nothing special. She said it was, quite simply, just: *one woman's life*.'

Acknowledgments

With thanks as always to my agent Juliet Burton, and to my new team at Piatkus, especially Anna Boatman and Sarah Murphy – for loving *Winter at Cliff's End Cottage* as much as I do, and helping to make it an even better read

Auntie Nellie's family Christmas cake recipe

This recipe would have been handed down through Auntie Nellie's family and passed on to Stella, who used it every year and – with Maisie's help – made the Christmas cake for the family Christmas she spent with Alec and Holly near the end of the story. I like to think that Holly, Alfie and Maisie now make the same cake each Christmas in memory of Stella.

INGREDIENTS

- 1½ lbs mixed dried fruit
- 4 oz chopped peel
- 4 oz glacé cherries
- 4 oz chopped almonds or walnuts
- 10 oz plain flour
- 1 teaspoon baking powder
- 1 rounded dessertspoon cocoa
- 2 rounded teaspoons mixed spice
- ½ lb butter
- ½ lb dark brown sugar

- 1 tablespoon dark treacle
- Grated rind of one orange or lemon
- Large pinch of salt
- 3 tablespoons rum or brandy
- Few drops of almond essence
- 4 eggs

METHOD

1. Three days before making the cake: put the mixed fruit in a large container, sprinkle with rum or brandy, cover the container and shake or stir occasionally.

2. Grease and line an 8-inch cake tin; Preheat the oven to 170 degrees (C), Gas Mark 3.

3. Add the cherries, peel and nuts to the soaked fruit, and stir.

4. Beat the butter in a large mixing bowl until soft, add the grated rind, then the sugar, and beat well.

5. Add the treacle, beat well again.

6. Add the eggs, one at a time, beating well after each one.

7. In a separate bowl, sieve together the flour, baking powder, cocoa, salt and spice.

8. With a metal spoon, gently fold about half of the flour mixture into the mixture in the large bowl.

9. Continue to gently fold in, alternately, some of the flour mixture, and some of the soaked fruit mixture (including any of the liquid that hasn't been absorbed).

10. Gently stir in the almond essence.

11. Spoon the mixture into the prepared tin and flatten the surface.

12. Put into the centre of the oven, bake at 170°C (mark 3)

for 1 hour, then reduce temperature to 150°C (mark 2) for 1½ hours. Check whether a sharp knife inserted into the centre of the cake comes out clean; if not, bake for a little longer. (*NB from Holly: today's fan ovens will probably need a shorter baking time or slightly lower temperature*).

13. Cool the cake on a wire rack, then store in an airtight tin for 1 to 2 weeks before adding marzipan and finally icing.

Stella would have made her own marzipan from ground almonds, icing sugar and eggs – and her own royal icing from icing sugar, egg whites and lemon juice. But I think Holly would be quite happy to buy these from the shops.